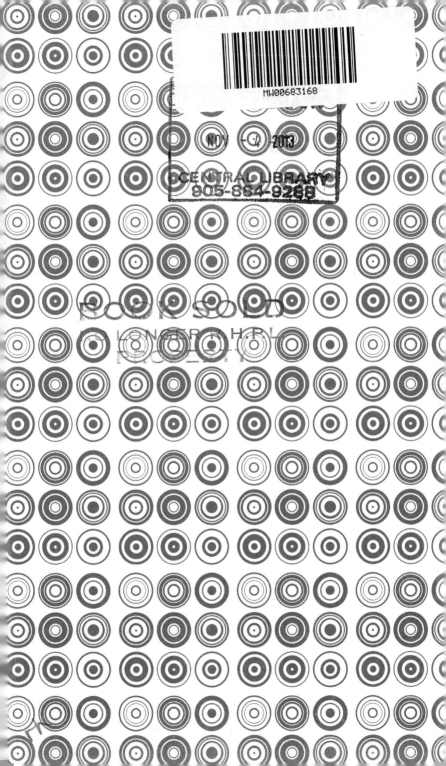

MW00683168

Accusation

CATHERINE BUSH

Accusation

(a novel)

GOOSE LANE

Copyright © 2013 by Catherine Bush.

Edited by Bethany Gibson.
Dust jacket and page design by Julie Scriver.
Dust jacket image detailed from "Self Portrait," copyright © 2012
by Sophie Schwartz, www.sophieschwartzphotography.com.
Endpaper design by PaperweightMemories.
Printed in Canada.
10 9 8 7 6 5 4 3 2 1

Library and Archives Canada Cataloguing in Publication

Bush, Catherine, author
Accusation / Catherine Bush.

Issued in print and electronic formats.
ISBN 978-0-86492-900-6 (bound). ISBN 978-0-86492-780-4 (epub)

I. Title.
PS8553.U6963A33 2013   C813'.54   C2013-902176-0
C2013-902177-9

Goose Lane Editions acknowledges the generous support of the Canada Council for the Arts,
the Government of Canada through the Canada Book Fund (CBF), and the Government of
New Brunswick through the Department of Tourism, Heritage, and Culture.

Goose Lane Editions
500 Beaverbrook Court, Suite 330
Fredericton, New Brunswick
CANADA E3B 5X4
www.gooselane.com

Into the street the Piper stept,
Smiling first a little smile,
As if he knew what magic slept
In his quiet pipe the while;

—Robert Browning, *The Pied Piper of Hamelin*

And how could we save ourselves from suspicion? There
is no deliverance from suspicion! Every way of behaving,
every action, only deepens the suspicions and sinks us the
more. If we begin to justify ourselves, alas! Immediately
we hear the question, 'Why, son, are you rushing to justify
yourself? There must be something on your conscience,
something you would rather hide, that makes you want to
justify yourself.' ...Everyone crouched, fell to the ground,
and thought in fear, 'I am accused.'

—Ethiopian palace official, from Ryszard Kapuscinski,
The Emperor

1996

She pushed her chair back from the desk as the awful word on the screen entered her, and the name of the man linked to the word.

Mid-afternoon on Labour Day Monday: heat filled the room, the upper floor of her house, the streets of Toronto, the air above them, and more sweat pooled under her arms and at her throat and across her chest, as she stood, trying to calm the blood speeding through her veins. Outside, when she paced to the window, beyond the Norway maple, a car passed and with it the ordinary mystery of strangers going somewhere. The cry of a cicada soared, and out of the stillness, a jet fighter, part of the holiday weekend air show, roared into tumult, shaking the walls and window glass.

If she had gone away for the weekend instead of lolling at home and, obsessive journalist that she was, following the news on TV of the Iraqi march north toward Kurdistan, if she had not gone upstairs to her computer to check what more she could find online in the scroll of press newsfeeds, she would not have come across this mention of him.

She turned back to the room, which seemed full of his presence. She saw him as she had first seen him, on stage in Copenhagen, alive with pride and adrenaline, a tall, light-brown man in a white T-shirt, head tucked beneath a red baseball cap, the child performers of the circus crowded about him.

Months later, she had met him. One night in July, a little more than a month ago, in the passenger seat of her car, he had canted forward in distress, urging her onward. She had driven him those long hours through the night, helping him get to Montreal and from there back to Addis Ababa and the circus children.

At her desk, quickened fingers seeking more, she located a day-old article from the *Sydney Morning Herald*.

> Nine performers in the Ethiopian children's circus, Cirkus Mirak, have defected and are applying for asylum in Australia, the migration agent representing the performers has announced. The performers fled the circus last Thursday night and claim that circus founder and director Canadian Raymond Renaud consistently abused them. The circus was on a ten-day tour of Australia, and appeared most recently at the Sydney Alternative Arts Festival, its acrobatic performances hailed by critics and crowds alike.

She knew nothing for certain. It was only an accusation. Abuse: the article didn't even specify what kind. Yet, as she knew, an accusation, regardless of truth, has its own life when let loose in the world. Experience had taught her this. The words, released, went on uncoiling themselves. A pulse rapped in her head.

What to do?

Do nothing. Or call Juliet Levin to tell her what she had discovered.

Sara had flown to Copenhagen at the end of March to attend a conference on migration, as the Danes called it—immigration, she would have said. She had been invited along with Rivka Mendelsohn, the Israeli-Canadian academic who worked with Tamil populations in Toronto. Rivka had recommended her to the Havn Foundation, which was sponsoring the conference, as someone who wrote about immigration and multiculturalism issues: this was now her beat. And how different this trip was from the ones she'd taken when working for the foreign news desk and in the years when she'd traipsed as a stringer through Eastern Europe and the Middle East.

In her room in the lovely old hotel by the waterfront, a wrapped chocolate lay like a scarab atop the linen pillowcase, and at the conference itself, in the breaks between papers delivered by the German, Danish, Dutch, and Spanish social scientists and bureaucrats, eleven in all, plus Rivka, a quiet young woman rolled a trolley bearing the finest coffee in bone china cups to one end of the long mahogany table.

All the Europeans, none an immigrant, spoke in clear English about the problems of the Turks in Frankfurt and the North Africans in Amsterdam and the flood of Poles into London. All Sara's expenses were paid, and she had no responsibility other than to listen and feel coddled and occasionally guilty about being coddled amid all this luxury and talk. No helmet, no fixer, no flak jacket. At dinner, they went out and drank a very good wine on the foundation's tab, and the Europeans asked her questions about multiculturalism and she got drunk as she talked about the possibilities of the immigrant nation, she, the granddaughter of Scottish and Welsh immigrants, sounding as optimistic as she could given that the Europeans were so curious about it.

At the end of the second day, she plunged out of the hotel into the early evening, desperate to smash through an invisible screen, gulping for air. Ropes clunked atop the masts of ships along the waterfront as a breeze carried in the tang of the sea, and with a long stride, turning a corner, she came face to face with a poster: on a blue background, dark-skinned children in leotards formed acrobatic poses. The words *Cirkus Mirak fra Etiopien* aroused her curiosity: an Ethiopian circus, here in Copenhagen. She had never had much interest in circuses, but given where she was and what she was doing, going to see this circus seemed suddenly appealing. She debated trying to cajole some of the others into joining her, but that would mean stealing them away from another boozy dinner. Back at the hotel, she left a note for the conference organizer, another for Rivka, then, like a truant schoolgirl, took off, foraged a quayside dinner of mussels and beer for herself, and caught a cab to the warehouse theatre where the circus was performing.

Inside a white room that functioned as a lobby, tall, blond people milled about, wide-shouldered men in grey coats with mufflers cinched at their necks, women holding the hands of babbling children. Being tall and blonde herself, in her black boots and black coat, Sara passed as a likely Dane among them. There were a few others not obviously Danish: a dark-haired woman glittery with gold jewellery who spoke what might have been Hungarian to her diminutive male companion, a handful of Ethiopian expats though not many: a quartet of older Ethiopian men in suits with firm postures and long, strong faces and arched brows conversed in the staccato sounds of what was probably Amharic; a few young men and two couples, along with a family of mother, father, and three boys accompanied by an older woman in a wool coat, a white veil trimmed with a glint of colour thrown over her head, also stood close by. Most Ethiopian immigrants, Sara surmised, would not have been able to afford the price of a ticket.

She had been to Africa once, to Kenya, five years before. The paper had sent her on from Istanbul, where she happened to be, to Nairobi, from where she'd headed north with a convoy of aid workers, in trucks and white Land Rovers, up through the scrub desert of Turkana, called by someone *the frying pan of the world*, to the wastelands of the Kakuma refugee camp. The van she'd travelled in had blown three tires on thorns on the last stretch of the journey, and each time the van juddered to a halt, she and her companions had clambered out to help fix the tire or crouched by the road in the appalling heat, the view a terrain of desiccated thorn trees and scorched riverbeds, which nevertheless was touched with austere beauty. Even when the land looked empty, people appeared: a Turkana woman wanting to change an American hundred-dollar bill; a teacher — dark skin shining, in dark suit and tie, despite the heat. After the third tire blew, a truck full of American evangelical Christians stopped and offered them a replacement tire. In the camp, children clutched at Sara: Somali, Ethiopian, Sudanese. Hands tugging at her clothes, they begged her to take them away with her. At night the earth became a field of tiny fires. All day she swept at the constant eye-bombing swarms of flies. It had been hard to contain her despair, though this was matched by admiration at the resilience of those who'd walked for weeks, even months, to reach this place, and there was reassurance in the thought that ordinary tasks — washing, cooking, tending children — went on here as everywhere. Out of these internal states rose the insistence that there was mean-ing in documenting the stories of people in a place like this: the thing she did. She hadn't needed a helmet or flak jacket here either, not that she ever went into front-line war zones, only into borderlands of turbulence and uncertainty. She had been drawn to extremity but had no appetite for deepest danger. And then, a year and a half ago, she'd given it all up, the risk, the search for authenticity by giving voice to the ground truths of such places, in favour of a life that kept her close to home.

Along with her ticket to the circus, she was handed a program in Danish, largely inscrutable, but there were photographs, in grainy black and white, of the child performers forming human pyramids and airborne in front of a crowd of children squatting on what was presumably an Ethiopian hillside.

As Sara took her seat in one of the raked rows, musicians filed to a cluster of instruments and amplifiers in front of a raised and curtained stage. Not children but late teenagers. A hush fell over the audience as one of the young men settled the strap of a saxophone across his shoulder, another took up an instrument that resembled a lyre, yet another cradled a long-necked, single-stringed instrument and shook out his other arm, which held a bow, and an older girl, willowy and slight in a loose white costume, curved a cordless mike into place over one cheek.

When the curtains parted, the young woman began to sing, her sinuous voice rising, the wail of the saxophone rising with it, above the pluck and vibration of the strings, a pulse starting. Across the stage lay a row of blankets, humped forms beneath them, all still, until the one in the middle began to stir, limbs in a bright-blue leotard protruding, limbs that then shucked off the blanket to reveal an elfin boy, who soared into a backflip. The blankets to either side of him shifted, rose up, and were tossed off as two other boys, clad in yellow and red, tumbled into somersaults, and beside these, two more forms lifted their blankets upward and were revealed to be girls, in looser white outfits, like that of the singer, bodies balanced on forearms and chests, legs arced back above their heads, blankets dangling and twitching from their feet.

There wasn't precisely a story, although the three boys who'd come from beneath the blankets seemed to be on a journey in which they encountered groups of other performers, who were eager to show off to the boys what they could do, as were the boys, in turn, so that an air of lighthearted one-upmanship passed back and forth. There was some comic miming: one of the boys disappeared and had to be searched for. A trio of girls helped. Jugglers appeared, and stilt-walkers, two slim earnest boys atop tall wooden legs. The boy in blue reappeared on a unicycle, arms waggling, chased by the boys in yellow and red, then by an older, menacing boy on stilts. The music was fervent, propulsive, at moments almost a lament. Some of the children seemed as young as eight, or ten, and others were teenagers, one of them tall and strutting, with the wisp of a moustache. All of this Sara imagined describing to her lover, David.

A fleet-footed flock of boys rushed into sight and rippled across the stage in barrel rolls, bending at the waist and diving into the air. Boys climbed atop the shoulders of other boys and sprang into somersaulting dives. A row of four boys held out their hands to three, who hoisted themselves upon the shoulders of the first row, then two more climbed atop those, toes curled around the shoulders of the boys below, and the boy in blue was lifted into place atop the pyramid, the boys at the ends of each row holding their arms out while the other boys gripped the legs of those above them, the tower wobbling yet intact, the boys' faces alight with exhilarated concentration, the boy in blue grinning at the top. To a shower of applause, he toppled forward, caught in the arms of two girls.

More girls shook their shoulders in a dance, a host of tiny braids tumbling around their ears, then arched into backbends and again formed a human pyramid; atop a row of three, two, an older girl balanced on arms and shoulders curved her torso and legs so far around that her feet dangled like hands beside her head. There were perhaps sixteen performers in total, although it was difficult to count, all the bodies in motion, their energy infectious, their agility so beguiling that Sara was caught up, entranced. Two boys entered carrying flaming torches and began to toss them back and forth. What she felt from them: such pleasure, such excitement.

The music, like the performance, reached a crescendo, sound and movement, the female vocalist's voice sailing high as if soaring among the bodies and pressing them onward, and the saxophone offered its own fevered surges. Two solemn, almond-eyed boys dragged out a span of thick rope and, from either side of the stage, began to turn it like an enormous skipping rope. The tall, moustached boy held a match to it and flame licked its way along the span, leaping along it as the performers began to hurl themselves over the flames, one after another, the blue boy, after a series of speeding backflips, hurtling over the burning rope last to land, still grinning, arms outstretched.

Applause erupted as the children bowed, sweaty, breathless, the flaming rope extinguished, before they, too, began to clap, and two boys slipped into the wings and tugged a man into sight.

Tall, he ducked his head so that his face was hidden beneath his red baseball cap, as if he were bashful or wished to reduce his height. Not obviously Ethiopian: he did not have the distinctive look of the Amhara, anyway. A muscled, supple-limbed, pale black man in a white T-shirt, who pulled off his cap to reveal cropped hair and a radiant and dimpled smile. He held up his hands to applaud the children before opening his arms to the audience and taking a deep bow himself. The children and teenagers crowded close to him, flushed and quivery, as if drawn to him, and he in turn vibrated in their presence, his gaze alight. He pressed his hands against his jean-covered thighs. After motioning to the audience to quiet themselves, he began to speak. In English. A young blonde woman, holding a microphone at the side of the stage, translated his words into Danish.

Thank you, he said, thank you so much for coming. His lilting voice unfurled itself, and Sara thought she heard the hint of an accent, although she couldn't place it.

We are so very thrilled to be with you on our second tour to Europe. We have travelled very far in five years. In five years the world knows of us, and we are happy to show the world what we have achieved in this time, to say this is what is coming out of Ethiopia, not starving children, but this energy, this accomplishment.

There was a touch of self-consciousness in the way he used his voice, as if he were playing an instrument, yet his warmth and combination of fervour and charm overtook whatever was manipulative. He breathed out a generosity that made him the kind of man you felt compelled to watch.

He waited for the young woman to translate his words before continuing. We have taken some of the traditions of Ethiopian music and dance and wedded them to circus. There is no tradition of circus in Ethiopia. Five years ago when I came to Addis as a teacher, I had no idea to create this. We began with nothing and made one show, and there was such enthusiasm that now we have a circus and a circus school, and other circuses are forming in other towns, and in other parts of East Africa, an entire movement. We work with children of the street, but this is not all we do. We work with all children who come to us, who wish to study circus, and we have a great amount of support from the NGOs, the non-governmental agencies, who love how we go into communities to perform and bring social messages to people through our shows and offer children this opportunity for self-affirmation and self-discipline. What I wish is to show children what is possible, create a magic, for children, for everyone, to transform things, to say this is what a circus can do and what children can do, wherever they are in the world. There are flyers about us in the lobby, and there is also a donations box if you wish to give more to our projects. We are grateful for any support.

He used his hands as he spoke, his flexible fingers shaping the air. Where was he from? Sara puzzled through what had to be his bio, in Danish. Raymond Renaud his name was. *Canadisk*. Canadian. *Fra Montreal.* A shift occurred in the nature of her curiosity once their shared nationality was revealed. Yet there was his placeless accent and occasionally odd diction. How, she wondered, had he come to be in Addis? His age was hard to determine: he looked young but not too young, perhaps close to forty, and therefore around the same age or slightly older than she was.

And the children, the performers, what was it like for them to be in Copenhagen, so far from Addis Ababa, breathing in the cool air and the smell of the sea, and already at this time of spring living through the great expanse of a northern twilight. How much did they see or get about in the places where they travelled? There were, yes, sixteen of them, plus the musicians. It would be expensive to tour a group like this. They were performing three shows plus two daytime performances for schoolchildren, funded, to judge by the logos in the program, by various levels of various governments.

Please tell all your friends, the young woman said, in English and Danish. The children were making their way offstage, the man — their founder, director, leader — stood out in his white shirt, guiding the performers like a shepherd, one hand briefly hovering between the shoulder blades of one of the younger boys.

In the middle of the next week, back in Toronto, Sara pulled open the door of a Queen Street art gallery, shaking off a skitter of rain, to find herself in the path of her old friend Juliet Levin and Juliet's partner, a photographer, on their way out of the clamorous opening of a show of pinhole photographs. Max, leather-jacketed and feline, had his arm around Juliet, gamine in a pink coat and shiny boots that ran up to her knees. Juliet had the same nervous prettiness and slant to her posture, as if she were rushing into a wind, that she'd had since their university days in Montreal.

Sara kissed Juliet's warm and perfumed skin and felt the press of Juliet's lips against her own, one cheek then the other. They exchanged the usual phrases — how are you, it's lovely to see you — while Sara scanned the room beyond Juliet's pink shoulder for a glimpse of Soraya Green, the friend and fellow journalist whom she was meeting and to whom she was going to give the lowdown on the conference in Copenhagen.

Every encounter with Juliet carried a whiff of the past that had to be shucked off or contained. There it was, fainter than previously, yet not entirely neutralized. Juliet, daughter of a socialist doctor, had once told a story about going into a bar back home in Winnipeg and asking for a whisky sour only to find that the barman didn't know what that was. In telling this story, she'd seemed to want to affirm how far she'd come from her place of origin. Juliet had been good to Sara. She had provided Sara with a place to live when Sara had nowhere else to go and had given her unwavering support in the months leading up to the trial, after Sara had been charged with theft and fraud. Juliet had offered of her own accord to stand as a character witness in Sara's defence. One night, early in her stay in the apartment on avenue de l'Esplanade, Sara had walked into Juliet's bedroom to find Juliet, wrapped in a wool cardigan and flannel nightgown and hockey socks, studying at her desk, and said, I did not steal that woman's wallet or use her credit card. And Juliet had turned, her face bright in the lamplight, and said, I know you didn't.

They had not become friends in the Feminism and Sexuality seminar in which they'd first met. Juliet had been one of the ones who took a lot of notes and didn't talk much, and who hesitated when she did talk. Once, during that semester, a year and a half before the trial, they had run into each other filing out of a dance performance in a loft on Saint-Laurent. Going to see dance was something Sara did on her own. Not many undergraduates went off-campus to see shows, but she was older than most, four years older, and already had, to her mind, an adult life, and was in a phase during which she liked to sit in the dark, immersed in the fierce movement and physical conviction of the dancers' bodies, feeling the sustaining heat of her still-secret relationship with Graham Finnessey deep in her belly and limbs. Most of the people she knew in political science, or historians, like Graham, weren't interested in dance. She wore a sheepskin coat and tall black boots and felt alluring and vital as she strode through the Montreal streets. And there was Juliet Levin, with some friends, fellow fine arts or humanities students, all dressed in black, congregating near the door where the dancers would appear. How upright, beneath her silky sweater and skirt, Juliet's posture was, how obvious her longing to be if not a dancer then mistaken for a dancer or someone like a dancer. In the gallery entrance, in Toronto, a trace of this moment still quivered in her.

We're on our way out to dinner, Juliet said as Max bounded ahead of her through the door and into the street, while Juliet allowed herself to be borne back inside, along with Sara, leaving the doorway to a laughing couple on their way in.

Juliet sounded apologetic, as if she hoped to give the impression of wanting to chat for longer, even if she couldn't.

I saw something in Copenhagen last week that might interest you, Sara said. The thought had not occurred to her until this moment. Although she and Juliet had not gotten together in some time, years in fact, there remained a sense of indebtedness in her toward Juliet for all that Juliet had once done, and simultaneously a violent longing to be free of this feeling. I was in Copenhagen for a conference and saw a children's circus from Ethiopia founded by a guy from Montreal. They were performing, they're great, they do a lot of acrobatics.

They tour internationally and are involved in social outreach, mostly in Ethiopia, from the sound of it. It might be a good fit for your show.

For the past three years, Juliet had been a producer for a national television arts show. Yet now, at these words, she looked strained. The show's been cancelled.

Oh, Julie, I'm sorry, I had no idea. What happened?

They want to reinvent it, they said. Make it more youth-oriented.

Are you definitely out of a job?

I don't know yet.

Well, this could be something youth-oriented. He'd be telegenic, the circus founder. There's the Montreal angle. And the kids. Maybe you can do something with it anyway?

Juliet nodded offhandedly and pulled a little black notebook out of her handbag. Do you have any contact info?

His name is Raymond something. Renaud, Renouf, something like that. And the circus is Cirkus Mirak.

Max, in his leather jacket, pressed his face to the gallery window and waggled a finger at Juliet, who stuffed her notebook back into her bag and, already in motion, said, Thanks.

Two days later an email arrived from Juliet repeating her thanks for the tip about the circus. The day after that, as Sara sat at her desk in the newsroom, within its enclosure of carpeted dividers, beneath the flash of TV monitors, spumes of paper covering the wide surface in front of her, her phone rang, and it was Juliet Levin.

I found a website, but can you tell me more about the show you saw? What the children do exactly?

There was a lot of juggling, stilt-walking, acrobatics and balancing acts, and live music. There's an Ethiopian inflection to all of it, to the music and the costumes. Oh, and a couple of them juggle with fire and they all leap over a flaming rope at the end.

So it's all children, and it was started by this Canadian?

As far as I know, yes.

And you thought they were good.

Yes.

And he'd be good to talk to.

I think so. Yes. He goes to Addis Ababa and founds a circus. There has to be a story there.

Have they ever been here?

I don't know that.

Almost two weeks in the past, glimpsed on another continent, the vividness of the elastic-limbed girl contortionist and the small boy in blue who had somersaulted over the rope of flame had begun to fade. They had touched and briefly intrigued Sara, but the daily swell of the newsroom diminished them: its warren of dividers and desks within cells personalized by a choice of mug or photographs or cute cat cartoons or the swoop of a screensaver across a computer monitor; the ranks of hunched bodies, the clocks, the map of the world above the wall of photo files, the blare of telephones, voices, the urgent rattle of fingers across keyboards pressed themselves around her. Then there was her need to add two hundred words to the piece on Romanian orphans who had found new homes in Canada and to do it in the next hour, since the piece had to be edited and filed by the end of the day. Nuala Johnson, the national editor, was waiting for it. After that, she'd have to come up with ideas for the next day's story meeting, something, say, about the recent influx of Russian criminals who were building mansions with their laundered money, and—she'd need something else. Meanwhile, the headlines in the newspaper open across Sara's desk shouted about the ferry sinking off the coast of Haiti and the massacres of Hutus by Tutsis in Burundi.

Okay, Juliet said. There's a number on the website. Maybe I'll see if I can get hold of him.

Three and a half months later, one Monday afternoon in mid-July, Alan Marker, deputy editor on the foreign news desk, made his way along the channels between office chairs, broad as a tugboat in his striped shirt, holding aloft a piece of fax paper like a sail, and boomed, An arrest warrant's been issued for Karadzic. Alan was as obsessed with justice in the case against the Bosnian Serb leader, former president, now indicted for war crimes, as another might be over a lover. In Sara's ear, from a law office in a tower mere blocks away, David said, The appointment's at twelve on Thursday.

And if he was taking his wife, Greta, in for a CT scan at noon on Thursday, it was pretty much a foregone conclusion that Sara would not see him on Wednesday evening, the night on which they usually met. Greta's last scan, three months before, had been clear, no sign of the return of the first tumour, nor any sign of the second one, the small inoperable walnut of an astrocytoma that had appeared, six months after Greta had received her last all-clear, in the left frontal lobe of her brain.

But next week absolutely yes, David said, and his tone conveyed a confirmation of all they did share, despite the circumstantial strangeness of their connection, the steadiness of a hand held out.

You know it's fine and I assumed as much, Sara said. How are you feeling?

Arctic winds poured from vents in the ceiling, so ferociously that Sara found herself longing for a toque and parka, her sweater no more than a flimsy second skin, the diminishing heat from her cup of coffee barely penetrating her as she hunched toward the phone and David through it, Alan Marker's voice surging in the background.

Hopeful but terrified. The doctors sound optimistic, yet I can't be a libertine with hope, it's too dangerous.

On the last scan all was well. Hold on to that. Hope. Better to hope. I'll be thinking of you and holding out all my hope from here.

What a peculiar angle of interest hers was: and yet impossible not to offer hope and mean it. What kind of monster would she be if she could not do this? Of course she wanted Greta to be well, to make a full recovery from the cancer and the attendant neurological symptoms, the fatigue, the memory loss, the slips in speech that David had described to her and which Greta had been in rehabilitation to overcome.

Thursday was Sara's birthday. David seemed to have forgotten, and how could she blame him. She would be a poor sport to remind him of it, at least right now. Anyway, neither of them had ever been the sort to set much store by birthdays and their attendant celebration, although Sara did remember the date of David's, February 22. Nor did they have the sort of relationship in which they spent their birthdays together. That was fine. This triangulation, entanglement, whatever you wanted to call it. She had chosen it. She was turning thirty-six; it was not an exceptional year, just one more on the road to forty.

David said, We won't have results for a while, so there'll be that agony of waiting.

Let me know how it goes, Sara said. Call at any point if you need to.

After she hung up the phone, she rose to her feet and paced back and forth on the patch of carpet behind her desk, as if walking along a humming wire, Nellie Wuetherick craning over her own phone on one side of her, Paul Rosenberg deep in the embrace of his keyboard on the other. She banged up against an internal wall with David, but this was exactly what she wanted because it stopped her from getting too close and if she kept this distance then he could not hurt her.

Months before, there'd been an evening when David had poured dollops of single malt into a pair of her mother's old crystal tumblers from the bottle that he kept in her kitchen, and they'd made their way, tumblers in hand, down the hall toward Sara's living room, and David had turned to her and asked, Did you know that Karadzic, the Serb leader, wrote poetry? Sara said she did, someone at work had told her, and someone she knew in England, another journalist, had even sent her a translation into English of one of his poems. The shocking thing, or one of the shocking things, being that, while it was bilious with anger, it wasn't as awful a poem as you might expect.

David, she'd said, I love that you'd know I'd want to know something like this.

His shirt collar was loosened, he was barefoot, showered, and when he touched his cool glass to her back, between her shoulder blades, the gesture moved through her body, her blood vessels pulsing in a thick, languid tock after sex. Beneath his surface formality lay a physical fluency, a fluency they shared. Then there was his care, their unusual intersection of interests, and the other ways in which he continued to surprise her. One night, they'd gone out for dinner, as they sometimes did in her neighbourhood, and he'd told the two men at the table next to theirs that she and he were Canadian journalists living in Russia home for a visit. The men, chatty, had begun by asking them what they did, and then wanted to know about Russia, and on the spot they'd had to fabricate this other life out loud. Sara had no idea what had possessed David to say such a thing, other than that he knew she'd spent a few years of her childhood in Moscow and could trot out a few Russian phrases, endearments: zaika moya, solnyshko moyo, my little rabbit, my little sunshine. Also, her parents lived in Moscow, her father having returned to work at the embassy there, after the years spent in Ottawa and in other overseas postings: Berlin, Brussels, Kiev.

When Sara asked David, later, why he'd done it, he said because it was no one else's business what they were to each other. Yet there were far more straightforward ways than this to create a veil of privacy around themselves.

In her living room, they'd folded themselves onto the old sofa, clasping their tumblers of Scotch, and debated why dictators and despots might decide to write poetry. Didn't Gaddafi write poetry too, or just prose? Sara asked.

Saddam Hussein wrote novels, David said, and poetry. Goebbels wrote plays.

Lenin wrote poetry before he became a dictator, Sara said. Maybe there's an impulse toward poetry not only as something potentially beautiful but also controlling, a way to give formal shape to experience, emotion, rhetoric, and so sway people. You think? There's probably no way to generalize why dictators or sociopaths write poetry. It could be from some private, dissociative urge.

A belief that words can sway, David said. Beautiful order brings power. Or there's a desire to create a façade of the sensitive and artistic. With his large head and compact body, he threw himself almost physically into a consideration of the question, neck torqued, forehead furrowed. Copyright lawyer, avid and complicated man, who held on to his own forms of self-containment. All Sara's attention, physical and mental, was drawn to him, and yet when he left the house she would be flooded with relief. Okay, David said, I've entertained that question long enough. But beautiful constraint. He clinked his crystal glass to hers, their thighs pressed together. Let's drink to that. Or let's put it this way, to the beauties of constraint.

He was talking about them. In their case, constraint also meant secret. David was not just her private life but a secret one, as she was his. By now they'd shared nearly three years together, and Sara was supposed to keep this to herself as, generally, she did.

No sooner had she swung herself back into her desk chair, the newsroom churning around her, more swirls of gelid air pouring from above, than her phone rang again, and when she reached to answer it, Juliet Levin said hello, then something like, Are you going to the Cirque de Lumière benefit on Thursday?

Am I what?

The Cirque's doing a benefit performance for Cirkus Mirak, the Ethiopian children's circus, and I wondered if you're going.

I don't know anything about this. That night in Copenhagen wafted back into view, the air full of twisting and tumbling children.

Oh. It was Juliet's turn to sound surprised. I thought you'd have heard.

I don't always pay attention to things like this. I'm sure Anne in the arts section knows. Are you going?

I'll be filming. Sorry, sorry, I've been meaning to tell you. I'm shooting a documentary about the children's circus.

You are?

I'm so busy. It's been a total whirlwind. Breathlessly, Juliet filled Sara in: how, back in the spring, she'd contacted the circus founder and director, Raymond Renaud, through the phone number listed on the website, and reached him shortly after his return from Europe.

I told him I'd heard about the circus through a friend. I said I was interested in doing something and asked if anyone had and he said there'd been a short documentary made for German television. But that was all. Nothing in North America, and since he's interested in bringing the circus to North America, he really liked the idea. Originally I thought I'd approach funders and broadcasters first but he told me to come sooner than later, as soon as I could, because summer's the rainy season and he said it didn't make sense to come then, and then they're touring again later in the summer and fall. And so I breathed deep and put the trip on my credit card and went in May, for two weeks, and brought along a Ryerson film student as my assistant and sound guy, and we shot on video, and I've decided it's okay for it to look a little raw. And you were right, he's been fabulous and generous, the whole story is amazing, the social circus angle, and the children, and he's great on film.

Sara was still trying to get her head around the idea of timid Juliet in Ethiopia, not to mention Juliet shooting a film there. So is this for your show?

Oh, no, Juliet said. That's over. I've approached various broadcasters. And funders. And everyone seems to totally love the story of him and the circus, and I'm hoping to make a feature. I can't quite believe it, but I am. And it's all thanks to you. Because if you hadn't told me about this.

There was no reason to feel jealous. Sara did not feel jealous, yet there was a twang of some kind. She had handed this story to Juliet. It was not her kind of story. And here was Juliet, effervescent and joyous, running with it; Juliet had run all the way to Addis Ababa, a city where Sara had never been and where she had trouble imagining the Juliet Levin she knew, with her neat and beautiful outfits and nervousness and downtown life, contending with bad roads and wonky electricity and all that was wild and unpredictable about a city in the developing world, the sort of place that had until recently been part of Sara's life until she had chosen to step away from it. So more power to Juliet. She had wanted to offer Juliet a gift and she'd succeeded.

Were you anywhere other than Addis?

Mostly Addis. They have a rehearsal space on the outskirts of the city, so we spent a lot of time there, then travelled south with them on tour, which gives me this built-in narrative. And everyone loves him there. You should see. Children flock to him, and people in the communities are so thrilled by the whole idea. One guy was calling circus the new religion. NGOs are mad about the work he's doing. Everyone says how transformative it's been.

And the benefit?

He's going to be there. There's a North American tour in the works now, and he's trying to raise money for that, and more awareness here generally. You should come and meet him.

How expensive is it?

Tickets are a hundred dollars. I think.

Knowing that the odds of seeing David were slim, Sara had planned to go out for drinks with friends. If Juliet had once known when her birthday was, she, too, seemed to have forgotten, as Sara had forgotten Juliet's, other than that it was, she thought, sometime in March. She felt no great need to meet the circus founder, despite Juliet's excitement, yet maybe the thing to do for her birthday was go to the circus. She had never seen any of the high-tech acrobatic performances of the Cirque, which had started out, she knew, as a gang of stilt-walkers and fire-jugglers bewitching crowds on Montreal street corners, back in the days when she and Juliet had been students there. Perhaps their early shows were not unlike what the Ethiopian children did. Going to the circus could be a way to embrace youthfulness, which wasn't a bad thing when you were on the road to forty, and supporting the children's circus was undeniably a good thing.

His amplified voice was the first thing that met Sara as she slipped into the back of the reception tent, late for the pre-show talk. Two tents, a smaller one and the big top, had been raised by the side of the lake in a west-end parking lot. He was standing at one end of an airy room, raised on a small platform, in front of a microphone and podium, the tent's thick canvas soughing in a breeze, traffic distantly surging, the scree-scree of gulls ricocheting down from the sky. She made her way along the side of a crowd of men and women in fine suits and shiny dresses, hands clutching wineglasses, in order to see him better, and there, from the front of the room, above the heads of the crowd, rose the furry pelt of a sound boom: someone, presumably Juliet, was filming him.

You have to understand a phenomenon that people there call ferengi hysteria, Raymond Renaud was saying. In my time I have travelled a lot and I have been a foreigner in many places, but I never experienced anything like the level of street harassment I found in Addis. I was biking to the school where I taught and people not only shouted at me but threw things. Stones, orange peels. Okay, they are not used to seeing foreigners biking in the street, but this was so disturbing. The word for a local person is habeshat and for foreigner it is ferengi. When people shouted ferengi at me, I called back habeshat. This confused people, but still they threw things at me. It was a terrible time. I was in despair. All I wanted was to leave this place, the hostility was so intense, and my life felt so restricted.

Instead of the white T-shirt he'd sported in Copenhagen, he wore a loose-fitting, checked yellow jacket, brown trousers, and brown socks with sandals. It was hard to tell if this was his idea of dressing up, or all that he could afford in his attempt to dress up, or if there was defiance in his attire, a resistance to wearing anything more conventional. And there was Juliet, face pressed to a video camera, roving in front of him, and a young blond man holding up the sound boom. The musical quality of Raymond Renaud's voice was as strong as Sara remembered, the charismatic ardour of its rise and fall, the hint of unplaceable accent. He gestured with his hands as he had in Copenhagen: his fingers pressed and squeezed the air. There had to be a waiter slipping somewhere through the crowd. Sara turned, needing a drink.

One day, he continued, I took my juggling pins and began to juggle in an empty lot. Whatever happened, it couldn't be any worse than what I'd already experienced. And I drew a little crowd of people. Then, out of the crowd steps a boy, maybe ten, a bit shy, who comes close to me and asks if I will show him how to do what I am doing. And I allow myself to feel a leaf of hope. Maybe this will change the nature of our interaction in a way that doesn't have anything to do with money. And the next day I brought along my pins and juggling balls and some plastic bottles and a bag of apples, and a few more children step forward and ask me if I can teach them. They spoke a little English and I spoke a little Amharic. They had never seen anyone juggle. Every day I went back and more and more children came and asked to join us and it was beautiful.

We found a garden where there was grass beneath our feet, which was better for practising acrobatics. We found some old mattresses and tied thick wire between two trees for a tightrope. I taught juggling and simple gymnastics and bought some wood to make a pair of stilts and taught them to balance mops on the ends of their chins. And one day the children came to me and said, Please, can we do a show, and I said, Yes, yes, why not. We had a boom box plugged into the cigarette lighter of my truck for music. We put up a sign, went back to the empty lot, and people came.

While all this was going on, you have to understand, the military dictatorship is falling. There are tanks in the street. The schools close. I lose my job. All foreigners are advised to leave. Before, because of the harassment, I wanted only to leave and now the children, they are begging me to stay with them. And I was beginning to understand what was possible, the true power of circus. And I was filled with the desire to be with them. So I stayed.

A waiter passed by, and when Sara reached out, a glass of white wine was placed in her hand and she swallowed the wine's winsome tang and felt its percolation through her body.

Many of the children are poor, they have very little, but they have families, they go to school, and if they hang about in the street, it is because they have nothing else to do. So what I do is I create a prevention against streetism, by taking all children

(37)

out of the street and giving them something to believe in. And more and more children found their way to us.

So after a year, when I came back to Montreal for a visit, I decided to go into the office of the Cirque and explain my project to them. I knew no one. I was doing this thing I believed in with my whole heart, but I began to see that to grow I really needed some support. I walked in the door and started speaking to people, telling them about the circus, and the children, and how we are using our shows to communicate social messages to communities, how a circus can be a new way to do this, and people started going, Wow, we really get what you're up to. And the next instant, they said, Tell us how we can help. That afternoon, I walked out with a cheque and a duffle bag full of equipment and costumes. All along, it has been like this. People are so generous. The Cirque is so generous. Tonight you are so generous. And in five years, we have grown like a miracle.

Yes, I am the director, but the true root of all this comes from the children. They led me to it. There is a Cirkus Mirak because of their work, their dreams, their passion. I gave them a beautiful idea, and I train them, but at heart, I am directed by them. They discover what is possible. The circus, it's theirs.

Two glasses of wine on an empty stomach might not have been the best idea, even if it was her birthday, and as Sara took her seat in one of the tiers atop a metal scaffold, the whole structure seemed to wobble. Juliet and her assistant, the young blond man who'd been holding up the sound boom, were on the far side of the ranks of seats, in another row perched high, while

Raymond Renaud was down near the front, with a cadre in suits apart from one gesticulating man. A woman in a black dress seemed to be working as his handler. He glanced about, as if trapped between these people. Then again, he was on show at every moment, which no doubt took effort, every gesture a performance.

David had not called. Sara had stopped briefly at home after work to change her clothes, and there had been no message from him; nor had he called her at work during the day. There were birthday messages from friends, but none from her parents. Her mother had sent a card from Moscow, which had arrived two days before. Their contact was sporadic and had been for years, since the turbulence of her adolescence, although the origins of her sense of estrangement from them lay further in the past. All of it had been exacerbated in the wake of the charges against her, and the trial: she'd felt that her parents had decided this was simply more trouble she'd got herself into. Still, it was odd to have no birthday call, and since it was already late in the evening in Moscow, it was unlikely that they would call now.

Once, David and Greta might have come to an event like this. Greta, also a lawyer, small and dark and vivacious to judge from the few pre-illness photographs of her that Sara had seen, had sat on the board of a small arts foundation. Lawyer *and* altruist. She'd had to stop working because of the cancer and the neurological impediments left in its wake, which, after months of therapy, were retreating. Greta should have died from her cancer. She hadn't. Everything now pointed toward — stability, this was the word that David used. He said Greta was preparing to return to work. The fact that Sara hadn't heard from him was impossible to read. They would not have results from the scan but possibly an intimation of how things had gone. A sudden image of David appeared: standing in one of the tent's entranceways, in a tux, casting about. Pure fantasy. Sometimes, especially in recent months, she found herself, when out, searching for a chance sighting of David with Greta. And if, or when, Greta began to reclaim her whole life, what would alter in Sara's own relationship with David?

She had met David at a benefit. One night, three years ago in June, Matt Johansen, one of the city reporters, had stopped by her desk and asked if she happened to be free because he was on his way to a charity boat cruise in support of lupus research or maybe it was diabetes and his wife had just called to say she'd come down with a fever. I think she's genuinely sick, but listen, I'm sure it will be awful and the worst part is if you hate it you're absolutely stuck because you're on a boat out in the harbour and there's no way off.

She went because Matt was good company, and she had no plans other than work for the evening, and there they were on the upper deck of a converted ferry, a jangly Dixieland band warming up below, neither particularly dressed for dining and dancing, Matt in a windbreaker, Sara in jeans and T-shirt and boots and leather jacket, when Matt ran into an old friend of his, Siobhan something, accompanied by a man in a tuxedo. A friend of hers, Siobhan said, making the introductions. David Ross.

Sara's first thought: a tuxedo! And: he has a large head! The man held out his hand. In her black boots she was taller than he was. Sara Wheeler, she said.

He had the air, she thought, of an alien; he did not seem ill at ease in his skin but radically perplexed to find himself where he was.

When she asked him what he did, as they leaned against the railing, Matt and Siobhan having moved off elsewhere, he said he had taken a leave from his job as a lawyer to look after his wife who was ill. He said he was out on his own for the first time in six months. He did not know what he was doing there. He had made a terrible mistake in allowing himself to be brought along. This was impersonal, she decided; it had nothing to do with her. She asked him the nature of his wife's illness and he told her: the diagnosis six months before, the surgery, the neurological problems, the radiation and chemotherapy. When he asked her how she came to be on the boat, Sara explained her connection to Matt and told David Ross how strange it felt to be floating around the harbour, two weeks after returning from Iraq.

That caught his attention. Where exactly? David Ross asked her.

I went with a group of reporters into southern Iraq. Najaf, around Najaf, looking at some of the post-war reconstruction. We visited an orphanage, a hospital. We did a lot of things.

Your first trip?

First to the south, second to the country, I was up in the north, near Kurdistan, last year.

Inky water roiled about below, the city beyond them transformed into a wall of scintillating lights both flattened and dense. What struck Sara, beyond the selfless commitment required to take care of his sick wife, was that to do it well David

Ross would need to be very good at looking after himself. Bombed buildings in Najaf floated in front of her. She tried to make them float away. Perhaps he sensed some similar quality of self-care in her.

She had not been looking to meet anyone. She had given her heart once, wholly, and having been betrayed by Graham Finnessey, having lost the life she'd thought would be hers, she did not want to go through that pain ever again. There had been other men since Graham, as there had been boys before him, but nothing that lasted, and if anyone came too close, she cut them loose, for how else were you to protect the tender self? Whatever frisson of attraction she felt for this man, he was safe, bound by the ropes of his marriage and his wife's illness.

A week later, he called her up and asked her out for a drink. They ended up back at the apartment where she was living. It was clear what she was to him: a release, an escape, and for one night she thought, I can do this, I can offer him this compassion. The next week, he called her again. He told her not then but sometime soon thereafter that he and Greta had met at university and been together since they were twenty-one. They had been through some difficult times, but they had a life together. They'd had a very long disagreement about children; she wanted them; he didn't; they'd talked of parting; then she got sick. He had no desire to leave this life. He couldn't leave her and he wouldn't; these were two separate things and both were true. He was such a lawyer, Sara thought, in his need to spell things out, in his insistence on certain kinds of clarity. About his life, his wife. And if he'd left Greta, at least while she was ill, she wouldn't have wanted him. But she wanted him, his body at least, in her bed, what their bodies did together. One night, she reared up, pulled herself free of the tangled sheets, and said, I can't do this if it's going to hurt Greta. For whoever and whatever else Greta was, Greta needed him. From the bed came his voice. Sara. There was nothing peremptory or demanding in his call. I told her there's a friend I see sometimes. I needed to tell her that much. What Greta said in return, he didn't mention. Friend, Sara thought, and the word repelled her—pawn in some practical accommodation between them. She did not want to be having an affair and was repelled by herself. He did not talk then, only later, about the neurological symptoms, and how Greta was altered by them. Nor could she believe that she was in bed with a lawyer. Though what she felt by then had moved beyond compassion.

From the beginning, there was a force of something between them. Of taut connection. The calm field of his body in the bed. The way he called her name in the dark. He had an ability to be present and available to the possibility of a given moment, and this drew her, a form of generosity that she wanted fiercely to be in the presence of. He did not want all of her; nor did she wish to give all of herself to him. He was such a mixture of impulsiveness and restraint. Early on, he told her he would not be able to use the word *l---*. They would not be able to, should not make such declarations to each other. But tenderness, he said, let that be our word. I feel very tender toward you.

Yes, there were moral contortions in being with him. And I feel very tender toward you, she said.

Those first months, she was often away travelling, and he was often exhausted by caregiving. There was the night when he wanted only to talk, the night when he said, I cannot do this, the night when she said it, the night when he came and fell asleep while she cooked him dinner, nights when they went out to movies in cinemas where they were less likely to run into people they knew. The week after Greta rang the bell at the end of her chemotherapy treatments, he arrived and lay on her sofa and sobbed and wouldn't tell her what so disturbed him.

When she skipped a period right after a trip to Israel and the West Bank, she put it down to stress: the aftermath of the massacre that she was covering, then being nearly attacked by the Zionist settler with a gun and a vicious dog. When, after the second missed period, her doctor told her she was pregnant, she was shocked; they'd been taking precautions, but she hadn't been using the pill, hadn't thought she was sleeping with him or anyone enough to warrant it. David, too, was shocked when she told him, but exemplary, said he'd support her whatever she decided to do, would offer all necessary financial support if she decided to go through with the pregnancy. She'd been so certain of what she would do until he opened up this other door of possibility. Having a baby had seemed unimaginable until it didn't. She'd never thought she wanted children, and though she felt David's fear and dismay, horror even, here was this other, tender life beginning its vertiginous hold in her. A baby. She told no one else. Eleven weeks. She had an appointment for an ultrasound. Until the morning she woke, body cramping, put out her hand, and felt the sticky, blood-soaked sheets, this discovery even more shocking than the first, the gash of grief so great it pulled her under, wave after wave of grief. She cancelled a trip to South Africa for the elections, the chance to meet Mandela, barely left her bed for a week. She told her parents, and most others, that she'd caught a parasite while travelling. David gave her space to grieve. He did not desert her.

Two months after that, he showed up one night without calling and stepped inside the apartment without taking off his overcoat and as he sat himself on the edge of her sofa, sandy hair greying at the edges of his large head, one hand in the grip of the other, she had an intimation of why he must be there. He said, We got the results of the scan two days ago and the first tumour is gone, but there is another, smaller one. They are doing a biopsy. He said, It is easy to feel you have done something wrong, you have done something to deserve this. This isn't rational. At every instant one has to fight against this. I don't know what lies ahead or what I'm going to do, but please don't tell me you can't see me right now.

She had a vision of what they were together, a huge, tensile creature alive in the room. In any relationship, you made a vibrating creature together, and theirs was jagged and roiling and kind and ferocious and tender, it was all these things. She had already put in a request to switch jobs, to do something that would keep her closer to home. She went to the kitchen and made them each a cup of tea with brandy in it: there was no adequate gesture in such a circumstance, and this was the best she could do.

She'd first thought of buying a house when pregnant; in her grief, she went ahead and did it anyway. Friends helped her move. Greta went back into treatment.

She and David had survived all this, and what they shared, whatever you called it, had burgeoned into its own form of commitment.

On the round stage below, two creatures with nubby horns protruding from their heads led a small figure in a blonde wig away from a coat rack and its mother and father, who were seated in two large armchairs. The armchairs vanished and were replaced by another realm in which, as the small blonde person and her companions watched, silver-clad figures descended from the heights of the metal rafters, bending and twisting within silver hoops clasped by a hand or a flexed knee. Tiny Chinese contortionists wrapped their limbs into helixes, as if their joints were liquid or air, while balancing silver balls on various parts of their bodies. Virile, Spandex-clad acrobats rode bicycles, hopped on and off them while keeping the bicycles continuously in motion, tossed the bicycles back and forth, until every one of them was upside down, legs in the air, atop a moving bicycle, balanced on one arm and a hand that grasped a bicycle seat. Sara wondered what Raymond Renaud thought of all this. She kept being distracted by the spectre of money, how much it must cost to mount a spectacle like this, as a woman spun her way down a skein of red cloth attached to a high crossbeam, her sequined body held in place now by a foot, now by a wrist wrapped around the ribbon of red. Violins surged. Everything she saw made her think of money or death. There was the peculiar and mounting exhaustion of watching

(46)

one act of extreme dexterity after another, the desire for more risk and possible disaster warring with the impossibility of one feat topping another. She found herself longing for the simpler, intimate vitality of the children's circus.

At the post-show reception, back in the smaller tent, Raymond Renaud stood in a corner surrounded by a cluster of hangers-on as Juliet filmed him and a photographer snapped his picture. His juggler's arms, in their yellow checked sleeves, swooped through the air, although Sara was too far off to hear what he was saying. The tiny Chinese contortionists huddled in another corner towered over by the hulking gymnasts. Around the perimeter of the room, on black-cloth-covered risers, large-scale photographs of the Ethiopian circus children were mounted. The photographs must have been there during the pre-show talk, but she had failed to notice them. Glass of wine and plate of canapés in hand, Sara drew close to take a look, all shot, a small sign said, by an Italian photographer.

The photographs were dense with colour: the saturated red of the ground, the oscillating blue of the sky, the deep green of a fringe of pine and skinny eucalyptus trees pulsed behind the children. In some photographs, they were costumed; in others, they wore street clothes. A team of boys in pink leotards, ribbons fluttering from their sleeves, soared, airborne, knees tucked to chests, arms clasped around legs, shadows like a flight of hawks against the blue canvas scrim at their backs. A quartet of girls in white held aloft a fifth girl, the older one who'd been the most extraordinary contortionist in the show in Copenhagen: once more, her weight rested on her arms and chest, and she inverted

(47)

her legs above her torso so that her body formed a circle and her feet dangled beside her head, the arc of her legs echoed by the refracted halo of the sun.

The children looked wholly absorbed in what they were doing, oblivious to the photographer or else ignoring him, the upheld girl's expression dreamy. A young boy in T-shirt and jeans and running shoes was the same slim boy in blue who'd been the first to spring from beneath the blankets in the Copenhagen show and the last to fling himself over the rope of fire, only now he held aloft two blackened metal torches, flames quickening at their tips. His physical beauty was such as to be almost discomforting, the full lips and fine arch of his brows and almond skin, even as the photographs touched all the children with beauty yet did not objectify them. What shone through was their insistence on being taken seriously, as performers, professionals — either the photographer wanted to suggest this, or they did, or both.

Someone called out her name. Juliet was approaching, pink-cheeked, without her video camera, in the company of the circus founder, who'd cast off his crowd of followers. Juliet looked, it had to be said, a little in love with him, and he, smiling, light on his feet, glanced at the photographs behind Sara before his gaze veered away.

Alcohol had widened her veins and made everything drifty. She had to figure out what to do with her glass and plate. Green-eyed, now that was a surprise, and older than when seen at a distance, if still youthful: pouches beneath his eyes, flecks of grey in the tight curls of his black hair.

Raymond Renaud. This is Sara Wheeler, Juliet said. Sara's the one who told me about the circus in the first place. She saw you in Copenhagen.

The grip of his hand in hers was warm and firm. Thank you for that, he said.

I was there for a conference. I happened to see a poster. They're wonderful performers. I'm not a circus person, but I thoroughly enjoyed the show.

Sara's a journalist, Juliet said.

Not an arts journalist, though. I write about immigration issues. And immigrant communities.

Maybe when we come here you can write something, he said, holding her in his green-eyed gaze. He had a supple physical presence, not slim but solid, taller than Sara, and projected a flexible strength. Or when Juliet's film comes out. When we travel we often do outreach into the diasporic communities. Or maybe one day you will find yourself in Addis Ababa. Have you ever been there?

I haven't, no.

You should come and see the circus in its habitat, or you and Juliet will come and you can write something then.

Juliet stood beside him, taut in her silky skirt and purple tights and Australian desert boots. Raymond Renaud touched Juliet's shoulder as if he sensed that she needed to be placated. Juliet says people here are very excited about her film, and I'm so glad to be bringing this momentum and awareness to North America. Now I have to ask you a question. When you saw the show in Copenhagen, tell me truly, what did you think?

His insistence puzzled Sara: she'd already told him that she'd thought the show was good.

They're fantastic performers, exuberant, daring. Do any of them have any prior training or is this all thanks to you?

What I've done is introduce the idea of circus and these particular skills. What is so important to me is that people see what genuinely good performers they are, talented, capable, that people do not watch the show and think charity work or social welfare project or see them as a curiosity.

I didn't think that.

He was alive to the need to bring Juliet into the circle of his attention, Juliet's lips parting as if she were about to speak. Or patronize them, he said, his gaze moving between the two of them. That is not what this is about. Because they are so good, they are so—

He broke off. Something caught in his throat. He froze, recovered, gathered them both in his radiant smile. It is so, it is so important, this work. I have been changed by it. It's greater than travel, better than anything I've ever done, better than sex.

Some distance from the entrance of the reception tent, across the parking lot, a light glowed above the metal frame of a payphone. Sara wanted and did not want to know if David, or her parents, had tried to reach her. With David, there was the perennial difficulty of not being able to call him, at least at home. She was ready to leave yet perhaps should wait a little longer for the wine to settle in her bloodstream. She walked toward the metal box, gulls swooping like handkerchiefs through the dark above her, slipped a coin into the slot, and called her answering machine: no messages. The silence fell into her.

The tent had a side opening, she noted as she returned, and beside it rose a stack of red plastic crates, the kind that held wineglasses, and two figures stood nearby: a waiter, in white shirt and black vest, who ground a cigarette beneath his heel, and Raymond Renaud, in his yellow checked jacket, close at the young man's side. His words of moments before, *better than sex*, returned to her. Her approach must have caught Raymond's eye, for he looked up and, as the waiter slipped back into the tent, called out, Do you happen to know the time?

A lake breeze hit her as Sara made her way toward him, and she tugged up the cuff of her linen shirt, aware of voices behind her leaving the tent for the parking lot. Almost eleven-fifteen, she said when close and held out her hand to him once more. Sara Wheeler, I'm—

Yes, yes, I remember. Something peremptory flared through him, though he kept his voice low and conversational, and they were far enough from the main entrance to the tent that they were unlikely to be heard. She was aware, even more intently than when they'd met earlier, of his solid yet quicksilver muscularity. Did you by chance drive here tonight?

I did, she said, although his question implied another question, and it was already forming between them while she waited to hear exactly what it would be.

Would you be able to give me a lift to the airport?

Now?

There is a late flight to Montreal. I hope to fly stand-by.

If her memory served her, there was a flight that left around midnight for Montreal. Even if they were to set off now, and as close as they were, a twenty-minute drive from the airport at this hour, she doubted that he would make it, but was it worth a try? His need to fly to Montreal at this time of night puzzled her, and there was also this: I thought someone said you were going on to Washington for another benefit.

I have a change of plans, he said. Now I have to get back to Addis. I have a flight from Montreal via Frankfurt tomorrow evening.

So you could take a flight from here tomorrow. There are plenty of flights. If the last flight's at midnight, I don't think you'll make it. Isn't the Cirque putting you up in a hotel?

Of course, yes.

She was trying to piece together various things: his urgency; the fact that he didn't seem to have asked any of his handlers for a ride; the hippie-esque look of his socked feet in their sandals; a wildness in his glance, as if he didn't want to be found. What are your plans for tomorrow? he asked, which if it was an attempt at seduction seemed a clunky route in.

Work, she said.

Is it essential for you to be there?

Yes, no, not absolutely essential. A cloud of curiosity sifted up through her.

What would you think of driving to Montreal?

Tonight?

Yes, tonight.

The proposition seemed outlandish: six hours of night driving, the two of them near-strangers, and what was she supposed to do when she got there? Maybe you would like to spend the weekend, he said.

It's Thursday.

Well, a long weekend. Whatever his urgency, he was also framing the whole thing as a dare. He winked. I will help with the driving, he added. And pay for the gas.

None of this made any sense, which in itself was intriguing. She was tipped into the vertigo of whatever propelled him, this mystery and the beating of its wings. He was not proposing that they spend the weekend there together.

There is so much I need to do tomorrow, he said. He slung his juggler's arms across his chest. I would like to get to Montreal as soon as I can. As if this semi-rational explanation was enough to overcome the preposterousness of proposing to drive through the night rather than his catching the first flight in the morning.

Did you ask Juliet? She needed to know this.

No. Juliet doesn't have a car. Anyway, I don't think she would do it.

Sara thought, That isn't true. For some reason, he didn't want Juliet to do it.

Surprise pushed away the last vestiges of the wine's fuzziness. What she should do, what she could do, was offer to drive him to the airport—and if they left instantly maybe he'd catch the last flight after all, however much of a long shot it seemed. If not, he could spend the night at the airport, or she could drive him back to the airport first thing in the morning. Yet his offer of the larger, crazier adventure had an odd effect. It made her feel recognized, as if he'd seen into her own capacity for impetuous, even reckless behaviour.

For at other times, and in other parts of the world, she had not been one to hurry home at the end of the evening to put herself to bed before it got too late. No, she had kept herself awake or *asked* to be woken deep in the night by a phone call or a rap on the door and pulled on her underwear inside-out and bolted mugs of syrupy coffee or tossed back caffeine pills or cold medicine laced with speed before hunkering down in the broken-springed back seat of a van, a nylon headscarf tied about her head, pressed between the exhausted bodies of colleagues, fellow journalists, their translator, often all men, as a driver bore them out, out along the road to Najaf, through the slowly lifting dark.

Years before that, in the wake of the trial and her acquittal, she had on impulse bought a cheap plane ticket from Montreal to Paris, hours after handing in the final paper that would allow her to graduate. She had bundled clothes into an oversized knapsack and stuffed the rest of her possessions into cardboard boxes, stored them under the bed in the spare room of Norbert McKibben, world-famous political scientist and department chair, in whose house she'd spent those last two months holed up, eating meals made by Norbert's kindly wife, Maureen, after she'd bolted from Juliet's apartment.

On her first day in Paris, she'd met some Gitane-smoking young Parisians in a café in the Marais. Late the next night, she huddled with them around a manhole cover while one young man pried the metal lid open with a crowbar, before the

Parisians stubbed out their cigarettes and, one by one, took hold of the supports of a ladder and climbed into the descending tunnel's mouth. She'd been the last to grab hold of the side rails and reach one foot below another onto the rungs, tugged by the promise of a trip through the catacombs and the chance to throw herself toward something riskily new, once the girl on the ladder ahead of her leaped into the dark toward the dank base of the tunnel, shouting, Sautez!

On a whim, she had written a piece on the catacomb-walkers and their traipsing and partygoing in the underground tunnels of Paris, and sold it as a freelancer to a New York newspaper. Days later, still gleeful, she'd stepped out of the communal shower in her Paris hostel to hear someone say in English that a nuclear power plant had exploded in the Ukraine and a radioactive cloud was blowing west across Europe. A Lebanese journalist, met at another café, said, Go to Beirut, and gave her the name of a fixer and of a small, cheap West Beirut hotel close to the one where all the journalists stayed. She'd decided maybe it made sense to get out of Europe, and thought, Why not Beirut? Two weeks later, she was stepping off the boardwalk onto the Beirut beach, stones pressing against the soles of her feet as she walked toward the sea.

And here was this man, the electric heft of his body felt across the space between them. She had no desire to go back to her empty house, to face, again, the fact that neither David nor her parents had called. She lived a life that left her free, if she wished, to take off in the middle of the night without consulting anyone. On the other hand, she had no desire to sleep with this man. It was her birthday, if only for half an hour more, which made any decision feel numinous. Returning to Montreal, which she did very occasionally for work, would be proof that what had happened to her there—the accusation, the trial, the collapse of her life with Graham—had lost whatever hold it once had on her.

Okay, she said. Let's do it. Do you need to go back inside? I'll get my car. It's a white Toyota Camry, and I'll pull up at the back of the lot—Sara pointed, beyond the tent, to the exit lane that led past where the looming, decommissioned battleship was docked.

I have a bag I must get, Raymond Renaud said. And presumably he would have to say goodbye to people. Thank you so much for this.

He left her side, loping toward the tent, relief making him buoyant.

Exhilaration knocked at the top of her head. She could not now go back inside to find Juliet. If Juliet had left while Sara's back was turned, surely Raymond would have seen her and called out. She could not say goodnight to Juliet and tell her what she was about to do. Nor did she want Juliet to see her driving off with Raymond Renaud. If Raymond told Juliet that he and she were going to drive to Montreal, that was his business. Sara didn't think he would. She did not want to admit that her own decision had anything to do with Juliet, her complicated feelings toward Juliet, a desire, now, to snatch something from her. She was stepping toward mystery, the lake breeze quickening in the threads of her shirt. Most immediately, she had to make it to her car, get Raymond into her car and the two of them away from this place without being seen.

.   .   .

Sara leaned across to unlatch the manual lock on the back
door of her car. With a murmur of greeting, Raymond Renaud
swung a nylon bag from his shoulder and tossed it amid the
sun-stained newspapers, snow scraper, sandals, handbag, the
pool of her pashmina on the back seat, then ducked into the
front passenger seat, jerking the seat backward until his legs fit.
She stalled the car, trying not to look out for Juliet, and had to
restart the engine, considered making a quick detour west to
her house, which wasn't far, to change her clothes and use the
bathroom, but rejected the idea.

Do you need to stop by your hotel?

I am checked out.

And you're absolutely sure you need to do this? There was
a gas station at the corner of Strachan and King; no, the one
at Bathurst and Lakeshore was closer.

Exhaustion seemed to press him into the seat cushions, his
hands stretched taut across his thighs. He looked at her with
an exhausted intimacy. Yes, he said. And then: Can we get a
cup of good coffee?

Sara had to laugh. Coffee, but I don't know about good.

There had been a lot of late-night travel in her childhood, by
train, across Europe, since her father, despite his career in Foreign
Affairs, hated to fly. The strained, bleached light of a nighttime
train carriage: she was six or seven, maybe on the train between
Moscow and Leningrad as it was then, her parents asleep on the
banquette across from her, holding hands, her mother's head

resting on her father's shoulder, and she had needed to pee and wanted them to wake, wanted her mother to wake, but her mother didn't, and there was desolation at this, at their love that excluded her, and also defiance, and she had stood and walked down the shaking train carriage by herself, past the huge one-eyed woman whose eye flickered open, the enormous man who smelled of sausage and whose head was wrapped in a scarf, the man with the nubs of horns poking out of his head who reached out a red hand and whispered something leering in Russian, crooking his finger and beckoning to her.

In the Esso station at the foot of Bathurst Street, Sara waited for Raymond Renaud to shift past the celebrity magazines to the cashier, the heat from her coffee moving out through the cup into her hand, a packet of cashews and another of beef jerky caught in the crook of her arm, and when he didn't move, she cleared her throat, and he started, as if he'd lost track of who she was and where he was.

Back in the car, he was silent as he set his coffee cup into the cup holder at the base of the dashboard. He had given up on charm, it seemed, and the withdrawn weight of him beside her made her fear she'd made a terrible mistake.

She tried asking, When did you learn to juggle?

Long ago. It was very accidental, all of this. He stared out through the windshield as they left the cave of Lakeshore Boulevard and sped up the expressway on-ramp. It would be almost morning by now in Addis Ababa.

When did you arrive? she asked him.

Here? Yesterday.

Were you pleased with how things went tonight?

He shot her a look as if either he didn't wish to be disturbed or found her questions inane. Probably the last thing he wanted was to talk about the circus, and she had no desire to interrogate him, only to engage in some far more basic form of interaction, to fend off the miasma of his exhaustion. Up the Don Valley Parkway they sped, through the cavernous ravine, not all that far from the house, on the east side of the ravine, where David Ross would be lying in bed beside his wife. When Sara switched on the radio, raving jazz poured out. She'd already lost the feeling of complicity that had catapulted her toward driving, that reminded her of urgent road trips embarked upon in the past with fellow journalists, that camaraderie. Being this silent man's chauffeur for six hours she would not be able to take.

As they neared the ramp to the eastbound 401, Raymond Renaud turned to her. Juliet said she met you in Montreal.

When did she say that? What she really wanted to know was if he'd told Juliet about the trip. And, at whatever point he and Juliet had spoken, how had Juliet described their shared past and, possibly, her own tangled history in Montreal?

I don't remember, he said, and as Sara aimed the car into the 401's express lanes, Do you think she's a good filmmaker?

So this was what he wanted to know. She's worked in television for years. I'm sure she'll do a good job with the film.

Really she had no idea what kind of filmmaker Juliet was. You're from Montreal, she said. I read that somewhere. You grew up there?

In Saint-Henri.

Which as far as she could remember was rough and working class and white and at one end of the island.

You were born there.

Not in Saint-Henri. We came there when I was seven. My uncle lived there. Before that, I was living for a year with my mother in Côte d'Ivoire. My father didn't come. He stayed with my uncle.

Your mother's from Côte d'Ivoire?

His face made a quick spasm: of course he recognized the racialized nature of this question. My mother's from Haiti, Port-au-Prince. My·father, from Rimouski. A hint of his former charm returned, or showmanship: his bright grin. That was not the usual thing in Saint-Henri, I will tell you. I was not the usual thing. But you learn, you survive. By now I am used to being not the usual·thing. You?

Born in Ottawa, spent some time in Europe.

Where?

First Moscow. My father was posted to the embassy. As a secretary. Then Berlin. Later, briefly, Brussels and Kiev. You've been to Haiti?

Never.

She told him she'd gone for a week to Port-au-Prince after Aristide was returned to power. Nights up the hill at the Montana, the hotel where all the journalists and UN workers stayed, and where rats as big as beavers had scuttled across the lawns, and fires had burned on other hillsides and the ak-ak-ak of gunfire was loud enough that she'd dosed herself to sleep with extra-strength Nytol. She didn't say that; she said, I went out with a couple of UN peacekeepers a lot of the time, and my translator, to talk to people about how they felt after the election.

He nodded.

Beyond Scarborough, then the Rouge Valley, the pale blank slate of sound bafflers rose up beside them, cutting them off from row upon row of swollen, immodest homes, all but their limitless grey peaks. Every time she passed out of the city along this highway, more good earth had turned into surging, self-replicating piles of brick. She would gun the accelerator and speed past the desolate ranks, weaving around the transport trucks, aiming for the stretches of highway beyond Ajax and Whitby where the lake appeared, on the right, glinting like a body freed from the confines of shirt or dress.

Maybe he, too, needed to feel himself in motion, to travel through this landscape rather than fly over it. This could not be his only reason for wanting to drive. She was aware of his lips, the wide bridge of his nose, the sleeve of his jacket, a hand's breadth from her arm. There was a wall in him, and beyond it some darker turmoil pushing up. He did not have to move for his restlessness to churn the air, swell, flood out through his limbs, fill the car, and press against her.

Why are you in such a hurry to get back to Addis?

Something happened.

Everything in him, she thought, resisted speaking to her. She thought, I can't do this. She would take the next exit, somewhere in Pickering, turn around, and ferry him west to the airport, or find a gas station, a truck stop and cajole someone else, a trucker, another driver, to carry him onward.

As if he sensed her retreat, his posture shifted. She felt him move. I am under a lot of stress. I'm sorry. One of my performers is injured.

That's not good.

When she glanced over, he was staring at his hands in his lap as if they were unattached, creatures that he was surprised to find there.

She waited to see if he'd say anything more before continuing, What happened to him, or her?

He fell during a rehearsal.

Was he badly hurt? She thought back to the show in Copenhagen, wondering which boy it was.

He can't move his legs. They say paralyzed from the waist down.

Oh, I'm sorry. His words hit her in the gut, entered her foot pressed to the accelerator, her hands gripping the wheel. Of course you want to get back.

Nothing like this has happened before. We are so careful. It is terrible that it happens when I'm not there.

Who is there, was there, when you're not?

Our trainer, Tamrat Asfaw. He works with them every day. He called me this afternoon. They are all in shock. This happened only today, yesterday, Friday morning.

So you knew during the show.

I felt sick. I wanted the whole time to vomit, flee, get away, be with them, and I couldn't. Half of me is there, not here. It was the hardest thing to do, all this talk tonight. A nightmare. I couldn't tell anyone there what happened. Not yet.

Is the boy in hospital?

Yes, for now, though I don't know how long he will stay or what kind of care he will need. He had angled himself partially to face her, seat belt pinning him in place, and he looked wide-eyed and small with fear.

How old is he?

Twelve, around that.

Do you know how it happened?

They were practising a balancing routine, Tamrat says. They do it all the time. They've done it a thousand times. They climb on each other's shoulders. There are four boys in the bottom row then three boys then two then Yitbarek on top, with one foot on Moses's shoulder and one foot on Bereket's, and he leaps into a somersault and lands. They were on mats. Tamrat says he lost his balance, maybe someone wobbled. He was beginning the jump, but he twisted and fell. He is not careless. He fell on his back. When they went to him he couldn't move his legs. They got him in the truck and took him to the hospital.

In a truck?

Yes.

Have you spoken to the doctor?

Not yet. Not his family. He let out a rasping sound.

Which one is he? Yitbarek — She was casting back again to the show she'd seen, the pyramid act, boys climbing up each other's bodies to stand upon each other's shoulders, what boy had been at the top, boys of around twelve, boys juggling, boys on stilts, the boy in blue.

He's, he's the — Twisting in his seat, he threw up his hands, as if to ward her off or distract her from the fact that he was near tears and couldn't speak.

She had to keep her eyes on the road. Maybe when you get back you'll find out it isn't as bad as you think.

You have no idea.

I don't. But people do recover from spinal cord injuries, some do.

He was silent. They passed the sign for Clarington. He said, You don't think of the worst until it happens. You don't think the worst will happen until it does.

Is there any kind of health insurance?

Not yet, he said. There should be, but there isn't. It's because of the UNICEF grant. We are supposed to have this money and we don't have it. In the beginning, you know, we were so small. All of it was voluntary, me and the children, we did it in the afternoons and on weekends, and then more children came, and we started the school and the school for street kids, and the NGOs heard about us and came onboard, but it was still so—Nobody has any money. The children can't pay. No one can pay for classes or equipment. We feed them. We are in a borrowed place, a local councillor has given us space for offices and to rehearse. We teach the street children so maybe they can go back to the street and busk and make money. No one has money to see the shows. And it's okay for me to give up my job and live on very little because I am called to do this, everything in my life has led to this. But I still need money for the circus.

He ran a hand across his mouth before continuing, and maybe it was easier to talk about all this than the boy. So UNICEF heard about everything we're doing, the work with children, the social circus work in communities, and said, We will support you. Big multi-year funding to help us as an organization, and I thought, Fantastic, this will be our breakthrough. There's an application, a grant. They say, It is a formality, and it is approved, we sign a contract. But this is over a year ago. There is still no money. I call them, I send emails, I say, What's going on, where's the money, and they say, It's coming, but it takes time. How am I supposed to plan? We have grown so much, and we are stretched so thin. We need things, we need insurance. I am not trained in all this, but I am trying to hold it all together.

In his lap, his fingertips pressed against each other and released, pressed and released.

It sounds like a lot for one person to do.

Yes, yes.

How much money are you talking about?

One hundred and seventy-five thousand US.

A serious sum of money by any account.

Yes. I want to buy land so we have a permanent home, and pay the children for their work and time. I've borrowed against it. There are other funders, but no one else can offer this level of support. I'm talking now to the Cirque about multi-year funding. But with UNICEF, we have a contract, they promised me money, and I'm trying to look after the children and go out into these communities and do the work, and they can't even tell me when the money will come. What do they want me to do?

I'm not offering excuses, but you're dealing with a very large, top-heavy, and rather dysfunctional bureaucracy.

Who are supposed to take care of the welfare of children.

Yes, only in an organization of that scale, there's no one person accountable, and things sometimes do move unconscionably slowly. I'm not trying to defend them.

You think I am naive.

It's a difficult business model. To be dependent in this way. I don't envy you.

So what am I supposed to do, he shouted. His voice dropped. I'm sorry. His hand reached out to touch her arm before skidding away. She had a sudden image of him flying through the air with his children, high over the ocean, and wondered if there were times when he shouted at the children too. No insurance, she thought, this wasn't good. I can't believe the thing that's happened, he said. It is so terrible, I think, if I go back, it won't be true, it can't be. When she glanced over, he was touching his knees with his fingertips, his thighs, the edges of his jacket. If I was there it wouldn't have happened, if I had stayed, if I had not come away. If he fell, I would have saved him. He is, of all of them, he is—

You can't think that.

But I do.

They passed the Welcome Port Hope sign, a trick, two places welling out of the dark, though Sara had no idea where Welcome was. An irradiating pair of halogen headlamps sped up from behind her, blinding her through the rear-view mirror before the car passed and became a pair of red taillights receding into the dark. Headlights flared from across the meridian, and the broken white line of the lane divider strobed up from the dark tarmac to either side, small flares glimpsed across his face, felt on hers.

She tried again: Would I have seen him, Yitbarek, perform in Copenhagen?

Raymond Renaud was silent, as if holding himself against all that churned through him. Yes, he said at last. You would notice him. He's small but not the smallest. He is so alive when he moves. He does the act with the torches. He came to us in Dessie in the north. After a show he found me and he was so excited to show me what he can do. He was imitating the others, and even then you could see—he was so quick, so flexible, so daring, he just has so much natural talent. I said to his parents, You must let him come with me. You must let him do this. He is that good. I will make sure he stays in school and does all his schoolwork. I will look after him, I promise.

He clapped a hand over his mouth, bent forward against the seat belt, as if he were about to be sick.

Raymond, are you okay?

He started up again, eyes shining. I am responsible for them. Don't you see? They are in my care. Everything has been so crazy, like a runaway horse. I am trying to hold on to the reins. When I get back, I will do everything for him, raise money for him, do all the rehabilitation, whatever it takes. I will tell them all, he will walk again. We will all be stronger, we will come through this.

She looked down at the speedometer to find herself racing along at one hundred and forty, past the sign for the Big Apple, then the Big Apple itself, round and large as a house, the car shuddering only when she lifted her foot from the gas. Raymond seemed unaware of their speed. He sat back, palms pressed to his eyes, breath ragged, body shuddering a little, wildness charging through him, as if, left alone, he would have gone galloping through the night, and in his grief he reminded her of David, which made her heart move toward him. I'm doing my best to get you back as soon as I can.

Other moments surged up, out of the dark and those delirious hours of night driving. Somewhere between Brighton and Trenton, calmer now, a presence more felt than seen, he said, The year we were in Côte d'Ivoire, in Agboville, my mother and I, I was bitten by a snake. It was under a chair, outside, I reached for it. She was a nurse, but she did not know this snake or its venom or its antidote so she took me to an old woman who sucked the venom out. She says it was in a clinic, but I remember it as a hut and dark. It was not at the hospital where she worked. I know she was terrified. She thought she had brought me to this place and killed me.

Your father didn't come with you?

They were having some trouble. He was often away. But she went back to him.

They met in Montreal?

He met my mother and my aunt. Angèle and Philomène. The Désir sisters. He had to choose. That is the story.

She told him how in Moscow, her father, the third secretary then the second secretary at the embassy, would come into the kitchen where she was eating porridge or a boiled egg and balance a spoon by its bowl on the end of his nose or pull a ten-kopek piece out of her ears. Of going out for pastries and hot chocolate on Saturdays in Berlin with Anna, the woman who looked after her. Of her amazement, upon returning to Ottawa, at ten, to discover how many different kinds of toilet paper there were in North America. Wandering the long supermarket aisle with her mother, she'd stared agog at the pictures of kittens and babies and snowflakes on the plastic packaging, the various patterns of dots and swirls imprinted on the bright white rolls themselves.

Neither she nor he had siblings, although Raymond said there were always cousins around in Montreal, and other children had lived with them that year in Agboville and he'd liked having them around, the almost-siblings.

He said, In those days when I was with my mother, and she talked to me and confided in me sometimes like a husband, what I wanted most of all was to be seen.

Then he spoke again about the boy, Yitbarek. He will come up to me in the hall or at the house and go, Teach it, or Teach it me, he was just always so eager to learn new things, always, a move or routine, whatever it is.

She felt that there was something he needed her to understand about the boy, that he was handing her this vision urgently.

A tractor trailer roared past, behemothic in the dark, and a yawn quivered through him, escaping from his mouth.

You can sleep for a while if you want, Sara said. It's okay. If I get too tired, I'll wake you and make you talk to me.

Maybe I will a little bit.

They were approaching Belleville, and she was glad of his calm, although it didn't mean his distress had vanished. He hiked back the seat so that he was near to horizontal, the top half of his body disappearing from sight, his hands wrapped around him, shadowy in the dark when she glanced over, and she listened to his breath slow and grow hoarse, and thought how strange it was to see him like this, strange to have a man in her car at all, since David was seldom in it, and she was used to driving alone, and here was this man, Raymond Renaud, founder of a children's circus in Africa, laid out now beside her in the vulnerability of sleep, and it was impossible not to entertain the thought that in this state she could do what she liked with him, take him anywhere.

She slowed in the exit lane that led to the service centre just beyond Odessa. If he didn't wake, she would leave him sleeping while she went inside to buy a coffee, needing that fuel to keep herself alert, but as the car decelerated, he stretched and yawned, then pulled the seat upright, and, yawning again, breath curdled, voice nasal with sleep, asked where they were. Sara told him they were near Kingston, and he could stay in the car if he wanted, she could get him something, but he said no, he'd come inside.

It was glorious to climb out into the cool night air in which crickets were singing, to stretch her arms, squeeze her toes in her blue sandals, tottery on the heels, creases furrowing her linen trousers and shirt, her party clothes. Beyond the grassy ditch separating parking lot from highway, the slipstream of trucks pushed waves of thundering air toward them. On the far side of the car, Raymond Renaud stretched too; then, as they made their way toward the glow of the circular service centre, beneath the hum of the mile-high lot lights, he said, In this country they eat a special food called doughnuts very late at night. No one knows the true reason they are called this.

Tell me what they're like, Sara said, both of them giddy and bumping shoulders as they passed the truck lot, where the great trucks, like elephants, flanked one another, some rumbling, engines idle, running their air-conditioning or refrigeration units. Giddiness didn't take away from the underlying horror of the paralyzed boy; it was bound to this, to the fact that the boy's plight was now shared knowledge between them. Then her perception shifted and all she wanted was to get this errand, this crazy thing she was doing, over with as quickly as possible.

Inside the women's washroom, Sara threw cold water over her face and patted her skin dry with paper towels before making her way along the curved corridor that led to one of two restaurants. As she turned the corner toward the right-hand restaurant, she looked about for Raymond and saw him not at the service counter, where she expected him to be, but out among the tables, beneath the shimmering fluorescent lights, stripped of his yellow jacket, in a black T-shirt, in front of two seated boys. He was juggling. *Juggling.* With what? She couldn't see. Then she could. Small, multicoloured balls. Where had he got them? Had he brought them from the car, stuffed in the pockets of his jacket, and she had failed to notice? She was stunned at the sight of him and—

Head tilted up to follow the arcs of the balls, how fluid he seemed, how assured, how calm, despite the balancing twitches of his hips and the shuffle steps of his sandalled feet. Once again, he was revealed to her in an entirely new way. She didn't dare move closer, didn't want to disturb him but to watch as others were watching, the boys' mother, or the woman at the same table who was presumably their mother, though darker-haired and more bony-featured than the boys. Bleary-eyed travellers at other tables were roused to alertness. The two women behind the counter where the doughnuts were had drawn close to its edge and whispered as they stared, and a man in a trucker's cap stalled in astonishment inside the side door. The coloured balls flew up from Raymond's hands and tumbled down, six balls. Sara had no names for the patterns he was making, the volleys, a spray of balls, his hands held up and open at the end of each muscled arm, releasing each ball with a flick, easy at the wrist. He spun around without missing a ball. She'd had no idea he was so good. The boys gaped at him in wonder. All that grief and turmoil had to be in him somewhere, transmuted, displaced, given this form, performative yet generous, as if he wanted to find and give others pleasure.

He called out to the women behind the counter for a dough-nut, weaving between the tables toward them, keeping the balls in the air, teasing the women, I will pay, do not worry, nothing with icing or glaze. Catching three balls while keeping three in the air, he stopped by the rack of utensils, plastic and metal ones, and grabbed, what, metal knives, three of them. The younger woman, in her brimmed visor and hairnet, looked at her co-worker, nervous, then tossed him a doughnut overhand, an old-fashioned, and he dropped a ball but caught the doughnut with a grin, adding it to his volley, catching the knives by the handles, grabbing the doughnut in his mouth when it fell and taking a bite before sending it airborne again.

Someone started to clap, the air alive with excitement and disbelief at this tall man juggling in the wee hours at a service centre on the 401, and the jaggedness of something so unexpected. Raymond finished the doughnut and caught the balls and knives, picking up the dropped ball from the floor, but he was not through yet, and, throughout all this, how calm he remained. He set down the knives, pulled out a chair, and, standing on its seat so that he towered over them all, launched the balls again while tipping the chair forward, not falling but stepping backward onto the back of the chair, rotating the chair beneath his feet, growing taller as he moved, feeling his way backward to balance now on the chair's legs, keeping himself upright, under the shimmering lights, not looking down as the pressure of his moving weight turned the chair beneath him while his hands kept the balls spinning through the air. Joy shone on his face, through a sheen of sweat. At last he caught all the balls in both hands and leaped free of the chair. When everyone clapped, he gave that shy, dimpled smile that Sara remembered from Copenhagen and dipped his dark head. Had she really seen what she'd just seen? As soon as he stopped and righted the chair, it seemed improbable that any of this had happened, or that it had happened like this, despite the surprised murmurings of everyone around her.

He was conversing with the boys, leaning over them as Sara approached, explaining to them about Cirkus Mirak, the children's circus in Ethiopia, did they know where that was, it was in Africa. He pulled a folded flyer out of the pocket of his jacket and gave it to them and told them some day they should come for a visit. When Sara came close, Raymond turned to her with a friendly smile, and the boys and their mother also turned and must assume, if she was the companion of this man, that all this was familiar to her. That she knew his secrets. Raymond introduced her to the boys, Ben and Matt, and their mother, Moira, who were on their way from Sarnia to Moncton, days and nights of travel to take up a new life there, and suddenly she was commiserating with the mother, and joking with them all, saying, no, she had none of his talents, could only appreciate his, this complicity, and wishing them a safe trip onwards, while Raymond offered to buy the boys more doughnuts. Their mother said, no, really, they'd had enough, she needed them to sleep. A near-intoxicated glow poured from Raymond, despite his underlying note of distress. Some sadness and bewilderment came from the boys too. He was gentle as he shook both the boys' hands.

On the way back to the car, Raymond carried a box of doughnuts along with his coffee, the juggling balls weighing down the pockets of his jacket. Sara was about to ask him where they'd come from but stopped herself: to ask meant the stubborn return to the practical, the stripping away of mystery.

In the car, he reached one arm behind his seat for a plastic bag that he seemed to know was on the floor, tossed the sand-filled juggling balls into it, knotted the plastic, and dropped the bag behind him.

You're incredibly good, Sara said, setting down her own coffee. You must practise a lot.

Not much, he said. I don't have time. Have a doughnut?

Pass me a cruller, please.

You are sure you don't need me to drive?

I'm fine for now. She loved driving, loved the control of it.

Something had shifted between them, a loosening coloured by her amazement at what he'd done, could do, those hands, those arms, that body now slurping from a cup of coffee at her side as she pulled back onto the highway, glazed cruller on a napkin in her lap. A loosening familiar from other journeys with fellow journalists in stranger places, on planes, in vans, in bars, in the aftermath of something harrowing or exalting, something extreme or risky, the intimacy possible in the intensified chamber of hallucinatory exhaustion and enforced closeness that you know will end.

Wiping icing sugar from his lips with the back of his hand, Raymond said, This is a thing I like to do. Juggle in unexpected places. Sometimes I carry a set of juggling balls and sometimes I use whatever I can find. When I was in Sri Lanka—

When were you in Sri Lanka?

Ninety—

I was there in ninety-one, covering the civil war.

We just missed each other.

Were you teaching? What was it like being there when you were, I imagine, quite tense.

I was on a break. A friend worked there. In an orphanage. So I went for some weeks. I went north and east, into Tamil territory, because I'd heard the beaches near Trincomalee were beautiful. There were a lot of soldiers. And armed rebels. I'd get off a bus and juggle. Or I'd go to the market and pick up fruit, breadfruit, mangosteens. Sometimes I juggled in front of the soldiers. Or the rebels. Once I juggled with street cones. It is about showing people an unexpected thing. Creating an anomalous situation. Which I also tried to do in Addis Ababa. And this, tonight. It's about changing things even briefly, because people are distracted. I like watching children be enthralled by something like this, when they are not sure what to think or why you, the outsider, are doing this thing. The expected interaction is overturned. If I give out money until I have nothing, it will not change a thing.

How did the soldiers or the rebels react to your juggling?

He gave another grin. They didn't kill me.

She told him that she had spent most of her time there travelling with soldiers, remembered driving past long stands of palm trees with the tops of their heads blown off. He, too, said he remembered palm trees with the tops of their heads blown off. A transport trailer, lit by the gemlike reflectors along its bulk, seemed to elongate as she passed it. Were you teaching before you went over there?

In Canada. In the north. Then I decided to take some time to travel.

And, after, did you have a plan to go to Africa, or go back there?

I applied for jobs in international schools. It was chance. I got the one in Addis. And you, he said, brushing crumbs or sugar from his knees, did you set off to be a reporter in faraway places?

I didn't really set out to do anything. I was trying to escape some things that happened in Montreal. I was in a relationship that ended. We were supposed to get married. And then a woman accused me of stealing her wallet and using her credit card. Which I didn't do. But I was charged and it went to trial, and that was a very long process. And the man I was with, I trusted him to support me, I wanted him to be a character witness in court, I didn't have a proper alibi, he was the closest thing I had, but he wouldn't do it.

She was startled to hear herself saying this because it was not the version of events that she usually told, and she had never spoken of these matters in exactly this way. There was still pain in mentioning the particular form of Graham's betrayal. She had never told anyone at work about the trial; Juliet Levin was really the only person among her Toronto acquaintances who knew of it. David didn't.

Why wouldn't he help? asked the man in the car with her, and his attention was keen and felt like velvet. If he had been sleeping before, he was now alert. Why had she told him this? Because he had opened himself to her about the boy. Because she'd watched him juggle, seen beauty in him as well as distress. Because by then a cord of intimacy stretched between them.

He didn't want to be made public in this way. He'd been my professor. He taught, he teaches modern American history. We met in a class of his. It sounds so sordid now to say it. I think he was genuinely in love with me. He asked me to marry him. And I was madly in love with him. But in the end he turned pragmatic. He was coming up for tenure and he didn't want this thing that was happening to me to jeopardize it. I became a liability.

Why did the woman who accused you think you did it?

How dark it was outside: there were no cars in sight, no headlights coming toward her, no taillights receding up ahead, only the extending pools of her own car's headlights. They were in the middle of a dark path, dark woods spinning past to either side. Sara felt utterly awake. And calm.

We were in the change room at the downtown Y at the same time, the only two women there. I had been in the pool, then we were both in the showers, but I came out before her and was dressed and about to leave when she called out her wallet was missing. I helped her look for it and asked at the front desk to see if it had been turned in. She could have lost it anywhere, but she seemed convinced she'd had it when she came into the Y and taken her membership card out of it. Anyway, I left and didn't think any more about it until I got a call from the police. She'd filed a report saying the wallet had to have been stolen from the change room and I must have taken it while she was in the shower when she'd left her locker closed but not locked. But then it became more surreal, nightmarish. There were all these store clerks who identified me as the person using her credit card later that same afternoon. They all signed statements saying I was the one they'd seen with the card, and it didn't matter that the signature on the credit slips didn't match the one I gave when the police asked me to sign her name. They said I was trying to cover my tracks. My lawyer found out later, after I was charged, that the clerks were shown this page of mug shots in which I was the only white and blonde woman.

Can that happen? The thing with the mug shots? She was aware of his curiosity, which was not judgment.

It did happen.

What about at the trial?

(78)

I was let off due to lack of evidence.

The words of her lawyer, Paul Kastner, the second lawyer, came surging back, from the hallway of the court when they'd stepped out at the end of the trial, his voice raised in vexation: Sara, the court is there to get you off, not declare you innocent.

Only a couple of years older than she was, garrulous, finger-nails bitten to the quick, a terrible taste in ties, he'd been assigned to her through legal aid, after the first lawyer, Charles Martel, a distant acquaintance of her parents, suave in his charcoal suit, had advised her to plead guilty: it was a first offence, it didn't matter what she'd done, it was expediency, she'd get off with counselling or a fine and avoid the risks of the courtroom and extended legal costs. Or her parents would avoid the costs. You want me to do what? she'd shouted before bolting from his office.

People, Raymond Renaud said, shifting in the dark, think they remember things that aren't true. And when they believe something is true, it is hard to make them believe it isn't.

Yes, Sara said. Touched. Intimacy, she thought, was a way of being seen by someone else, touched, a form of bearing witness. She felt a sudden, deep connection to him. That's it exactly.

I'm sorry, Raymond said after a moment. I have to ask. What did the person with the credit card take from the shops?

I'll probably never forget. A pair of lambskin gloves from the Bay, a bottle of Chanel perfume from the perfume counter, twenty cassette tapes from Archambault. A leather coat from a Danier outlet. The horrible thing is they're not so far from things I might have bought except I'd never, ever buy albums by Sting or Madonna.

The wind through the air vents felt cold. The blue numbers of the digital clock on the dashboard read 4:06 a.m. Sara's fingers shifted to find a comfortable place on the steering wheel, her eyelids itchy as if grit pressed against them. It struck her that she had not told him about Juliet Levin's part in all of this, but the opening into which she'd spoken already felt closed, and besides, it had all happened so long ago. The release she felt in telling him, freedom in the wake of it, confirmed that all of that was long ago, and had been passed through, and was now behind her.

Glancing over, she took in Raymond's slump, the sideways loll of his head, chin dropped, breath like a rustle through fur. That he had fallen back to sleep didn't matter. There was something for her in driving to Montreal, proof that the past was in the past.

Without flinching she imagined entering Graham Finnessey's class, then his office, her glide of sexual confidence, the feel of her jeans tight at her hips, the pressure of their secret; she'd thought of herself as worldly when she had really been so young, so innocent. That was before she'd really fallen, allowed herself to believe she'd found a haven with him. His hands in her hair as they walked in Parc La Fontaine. He'd invited her to come on a trip to New York. He'd said, You are so astonishing to me. I have never done anything like this before and I'll never do it again. The books, the Westmount apartment, the travel, the bottles of wine, the sex, their entwined lives. They were in bed when he asked her to marry him. He took her home to meet his parents in Kitchener, a slim silver engagement band on her finger. A year and a half later, Graham stood behind a kitchen chair, a short, slim man with mica-bright eyes, violent in his self-interest, and said, Isn't there some other friend you can say you were meeting at the end of that afternoon rather than me?

The light began to shift — the blink of an exit ramp as Cornwall passed. Plush shadows lost their depth, as objects, pulled out of the dark, grew more solid. Steering wheel, dash-board, doughnut box. Sara gnawed on a piece of beef jerky and the action of her jaws kept her awake. All those years ago in Beirut, she had only begun to formulate a plan after Hanni, the fixer recommended to her by the Lebanese journalist in Paris, took her, bundled in coat and head scarf, to meet a young man connected to the group who'd kidnapped the Irish and the British journalists. This young man, probably younger than she was, who would not show his face, wedged his cigarette into his lips around the folds of his cloth mask, was angry in a more lethal way than she was, yet willing to talk. Her anger, in the wake of what had happened in Montreal, needed to find some form. Selling the interview to a wire service, reading her handwritten words down a telephone line, felt like vindication. People trusted her and listened to her. She was smart, she could do this, and would prove her trustworthiness by channelling the voices of others in greater extremities than anything she had been through. She approached Canadian papers as a stringer because she wanted Graham, and others, to see what she was doing. Another journalist gave her a name of someone at the LA paper. Her reasons for doing what she was doing were so personal in those days: her need to prove herself in the eyes of others. She'd wanted her parents, out of the direct line of Chernobyl's radioactive cloud in their Moscow apartment, yet close enough, to see what she was up to as well.

Raymond Renaud stirred in his sleep. Dawn light gilded him. Soon he would vanish, and whatever she had confided to him, the self that she had revealed, that he had called out of her, would vanish with him, along with the selves that he had revealed to her. Talking to him was like whispering a secret to a tree. Perhaps they'd say hello if he came on tour with the circus, but they'd likely never do more than that, and that was fine.

He woke just before they crossed the border into Quebec. As she followed Route 20, the southern route, into the city, which became at times less highway than wide suburban boulevard, blinking traffic lights swinging above the trees, Raymond told her about his year as a teenager in a Jesuit seminary outside of Hull, across the river from Ottawa, in Quebec, which must, they worked out, have been around the same time that her parents, heading back to Moscow, had enrolled her in an Ottawa boarding school, not the fancy one but the one she'd always thought of as the school for wayward girls. By then she'd already run away from home, threatened to drop out of school, told her parents she didn't see why they couldn't leave her to live somewhere on her own.

Is there anywhere in particular you want me to drop you? Sara asked. Words rolled out of her mouth like odd-shaped animals. As they passed along the southern perimeter of Dorval, a jet lifted itself into the air. Do you still have family here?

She could no longer remember if he'd said something about meeting someone, there was only this astonishment: to find herself, at dawn on a Friday morning, sleepless, driving into Montreal. What had she just asked him?

Any Métro station will do.

Meanwhile, other scenes flashed before her: an olive grove; scarred Beirut high-rises; a bombed-out tank; the interior of the house of a Kurdish family in Kirkuk; children crying in a hospital in Najaf. A gym change room, yellow lockers, she was pulling on her jeans, a woman's voice called out. Places that remained inside her and that sleeplessness brought back.

They approached downtown through the dayless-nightless tunnel of the Autoroute Ville-Marie. There was a hotel that used to be on Sherbrooke at the corner of Peel, or was it Stanley or de la Montagne, not far from the McGill campus, the Château something, which had once been plain and not too pricey, and Sara poured herself toward the hope that it was still there, the street unravelling like a sheet before her. If no one would let her in, she would kick off her sandals and fall asleep in her car. And later she would call David, ask about Greta's scan, and tell him what she'd done, the thought of speaking to him hovering before her like a beacon.

At the corner of Stanley and de Maisonneuve, she slid to a stop in front of one of the entrances to the Peel Métro, the street wide and grey and empty of people, just as a uniformed man unlocked the station's glass doors. Raymond reached into the back seat for his nylon bag.

Did you tell the people at the Cirque you won't be going to Washington?

I'll call in an hour or so, when the time is a little more reasonable.

Sympathy seized her, at the thought of all that he was hurtling toward. Good luck with everything. I truly wish you the best and hope for the absolute best for the boy. She pulled her handbag from the back seat, fumbled through her wallet, and extracted what bills she had, five twenties, offered these, and Raymond took the money with a nod.

You have been so generous. If there's ever anything, I don't know what I can do, but something. You must ask. He touched her arm.

Out on the sidewalk, he in his rumpled jacket, she in her creased clothes, they hugged, and he kissed her three times, cheek to cheek to cheek, the Ethiopian way, he said. She kissed him twice, the Montreal way. I can't thank you enough. For an instant she thought he would say something more. But, no. His hug deepened, hard and close, before his arms released her.

He didn't slip into the Métro. Picking up his bag, he set off at a jog along the street.

What? Juliet said, and her voice rose.

It was dusk on Labour Day Monday. Sara had not tried to reach Juliet earlier in the day to tell her about the circus performers' flight, since it was a holiday and Juliet might not be home. When she did reach her, Juliet said, yes, she and Max had been away for the weekend, they'd just got back, traffic was awful, while outside Sara's kitchen window, rays of light grew long in the west, and crickets hummed, and the soul-destroying racket of the air show had rumbled off for another year. On the expressway down by the lake, as on every other highway in the city, people would be stewing in their cars. On the table in front of Sara, ice settled in her tumbler of Scotch. She had not spoken to Juliet since the night of the circus benefit in July.

Even if they're speaking about abuse, they're only allegations, she said. And it didn't mention what kind of abuse, just consistently.

Did it say who? Juliet asked in the same keening tone. Which of them ran off?

No names, only that there were nine of them, and they were older, mostly teenagers.

Boys, girls?

The article didn't specify so I assume both.

What kinds of abuse are there?

Physical. Sexual. Her elbows on the table, one hand raked into her hair, internal discomfort contorting itself within her, Sara swallowed a sip of Scotch and the ice cubes chattered, and Juliet heard this.

Her hearing it registered as a pause, before Juliet continued, He told me he was going to send me some tapes from the Australian tour, either something he'd shot, or media clips, or he'd put me in touch with someone else, and I heard from him right after they got there and then nothing even though he knew I was on deadline and in the midst of editing.

An ordinary airplane groaned through the sky. Julie, Sara asked, using the old name, the one that Juliet had gone by in their Montreal days, I have to ask, did you notice anything, anything at all, when you were in Addis?

No, Juliet said vehemently. No. They all seemed so—happy. Busy and sometimes stressed but happy. He wasn't violent or brutal. Or—inappropriate? There were always children around him, but he was working with them. Nothing was the way it would be here. But they were all so committed to the circus.

All afternoon Sara had gone back over the hours she'd spent with Raymond Renaud in her car: his urgency to return, his upset over the boy, his juggling in front of the two boys in the service centre. His being distraught about the paralyzed boy or juggling in the service centre weren't necessarily suspect; nor, at the time, had she felt anything unusual in his attention to the two boys. He had seemed kind and overwhelmed. Mercurial? It would have been monstrous not to be upset about the boy so badly hurt while in his care. There had been a sense of intimacy between them.

I know it's selfish, Juliet was saying, especially now, but I can't help thinking about my film, what's going to happen to my film?

It's not good, Sara said and felt a twinge of responsibility at having set Juliet up with this story. But you don't know yet that he's done anything. You don't know what's happened. Nothing is certain. I'll hunt around and see what more I can find out.

Thank you, Juliet said and her voice wobbled, as if on the verge of tears.

Upstairs again, in the blue of twilight, Sara reconnected the modem and pulled the article from the *Sydney Morning Herald* back onto the screen, still in her sundress, bare feet wrapped around the rungs of her chair. David was probably home by now. He'd told her that Greta's parents were throwing a party for her, for them, everyone breathing now with cautious optimism, two more months since her last clear scan in July. The most important thing, she told herself, was not to overreact.

> Nine performers in the Ethiopian children's circus, Cirkus Mirak, have defected and are applying for asylum in Australia, the migration agent representing the performers has announced. The performers fled the circus last Thursday night and claim that circus founder and director Canadian Raymond Renaud

consistently abused them. The circus was on a ten-day tour of Australia, and appeared most recently at the Sydney Alternative Arts Festival, its acrobatic performances hailed by critics and crowds alike.

The youngsters, aged 15-19, are recovering from their ordeal, according to migration agent Sem Le. The youngest of the group were put in the care of child protection authorities. The oldest were offered temporary housing.

She had already worked out that migration agent was an Australian term for what she would have called an immigration consultant, and that Sem Le was in fact an immigration lawyer. She had tracked down his Sydney office number; he seemed to run his own firm. His was a Vietnamese name, and so perhaps he was an immigrant, and had even been a refugee, his parents fleeing across the sea by boat, bringing him as a small child with them. He might have intimate knowledge of harrowing journeys to outrun the past. It was nearly eight o'clock in the evening in Toronto, which meant that it was nearly ten on a Tuesday morning in Sydney, fourteen hours ahead.

And it made sense to try him first, to see what he would tell her and if he would prove a possible route to Raymond Renaud's alleged victims and accusers, whom she must have seen perform all those months ago in Copenhagen. The older ones: among them, the girl contortionist, the boy with the hint of a moustache. The sweet scent of trees blew in through the open window.

G'day. His receptionist's voice sounded young and twangy, full of wide-open vowels cantering across a sun-baked landscape. How can I help you?

I'd like to speak to Mr. Le. And how should she introduce herself, since she had no intention of writing about this, yet if she did not identify herself as a journalist, what reason would Sem Le have for speaking to her, or she for trying to solicit information from him. Sara gave her name and the name of her newspaper. I'm trying to find out more about the children who ran off from Cirkus Mirak, the Ethiopian circus.

Can you hold on, please, the receptionist said, and the line beeped in a different way than it did at home.

A new voice, male, cut in, brisk and cheerful. Good day, good day. Australian, with a hint of somewhere else.

Sara explained: who she was, where she was from, that she was looking for more details about the circus case, why the performers had run, what precisely their allegations were.

Yeah, it's a very sad story, Sem Le said. Terrible. The allegations are of profound mistreatment. Physical and sexual abuse. Working under unsafe conditions. Failure to pay a basic wage. Are you writing about this?

Part of her floated, suspended, as Raymond Renaud contracted in front of her. Possibly. He's from here originally, the circus founder, and is he —

Yeah, he's the one they're alleging did these things, Renaud, the bloke who runs the circus.

Confirmation made her heart race. Did they say these, all these things occurred on an ongoing basis?

We're trying to pin down details. Their English is not great. We have a translator working with them. And a counsellor. They called me in, yeah, after they took off. I've worked with a few prominent cases, but never so many at once. Kids running from a circus, not to a circus. They're in shock. Pro bono, but how could I say no to that?

Where are they now?

Still in Sydney. There's a church group helping them that works with asylum seekers. It's a challenge because there's so many of them. Six boys, three girls. And for the moment they can't work. The older ones. And they have no money. We're thinking of moving them to Melbourne, where there's more of an Ethiopian community.

And they're all making these allegations?

Yeah. So far. Sounds like there was something nasty going on over there. Looks good from the outside, but they're trapped under this bloke's thumb. This is what they've told me. Tragic, really. They're quite shaken up. Obviously we'll be working closely with the Ethiopian authorities.

Was it hard for them to get away? Given there's so many of them.

They waited until the night before they were to fly back, then had to choose their moment. Naturally he was keeping a close eye on them. They couldn't take anything with them in case he spotted them. They were all in the same hotel. Two of the boys did run into him, the director, in the elevator, and had to act like nothing was on. Three of them got out in the service elevator and spent the night in a park. One of the others saw him in the lobby and had to hide and did a runner anyway.

The girls caught a cab and ended up at a hostel. The rest of the boys spent the night at the coach station.

And they knew how to make an asylum claim?

I believe they had some contact with people beforehand who told them what to do.

Is one of the girls a contortionist?

A what?

In the circus, in their acts, there's one who's particularly flexible —

So you've seen them?

I saw them perform once.

Well, I don't know that.

Would it be possible to talk to any of them about what they went through?

No, Sem Le said. They won't be giving interviews.

Sara set down the phone and unclenched the hand that had been cinched around the receiver and went on listening in the silence to what she had just heard. Had the older ones fled because they were the only ones able to get away? Across the world, they moved into a new day, circus-less, perhaps still clad in clothes that smelled of home, and Sem Le, their champion, whom she imagined as compact and stocky, rose briskly from his desk, smacked his hands, or called out to his receptionist, or once more grabbed the ringing phone.

She had the number of the woman who ran the Sydney Alternative Arts Festival beside her. After Sara introduced herself, Holly Mercury's assistant said, I'm sorry, she's not available, with the air of one distracted by someone else vying for her attention. Just a moment, please. The line clicked into a hold, and then an older woman's voice came on, blunt and low, and identified herself as Holly Mercury.

I'd like to make a few things clear, all right? There were absolutely no rumours preceding their arrival. They played in festivals across Europe, and I had no word of any issues. And there was no sign of any inappropriate behaviour while they were here. They were here for a week, and in Melbourne and Adelaide before that. Also, I had very little contact with them. I saw them in rehearsal once and on opening night, and then I happened to be at the hotel to say goodbye when he found out they'd taken off. He was trying to round them all up, there was a bus waiting, it was chaos. One of the others told him they'd split. I suppose some of them must have known.

What did he do?

He seemed shocked. He had to get the others to the airport. I told him I'd see what I could do to help. This was before I got word from the police and their legal agent.

So there had, Sara thought, been this much planning. To bolt on the verge of their return to Ethiopia left Raymond Renaud no time to track down the runaways before he had to race to catch a plane with the rest of the children. They had known to make an asylum claim: someone at some point had told them what and how. Perhaps they had been plotting their escape for months. In March, as she'd watched them onstage in Copenhagen, performing and taking their breathless bows, the idea had already been coursing through them. They had whispered about it behind his back. In a hotel room, behind a closed door, someone said, This is what we will do.

Or they had not considered running at all until after arriving in Australia: something had happened there, or things had reached a breaking point. Or, *or*—Australia itself had beckoned: the lure of taps that ran endless water and large TV screens filled with multiple channels and shops as bright and glittery as peacocks' tails. All of this tugged at them. There was a leader. They had come up with the plan together. There was horror here somewhere but what kind of horror.

From downstairs came the thud of the back door being pulled tight against its frame, which marked the return of Kumiko, her basement tenant, without whom she would never have been able to afford the house. The house that she was glad to have despite the grief tied up in its purchase, the stability of a place that she could call her own.

In the kitchen, to a warble of Japanese making its way from Kumiko's answering machine up through the floorboards, Sara poured herself another drink and, in front of the fridge, pressed an ice cube to her forehead, felt the sear of its wet cold. There had to be two or three legs to the journey from Sydney back to Addis Ababa, via Bangkok or Dubai, and he was trapped in his seat as he had been in her car, nine empty seats around him, the other children silent or upset or whispering, the rift between him and them widening. Would he have the strength or the self-composure or whatever it took to try to comfort them? Or had he willed them to stay silent, desperate that they not speculate among themselves. She had never followed up to find out what had happened to the paralyzed boy. Perhaps Juliet knew. Ahead of him: the calls or visits he would have to make to inform the parents of the runaways that their children had vanished. Since he was responsible for them. Either he had every reason to know why they had done what they'd done, or he had some intimation, or he was caught entirely by surprise. On the plane, there would be time to think. She rubbed the ice cube across her forehead. She had no idea how to think of him. On the plane, all he would have known for certain was that they'd taken off.

Drink in hand, she made her way back upstairs to the warmer second floor and her home office at the front of the house, where the coloured swirls of the screensaver made blue swoops across the darkening walls until her fingers touched the keyboard. When she searched, she found no news from Addis Ababa, nothing posted online from the English-language paper there. The press newsfeeds were full of thickets of postings about the Americans threatening air strikes against Iraq.

One night, sometime after his return, he would have answered the phone and heard someone say, There is an investigation. This is what you are alleged to have done. Afterward his clothes would be the same and the room around him and nothing else. She had seen him in distress, glimpsed his particular tincture of fear and rage. One kind of horror if he'd done what he was accused of and another if he had not.

He was out there somewhere, and something led from her to him. She rose to her feet and swallowed a mouthful of whisky. What she owed him was the space in which to be innocent without dismissing the story of his accusers. The internal juggling act was trying to hold both these things in her head at once. He was not charged with anything. Her body coiled in horror and disbelief and fear and compassion and with the desire not to judge, because legally it was wrong as yet to judge him, either him or his accusers, but him in particular because he was the accused and as yet only accused and in some small way she knew what this felt like.

Downstairs and out the front door, she took a seat, hugging her knees, on the top step of the porch. A breeze sighed through the maple tree, lit green from behind by the street lamp. She balanced the moist circle of her glass first on one knee, then on the other. The past came flowing back.

After her first police interview, she'd told herself it was natural that the police wanted to speak to her, since she'd been in the vicinity when the theft was discovered. And Graham had been offhand yet reassuring: it was a stolen wallet and credit card, a small thing. He'd asked about the woman whose wallet was stolen and Sara had tried to pull the blurry stranger into focus. In truth, she'd barely noticed the woman, maybe late twenties, not overweight but soft around the edges and frankly a little hysterical when she'd discovered her wallet was gone.

The day the two police officers showed up at their door to search the Westmount apartment, the first thing Graham asked, after the officers had left, was what address Sara had given them. He persisted: why hadn't she used the address of the apartment on Saint-Viateur, where she kept a room at his request? Because, Sara said, it seemed a bad idea to give an address and phone number of a place where she didn't actually live and never was. He was standing on the far side of the living room, her fiancé. She couldn't believe they were having this argument, her mind full of policemen's hands in transparent gloves working their way through their underwear drawers and cupboards and closets. The police, so callous and insistent. She wanted Graham to say: This is outrageous. She yelled at him: Aren't you on my side? She had the alarming sensation of the whole world tilting sideways.

After she was charged and booked and allowed to go with restrictions—unable to use a credit card, not to approach within twenty metres of any of the stores from which goods had been stolen, including the two big downtown department stores—she took a bus back to the apartment on de Maisonneuve, which was still technically Graham's, locked and bolted the door, and didn't call Graham but lay in her boots and sheepskin coat and the cheap sunglasses she'd bought on the way home on the sofa that was also his, and in those moments the most stunning sensation had been her absolute loss of control, a vertigo of wondering what she had done to make Colleen Bertucci convinced that she was the thief, the police believe Colleen not her, the store clerks unwavering that she was the one, her own helplessness. Her adamancy that she had done nothing made no difference. Lying on the sofa, she began to cough and couldn't stop.

All this remained alive in her. The catch in her throat. Such a thing could happen to anyone. Couldn't it? Small things cast long shadows. Somewhere a raccoon shrieked.

The next morning, Tuesday, the streetcar that Sara rode to work was filled with children, teenaged girls in tiny kilts, small kids weighed down beneath oversized knapsacks, all of them chattery with the return to school. The newsroom had an autumnal buzziness, despite the heat of the day outside, or else simply a social fervour after the long weekend. People gathered, mugs clasped in hands, to chat about the American air strikes against Iraq *and* the royal divorce. Within the flimsy barricades of her cubicle, Sara swung a sweater over her shoulders and called Juliet at home, and Juliet answered on the first ring.

Keeping her voice down, she explained how the performers had fled the hotel at night and spelled out what the allegations against Raymond Renaud were.

All those things, Juliet said.

Julie, when you were there, I have to ask again, did you notice anything, anything at all that struck you as suspicious?

No, Juliet said, and I really didn't feel like he was trying to hide anything from me, but now everything looks suspect.

What about your assistant?

I haven't called him yet.

Julie, are there people I can talk to, in Addis, say, who might know more?

Are you going to write about this?

No. No. That isn't why. I'll pass on to you whatever I find out.

Maybe I should be the one doing this, Juliet said. But right now I feel so stunned, I can't.

Would you be willing to show me some of your footage?

I guess. Sure. Why?

I'd be interested in seeing what there is to see, of him, and the circus. I'm curious to see what it looks like. You know there's still a film to be made of all this.

Sara wanted to see him again in whatever way she could. She needed to sense if there was something crucial about him that she ought to have noticed. And, if she had missed some sign of deeper corruption, after spending all those intimate hours in a car with him, what did this reveal about her? Not to mention her uneasy sense of feeling implicated because she had helped him return to Addis Ababa and the circus children.

Juliet said, Only I don't know if it's a film I want to make.

Tomorrow's not good, Sara said, but what about Thursday after work?

Juliet held open a glass door that led into the cool, dim vestibule of a small warehouse building on Bathurst north of Queen. Immediately behind her, a flight of stairs led upward. Sunglasses off, eyes adjusting, Sara stepped in from the heat, the outside air thick and sultry even though it was September and afternoon shadows were creeping down from the western housetops as the sun slid low in the sky. A crease quivered between Juliet's brows, and strands of her hair, most of it clipped back, wisped about her face. In a black dress and little turquoise cardigan, she led Sara up the flight of stairs, through another door, past a small seating area where two sofas were set in an L, and down a corridor of closed doors to the one marked Suite C, which Juliet, shoulders hunched, unlocked. Inside the edit suite, the walls were covered in black felt, and metal shelves climbed up one wall, and there were two monitors, one set upon a metal cart, the other on a desktop. A blue-white tube of fluorescent lighting trembled overhead.

It had been a long time, Sara thought, since she and Juliet had been alone in a room together. In the early years after their separate moves to Toronto, they had met in bars and restaurants or galleries, and a couple of times, at Juliet's invitation, had gone to see dance together, although in those days Sara was often out of town. The last time they'd been alone in a room with this kind of privacy had been when Sara had come to live with Juliet and her roommates in the apartment on avenue de l'Esplanade in Montreal, after she had walked out on Graham or Graham had thrown her out, and Juliet had bumped into her one February afternoon as she sat near the campus in a Van Houtte coffee shop, a knapsack bulging with her belongings at her feet.

It was strange to think of Raymond Renaud as the agent of their new proximity, and uncomfortably strange to find herself once more wanting something from Juliet. As Juliet tucked her keys into the leather handbag that hung from a hook on the back of the door, Sara tried to determine if Juliet seemed resentful of her, given that the circus story had altered so radically since she'd first told Juliet about it. Not noticeably. Juliet must have considered how Sara's history would shape her interest in Raymond Renaud's predicament, although neither of them had mentioned this.

How's Max?

Great, Juliet said. He's working on a new show. Actually, he's kind of gone off in a new direction. He's using images from surveillance cameras broadcasting on the web, so capturing pictures from a stream of images rather than taking them but still choosing them or creating them?

Sometimes Sara found herself wondering what kept confident Max and anxious Juliet together: Juliet's loyalty and admiration and adoration? Something sexual? They'd been together for around five years. These days, Max's photographs of derelict urban landscapes and ruined industrial sites sold for far more than she could ever contemplate paying for a piece of art. No doubt Juliet had hoped her film would be her own way to step forward artistically. Now this had happened.

Juliet, I am so sorry about this whole business.

With a grimace, Juliet took a seat in front of the monitor on the desk, wrapped a loose strand of hair behind her ear, and, aiming for a smile, patted the chair next to her. A black bound notebook lay on the desk, a pair of speakers to either side of the monitors, some papers scrawled with what Sara thought were called time codes, and, beside an ordinary keyboard, a contraption with a joystick on it, presumably for manipulating the tape. Businesslike, Juliet plucked a mini cassette tape, small enough to fit in her palm, from a pile on the desk and slid it into the mouth of the videocassette player, which swallowed it with a mechanical gurgle. I wasn't sure what you'd want to see, and there are a lot of rushes, and I could have shown you the rough cut I've been working on, but now I feel too weird about it, so I've cued up a few other things.

Weak air-conditioning attempted to cool the room, stuffy with odours of dust and sweat. A small plastic fan clamped to the side of one metal shelf waved some air across them. Juliet reached to switch off the overhead light as an image flared onto the monitor screen: a dirt path by the side of a road sped past, presumably shot through the window of a moving vehicle. There were trees and people walking along the tamped red earth, women in sweaters and flowered dresses with plastic bags swinging from their hands; a man in a suit came close then vanished; a flock of goats or sheep skittered from the road into the comfort of a ditch; a barefoot boy trudged behind a wooden wheelbarrow; voices outside brayed and were whipped away like flags while voices from within the car mumbled and fluttered. The footage felt real because it was raw.

This is our first full day, Juliet said. We're on our way to the circus compound. Where they rehearse? We saw them perform the first night we arrived, in a field outside the Italian embassy, but you've seen them perform so I decided not to show you that.

A donkey trotted along, skinny poles of wood lashed to its sides; a gas station appeared on the right as the car made a sharp turn to the left and scrunched to a stop on dirt and stones. Whoever was holding the camera climbed from the car, footsteps crunching as the view lurched across more scrubby trees and the dusty yellow planes of the car, before rising up the length of a wooden pole at the top of which the cut-out wooden figure of a boy balanced on his hands, legs in the air. His unitard was painted pink, his body red-brown, a splash of black hair daubed atop his head.

Did you get hold of your assistant? Sara asked.

Juliet muted the sound as the car and its passengers jolted up a steep hill, stones projecting from the craterous red dirt, a scrim of trees bouncing outside the car window.

Justin was totally shocked. He spent more time hanging out with the performers than I did, the older ones. But they didn't speak much English and mostly they were goofing around or trying to teach him to juggle or playing soccer. He said he didn't notice anything. They didn't seem upset. They didn't talk to him about Raymond.

On the screen, at the top of the hillside, where the land levelled into a flat parking area, a white pickup truck, coated in a skin of red dirt, was parked alongside a couple of older, smaller cars. Light glinted off the windshields. Across a hummocky expanse of dirt and grass rose two yellowish single-storey buildings, a fringe of trees beyond them, and on the ground, in front of the buildings, moved a clump of human figures, all of them small, maquette-sized.

Everything felt compressed and intense and mostly we were going crazy trying to make the film, Juliet said.

Something Sara had seen previously, in a photograph, sprang to life: older boys in pink leotards with ribbons dangling from them tossed juggling pins and wandered around the perimeter of a brown square of tarpaulin spread on the ground. A scrim of blue canvas was mounted behind them. A lean, olive-complexioned man in a khaki vest stepped back from a tripod-mounted camera as a human pyramid of girls in white outfits dismantled itself; the girl at the top, whose feet had waved alongside her ears, unwound first one leg then the other in a graceful arc, her feet resting briefly on the torso of the girl beneath her before she jumped free. So at ease in her body, seemingly at ease, even languid. And so extraordinarily flexible. Raymond Renaud, red ball cap on his head, sunglasses shielding his eyes, turned, separated himself from the children and the photographer, and waved.

The photographer's name is Paolo Sabatini, Italian but shooting for a Dutch magazine, Juliet said, and he was only there for a couple of days. There was an Italian sociologist studying the circus, but he didn't really interact with anyone, just sat around taking notes, so I don't know how much use he'd be. There were always people around, always people observing him. Apart from when we interviewed him and once when we went out to dinner, I don't think I ever saw him alone. And he let me film what I wanted, where and when I wanted.

Can you pass on Justin's email or phone number to me?

Sure, Juliet said.

Behind Raymond Renaud's back, the teenaged boys patted one another's shoulders with carefree bonhomie and the girl contortionist walked with an effortless stride toward them.

That's Gelila Melesse, Juliet said, pointing to the contortionist. And Alem and Dawit and Kebede Gebremariam. Do they look —? I don't know, I don't know what I see when I look at them now.

Sara peered at them. As the photo shoot came to an end, Juliet stopped the tape, extracted it from the player's mouth, and fed in another from her pile.

Sara had a sudden impression that Juliet didn't want to be doing this.

In an echoey hall of painted cinder blocks, Raymond huddled with a quartet of girls, including Gelila, demonstrating something with his arms. Two of the girls made their way into backbends, while Raymond seemed to be discussing with Gelila and the other girl how the two of them would balance atop the bodies of first two. With one hand, Raymond adjusted the feet of one of the arched girls, as if to secure her weight, then touched his fingers to the back of her ribs as if to nudge the curve of her spine higher. His manner seemed kind but exacting, as if he had a clear idea what he wanted.

Isn't it natural for there to be some kind of touch when you're doing physical training like this? Juliet said.

I guess so.

A kitchen, a room with yellow walls: three younger boys sat at a table covered in dirty dishes eating what looked like bread and jam and chatting in Amharic.

Is this his house? Sara asked.

Juliet nodded.

And the boys live there?

Three of them do. But there are almost always other kids staying over or coming to use his computer or get help with schoolwork or playing in the courtyard.

The camera swung across the room, and Raymond looked up from stirring a pot on the stove.

Where do the boys sleep, or any of them sleep when they're there?

They have a bedroom. If there's too many, then on mats on the floor. Or the sofa. He said something about how they need a proper address to get registered in school.

Did he have favourites?

He looked out for the ones who lived with him, who didn't have other homes. But usually there were lots of kids, he'd be driving them around in the back of his pickup, and like I said, they were always running in and out of his house.

Was he affectionate with them?

Sometimes it was more like they, especially the younger ones, were physically affectionate with him.

There were situations in which Sara herself had found it difficult to escape being touched by children: touching and being touched. Visiting orphanages, she'd been swarmed by children who'd clung to her, who would not let go of her body, her hands. And it had seemed wrong not to allow this contact, invite it even, given the extremity of their need for touch. Perhaps, under similar circumstances, his touch had been misconstrued—by someone.

Did he ever take kids off on their own?

All I can say is, not that I saw. A couple of kids, maybe, but mostly he'd be with a whole gang of them.

The camera swung into a dim hallway, moved past what looked to be a study, where the flash of a round wall clock read ten past nine and daylight streamed through a window, and pieces of paper and a small Canadian flag were pinned to a corkboard. A door led out into blinding brightness.

And the older ones?

Maybe it was hard because he also had them training the younger kids and leading classes for street kids in addition to their own training so they worked a lot, but the idea was that they would take on this work as they grew older and help run the circus or found other circuses in other places. And I thought they were genuinely excited by this. That's what Gelila said to me. They seemed excited. She said she wanted to work for the circus for the rest of her life.

Raymond, visible from the waist up, clad in a pinkish T-shirt, sat on a wooden chair, piney fronds and the orange beak of a bird of paradise flower swaying behind him. Familiar and not familiar; the coiled dark hair, his smile. Sara's heart leaped. Victim? Or a monster ferociously hiding his true self? Or someone caught between...? How different it was to stare at him fixed in the past from the perspective of the present, with the knowledge of what he might have done. To observe him with this new intensity.

Onscreen, he looked good-natured and expectant, innocent if for no other reason than that he had no idea what was thundering toward him. Through the speakers came breezy flutters from the mike pinned like a spider to his T-shirt, and some off-camera mumbles from Juliet about wind and the quality of sound; then Justin: I think it's all right.

Still off-camera, Juliet asked Raymond how he'd come to Addis Ababa, and he launched into the story of how he'd arrived to teach English and French at the international school and, as he biked through the city, had things thrown at him, and, on a whim one day, had taken a set of juggling pins and juggled in the street. He wasn't simply repeating the story as Sara had previously heard it, using the same words, like something memorized. His voice, addressed to Juliet, had a different, thoughtful lightness.

She wondered what Juliet felt as she watched him. After a few minutes, Juliet stopped the tape. Do you want to see more of this or should we go on to something else?

Nothing felt clear, or clearer. Taking in his image, Sara didn't feel monstrousness. Which didn't mean it wasn't there.

A little more.

In his pink T-shirt he said, There are maybe twenty thousand street kids here so we work with only such a tiny number. First we have to train the kids to busk and then we have to get permission from the police.

Was he ever verbally abusive? Angry, shouting, physically rough with them?

He said, They are working in an environment that is very unusual here. It is very cooperative. When they build a pyramid, they have to work together to do it.

Juliet ejected the tape. No. Well, angry, maybe. Frustrated. He shouted. Especially around the time of the trip to Sodo. But nothing that felt outrageous, and none of the kids seemed that upset. We were supposed to go in a bus. They travel in this bus, but the bus broke down at the last minute so he had to organize something else. We ended up going in three different minivans. Plus there was all this equipment that had to be loaded in and didn't fit properly, and we were supposed to leave before dawn so we could get there in the afternoon, but we didn't obviously, and it was a nine-hour trip south on not great roads.

Maybe he felt guilty about getting angry at them? That evening we stayed up late in the hotel and talked. There was like an outdoor corridor outside the rooms. Really it was more like a shabby motel with barely running water and all these trucks parked in the yard. He did say how exhausted he was and how he never got a break. Then he talked about how he wanted to create the first black African circus, and make it one of the world's big circuses. How he thought that was possible. I told him I wanted him to repeat all this for me on tape because I wasn't filming, which was dumb, but somehow we never found the time.

So anyway, Juliet went on, shoving in a new tape, this is Sodo.

Raymond, in his red cap, caught a handful of white juggling pins and turned and, like a lithe piper, waved at the crowd of people who followed him.

There was a parade through the streets before the show, and by the end it was like everyone in town had joined in, Juliet said. And at the time it seemed completely magical.

Two boys on stilts clumped along, tall above those around them; a musician in a green felt hat arched over his saxophone. Gelila and another girl laughed as they strode in their white costumes, and more costumed boys wove among and around men in dusty jackets, women in traditional white veils, a woman in white shirt and dark skirt, children skipping and running alongside them. There were goats, and two boys passed juggling balls back and forth against a backdrop of small buildings with flaking plaster walls, and everyone projected an air of shambling anticipation.

Sara thought, I should tell Juliet about Raymond's juggling in the service centre on the 401, that other magical moment.

In daylight, on a large rectangle of tarpaulin spread on the ground, two girls, older and younger, mimed actions. The older girl wore a vest with the emblem of the Red Cross sewn on its back and seemed to be showing the younger how to wash her hands with soap; equipped with cordless mikes, they spoke in Amharic. To one side of the stage, a large rectangle of canvas, laced with nylon string to an upright metal frame, featured a series of cheerful, painted illustrations, of a sick child in bed, a boy with a crutch, a veiled woman holding a baby in a doctor's office while a white-coated doctor held out his hands to her, the illustrations tagged with phrases in Amharic script. Raymond

Renaud stood beside this banner, cap in hand, intent on the performance, as other costumed performers waited solemnly, one boy with hands on hips, close to Raymond, not avoiding him. There was nothing obvious to be gleaned from Raymond's stance or the boy's stance other than their absorption in the show. Across a low dirt slope, the dark heads of seated children bobbed, engrossed, and curious adults formed a ring around them, mostly men but also a few white-veiled women standing beneath a line of skinny eucalyptus trees.

Better than sex, Juliet said, Do you remember him saying that the night of the benefit?

Yes, Sara said, and this was her cue to say something more, to tell Juliet about the trip she'd taken with Raymond Renaud.

It keeps coming back and I keep trying to remember the context. I thought at first he meant he was choosing this work instead of sex. Because it was so important and necessary. But it doesn't have to mean that at all.

I did feel, Sara said, there was something shut down in him. Sexually. Something closed or blocked off.

Really? Juliet said and ejected the tape. Can I show you one more thing?

The grounds of the circus compound back in Addis Ababa were recognizable. Dusk once more: the sky still light-filled while shadows pulled the trees toward darkness. Raymond Renaud, in a black T-shirt, was out on the bumpy grass with two of the boys, who were juggling and moving as they juggled, which seemed to be part of the challenge; they were performing a kind of dance, flipping balls and pins and what looked like oranges and water bottles back and forth, their elongated shadows also dancing, while Raymond directed them, conducted them might be a better word, arms in motion, body, visible from behind, lunging forward and back. Some faint and tinny music wavered from a boom box on the ground, and the music entwined with Raymond's inaudible words, his tone concerned, emphatic, at moments not quite a shout. One of the boys was the boy in blue from the Copenhagen show, the elfin, dexterous boy who—

The other boy scampered off, hugging the juggling pins to his chest, leaving the elfin boy to kick the rest of their juggling implements into a pile. Raymond pulled three metal cylinders from a white bucket in which a handful of similar cylinders were upended—torches, that's what they were, which the boy had been holding in the photograph that Sara had seen at the benefit, torches that Raymond now tossed toward the boy.

From the pocket of his jeans, Raymond drew something: from the back, it was only clear what he was doing when he held the small thing to the tips of the torches and flames gusted from them. The boy did not flinch. There was tenderness to Raymond's gestures. He was explaining something. He reached out and adjusted the boy's hand on the torch. Again, the boy did not flinch but cast one fiery torch aloft, catching it on its descent as he sent the next upward with a whoosh, and the next, the flare of flame washing over his skin. The sun set.

He knew you were filming all this?

Yes, Juliet said. We all walked out together. Now when I see him touch Yitbarek's hand, I think—. But maybe he's just trying to show him how to do it right. And he knew he was being filmed.

Leaning over, Raymond plucked the three remaining metal cylinders from the bucket and, clasping them in one hand, set them alight, and he and the boy passed the torches back and forth, before, at a signal from Raymond, Yitbarek tossed the torches one by one to him, and Raymond, face raised, feet shuffling over the bumpy earth, rotated all six. He turned toward the camera, smiling, and, as at the service centre that night in July, didn't seem to be showing off as much as demonstrating the possibility of something, and there was beauty here, and he knew it, he was making it, and Juliet must have known it, since her eye, filming, was also creating the scene. In this moment, he was performing for her. They were collaborating. Or he was trying to distract her. To convince her that beauty outshone other things. Onscreen, he refracted all these possibilities.

The flames rose and fell, the light truly fading now, and Raymond's body, in its black T-shirt, began to disappear, and the boy, too, receded from sight, leaving only the smear of their faces and the hungry flames to grow brighter and brighter.

Yitbarek's the one who had the accident back in the summer, Sara said. Isn't that right?

What? Juliet said. What accident?

The night of the benefit. Raymond Renaud told me. And now there was nothing to do but go on, explain all of it, Raymond Renaud's bizarre request that she drive him to Montreal, to which, in the heat of the moment, she'd agreed. His urgency. His admission that there'd been an accident, his fear that Yitbarek was paralyzed. As she spoke, she was aware of Juliet's physical retraction.

Paralyzed? Juliet said.

Maybe he isn't. If he didn't say anything to you. Maybe he got back and it wasn't as bad as he thought.

Maybe, she thought, Raymond had assumed she would say something to Juliet.

I can't believe you didn't tell me about this, Juliet said, taut in her chair, while on the screen, in the hall of painted cinder blocks, smaller boys, including Yitbarek, vaulted over the backs of bigger boys, and girls in T-shirts and leggings stretched their limbs. With an almost violent gesture, Juliet stopped the tape.

It was a wild thing to do, but once it was over, I got busy, and I didn't think that much more about it. I'm sorry, Julie. All of which was partly true. And the episode had felt private, not something she wanted to share with Juliet because she wanted to avoid Juliet's reaction. I really assumed, since you were in pretty close touch, that he would have mentioned the accident to you.

Everything's a mess, Juliet said. There were tears in her eyes.

That February afternoon in the Van Houtte coffee shop when Juliet, the unassuming girl from the Feminism and Sexuality seminar, in her trim, dark coat and red knit cap, had walked in the door, Sara had sensed approachability in her. And so she'd waved. Takeout cup in hand, Juliet had come over to Sara's table by the window. So much was pent up in her, and Juliet, who took a seat across the table, was willing to listen, her cheeks growing pink with appalled solicitude as she took in Sara's story, and there was such relief in this, until at last Juliet reached out and laid a hand on Sara's arm and said, If you need somewhere to stay, do you want to come to my place?

There had been such relief at this too. Sara still had the room in the flat full of girls on St. Viateur, but the thought of going back there had felt so lonely and mortifying that she couldn't bear it. In Juliet's eyes, she might be a victim, although Juliet also seemed a little in awe of her. An exotic victim. Above all, Juliet seemed trustworthy, ready to believe her, willing to help. She could relax her guard a little.

In the edit suite, Juliet rose and rustled a tissue from her handbag and, with her back turned, blew her nose. Was it also possible that she was hiding something?

Ed Levoix of the International Red Cross in Addis Ababa, whom Juliet had interviewed back in May, answered his phone himself. Juliet had shown Sara a glimpse of him on one of her tapes: a large man with sandy hair seated behind a desk, tigerlike in his self-satisfaction, who winked at his invisible interlocutor and joked, Who'd have thought I'd come to Addis and end up in showbiz?

Sara had tried him at the number that Juliet had given her, from home, first thing on the Friday morning, the day after meeting with Juliet in the edit suite, hoping to catch Ed Levoix at the end of his workday. Before him, she had attempted once more to reach Raymond Renaud at the number on the circus website, which was the only number that either she or Juliet had for him. Again, after several rings, the answering machine clicked on and Raymond's upbeat voice asked callers to leave messages for him or Cirkus Mirak. It seemed surprising that he hadn't changed the recording, less surprising that he hadn't returned the one message she'd left for him.

Ah, so you're a friend of Juliet Levin's, Ed Levoix said. He, too, was Canadian, Juliet had told her. I think I recognize your name from the paper. I read it sometimes at the embassy.

Can I ask you a few questions about Raymond Renaud?

I had a feeling that's what this might be about.

A yellow legal pad open on the desk in front of her, Sara asked him what he knew.

That some of the kids ran off in Australia and are seeking asylum and, you know, I'm sure you know, have made some rather disturbing allegations.

Has the news been reported there?

Not yet. Not that I've seen. But everyone in the expat community, everyone who worked with him, knows. And all of us are reeling.

Has he issued any kind of statement?

I've not heard a peep. It's early days, though.

He's there, as far as you know?

He came back here from Australia. I know that much. He's not showing his face anywhere now. I might have seen his truck once.

How are people responding?

People? Well, those of us who worked with him are, what can I say, heartbroken. There's so much broken trust. It seemed like such a fantastic new model for working with children and communities and was attracting so much attention. A circus, brilliant idea, and here's this fantastically energetic guy with a huge vision who looked to be doing a whole lot of good.

And no word from the circus organization.

That would pretty much be him. Though there's that other man who works with him. No. I don't think so. I saw somewhere they're supposed to do a show in some part of town next week. I've no idea if they will. The whole thing may be kaput.

Did you ever observe anything that seemed troubling?

Me? No. He looked like a workaholic who liked to work with children. No, ah, scratch that.

What about a boy who was injured and possibly paralyzed back in the summer. Do you know anything about it?

Really? Paralyzed? I've heard nothing.

In bed with David, empty whisky glasses on the floor beside them, her body flooded with heat and a deep internal ticking that was also a settling, the room full of the scent of peat and trees and sex, Sara said, I'm thinking of going to Addis Ababa.

You are, David said, body turned to hers, sweat at his temples, her hand on his hip. Because of the circus man? Is it for work?

Not exactly. No one's paying me to go. I want to go. It's impulsive and I know it.

Are you sure he's there? David asked, in the calm and measured voice that was so much a part of him.

Not sure, no. But I know he went back there and there's no word he's gone anywhere else.

Or that he'd talk to you?

Well, if I go, it's not just for him, there's the children, the circus, and other people to talk to.

What had his words been on parting: if there's ever anything

I can do for you, ask. Something like that. There was no knowing, now, that she could hold him to such a promise. Ask him to tell her his version of what happened; insist that he owed this to her. Spoken out loud, her plan, if you could call it that, sounded more than impulsive. Ridiculous even. Maybe impulsiveness was a quality that Raymond Renaud called out in her, only this time the urgency was hers. As David, too, had something invested in her impulsiveness and failure to play by the rules.

So you'd go, hoping to write about it, David said.

Sitting up, Sara took his hand and pressed the webbing between his thumb and forefinger, massaging it. There he lay, in her bed, beautiful in the lamplight, watching her. Looking at him gave her pleasure. Touching him. Being touched by him, his fingers tangling in her hair, working their way against her scalp. For all that he was not hers. Still, there was his ability and hers when with him to live entirely or almost entirely in the present. Or I'd figure out some kind of travel piece. It's true, I'm kind of taken up by this. Who and what he is. In the wake of that drive, agreeing to it, spending all those hours with him. Was I completely duped or not? It's about what we call ground truths, the things you can only learn by being on the ground in a place, that you can't know any other way. I want that. It's a bit mad, but I'm sure I can find a way to write it off.

When?

In a couple of weeks. If I can get the time. As soon as I can book a ticket and get a visa. I don't think I'll be able to get away for more than a week.

There was the piece she wasn't giving David, the piece of her past that was also propelling her toward Raymond Renaud.

Her sense of identification with him; the possibility of helping him if by chance he had been wrongly accused. But it wasn't necessary, it was merely complicating to tell David about this. All truths were partial. There were plenty of other reasons for her to want to re-encounter Raymond Renaud. She had never been to Addis Ababa. There was the mystery of the boy.

When, after the night flight from London, Sara stepped from
the metal stairs leading off the plane and onto the tarmac of
Bole Airport, a furious wind attempted to clear her jet-lagged
head. Men in uniforms stood guard with guns, and this felt
familiar from other places she had travelled, just as the musk of
the official inside the terminal, who waved her toward an endless
passport-control lineup, tugged her back to places where people
didn't use deodorant or shower as often as they did at home,
where the scents of the body were normal. At long last, the man
with the metal stamping machine stared at her photograph
and visa and asked her the purpose of her visit. He did not
ask if she had a police record. In the early days, after she'd left
Montreal, this was a fear. She hadn't been convicted but had
been fingerprinted and charged. Once, driving up to a border
crossing into New York state, the uniformed man in the booth
had asked, Have you ever been charged with anything? She'd
said, Yes, but I was cleared. It was a mistake. He had taken her
passport and disappeared, returned, asked her to come with

him. She'd waited for two hours in a small room, so late for an interview in Syracuse that the whole exercise grew pointless. The man came back and said he could refuse her entry but this was her lucky day, he would let her go this time. Since then, she'd gone through the formal process of having all traces of her record removed. She'd had to go back to Montreal to do this, back to the Palais de Justice. *Palace of Justice.* To the Ethiopian official she said, Tourist.

As she endured a second long wait, this time for her bag, an old sensation of sharp competence and ferocity bubbled up in her. Outside the terminal waited blue-and-white taxis among which men wandered; Juliet had told her how much the trip into town should cost. It would not be hot in Addis, Juliet had said, because of the elevation, and it wasn't. The late-September morning was damp and cool. Sara zipped up her fleece jacket. Goats or sheep or goats that looked like sheep milled about the wide road, while files of people in jackets or sweaters made their way along footpaths ground into the dirt by the side of the road.

At the front desk of the Hotel Berhailu, which acquaintances of Juliet's had recommended when Sara had asked for the name of somewhere clean, with a restaurant, and if possible at least three phone lines, in case one or more than one failed to work, she was handed a metal key as long as her finger. A guard, or watchman, stood in the entryway, eyeing the small gated compound outside. An elevator barely big enough for two, which shuddered with every lift of its cable, carried Sara up to the fourth floor, where she wiggled the key into a keyhole large enough to spy through and entered a room, courtyard-side, that might have been any number of hotel rooms in her past: the twin beds had thin brown covers and plain, wood-panelled headboards, the desk and clothes cupboard were stained a shiny brown. In the bathroom, a red webbed plastic garbage pail set beside the toilet was presumably to be used as a repository for toilet paper, although no sign explained as much, and the shower water, when she tried the tap, burst first in an explosively hot stream then petered to a frigid trickle. None of this dismayed her. Instead her arrival felt like re-entry into a world and way of being that she hadn't realized she'd missed.

After fortifying herself with a bottle of water, *Ambo* written in orange letters on its sky-blue label, and a not-bad macchiato from the bar downstairs, she left messages at the embassy and the city police department seeking word about the status of any investigation into the allegations, another message for the Larsens, Juliet's contacts, who had arranged a driver for her, and confirmed a meeting with Ed Levoix. She did not try to reach Raymond Renaud directly, having decided, after purchasing her airline ticket, that surprise might be her best option, which left him no opportunity to avoid her.

Juliet had been surprised by her decision to make the trip. Juliet herself seemed to have no inclination to return. Anyway, I can't afford to, she'd said. But I'm glad you're doing this. At work, Sara had asked her editor, Nuala Johnson, for a week's vacation but had not told Nuala or anyone else what she was up to, just that something had come up. You okay? Nuala had asked, and Sara had said fine. As soon as she paid for her ticket, her plan seemed more foolhardy than ever, but by then it was too late to do anything other than throw herself into it.

After lunch, she took another taxi to the National Museum, through streets crowded with people, children, wandering boys with small wooden crates. Locked on her arrival, the museum's doors were opened at last by a sole guard-cum-tour-guide who led Sara and an American couple from room to room, switching on lights and opening shutters as they went, until, ahead of her, Sara heard the American woman squeal in delight, Here's Lucy. It wasn't until she returned to her hotel that she discovered that the real bones of Lucy, famous little Australopithecus, millions of years old, found in an Ethiopian valley, were elsewhere, that the ones on display were fake.

The next morning at nine, as she entered the hotel lobby, a man, darker-skinned than the others around him, in a much-washed T-shirt and ironed khaki trousers, launched himself out of a vinyl armchair at the sight of her.

Alazar Wolde?

I am he. His handshake was firm, and he had a very white grin, offset by a questing tilt to his head. From her daypack, Sara pulled out her notebook, into which she had transcribed Juliet's directions to the circus compound and to Raymond Renaud's house, and showed the directions to Alazar. Her mini tape recorder, wrapped in a bandana, was a small weight in the pocket of her jacket, her camera stuffed in her bag.

Can we go there?

It's possible.

Is it difficult to get to?

No, no, he said. We will take the Wollo Road.

Have you ever seen Cirkus Mirak perform?

I have heard of it, but I have not seen it.

He offered to carry her daypack, but she shook her head as they made their way out to the hotel's pull-in area, where an old beige Fiat lounged beside a bank of scrubby rosebushes, the uniformed watchman alert by the open gate. Circling the car, Sara climbed not into the back but into the front passenger seat.

When with a hired driver, she preferred to sit in the front, especially if in a car rather than a van. Unless sitting in the back was unavoidable, for safety reasons. You saw more from the front seat. You were not always staring at the back of someone's neck. Things did not feel so obviously hierarchical, although they were hierarchical, she wasn't kidding herself.

Here, she needed no headscarf — unlike the time in Islamabad when, as she'd stepped out of her fixer's fumy car into an eddy of wind, her scarf had fallen back and all the men lounging in polyester pants against a row of street stalls had hissed, and the journalist with whom she was travelling, male, who'd exited through the car's back door before her, had, before she could do anything, reached over to tug her scarf back into place. For her sake, he'd insisted afterward, although as he said this he couldn't meet her gaze. Probably, if wearing a skirt or dress in Addis Ababa, she wouldn't have wanted to expose her knees, but when it came to attire, she did not so far feel more restricted than this.

Through the closed car window, as Alazar set off, came the scent, at every moment, of something burning. It was true, as Raymond had said, as Juliet had said, that people — children — shouted at you. Whenever the car slowed, children ran toward them shouting. As they hadn't in Kenya, where people waved and, even at gas stations, held out their hands for

(123)

you to shake. Along the side of the road, small boys carrying wooden shoeshine boxes called out, Listro, listro, to all passers-by, and at one intersection, an Ethiopian man in a business suit stood in front of one such crate, reading a newspaper as a boy knelt in front of him and rubbed his raised shoe with a rag.

Can we stop at a supermarket or somewhere I can buy a few supplies?

It is possible.

When Alazar pulled up at the curb in front of an old, wide-fronted shop with a wooden sign, Sara asked if he minded waiting in the car.

It is possible.

Inside, among a warren of narrow aisles full of shelves of dark wood that reached to the high ceilings, she found water, bananas, packets of the high-protein soy biscuits given to children for nourishment in refugee camps. It was only as she returned to the car that it struck her that Alazar's repeated phrase wasn't the deflection she'd first heard but something closer to No problem or Sure, okay.

The road they followed led away from the centre of town. At every intersection, more children, spying Sara, ran toward the car shouting. Some long minutes after that, on her right, as Juliet had said, appeared an Agip station, the fire-breathing black lion rearing on its yellow sign, and there, on the far side of the road, rose the pole with the painted wooden circus emblem at the top, of the boy standing on his hands, legs upraised, bright paint grown worn.

The surprise of seeing things you'd first glimpsed on film, beyond the confirmation of their actuality, was that nothing ever looked as you'd imagined it, those glimpses being no more than distorted signposts to a world that was inevitably wilder, deeper, and more unpredictable than what you had imagined. The road felt less wide and there were buildings, shacks, close to the circus sign, and more greenery enclosed the hillside that rose on the far side of the road, all thickly coloured beneath a slate-grey, rainy-season sky. When Alazar slowed and pulled into the gas station lot, a man in greasy coveralls stepped out of a cinder-block building, wiping his hands on his thighs, and children burst from behind the station building and out of shacks whose rust-red, corrugated metal roofs were held in place by stones and began to shout.

Sara pointed to the lane, on the far side of the road, that led up the hillside into trees. Without another word, Alazar swung out of the gas station, making a U-turn so jolting in its force and speed, especially given the transport truck barrelling toward them and the women walking in single file along the dirt path on the far side of the road, that Sara's seat belt was jammed against her chest. Then they were pulled up on the verge on the other side, and more children were running toward them from behind more shacks and ranks of skinny eucalyptus trees.

Alazar scanned the dirt lane that led up to the circus compound doubtfully. And, indeed, the track looked more eroded by rain and fissured with deeper channels than when Juliet had filmed it in the spring. You want me to take that road? he asked.

Do you think you can make it up without getting stuck?

He gave a grin that made the seams of bone across his wide forehead grow more prominent, and said, not, It is possible, but,

I think not. Stones protruded like teeth from the red path. If they'd had four-wheel drive, they might have made it up, but the Fiat didn't.

So then I'll walk up. Shouting children crowded around the outside of their parked car.

I will come with you. He was torn: she could see that he did not want to leave the car untended.

You don't need to, Alazar, I'll be fine. She handed him some money for a Nescafé and told him, glancing at her watch, to meet her at the Agip station in two hours, hoping that would be long enough. Okay?

Ishee, he said.

The moment Sara stepped out of the car, avoiding the puddle at her feet, children surrounded her, jabbed at her jacket with their fingers, brushed her with their arms and worn clothes, shouting, Ferengi, give me money. A girl in a ski jacket held out a plastic comb, a lottery ticket, and said, Buy it. A boy in a wool hat shouted, Where you go? You go to circus? Who are you? What is your name? Far more English than she knew of Amharic. A chorus of voices: What is your nation? What you do?

Are you artist? This last, from another boy, wearing a fedora, assertive and businesslike.

She was amused, intrigued. What makes you think I'm an artist?

He pointed at her clothes: jeans, fleece jacket, boots. Maybe anyone, or any white person making her way up the hill to the circus compound, was viewed as some kind of artist. Or it was flattery.

She told him her name was Sara, and she was from Canada. Have you seen the circus?

Some of the children said yes, some said no, and it was impossible to be sure who was telling the truth.

Do you know the man who runs the circus?

Mr. Raymond. We see him.

Have you taken any classes at the circus? For both Raymond and Juliet had mentioned classes for street children.

Yes, said the businesslike boy, and gave another tug to her clothes. Sister, give me money.

What's your name?

Berhailu. Which was also the name of her hotel.

What did you do in the circus class?

He hopped and skipped and glanced at his feet, as if a steep track was not the best place to show off such skills.

Why aren't you in school?

When they reached the top of the hill, he and all the other children fell back, drifting down the lane they'd climbed on. Ahead, on the stretch of dirt that passed for a parking area, two aged and mud-spattered cars were parked. Through will or tenacity or practice or faith they had managed the climb, but there was no sign of Raymond's white truck. Beyond the vehicles, across an expanse of scrubby grass and dirt and within an outer ring of pine and eucalyptus trees, stood two yellow buildings, the administrative building and the community hall, as Juliet had called them, the hall being where the circus rehearsed.

There were children out on the grass, practising a series of exercises atop a large square tarpaulin. Spotting Sara, they stopped, whispered among themselves, then dashed back toward the door of the farther building, the community hall. Through its open windows travelled a lilt of children's voices, the stamping of feet. More corrugated rooftops winked behind the trees, the smudged scent of charcoal drifting close.

Through the doorway of the first building, the one with the porch that, Juliet had said, housed the offices of the community leader and the circus, surged a boy in nylon trackpants and sneakers worn without socks. He marched down the wooden steps and, when he reached Sara, said, Please. You go. No visitors today.

I'd like to speak to Mr. Raymond. Which was what the street children had called him.

He is not here. A light voice, still unbroken. The boy was perhaps twelve, not yet adolescent, amber-skinned and slim, his furrowed forehead giving him a preternaturally aged air. He looked possibly familiar from Juliet's tapes.

Is he at home? Will he be back later? Presumably, even if Raymond was not, other adults lurked somewhere.

He is not here.

My name is Sara Wheeler. She held out her hand and, after a flicker of hesitation, the boy took hold of it between his cool, dry fingers. And you are?

Segaye.

Segaye, are you in the circus?

He nodded.

Are you an acrobat, a juggler? She mimed juggling.

Once more he nodded. I do it.

Have you been in the circus a long time? His glance skittered, as if he'd been told not to enter a conversation with the stranger.

Two year.

Do you like being in the circus?

Yes, is good.

Is Mr. Raymond good to you?

Yes, good. But his body was pulling away.

Have you been on tour with the circus?

She could feel as much as see his withdrawal from her.

Wait. Segaye, is Mr. — she had to dive into her daypack for her notebook, ruffle through its pages — Mr. Tamrat Asfaw, is he here?

He work.

Perhaps even now someone was watching them, fluttering in the shade behind a window. Was that not, from the near building, the percussion of a typewriter, the click of a latch.

Can you give him my name and ask if I can have a word with him?

Sara lowered one knee to the red dirt, balanced her notebook on the other, and wrote out her name in printed letters on a clean page, then deliberated over what else to write: friend of Juliet Levin did not seem useful, since she was not convinced Tamrat Asfaw would remember Juliet by name or that he'd feel anything but aversion at the prospect of Juliet's film; friend of Raymond Renaud was stretching it, and she had no idea how Tamrat Asfaw would respond to that, so she simply added the name of her hotel and its phone number, and beneath her name, from Toronto, thinking that perhaps her message might find its way to Raymond himself. She wrote, I would like to talk to you, then, impulsively, added another sentence, Raymond Renaud asked me to get in touch, hoping that covered all bases.

With the edge of the paper held in his hand, as if he might at any instant let go of it, the boy set off, shoes flapping at his bare heels, in the direction of the second building, the rehearsal hall.

Sara started to follow him, then thought better of it, and sat to wait on the porch steps of the first building, under the roof's wide overhang. How odd to think of Juliet Levin as the only person she knew, save Raymond Renaud, to whom she could say the rehearsal hall, or the administrative building, or the circus compound and Juliet would know exactly what she was talking about.

The door behind her had been left ajar and through it a faint conversation between women could be heard. Sara could not stop herself from rising and stepping across the threshold into a dim hall along which the scent of spices and more children's voices drifted. Juliet had said there was a room used as a classroom, and a lunchroom, where a woman prepared the children's lunches over a propane stove. What was the name, again, of the local leader, of the kebele, the district, Mr. Yonas Something. Juliet had written it down, along with a phone number, and Raymond had mentioned how this man had generously offered the circus office space and a place to rehearse. Circus is the new faith, he'd said on tape. Sara pulled out her notebook.

There was no one in the first small office along the dim hallway, but in the second, a woman in a jacket and flowered skirt rose to her feet behind a wooden desk, and there were no lights on in this room either, no power at all perhaps, which might mean this quadrant of the city was in the midst of its weekly day without power, for the city and the entire country were rationed in this way, so someone at the hotel had told her.

Is Raymond Renaud here, or Mr. Yonas Berhanu?

No, they are not here, the woman said in strongly accented English. Some perfume clung to her, or hint of frankincense. Please, I ask you to leave.

Already it felt as if the circus had a cordon thrown up around it, and it was not possible to be a curious visitor only a trespasser in a place where once people from nearby neighbourhoods had wandered over in the evenings to be ushered into the community hall to waiting rows of benches or had stood outside the windows to watch the children rehearse, as Juliet had described, and an Italian photographer and Canadian filmmaker and even a sociologist had all been welcomed to observe the circus.

Can I ask you when they will be here?

I do not know it.

In her years in the field, she had of course dealt with far worse setbacks.

When Sara stepped outside once more, she found no sign of the boy. Through the open windows of the community hall streamed shouts, the magnified slap of hands and feet against mats in a high-ceilinged room, and when she approached across the grass and dirt, and edged close to a window, there were the children, older, younger, in T-shirts and tights and nylon trackpants, moving about in the wide room of painted cinder block that she had seen on Juliet's tapes. Through the middle of the room ran a row of cinder-block pillars, and large squares of diaphanous cotton hung from the ceiling. Directly in front of her, boys tumbled into somersaults on mats that looked identical to the blue vinyl ones tossed on the floor of every gym of her childhood. Four girls worked in pairs, also on mats, one on her stomach while her partner stood between her extended legs and pulled upon the first girl's arms and torso to stretch her body back in an inverted C. Was that safe? And yet all this seemed ordinary, the T-shirts, the trackpants, the children's absorption in what they were doing. They exhibited no obvious signs of stress—

She looked again: in one corner of the room a boy kept his balance on a rectangular piece of wood that teetered on top of a piece of metal pipe while juggling, was it five?, small white balls in the air as another boy reached from behind him, stole a ball from one side then tossed it back into play on the other. In another corner, a girl of perhaps twelve or thirteen in a backbend so deep her head nearly touched the floor juggled three balls in this position, while four younger girls reached the apex of a balance pose: one girl extended upside down in the splits, hands gripping the hands of the girl who supported her from underneath, this girl balanced in turn on the torsos of two girls arched over, feet and hands on the ground. None of which was ordinary.

Were they ordinary children who had trained to perform such marvels or were they children gifted with extraordinary flexibility and daring who had found their way to the circus, or some of each? And what knowledge did they carry within them, in their minds, in their bodies, of what had happened between Raymond Renaud and the runaways?

On the far side of the room, near the door, an Ethiopian man, not tall but muscled, in a white T-shirt and green nylon trackpants, was talking to two boys. Nearby the boy, Segaye, sat on a bench, waggling his feet. Sara could see no sign of the note she'd given him. On the wall above him hung a flag with horizontal bands of green, yellow, red, the Ethiopian colours. Presumably the man was Tamrat Asfaw, who had been a wrestler, Juliet had said, until the day he saw the circus perform and showed up at the hall and said to Raymond, I want to help. She must have moved, or her presence made itself felt like a touch upon Tamrat Asfaw, who glanced over his shoulder and across the room. When she called his name through the open window, he didn't respond, only turned to say something to Segaye, the mood in the whole room shifting, the children halted in their practice. The boy bolted out the door as Sara made her way toward it.

In the open air, Segaye waved his arms. He work.

Can I make an appointment to speak with him?

Yes, she could barge in on Tamrat Asfaw and the circus children, but perhaps she had been precipitous in setting off without Alazar Wolde, Amharic speaker, in her desire to do a reconnaissance by herself.

Please, will you tell Mr. Asfaw that I will come back later or tomorrow? Oh, and, Segaye, do you know a boy named Yitbarek Abera?

Recognition registered on his face, also his surprise at hearing this name come so unexpectedly out of her mouth. His yes sounded like a question.

A few months ago, did he have an accident?

He gave a barely perceptible nod.

Did he get hurt?

He looked extremely nervous, as if he'd been told not to speak of this, or the very idea of Yitbarek's accident frightened him.

Did he fall?

He fall.

How is he now?

Okay.

Segaye, where is Yitbarek?

His house now, Yitbarek house.

And where is that?

That way. He pointed back toward the lane, his extended hand taking in an indeterminate stretch of trees and sky.

Where that way?

He shrugged.

Before he was in his house, where was he?

This question seemed to confuse him, so she tried again. Where did Yitbarek live before?

Mr. Raymond house. The boss house.

She showed Alazar the little map on which Juliet had drawn the location of Raymond Renaud's house, marking the corner lot, which they were approaching in Alazar's car, the house enclosed within a wall of red brick topped by spears of glass, broken pieces of bottle embedded in a line of cement, their points piercing upward. The sky still threatened rain, slate-coloured clouds turning yellowish where the sun tried to poke its way through them. Emerald fronds of bamboo shimmered above the height of the wall. Raymond's garden, where he had sat in a pinkish T-shirt, on a white wooden chair, in a rustling breeze, and spoken to Juliet. The rusty cylinder of a water tank perched on the roof of the house, which was modest in size as glimpsed through the front gate. *The boss' house*, the boy had said. The house where three boys had also lived and other children had stayed over and hung out. Maybe Yitbarek had indeed recovered from his fall, which would be the best news. From his side of the locked gate, a watchman in a yellow rain slicker stepped toward them, a little brown dog yapping at his feet, but the man made no move to swing the gate open. There was no sign of a white truck, and the windows offered no clues as to what life lay within.

In the car, Sara had told Alazar that she was hoping to speak to the man who ran, who'd run the children's circus. She'd seen the children perform in Denmark, met the man in Toronto, and wanted to visit them here. She was a journalist but wasn't, strictly speaking, working, she was helping a friend, a filmmaker, who was making a film about the circus. This seemed to be the best explanation she could offer for herself, for what she was doing, for the moment.

On foot she and Alazar stepped up to the gate, her blonde hair pulled back in a ponytail, his T-shirt, she noticed, coming loose over the waist of his trousers. The difficulty, always, in the matter of translators, was the surrender of control. The watchman wore a pressed dress shirt and neatly ironed khaki trousers beneath his yellow slicker. She had to trust Alazar—

Since she could not understand a word that he and the watchman were saying. In Spanish, she caught some sense because of her French, which was on the way to fluent, and in Russian and Arabic and even Polish, gleaned greetings and occasional phrases, depending on the speed of the speaker, but in Amharic, as in Pashto or Urdu or Tamil, not much at all. Okay, one word, amesegenallo, thank you, in a day she'd learned that much Amharic, no, two, ishee, okay. All else was reduced to intonation, gesture, the music and choreography of speech. The little foxlike dog sat alert at the watchman's side.

There was also the question of where to look, at Alazar as he spoke for her, in order to help channel her thoughts through him, or at the watchman, to whom Alazar was speaking, and addressing for her. Alazar kept glancing at her, his gesture of inclusiveness. What she could make out so far: he was voluble, genial, and would probably attempt to extract information by generating good feeling. The watchman's replies were monotone, and when he spoke, he rubbed a cautious finger back and forth along his right sideburn, ducking his head every now and again to keep an eye on the perked ears of his little dog.

He is not here, Alazar said at last.

Not here right now or he's gone away? She felt a sudden spasm of anxiety.

He has gone away, and he does not know where he has gone or when he comes back.

Did he take the truck? Is he in the country or has he left the country? Does the watchman know where he is? Sorry, that's a lot of questions.

Maybe the country. The watchman is not certain of it.

When did he leave?

Last week, he says.

Is there anyone living in the house at the moment?

Right now he says not.

So the boys, the children who lived here, where are they?

I will ask it.

Oh, and does he have any idea when Mr. Renaud's coming back?

After a further exchange in Amharic, Alazar said, He says you must speak to the people from the circus for this information.

Okay.

Do you wish me to ask anything else?

Did he leave in a hurry, pack up his things like he was moving, or like he was going on a trip?

I already ask this. He says, all the big possessions are still here. He left like he is making a trip.

Who's paying his salary, the watchman's, now, is it still Mr. Renaud?

You want me to ask this?

Yes, if you would, please.

The watchman's gaze jetted between them and a vinyl-covered kitchen chair, the padded seat cover moulded by long use, set up in the compound to one side of the gate, and was he the gardener or was it Raymond himself who had made bougainvillea bloom and ferns flourish? Through the watchman's flat volley of speech Sara made out two names.

He says, he believes it is Mr. Renaud who pays but Mr. Asfaw gives the money this week.

Can you ask him if a boy named Yitbarek Abera lived here, and if he was injured, and if he knows where the house of Yitbarek Abera is?

Yitbarek Abera?

Yes. He was in the circus. Can he tell you the way to Yitbarek's house?

Back in her hotel room, Sara tossed her jacket and daypack onto the bed, her key onto the desk. It was hard, now, not to surrender to disappointment. And self-recrimination. In the field, there was always that initial, elusive hope that the people you wished to meet would materialize exactly where and when you wished to speak to them. If you had a good fixer, as they were called, that helped: driver, translator, all-around facilitator. You landed on the ground and depended, often enough, on your fixer's contacts to get you to whomever and wherever you needed to go. Alazar seemed a good translator, a good-enough driver, not quite an ideal fixer. That Raymond Renaud was gone was not Alazar's fault. But they had failed to find Yitbarek Abera's house. Of course she had no idea what instructions Renaud's watchman had given. Perhaps they had been designed to confuse. The boy is lame, Alazar had said to her. He cannot walk.

Is he paralyzed? she'd asked, which would seem to be the case.

It is possible, Alazar said.

They'd ended up on foot in a warren of un-signposted lanes, craterous, full of puddles and open drains, too narrow for the car to drive through, surrounded by yelling children, but found no one who seemed to know about the boy or where he lived. Alazar had been profuse in his apologies. Fear underlay them: that he would not measure up and she would find someone else. I will find the way, he said. Tomorrow.

And Raymond Renaud. He had not lied about Yitbarek's accident, she had to hold on to this. In his story there was this much truth.

Sitting on the end of the bed, Sara unlaced her boots and slipped her bare feet into flip-flops. There was no power, she realized, when she flicked the light switch in the bathroom, and no hot water, and the faint diesel odour wafting from the hall into her room likely came from a generator chugging somewhere outside, which was powering some things but not others. Then, mysteriously, the light came on, flickered and fizzed, and settled at a lower wattage than usual. A generator and/or possibly a voltage stabilizer. The ambient sounds of a place like this.

She poured herself a sliver of duty-free whisky and added some water from the bottle labelled Ambo. She'd noticed people asking for water by this name, as in, *I'd like a bottle of Ambo.* Then she fought successfully with the catch on the door leading out to the tiny balcony.

There had always been the risk that he would not be here, and it was ludicrous to think that giving him advance notice of her visit would have provided him with any reason to stick around.

His truck wasn't at his house, and so perhaps he was somewhere in the truck, as in not far away, and would return.

Someone would pass on to him the written message that she'd left at the circus compound. He was still in shock. He was somewhere close by, hiding out, and only saying that he was gone. Guilty or innocent, he would have to create some distance between himself and the circus while whatever investigation there was took place.

In the garden below, a path led through pine trees or cedar to the gauzy blue of a swimming pool, where despite the chilly air an Ethiopian man seemed to be teaching an Ethiopian woman how to swim, their chuckles rising. The circus children whom she'd seen rehearsing that morning had not looked terrorized or kept against their will. The ones who'd returned from Australia, including Segaye, hadn't fled. She had not, despite Tamrat's ire at her, sensed fear and quaking submission in the room. This was no more than a first impression.

Inside once more, she picked up the receiver of the old black phone and punched in the circus number from the website. Juliet had said she thought the line rang in Raymond Renaud's house.

Raymond, Sara said into his answering machine. It's Sara Wheeler, from Toronto. I'm in Addis Ababa. When I dropped you off in Montreal, you said if there was ever anything you could do for me to ask. So I'm asking. I came here because of the circus. I'd like to talk to you. I'd like to hear your version of what's going on.

The phone rang and she swam up from sleep toward the braying sound, opened her eyes to the brash face of her travel alarm clock, just before seven a.m., somehow she'd slept through the amplified Orthodox Christian call to prayer that, like a muezzin, had woken her before six the previous morning—and was it David, to whom she'd spoken the night before, for whom it would now be nearly midnight and who almost never called her from home unless it was an emergency, who'd reminded her, during their conversation, both that she'd missed Thanksgiving and that Greta was going in for a new round of tests that week. Or could it be Raymond?

Wildly, Sara plucked at the receiver and managed a hello as she scrambled to sit up. The voice that greeted hers was male, Ethiopian, not Alazar's, more strongly accented, blunter, saying, This is Sara Wheeler—the words a question.

Yes. Within the casing of the sheet, she propped herself against the headboard and placed the squat black telephone, attached to its cord, between her feet.

I am Tamrat Asfaw.

Yes. Thanks. Thanks so much for calling. She did not know if there was aggression in his calling so early, an intention to disturb her as she was so obviously disturbing him, or if the timing was a matter of necessity. She was desperate to pee, needed pen, paper, glass of water, tape recorder, another minute in which to clear her head.

Who you are and what you want?

She told him: she was a friend of Juliet Levin, the filmmaker who'd been shooting in May; she'd met Raymond Renaud in July in Toronto through Juliet and he'd invited her to visit the circus; she was travelling through Addis and hoped to meet some of the children and speak to Raymond.

He is away.

Okay. Can you tell me where he is or how I might get hold of him?

I cannot.

She did not know if this meant he truly could not or would not tell her.

Is he still running Cirkus Mirak?

I do it.

So he's not involved in the circus at the moment?

He is exhaust.

Is it because of what happened in Australia?

What you know of it?

I know that some of the performers ran away, asked for asylum, and made some allegations against him.

The one who say these thing. They decide it. Then they say these thing.

So you—she found a pen on the night table, a museum brochure to write on, her tape recorder nowhere in sight. The phone cord was not that long and it seemed unwise to ask Tamrat if she could put down the receiver in order to search for the recorder in her jacket pocket or bag, given that her connection to him and his willingness to speak to her felt so tenuous. Why do you think they ran away? Is there any truth to their allegations?

They want to run, that is it.

Were you in Australia?

No, I stay. He go.

What did Raymond say about what happened?

I said it.

Has he made any kind of statement or denial?

He deny. And I am here. I see.

The other children in the circus, the ones who were on tour in Australia, or here — what do they think happened, or has any of them made any similar claims or complaints —

The ones who run, they say these thing, the others do not say it. We work hard to make circus. We do it. For good of circus. How else to do it? They want it. I want it. And I say, if any run, we never go away again.

You told them they mustn't run away from the circus. And they say —

Yes, yes, they see it. I go —

Tamrat, there's a boy, Yitbarek Abera. Back in July, Raymond told me he had a fall —

One time this happen. One time. It is accident. We watch. We take care.

I'm not implying you don't. So he did have a fall —

Yes.

How is he now?

We work.

What was that?

I go.

What about an investigation, into the allegations against —

I go.

Tamrat, can I visit you at the circus? Today, tomorrow, any day this week?

Not possible.

She sat with the phone receiver in her hand, the line dead, a confusion of sensation welling in her, a wild top note at Tamrat's word that Raymond had denied the allegations, which registered as relief.

At eight, Alazar picked her up and Sara settled herself in the seat beside him. Out along the Wollo Road, streams of schoolchildren in uniform traipsed along the dirt path at the side of the road, some sweatered, some in white shirts, girls in dark skirts or pinafores, puddles yawning in the reddish dirt, the clouds piled high and swelling. He told her, as he drove, how one of his first jobs as a driver had been during the big famine, many years ago now. He had been part of a UN convoy transporting food-aid workers into the north. It had been good work, full-time, good pay, he'd never had such good work since, he had even met the rock star Bob.

Goats lolloped along the drainage ditch in front of them. Exhaust spewed from a passing truck. They would find the lame boy, he said. And then, carefully: Did she have any plans to travel north? Did she know anyone who needed a full-time driver? Sara said she didn't but would ask around, didn't know yet if she planned to leave the city, told Alazar about her own trip up through the Kenyan desert to the camps near the Sudanese border, where there'd been no rock stars.

They pulled in and waited in the car in front of the Agip station. Although the circus children had been rehearsing up in the community hall the previous morning, Sara had no idea if they arrived at that hour every day, if they rehearsed and did their schoolwork onsite rather than going to a regular school.

No children appeared and began to make the steep climb up the laneway, nor was there any sign of Tamrat Asfaw in his dark-green tracksuit. Some of the local children whom Sara had encountered the day before shouted at them from outside the car and, when she rolled down the window, called out, Sister, mother.

Alazar said, They think you are a missionary. All the white people who first come here are missionaries so now they think all white people are this. It is where these names come from.

When Berhailu, the boy in the fedora, approached, Alazar rolled down his window and asked something in Amharic that involved Yitbarek's name. Berhailu opened the back door of the car and settled himself inside.

He says he will show us where the boy's house is, Alazar said, then turned and shouted at the other children who had crowded around the car windows.

Are the circus children coming today? Sara asked, turning to Berhailu. Beneath the brim of his fedora, he had long, beautiful eyelashes.

Yes, sister, he said.

Are they there already?

He shook his head.

Juliet had given her names: Tesfanesh, Kidsit, Lelise, Girma. Do you know Kidsit or Lelise? Are they coming?

Yes.

Tell me about the classes you take at the circus.

Is good.

Where did you learn English, in school? Although she had doubts about whether he went to school.

Circus.

Does Mr. Raymond teach the classes?

They do it.

By them she assumed he meant the circus performers. Even English classes?

Mr. Raymond do it.

What do you think of him? And the others, do they say he is a good man, or a bad man?

Good, sister. Though he might be telling her what he thought she wanted to hear.

Can you show me something you learned in the circus class?

She had to ask Alazar to repeat the request in Amharic. I'll give him money, she added.

He has no mat, Alazar said, after the two of them had conferred.

Nevertheless, Berhailu, shoeless, leaped out of the car and, after some urgent discussion with another boy in a windbreaker, performed a dance that involved foot stomping and hand clapping and eager waving of their thin arms, though these boys lacked the obvious skill and grace of the trained performers. Sara snapped a couple of photographs.

Back in the car, while Berhailu folded coins into a pocket in his grimy shorts, Alazar said, He says the circus children, they will not come until later because this evening they have a show.

A show?

A small show, a practice show.

Sara turned again to Berhailu. Can you tell us where?

.·.

Alazar, in conversation with Berhailu, drove the car at a crawl through a different warren of stony, rutted streets than those they'd navigated the day before and pulled up at last in front of a corrugated iron gate flimsy on its hinges, gaps around its frame, its two wings secured with a padlock, locked from the outside. A hint of a rusty metal roof and a black meander of an electrical line were visible overtop the gate. A crowd gathered: men in wool hats, women with cloth wraps hiding their hair, a throng of children. Sara joined Alazar among the shouting children as he rattled the gate and they both peered through the gaps at the dirt yard inside, the glimpse of a worn wooden door, blue paint flaking from cracked plaster walls. All he could confirm, Alazar said, after speaking to those assembled, was that the woman who lived in the house was out. She had lived in the house for about a month. There was a convoluted story about who had lived in the house before this. And Sara, too, from the few who spoke a bit of English: Yes, a boy lived there. The boy who stayed in the house. When he left, he travelled in a chair.

A capped guard in a booth activated the security bar that rose and allowed them to enter the walled parking compound of the Red Cross offices, downtown near the central stadium. Row upon row of white four-wheel-drive Toyotas greeted them, a shining army, along with a few ranks of motley cars, some with drivers leaning against the doors, the building itself brick and bunkerlike. Up on the third floor, Sara stepped from the elevator to find a large man in a tweed jacket surging down the hall toward her.

Once in his office, door closed, Ed Levoix said, Have a seat. Renaud's left town. Have you heard? I just heard. What a disturbing business this is, and I can't say it looks good he's taken off.

Sara took the chair in front of his desk while Ed Levoix moved to the far side of the desk, the window at his side. He made no move to sit but scanned about, as if searching for something else to be revealed. A large man but not flaccid, with a kind of restless strength like that of a Percheron horse. Back in the spring he'd sat at this desk while Juliet filmed him joking that he'd come to Addis and ended up in show business.

How did you hear he'd gone? Sara asked.

From someone who works for Save the Children UK who was supposed to have a meeting with him and ran into the man who works with him —

Tamrat Asfaw.

Ah, you know him, you've met him? A keen gaze atop the restlessness.

Talked to him.

And you're here because, tell me again. You're writing something or it's to do with your friend's film?

It's a curious-enough story. I wanted to see what more I can find out.

So you might be writing something.

I don't know yet.

You don't need to be coy with me. Why wouldn't you? The cocked eyebrow. That keenness. He looked as if he knew the usual thing would be to sit but for some reason unwillingness gripped him and he scanned the room again. When Sara asked him if he knew where Raymond Renaud had gone, he said he had absolutely no idea. He checked his watch. I know it's early-ish, but do you feel like going somewhere for lunch? Or coffee? Have you had the coffee ceremony yet?

Sara offered her car for transport, but Ed Levoix said, Oh, no, we'll walk. The Finfine. Unless you want to drive and meet me there. We'll stop and tell your driver where we're going. It's not far. He'll know it.

Out in the street, beyond the attendant's booth and security barrier, the usual mayhem met them: a furious stream of vehicles, a clamour of street children, mostly boys. Without a word of preamble, Ed Levoix set off across the road, not at an intersection, surging into traffic while dodging both speeding cars and children, almost balletic, as if this were sport to him, a mad sport, while Sara tried to keep to his side.

He did not slow until they were within another gate and walking up a paved drive through a garden, at which point, mildly breathless, he said, My daily exercise. Otherwise there's what, there's polo. You can't walk too much here.

Do you have a driver?

Oh, no, I drive.

A maître d' in a white coat led them to a table laid with a white cloth in the spacious restaurant through which were scattered a few tables occupied by men in business suits and two nicely dressed women, then to a second, more secluded table that Ed Levoix approved of.

Do you eat meat? he asked from his carved wooden chair.

Do you eat raw meat? I do, or I do here, but don't feel any compulsion to try it. There was a discreet little maple-leaf pin on his lapel. He had a wide mouth, told her he'd grown up in Moncton, New Brunswick, good Catholic family, made it out of town on a university hockey scholarship. She figured the best thing to do with a man like this was sit back and see, amid the self-display, what he revealed to her. There was some skittishness beneath all his bravado. It's almost noon, he went on. No beer until noon is my modus operandi, but we can at least order before noon as long as you have no objection. He clapped his hands to attract the attention of a waiter, as one of the Ethiopian men had done.

It's a long way to come out of curiosity, he said with another keen look.

Sara asked him if he knew if there was an investigation underway.

Oh, undoubtedly there will be, but in a place like this, and especially since this all got started in Australia, it may take time. Do you know many people here?

Mostly Juliet Levin's contacts.

After he'd ordered two bottles of Axum beer and food for them both, she asked him about rumours, were there any, and he said, settling back in his chair, Not about the sort of things he's been accused of. Or not that I heard over the last four years, which is most of the time he was in operation. Possible money trouble. Recently. That they were running out of money, and he wasn't the world's best administrator and had a few grandiosity problems. I am so very, very sad about all this.

Her bag was wedged between her feet. She was trying to decide whether to take out her notebook.

He liked to think big, Ed Levoix said. Not necessarily a bad thing, but he might have been better off sticking closer to home. One circus. With a social mission. Working with needy children here. That's it.

He poured the beer when it arrived into two glasses and clinked his to hers.

What about embezzlement?

No, no, not that I ever heard. Oh, I don't know. You're not recording this, are you? Ed Levoix looked around him. If you are, I won't say another word.

He leaned in closer. Sometimes, you know, it's just children, the problems of working with children, they're so — risky — or organizations that work only with children are. What is one to do? Give anyone who works with children monitoring bracelets? Was it suspect that he didn't have a team of people working with him? Should he have thought of that? There's the issue of money and what one can afford. We knew children lived with him, we knew it informally, but where else were some of the ones from out-of-town to go. Maybe he should have boarded them with families and paid the families. Or set up a dormitory? Where? He had space other people don't have. He didn't seem like one of those guys who bounce from one child-service organization to another, the creeps. I really don't know what to think. He seemed very committed to this particular project, not like it was an excuse for — and it was a heck of a lot of work, I'll tell you that much.

He frowned. Their food arrived, dolloped portions of meat and curried lentils, including a raw beef mixture called kifto, atop a wide tin plate of pancakelike injera, and Ed Levoix dove in, shaking his head, ripping off a piece of injera and swabbing up the meat mixture with it, all with one hand, red spice staining his fingertips. What's sad is that we won't be able to fund while there's this cloud of suspicion. Who knows if the organization's sustainable, which is a shame for the children.

Did you see him socially?

Oh, once or twice.

He has only been accused, Sara said. Not charged.

Yes, Ed Levoix said, staring at his red fingers. You saw the circus perform, didn't you? Did you have any contact with him?

I met him in Toronto.

Again, the keen look. Oh, you did, and spoke to him?

Yes.

And?

He seemed intensely committed to the work.

He stared into the middle distance, wiping his stained fingers on his napkin. It's all so tricky, he said. Moral outrage on the one hand and on the other not wanting to scapegoat and trying to figure out what to do or think.

Then, with a gust of spirit, as if he'd come to some decision: There's a thing on at the Larsens' this evening. The people your friend Juliet stayed with. A little soirée. Did they mention it to you? You should come along with me. I'll let them know. I'm sure they'd be delighted to meet you. There's someone who may be there. You might want to talk to him, and I know he'll want to talk to you. If he's not there, we'll figure something else out.

. . .

At the end of the afternoon, as the light began to soften, Alazar parked the car near a cluster of small shops and pointed across the road to a stretch of open ground backed by trees. When Sara stepped out of the car, the smell of raw meat, flesh and fat, curdled from an open-fronted shop, the wooden sign above its roof outlined by white fairy lights spelling the word *Butchery*. From elsewhere wafted the odour of grilling meat, and the tremolo of a song from a radio, and up on an electrical wire, stretched across the shifting blue of the sky, the receiver and cord from a telephone dangled plainly yet mysteriously.

After lunch, they had gone back to Yitbarek Abera's house, but the gate was still locked from the outside. From there, they returned to the Agip station, rain smearing across the windshield, hard drops drumming on the roof of the car. As the rain abated, Sara caught sight of Tamrat Asfaw in his dark-green tracksuit, walking on the far side of the road from the direction of town, gnawing on a cob of roasted corn. As he, in turn, with a glance across the road, seemed to catch sight of her, or at least saw something, a white woman through a car window, that brought an irritated flex to his features. From the other direction, a file of children in school uniforms appeared until Tamrat was encircled by them, chattering, wheeling, darting, black heads, lithe limbs. A bus blew past, dirty, mid-century in design. With a baleful glance across the road, Tamrat steered the children up the laneway. Sara wanted to yell after him, This is not a stakeout.

She said to Alazar, I would really like to speak to some of the circus children and if possible to their families. Can you help me arrange this?

I will do it.

Is this your car? she asked as they set off once more, because, returning to it, and him, after her lunch with Ed Levoix, she'd had the sudden feeling that it wasn't, its interior too impersonal, Alazar's belongings — money, two cassette tapes — reduced to what he could carry in his small black nylon bag.

I borrow it.

He told her as they drove off that he was waiting to get married until he found a full-time job.

Under an early evening sky now cleared of clouds, amid the bustle of the small, tin-roofed shops, they waited for something to happen on the far side of the road. At last, an old minivan pulled up beside the open area, and the side doors slid wide, and circus performers, in costume, some of whom Sara was beginning to recognize, spilled out. From the driver's seat, Tamrat exited, and then, also from the back of the van, climbed two men in suit jackets, whose presence felt initially forbidding, until the men began to help unload equipment — mats, speakers, unicycles, an amplifier, musical instruments. It became clear, as they set up, they were musicians, presumably replacing the other, younger musicians who'd fled.

There was no way to make herself invisible. No headscarf would truly hide her; it wouldn't alter the colour of her skin. Sara had to hope that Tamrat, directing the performers to spread a large tarpaulin over the ground, was too preoccupied to notice her among the stalls on the other side of the road from where he was. The old frisson: how one's motives, desires, one's very self could be mistaken without one being able to do anything about it, and come to have a life of their own.

Atop the tarpaulin the children lined a double row of blue mats, then spread a second tarpaulin over the first. People drew close, some running across the road, as Sara did, along with Alazar, once the performance had begun.

Two boys set metal pipes on top of a smallish circular platform mounted on what looked like blocks of wood, and, on these, side by side, they laid wooden boards on which they stood tippily. As in the rehearsal hall the day before, they began to juggle. From the back of the crowd, Sara had to weave between heads to see them. One girl helped another climb up the boys' bodies to stand, one foot perched on the shoulder of each, all three keeping their balance as they circled white pins through the air. Someone trilled and ululated. The musicians, off to one side, tugged at guitar and bass, creating a twangy, rhythmic accompaniment. From the front of the crowd Tamrat watched, arms gripped across his chest. When Sara glanced beside her, Alazar was grinning. The scent of his body offered a kind of comfort. A boy balanced a wooden chair on his chin, then hooked it by the back legs onto another, and raised them both, building a delicate tower of four chairs in the air. How had all these items, the chairs, the wooden platform, come out of one small van?

After the balancing acts, and the tumbling, bodies soaring horizontally above other bodies, as the light began to fade, two boys lit torches, two each, and were helped onto unicycles by some of the others. Space was cleared for them in front of the tarpaulin. When Sara looked again, Alazar had vanished, and it took her a moment to spot him, near the van, talking to one of the girl performers.

All of this felt suddenly fragile, despite the performers' daring and courage and engagement, the strength of their bodies. There seemed to be no social message to the show other than shared joy, a surfeit of it. As the boys on their unicycles tossed the flaming torches back and forth, the crowd whooped and clapped. The lure of the circus. How excited Raymond Renaud must have been to bring this joy into being. Yet was the circus an ephemeral curiosity in this place and doomed to vanish? How heartbreaking that would be. Cumulonimbus clouds gathered again on the horizon. A boy in a pink leotard, the chair balancer, stood in the middle of the tarpaulin talking in rapid-fire Amharic, and Alazar, back at her side, was murmuring, Maybe we will speak to Kidsit tomorrow.

Alazar, what's he saying?

He is talking about the wonder of the healthy body.

Sara glanced at her watch. We really have to go meet Ed.

As they hurried back to the Fiat, Alazar said, I am so happy to see this circus. In the car, he sped them toward her rendezvous at the bar that Ed Levoix had named.

Ed Levoix's white Pajero rode much higher off the ground than Alazar's car. In a brief stop at the hotel, Sara had changed into a linen shirt and exchanged her boots for her blue, heeled sandals. Through the thick dark that fell swiftly after equatorial dusk, along the hilly roads of a sector of the city still without power, oil lamps glowed in the street-side storefronts. The shadows of people flickered around the lamps, and bodies on foot, *people walking*, moved ceaselessly around their vehicle, jackets and skirts and the backs of heads briefly illuminated in the glow of their headlights.

They were talking of Nairobi, where Ed Levoix had previously worked. On either end of her trip to the Sudanese border, Sara told him, she had, on the advice of a friend, stayed in a nunnery there, which had been cheap and safe.

He said, There's a woman you'll meet tonight. Anna Quinn, a friend of Elsa Larsen's. Nun, from Nairobi. Man broke into her room, attempted robbery and who knows what else. Slashed her face. She's here recuperating, but she's going back. It's tough there, these days. But it sounds like you've been through worse things.

She'd told him some of the basics: Beirut, the return trips to the Middle East, other trips to Pakistan, Sri Lanka, Iraq, Haiti. Also the time in Eastern Europe. Not specifically about gunfire, rocket fire, the carjacking in Najaf, the memories she preferred to deflect but were recalled in her coiled toes and up into her gut.

Islamabad had not been so bad, and yet one night when she'd been out on her own, talking to an ex-army officer whom she shouldn't officially have been talking to, a little later than this hour, her driver had raced through the streets, hurtled through red lights and police checks, his own urge for self-preservation as strong as his desire to protect her and get her back to her hotel, the scent of his fear of being pulled over or shot as sharp as the stench of his cigarette smoke. They hadn't hit anyone, though there had been moments—people leaping out of their way, fleeing at the sight of them, men waving guns—she, her blonde head covered, hunched in the back seat—when she'd feared they would.

Amid the flicker of charcoal braziers and the scent of diesel, the hilly road that the Pajero travelled was too narrow and crowded with bodies for Ed Levoix to drive fast. Sara felt no obvious danger here and had needed no complicated travel insurance before setting out in case she got killed. Alert, avid, buoyed by the circus show, alive with the hunger to pay attention — this was what she felt now. It was the reason she'd done what she'd done so far with her life.

The lights will come back on at seven, Ed Levoix said.

Do you live on your own?

So far he'd been gallant not unctuous, but the sexual loneliness of those who lived in places like this had to be taken into account.

Yes, was all Ed said. The soiree, he'd told her, was a send-off for one of Peter Larsen's Ethiopian co-workers who was leaving for another job.

Who's the person you want me to meet or you think wants to meet me?

Gerard Loftus. He's been working out of town at an orphanage, but he's on his way back to Canada. He's a very determined personality. You'll see.

Lights. A wrought-iron gate loomed up before them, as, on the inside, a watchman raised a hand, blinking in the headlights' beam, before drawing the gate open upon a forecourt where other vehicles were parked. Incandescence spilled from a house, larger than Raymond Renaud's, in the open doorway of which a blond man bobbed.

A tall, slim woman with a greying ponytail appeared at his side. The Larsens, Juliet had told Sara, worked for a small NGO involved in setting up early warning systems for monitoring food scarcity: he was Norwegian, she American. Hugs all around, as if they'd been acquainted for years. Peter. Elsa. Sara. Peter Larsen energetically asking, And how is Juliet? So what's going to happen with Juliet's film?

Whippetlike in a long skirt, her ponytail falling halfway down her back, Elsa Larsen led the way into a dining room where people stood around a table on which were set out local, brightly woven baskets filled with dips and rolls and peeled sticks of carrot and cucumber, and distinctively Ethiopian silver crosses hung on the walls. Getachew Mengestu, in a natty black suit, on staff at Irish GOAL, another NGO, held out his hand and said, You are here on a visit? Where do you stay? Mariam Hailemariam, who was moving on to a job at Save the Children UK, had a broad, infectious laugh. Ian Flood—yes, that is my name—did drought-related work along with Agnes Strauss, originally from Strasberg. Administrators all, or almost all. Peter Larsen's ebullient voice rang from the hallway. Ed Levoix handed Sara a glass of red wine and said, I don't see Gerard, but I'll have a word with Elsa.

Across the room, a raw red seam crossed the cheek and jawline of a vivacious woman with short dark hair in nondescript skirt and shirt and cardigan: what must it be like to be forced to wear your trauma like that? Was the nunnery where Anna Quinn had been attacked the nunnery where she had stayed?

Elsa's long skirt disappeared around a corner. Ed Levoix, in his tweed jacket, was nowhere to be seen. Nor was he in the kitchen, where Sara found Elsa speaking to an Ethiopian woman in slippers and flowered dress and wrapped headscarf who sliced a baguette on a wooden countertop as a vat of water boiled on the stove.

Desta, Elsa said, introducing Sara to the woman, then: Ed says you're doing something on the circus?

I'm not sure yet. Do you, did you know Renaud?

Know, Elsa said. She peered into her glass, then up with a kind of scrutiny. I always thought he looked down on all of us a bit. We weren't authentic enough. Or creative. Or something. That's what I thought then.

Authentic?

He seemed to prefer the company of Ethiopians. The man he works with. It's horrible, what's happened. Whatever happened.

Have you by any chance heard anything about a boy, one of the circus performers, being injured?

I don't think so. Injured how?

In a fall.

No, nothing.

Maybe, Sara thought, he'd worked very hard to keep Yitbarek's accident a secret, at least from his funders.

Darling Elsa, said Ed Levoix, large in the doorway, sandy hair on end. Is Gerard likely to put in an appearance this evening? He isn't staying here, is he?

I gave him a night here when he first got to town, Elsa said, but then I told him he had to find somewhere else because of Anna. I think that annoyed him. I don't know if he'll show up. He keeps saying he has a lot of people to meet before he leaves and he's very busy.

She turned to Sara. Do you want to see where your friend Juliet slept?

Sara stepped through a set of French doors off the living room into a large, walled yard, the presence of the wall a deeper shadow in the dark. A path led toward a small, wooden, what would you call it, gazebo, the moist air perfumed by roses. It was true, she thought, she felt, he would not have fit in among these people, they would have chafed at him, as generous as the Larsens, as Elsa Larsen seemed to be. Why? Because they were the sort who played by the rules, who made the rules, and he didn't want to play by their rules, he wanted to do things his own way, because he thought he was better — what was Elsa Larsen's word?, more authentic — than they were. Or he hated the fact of their money and his need of it. She understood this. To be in that room made her irrationally long for the crazier company of front-line aid workers, war-zone journalists, the ones given to raucous and stupid behaviour; you walked among them and immediately felt the swirl of jagged displacements of people wildly fending off trauma even if they refused to speak of it.

Someone on the path behind her, quiet as an intruder: Sara turned with a start. A young man, caught in the light from the living-room window, voices from inside pressing themselves against the glass. Youngish, a mess of hair, wearing one of those bulky sweaters, Nepalese or South American, that students often wore, pocked cheeks, the most astonishingly soft and voluptuous lips, a shock in that face. She hadn't seen him inside. His stare had the fervour of a wild dog. He held a bottle of beer in one hand, sneakers on his feet. Not old but not as young as she'd first thought.

The figure said, Ed said you're looking to talk to people about Raymond Renaud. I'll talk to you.

Sara stepped forward and held out her hand. I'm Sara Wheeler, and you are?

Oh. Sorry. He juggled his bottle of beer awkwardly from right hand to left before clutching her palm. Gerard Loftus.

Ed wasn't sure you'd be here.

No. Well. I showed up. Lucky. He reclaimed his hand. Lucky for me, lucky for you. An oversized smile. It was hard to move her gaze from his lips, or the combination of his lips, his skin, his possibly sun-worn brow. Had he slept in the double bed covered in diaphanous sheets of white cotton in the room that Elsa Larsen had shown her, in which Juliet had slept?

Ed said you don't live in Addis.

No, Gerard Loftus said. And I'm flying out the day after tomorrow.

Were you involved with the circus?

Oh, no, not *involved*.

But you knew Raymond Renaud?

He glanced about, twitchy, despite the fact that they seemed to be alone in this part of the garden. From closer to the gate came the drift of a couple of voices as a car door slammed. I don't want to talk about it here. I can meet you tomorrow, like say tomorrow morning. My time is a bit full up but—

Do you want to come by my hotel?

Which is—

She told him.

No, he said. Then with an air of imperiousness, I would prefer the Hilton. I'll meet you at ten at the pool bar at the Hilton.

At the Hilton, Sara said, nonplussed, for the high-end Hilton hardly seemed the sort of place Gerard Loftus would frequent.

When, at the end of the evening, she stepped into the lobby of the Hotel Berhailu, Ed Levoix's Pajero accelerating out of the gate and flying down the street at her back, music poured out of one of the common rooms on the main floor, along with people in fancy dress. The voice of an unseen male singer surged against the clapping of hands, the winding line of a guitar, the melody broken open every now and again by a fanfare of ululations. It was a wedding, the man at the front desk told her, handing over her enormous key.

The music carried her upstairs to her room and poured into the room through the window that opened onto the balcony, while voices wandered amongst the trees in the garden like a flurry of gazelles, other people's happiness brushing against her hectic need to sort through what Ed Levoix had said before driving off, the meeting with Gerard Loftus lurking inside her like an unsettling present that she wouldn't able to open until morning.

He's an odd one, isn't he, she'd said as Ed had driven her away from the Larsens' party. Clownlike was her thought; she was having a hard time imagining Raymond Renaud close to this awkward man. Do you know what Gerard wants to talk to me about?

Eyes on the road, Ed Levoix said, I've heard his version. Or the short version. But I'll let him tell you what he wants to tell you. Listen to him. That's all. He'll be persistent. Adamant, even overwrought. He is an adamant and persistent person. Hear him out. Then do what you have to do. Make up your own mind.

He was drunk, she realized, or not drunk but he'd been drinking enough to heighten the blunt energy with which he'd met her at lunchtime. He wasn't oozy, but something had loosened: she caught a glimpse of the ghost of the hockey player he had once been. A fluid young man darting down the ice. And something else. Lattices of lines crossed in the pouches beneath his eyes.

Once through the hotel gate, he pulled up the Pajero before reaching the hotel door and, activating the automatic locks on all the doors, waved off the watchman, who, with a backward glance, returned to the entrance, swinging his nightstick. Sara felt more surprise than unease; the hotel was close. She could yell if she needed to. No threat. What they had was privacy. In a car, you could speak without looking at your companion, as Ed Levoix was doing.

Maybe it happened the way they say it did. What they're accusing Renaud of. Something systemic. But maybe it didn't. It's impossible not to speculate. I find it impossible not to. Maybe it was something smaller. You slip up, you reach out, once, maybe no more than once, you shouldn't but you do and you are never allowed to forget it. You hand over all power.

A couple in dress clothes, man in a black suit, woman in a shiny dress, black hair waxed and coiled atop her head, teetered into the open air. Sara had to wonder if he was talking about

Raymond Renaud or himself, and what spoke through him: guilt or pain or shame or self-recrimination. Did he know something or had he done a thing like this?

You do know that homosexuality is completely forbidden here. Anything that goes on is utterly furtive and hidden. That may not be relevant. But you should be aware of it. It is distorting. The hidden always exerts a pressure. Silence is cunning. Forget I said any of this.

With astonishing velocity, he'd unlocked the doors and was hurrying around the front of the Pajero to help her out on the passenger side. He shook her hand with brutal formality, his internal retreat so swift and total it left her reeling. Ed—

Make up your own mind, he repeated.

Ed, are you, can we—? She wanted more, needed more clarity.

Good luck with your work. Good luck tomorrow. Very good to have met you.

It was not until Sara stepped, just after ten the next morning, from a boutique-lined corridor through a bar and out onto the Hilton's patio, and wove through the unoccupied tables and past two breeze-frilled, empty swimming pools, that she registered the desire of Gerard Loftus to meet here as something more than presumptuous insistence. The air was not warm. He sat alone in his bulky sweater beneath a thatched umbrella. No one was likely to come near them.

He stood as she approached, as unkempt by daylight, his hair as mussed, his lips as startling. There were two spots of colour high in his cheeks. He looked like he might have spent the night balled up under bushes in this garden.

You didn't spend the night here, did you? She was needling him; there was something in him, she realized, that made her want to needle him.

Oh, no, at the Selassie Guest House. On the Dessie Road?

He sat, and Sara, in her fleece jacket, took the chair opposite him. I don't know it. And you're flying out tomorrow?

Back to Calgary. My visa's been terminated.

Because?

I lost my job. But I'll be back.

At the orphanage in Awassa, isn't that it? Ed Levoix had given her the name of the town and she had looked it up on a map, some distance south of Addis Ababa, a couple of hundred kilometres, somewhere that, to judge from the map, Juliet had likely passed through on her way farther south to the town of Sodo. Are you and Ed Levoix friendly? She had to ask.

I guess. We see each other occasionally when I'm in town. Gerard looked puzzled, even perturbed, as if she were leading the conversation down a branch that he did not wish to follow. Do you know what the Hope Villages are?

I don't.

It's not a religious organization, it's a foundation, a private foundation, based in the US. They run these villages for orphans. Here and elsewhere. With schools and they help train them for jobs? There's been one here since the big famine in the eighties. That's where I worked.

A waiter in a white jacket, a piece of towel tucked into his pocket, approached from the interior bar and had an air of being about to ask them to move indoors but changed his mind. Sara ordered a coffee — and buna; Gerard a glass of orange juice and a glass of milk, a childlike and rather revolting combination.

Ed said he thought you taught but wasn't sure.

I taught a class and I was the site manager. I did a lot of maintenance? He was staring furiously at her hands, her bag, her jacket. Aren't you going to record this or take notes? His tone was so admonishing that he made her want to resist doing the very thing he wanted so badly.

I can. She took her tape recorder from her pocket and unwrapped the cloth around it slowly and turned the recorder on and laid it on the table between them, then checked to make sure the reels were turning. Gerard seemed relieved. You didn't live in Addis, but you did have contact with Raymond Renaud, Sara said. Do you want to tell me about that?

I'll get to it. I need to tell you the other stuff first. Did Ed tell you how I lost my job?

No. She felt like she was tugging something out of him, a ribbon out of his mouth bit by bit, out of the knot of desires twisting in him. How did you lose your job?

I got fired. For helping the boys go to the police. The boys who were the victims of the former director, Mark Templeton. The sexual predator. You haven't heard about any of this? No one's said anything to you?

No, Sara said. The important thing was to stay calm, not leap to any conclusions, go on eliciting information, the trick of professionalism, of necessary dissociation whatever her throat was doing or her heart. Or her hands. She had her notebook in her lap; she wrote down the man's name. In front of her the lips of Gerard Loftus were saying these things.

What happened between the former director and the boys?

I was there for like a year, okay? And I'd be doing things, fixing things, because that's part of my job. And I'd see boys coming and going to his house. He had them bring him dinner sometimes. Because he had to work late. He said. Or he offered them special English lessons. One at a time. He liked the smart ones. He never wanted the same one to come too often. That would attract attention. But I noticed. It was only boys. When I asked, one or two of them said he paid them. I thought that was strange. There was one boy, Abiye, he was a little older and he went kind of often. So I asked him more questions. And he told me what was going on. I said I would help him write a statement and take it to the foundation and the police.

Gerard was staring at her, gauging the nature of her attention to him. He kept an eye on her hand taking notes. He leaned across the table to check the tape recorder himself.

What about other people on staff? What were they doing? Didn't anyone else notice anything?

No one else wanted to notice, but I knew because I used to work in this other school, in northern Alberta, where the same thing happened. So I knew what to look for. Anyway, maybe as soon as Abiye and the other boys stopped going to him, Mark figured out something was up. Before he heard from the foundation or the police. One day he said he was going to Addis and never came back. Then the new director, Richard Langley, he came out and he didn't want to talk about Mark or where he'd gone or what had happened. He said he'd left the organization, and then he read out a statement to all the staff saying there'd been an episode of misconduct and mismanagement, something like that, but they had dealt with it internally and it would never happen again. And we were supposed to protect the children by not talking about it. And he was furious with me because Mark had vanished. It was like because I helped the boys, it was my fault. But there were others. And they needed to get compensation too, because they were also victims.

Other boys? What sort of compensation?

Money from the foundation. Like Abiye got.

So more boys came forward?

I helped ten more make statements.

Ten. After they knew they would be compensated.

Yes.

Though that compromises their testimony. Don't you think? If they know they're going to get money for it.

Yes, but they're victims. Why shouldn't they get something for all they'd been through?

Gerard — She took a deep breath. Okay. Do you have any idea where Mark Templeton is now?

Maybe the US. Someone in Addis said they saw him getting on a plane. Listen. The foundation doesn't want to see it. They want it to be one boy, one man. They fired me because I refuse to be quiet about it. It wasn't just him, Mark, either. He'd have friends over to visit. They knew where to go to do their thing. Where they think they'll be safe. It was a ring of them.

A ring?

There was another man, Leo Reseltier, he works in southern Sudan, he came, and I know he propositioned one boy, Tedesse, because Tedesse told me, he told him he'd pay him money, three birr, Tedesse said, to come to his room. But Tedesse wouldn't do it. And Renaud visited. He knew Mark from before. I bet you didn't know that. Mark told me. They're old friends. They'd met years before in Sri Lanka.

How often did Renaud come—alone, with the circus?

Once with the circus. Twice by himself. He was supposed to be starting up a program at the Village, like a proper circus. So he taught a few classes, but the circus thing never happened. He taught a bit of juggling, stuff like that. You know, like, his cover.

How fervent he was, she thought, spit on his lips, the craning body, how nearly lascivious in his need and his certainty. Did you see anything, or hear anything about anything happening while Renaud was there?

Not specific, but he'd hang out, and he'd take kids off in ones and twos to teach them.

Boys, girls?

Boys and girls.

Did any of them ever say anything, complain, did you ask?

No. But everyone wants to do the circus thing so no one's going to interfere with that. And now there are the other allegations against him.

So you know about those.

Everyone knows about them.

Allegations he denies. People should know that too.

Well, they all deny them. Someone has to do something. You need to look into this, you know you do.

Are you religious? Evangelical?

Am I what? No. Why? What sort of question is that? Not anymore. What does that have to do with any of this?

You're from Alberta. I wondered. Doesn't matter. How old are the boys, and where are they?

Ten, eleven, twelve. They're at the Village. Where else do you think they're going to go?

I don't know what to do, Sara said to David from the bed in her hotel, where she was sitting cross-legged, the squat black phone in front of her like a body that she was addressing, or the receiver was her route to David's body, the magic capsule into which she poured her voice as his poured from it, from high in an office tower in downtown Toronto, where he was at work in the middle of his afternoon. In Addis Ababa, the lamp at her side glowed orange rather than yellow but did not go off, and a moth swung out of the dark and began to bash itself against the window. I don't want to go. I barely have time to go all the way there. And my driver's car has broken down. Then there's this. The thing about him that makes me not want to believe him. Because he's so insistent about his version of things. It's a question of tone, his voice, his manner. Which makes me not want to trust him. Because he makes me so uncomfortable, I have a hard time imagining him being taken into the confidence of these boys without his somehow forcing himself onto them. Maybe that's wrong. And he's making these insinuations about Renaud without offering any proof. Which is also a reason to go. Maybe he's done nothing but good and this is all me.

How she'd wished, as soon as Gerard Loftus had loped away from the interior bar, while she waited to pay, that she had never met him. That Ed Levoix had never taken it into his head to introduce them. She felt a senseless anger at Ed, at Gerard, at herself. Longed for Gerard Loftus, his matted hair, his bulky sweater, his lips, his presumptions, his vindictive if crusading ardour, his moral certainty, to vanish off the face of the earth. This was not helpful, it was real but radically unhelpful. Her desire to, well, punch him out. This energetic mirroring in which her dislike made her more like him. She and David had discussed such things before: the antipathy she sometimes felt toward people she interviewed, his toward clients. And what was Ed Levoix's stake in all this. *Make up your own mind.* Yet he'd felt she needed to know Gerard's story.

Having paid the very dark-skinned bar man with the slash across his cheek, either a former wound or ritual scarring, Sara had made her way back through the corridor of tony boutiques filled with crafts like those in the Larsens' house and out the front door into the spreading, treed grounds that surrounded the Hilton, where she found no sign of Alazar and the Fiat. Nor was there any sign of him after half an hour, or after an hour, although, on the doorman's direction, she vigorously searched the lot full of drivers, brown-skinned men in T-shirts lounging outside their cars. He must have dropped her off and left immediately; no one had seen a man or car that fit her description. After an hour, in exasperation, she took an ordinary taxi back to her hotel.

The question you need to ask yourself, David said in that

calm, calm way of his, is if you come home and don't pursue this, how will you feel?

I can't not go. I know how I'll feel. I won't be able to live with myself. I'll chastise myself. I can't not do it.

It was as if all those with an interest in Raymond Renaud were mapping themselves or versions of themselves on top of him, she thought. That's what it felt like.

There had been no message waiting from Alazar when she arrived back at the hotel. When she'd tried to phone the number she had for him, which, she remembered him saying, did not ring in his home, he didn't own a telephone, the line rang fifteen times before an ancient-sounding man answered, who barely spoke English and who vanished for several long minutes before returning to tell Sara that Alazar, he work. That afternoon, she and Alazar had been supposed to visit Kidsit and her mother, try once more to speak to Yitbarek, also Yonas Berhanu, the kebele leader. She had three days left in her trip. She'd heard nothing from Raymond Renaud in response to her phone message. He wasn't here or anywhere near here. He'd gone as far away as he could.

How long will it take you to get to the orphanage? David asked.

A few hours, several. I don't think it's possible to get there and back in a day. She'd asked the taxi driver who had returned her to the hotel and he'd said five or six hours and for an astronomical sum of money he'd drive her. Alazar, when he reached her at the hotel at last, his anxiety like a force field through which he pushed words, said, The car broke. Awassa, Mrs. Wheeler? It will take six hours. When do you wish to go? Sara felt him strain to hold back the new wave of anxiety breaking over him. Is tomorrow possible? she'd asked, and he'd said, I will see.

Anyway, whether I go tomorrow is dependent on if my driver shows up or if I have to hire someone else. And that I won't know until the morning.

You're good at improvising, David said. You've been in these situations before.

And you're so good in emergencies. Your fabulous ability to stay calm.

This isn't an emergency.

No, okay, it's a general statement.

Will you be all right? I really should get back to work.

I'll go. I know I have to go. Take good care of yourself.

Take good care of yourself. It was the thing they said to each other at the end of every conversation. Tenderly. They had not spoken directly of Greta. Yet she was there.

No sooner had Sara hung up the phone than the other word, the forbidden word, came surging up, up through her abdomen, like a fist, making her leap to her feet and double over. Love, the force of it. She loved him. Of course she did. Love coursed its way through her. She missed him, far away. Love clamoured. It was not just longing and desire but grace, forgiveness, tenderness. It was in her body, a physical thing struggling to get out. It had followed her around the world. It tumbled down the phone line, came in through the closed window here in Addis Ababa, where the moth still battered itself against the glass. She had tried to deny it. It did no good. She opened her mouth. If she said these words to him, he'd freeze.

He would say no, and don't. He had said, Don't. He would turn away from her. It is not possible.

Did she love him because he was forbidden? Married, claimed, and therefore not accessible. She'd had time to wonder this about Graham too. If part of Graham's appeal, at least in the beginning, had been the transgressive pleasure of sleeping with him and then walking into his classroom, knowing she shouldn't be doing this and how perturbed and excited their secret made him. Was the forbidden a thing she did, a thing she longed for? Not forbidden in the same way as what Gerard was talking about but still.

She would have said, given her complicated history with lawyers, that to be intimate with a lawyer was also the last thing she wanted. Unless her very antipathy had made David attractive, a desire to transgress against herself. He was not a criminal lawyer. He represented patents, not people. All his work was, you could say, about potential theft. He put it this way: he was interested in the rights of people, particularly those who made things up, discovered things, and needed to secure their rights to these things, in definitions of originality, fairness rather than truth.

Working out a good contract is like playing a good game, he'd said, and is as revealing of the crazy parade of human nature and all that people try to get away with. Isn't everyone in the business of seeing what they can get away with? He'd given a funny smile at that, then asked Sara whether she cared, as a journalist, if the people she spoke to were telling her the truth. They were in her kitchen, newly showered, leaning against the counters. Yes, she said. At least I want them to want to tell me the truth, or what they think is the truth, even if many people aren't very good at it. My job is to try to report what they've said accurately.

He hadn't been practising when she'd met him. There were wanderings in both their childhoods, David's military father having taken his family from a posting in Venezuela, where David was born, to a base in Germany, before their move back to Canada, to Trenton, Ontario, when David was eight. One of those first nights, maybe the first night, as they lay in her bed, by lamplight, after sex, he told her, The first word I ever spoke was door. I was nearly two. And that was weirdly prescient, since when I was thirteen my mother walked out the front door of our house and we never saw her again. He went on staring at the bedroom ceiling. When Sara laid a hand on his arm, his body had a kind of braced calm yet registered her touch.

Did you ever hear from her?

No. My father tried to track her down but gave up. My sister and I tried again when I turned eighteen and we got an address, but then we decided there was no point really, what was the point of contacting someone who didn't want to be found. I think we all felt that way.

Did she love you? The question burst from her. Oh, the unbearable, damaging things that people did to each other.

Yes. He turned to look at her, still that teenager, holding her gaze, wanting a witness or something more. And then something broke, he said.

It's hard to explain what happened with my parents, she said to him, then or on another night. More lamplight in the bedroom. It had to do with my father's neediness and my mother's inability to look after both of us. There's something very insulated and insular about them. It's as if having a child bewildered them. And then they were away, not like your mother, but they did go away and there was a gradual falling out of regular contact.

In the hotel room, she paced across the dingy carpet and peered through the large keyhole into the hall, while the moth went on thrumming against the window.

She did not know what David felt, what he let himself feel. Greta's next round of tests was coming up in a couple of weeks. In January, Greta would, if all continued to go well, be cancer-free for a year, and thus truly in remission. She did not know what to think of herself, that she'd let things come to this pass, love returning to her, though she'd sworn she wouldn't let it, her longing to be with this man always. Did she want love in this form? Could things go on and on like this? Was there another way? What did she truly want, what did he? All these questions knocked against her in Addis Ababa. Yet here was love, unsayable, undeniable, and it was hers, whatever David felt, and maybe in its beautiful uselessness was where its meaning lay.

Alazar led her out of the hotel to where a small yellow car waited, a Lada, Sara noted as they drew close. He seemed cheerful, filled with compensatory hopefulness, wanting her to be pleased, to make amends for the day before, for everything to work out.

This is a good car, he said. Look. He knelt, and beckoned Sara to kneel beside him, and showed her the steel plate bolted to the bottom of the chassis, rapping at the metal with his knuckles so that it gave a sharp tong. Then he stood and kicked the metal, and Sara, after giving the steel a knock with her own knuckles, nodded. A Russian-built Lada, butt of so many car jokes, hardly instilled her with confidence, but, what the hell, she would trust herself to it, and to Alazar. Okay, she said. Looks good, let's go. She handed him her suitcase, which he loaded into the trunk beside the small satchel he'd brought for the overnight trip to Awassa, their bodies beginning to move in a synchronized dance, his gestures and manner growing familiar. How intimate, and domestic, the relationship with one's driver could be.

I know Awassa well, Alazar said as they headed out of the city, past the Edible Oil Factory and the Jesus Rendering Plant. I am from this part of the country, near Shashemene. This is the junction town where we will take the road that leads to Awassa.

Do you know the orphanage called Hope Village?

Maybe, but I have not lived there for a long time.

She told him that the man from the circus, the former director, had visited the orphanage. She did not know what Alazar might have picked up over the last few days, what rumours he might have caught in the midst of conversations in Amharic that Sara did not understand or conversations with other drivers and watchmen that she had not been party to. If she were to reveal more about Gerard's story and her interest in the orphanage, Alazar might feel uncomfortable, even morally compromised, especially given Ed Levoix's assertion that any sort of homosexuality was an abomination here. Allegations of pedophilia might completely repulse him. If he discovered exactly what she was investigating, he might refuse to accompany her any farther.

As they crossed flat plains in which the only trees were carried in chopped pieces on people's backs, then through leafy copses strangely reminiscent of southern Ontario, Alazar spoke carefully about the growing restlessness of the Oromo, his people, since the current government, which had come to power five years before, after the dictatorship had fallen, and about which so many had had so much hope, was giving power to certain groups and not others, which led to the wish, in certain parts of the country, for greater autonomy. I myself have hoped for more change, and more opportunity, especially more economic opportunity, he said. It is hard to hope and then lose this hope.

By the side of the road stood a man in a long white robe under a parasol glittery with gilt thread, beckoning.

Alazar, sorry to interrupt, but what's that man doing?

He's a priest. He wants us to visit his relics.

Raymond Renaud had travelled through this country, likely many times. Juliet, too, must have travelled this road on her trip south with the circus, another layer in a palimpsest of journeys.

Okay, please go on.

There, Alazar said as they entered the town of Shashemene, passing two men in a pony trap with bells jingling on its harness and boys playing at an ancient foosball table set up by the side of the road. See that flag with the tree on it, that is the flag of the Oromo, my people.

What will you do, Alazar?

What will I do?

Given the way things are going politically.

Oh. He grinned as several things flashed across his face. I will look for more work.

The nice hotel, as Alazar called it, and to which he brought her, was set close to a lake, Lake Awassa, where fish hawks perched in the trees near the water's edge and monkeys swung among the green branches. Mosquito nets screened the windows of the room to which Sara was shown, a good sign. Having dropped her off, Alazar seemed anxious to be on his way—he would stay in town, he said, and pick her up at eight the next morning.

They had located the orphanage on a road outside of town before coming to the hotel. They had also stopped in the town itself, first at a roadside market, then in a café for espressos and spaghetti bolognese. Sara had asked Alazar to ask people what they knew of the orphanage and what they thought of it. No horrific rumours came their way. White men run it, Alazar told her after one conversation. Men? Yes, men, and it is a neat place. Neat, Alazar? Clean, they say it is tidy. Better to make their approach first thing in the morning, Sara decided.

At dusk, as she returned from a walk along the lake, distant bluish mountains visible over the indigo water, frondlike leaves quivering above gnarled tree trunks, Gerard's words kept springing from under her feet: *a ring of them.*

It seemed too early for dinner, but after washing up, Sara set off down the hall to the dining room, ready for a drink, voices burbling ahead of her. Sometimes, even in the most remote places, she was beset by the possibility that, upon entering a room, she would find Colleen Bertucci, her accuser. Or Marie-Hélène Laberge, the Crown prosecutor, so ferocious behind the demure disguise of her baby-blue shirt in her attempt to undermine anyone's, everyone's belief in Sara. Would they recognize her after all these years? She was pretty certain, if not absolutely convinced, that she would recognize them. What a mess of emotion these thoughts aroused. Something riotous and charred. And rage. What could you possibly say to people who professed not to believe anything you said? Do you believe this? Or this? Or this?

Had Colleen Bertucci ever succumbed to any wrinkle of doubt, or did she, all these years later, remain self-righteously fixed in her conviction that the theft had happened as she said it did. The wallet: brown, leather, containing a Visa card, a YMCA membership card, her driver's licence, fifty or so dollars in bills, some change, a fortune from a Chinese fortune cookie, a snapshot of her niece. As for Madame Laberge: had she simply been doing her job and fought for Colleen because she'd been paid to do so, or did she have to convince herself, at least partly, of her client's version of events?

Sara had fantasized about running into Graham too but never had. He was married, she'd heard, to another much younger woman and had two small children.

Don't get angry, Paul Kastner had insisted before their day in court. They had practised cross-examination techniques for hours. There was, in her story, the problem of having no good alibi after she'd left the Y for the span of time when the transactions with the stolen credit card had taken place. Alone, she'd wandered up Saint-Urbain and west along Sainte-Catherine, knapsack on her back, in no rush to get back to the apartment on de Maisonneuve, knowing that Graham would not be home until after five, oblivious to the fact that someone had decided she was a thief. The only shop she'd entered had been a drugstore, a Jean Coutu, where she'd bought a packet of condoms. Yes, she'd admitted that in court. The relationship had ended, she'd also said. This had been if not the most, then one of the most painful and humiliating moments on the stand. Paul Kastner's voice kept repeating itself in her head: The most important thing is to stay calm. Don't sound angry. It won't help at all.

In the dining room, two white men, Australians by their accents, waved Sara over to their table. From Adelaide, they said. They were biking across Ethiopia. Yeah, it's mad. We have stones thrown at us every day. Ah, but the country's beautiful and we're masochists. Fancy joining us for some doro wat?

I have to work, Sara said. She nodded to the notebook and pile of paper that she'd brought from her room. I'm a private consultant looking at some child-focused organizations and in the midst of a report.

They looked offended that their company didn't suit her, or at the clumsiness of her excuse, but let her wander off to a table by the window, where night was eliminating the mountains and the lake and leaving white fairy lights to wind their way among the branches of the trees.

There were so many different kinds of lying: the conscious, expedient lies of social navigation, lies told to protect others and to shield yourself, the elisions, partial seeing, necessary secrets, deeper lies told to spare the self from pain, not to mention the inevitable rearranging of memory and the lies that weren't really lies at all but alterations believed by those who told them, the problem of getting things wrong and needing to get things wrong because the truth was impossible to reach or impossible for the self to contain.

At the end of their time together, Sara had asked Paul Kastner if it mattered to him whether his clients were telling the truth. She had been genuinely curious about this. And Paul Kastner, the now so-very-successful Montreal criminal lawyer whose name cropped up every so often in the news, usually when he was defending someone notorious, had said no, he worked with what people told him, although what he liked were cases where the credible version of what had happened was not the obvious one. Then there were cases, like hers, in which nothing was resolved, other than that Colleen Bertucci's version could not be proved beyond a reasonable doubt. Anyway, he'd said, people can believe they are telling the truth even when what they believe is far from what actually happened, as in, they aren't, psychologically or physiologically speaking, lying.

From the waiter who appeared at her side not in a jacket but something that more closely resembled a white lab coat, Sara ordered a beer, a St. Giorgis. Rain began to drum against the windows. An Ethiopian man in a business suit stopped by her table and asked her where she was from. She said Canada.

Every journalist she knew who'd worked overseas had performed the toe-touch, a kind of lie. She had, on more than one occasion, the last time on the road to Damascus, of all places. St. Paul had had his conversion, and Sara had sat in the back of a car being driven from the airport into Damascus, close to midnight local time, desperately listening to interviews recorded by locals on the ground and brought to her by her fixer so that she could scribble notes taken from them and claim to have been on the ground in Damascus, which she was, technically speaking, when she signed off on the piece two hours later, even if she'd never left her hotel room or spoken directly to anyone she quoted.

In interviews people had lied to her. The Pakistani ex-army officer: I know nothing of those bombings.

She did not know what she would find at the orphanage. She would allow Gerard's suspicions to enter her, his intimations of the worst, but not give in to them. She had to permit him the possibility of belief while maintaining her own vigilance. She should at least be able to confirm whether or not Raymond Renaud had visited. She'd come searching for ground truths, whatever the search would bring. She did not know what she hoped to find.

Two cinder-block pillars flanked a wrought-iron gate. Over the gate a wooden sign arched like a rainbow, hand-lettered words across it, *Hope Village* in English, and presumably the same in Amharic. As soon as Alazar stopped at the gate and rolled down his window to shout at the watchman, children tumbled out of the bushes — in T-shirts, sweaters, a padded vest, an old duffle jacket, all brown with dirt. There were children everywhere. It was as if the bushes had turned into children, who came running toward the car, shouting. They ran their fingers over the dust-covered, mud-spattered metal, and, spotting Sara, cried, Mother, how are you? Mother, we are hungry. We come with you. The watchman opened the gate, shooing the children away with a stick, while Alazar, with a sideways grin, said, I told him you have an appointment.

They pulled up to one side of a wide dirt compound. Beyond them, an Ethiopian woman in a flowered dress watered greens in a vegetable garden with a plastic bucket. Low buildings, some of whitewashed cement, others of prefabricated metal, formed a loose circle around the yard. An enclosure of fencing was visible in the distance: some children were secured inside the ring while others were desperate to get in. A white Toyota truck napped beneath one of two trees, and at the sight of the truck Sara's heart leaped, but on second glance it was bulkier than Raymond Renaud's as she remembered it from Juliet's videotapes.

Everything appeared outwardly in good repair. The red dirt that sprayed up the white walls looked to have been splashed by water thundering down in recent rains and tumbling unchecked from the runnels in the metal roofs. A chicken strutted across the ferrous earth. Through the door of one of the closest buildings stepped a white man in a pale-blue shirt, who stared at them with belligerent surprise, then hurried in their direction.

Something about his clothing, the button-down collar of his pale-blue shirt, his tan trousers, identified him as American. Of a certain kind. Almost blond. Not quite handsome. A too-strong jawline. When Sara stepped out of the car, he adjusted his expression. She might be a wandering idealist with money to give. As she approached, he held out his hand. Richard Langley. Welcome to the Hope Village. Do you know about our work with orphaned children? Would you be interested in a tour?

She asked, though she recognized his name, if he was the director. He said he was. She handed him her card. She said she'd met Gerard Loftus in Addis, and he'd told her what had gone on between the former director and some of the boys, and she wanted to talk to him about it. He stopped. Everything open in his face shut down although he went on smiling. He didn't want to talk about it, yet if he refused to talk she might accuse him of trying to cover up a crime. She knew it. He knew it. Then she would pull out Gerard's other revelation: that all those who worked at the orphanage had been told not to talk. That he seemed so taken aback suggested that she was the first of her kind to arrive.

You can't be surprised that Gerard would speak to someone, that he'd want to get the word out. I'm here because I want your version of what's gone on.

Come into my office. He still held up her business card.

Sara leaned through the open car window and told Alazar she'd find him if she needed him and he offered up a comradely if guarded smile.

Richard Langley led her into the building from which he'd appeared. Inside, the air was awash with the loud whirr of old and bulky computers, the high-pitched buzz of bluish fluorescent lights. In an outer office, he introduced her to his secretary, Mrs. Fesseha, a grey-haired Ethiopian woman, who nodded hello, and Barney Wilcox, a pink-faced Englishman on a volunteer placement, whose enthusiasm subsided when Richard Langley failed to offer any explanation for Sara's presence.

Inside his office, he shut the door but did not switch on the overhead light. There was clearly power, since lights were on in the outer office, so this meant he'd made a choice. He was not going to do anything to make her feel welcome. If he didn't turn on the lights, maybe she would leave faster. He stepped behind a large wooden desk, the kind a teacher might have in a classroom. The squat bulk of his computer, also switched off, lurked on a side table to his left. A pad of yellow paper lay open on the desk's surface. From the window to his right, which opened onto the side of the building, he would, at an angle, be able to view the front gate and any arrivals. Facing him, Sara saw only the white cement wall and metal roof of another single-storey building. She wondered if he'd been sent out by the foundation to clear up the wreckage that had been left by the former director, if he was seen as the sort who would be good at this, or if he had chosen this assignment. He wore a wedding band, she noted. If he had a family, had he brought them along? A low shelf, beneath the window, held a few books: Stendhal's *The Red and the Black*, some Ian Fleming.

Richard Langley motioned her toward an armless wooden chair, a student's chair, in front of his desk. Please take a seat, he said.

He placed her business card in the far corner of his large grey blotting pad. He did not offer her anything to eat or drink, no tea, no water. He seated himself, and the straightness of his back had its own force. A man, Sara thought, who liked things to go his way, his strength and weakness being that he wasn't bendable. What exactly have you heard? he asked.

She took her tape recorder out of her pocket, placed it on the desk, and asked him if he minded her taping their conversation. Richard Langley stared at the recorder as if it were a small, spiky creature and said, Go ahead.

Gerard told me what he'd observed, the boys going to the former director's house, that he talked to Abiye and helped him write a statement and go to the police. That the former director left or took off. He attempted to help other boys who were also victims. He implied he was fired because of this.

Gerard wasn't fired. He was asked to leave and offered severance. I told him it was impossible for him to go on working for an organization he seemed to want to destroy.

Destroy is a strong word.

Yes, he said. But he didn't retract it.

The place seemed very quiet for somewhere full of children. The children, or most of them, were presumably in classrooms on the grounds, in other low-slung white buildings. Sara's experience of orphanages, in Haiti, for instance, had been of more mayhem, smell, need, children wandering in compounds that were not—what was the word that Alazar had used—neat. Of course the nature of her visits had been different: she had usually been on tours, taken to see the children.

How are you funded? She wanted to get to the matter of Raymond Renaud but had to take her time.

Through private donations. We're a charitable organization.

And you've been out here how long?

Me? I was brought out four months ago. I was at headquarters in New Jersey the two years before that. Before that at our Village in the Punjab.

Do women work for the organization? Or here, in the Village? Gerard didn't mention any.

Yes. You saw Bethlehem in the garden.

Bethlehem?

The cook. She was watering vegetables when you drove in. I am alert to the need for gender balance in staffing, particularly in the case of international hires. And volunteers. Though we remain dependent on whoever wants to venture to a remote place like this.

It wasn't really that remote, Sara thought. There were tourists and businessmen at the hotel, and the town itself was relatively large. The orphanage was set off on its own perhaps five kilometres outside of Awassa but wasn't inaccessible. She said, Gerard described a situation, an abusive situation that was systemic or at least that went on for a couple of years and involved a number of boys.

Abiye. Yes. And we now know there were a few others. Three. We have also discovered there are those who said they were harmed and were not. They have confessed to this. They made statements with Gerard's help, which they now say they did for money. They wanted the compensation money. We've brought in a counsellor to talk to them, the victims and all the children. It's an extremely unfortunate situation. For all of us.

Does Gerard know about this? About the retractions?

The false statements have come to light since he left. He's been made aware. He could be charged because of it. I can't comment further since all is in flux.

He's leaving the country today, isn't he?

I'm not privy to his exact travel plans. He is leaving.

If he leaves, how can he be charged?

Listen, I'll grant Gerard this much. I believe he acted in good faith. I am grateful for his bringing this utterly regrettable situation to light. However, he also made a difficult situation worse.

Did anyone else notice what was going on or try to do anything?

Gerard was particularly observant. I cannot fault him in that regard. Most of the local staff wouldn't know what to look for. They simply wouldn't think of it. We believed we had a sufficient screening process, but we did not and we have put new measures in place. We wish to be accountable, but, you must understand, there are challenges when screening candidates primarily with overseas experience who wish to hide aspects of their past. And who've never faced charges. As an organization we were infected by an evil individual and have, in our own way, been victimized.

Victimized. She was trying to work out Richard Langley's feelings for Gerard Loftus. She would have said Gerard aroused a mixture of disgust and anger in him, that he thought Gerard a wild card and paradoxically, the intensity of this man's dislike made her feel warmer toward Gerard.

Infiltrated, Richard Langley said, and held her gaze, and his holding felt like a wrestling match.

What about Mark Templeton, where is he and has he been charged?

That is another thing Gerard did. It's my understanding Gerard told him about Abiye's statement and tipped him off. Pure stupidity.

Do you have any idea where he is?

Templeton? I believe he left the country. I wasn't here when he left.

But you were with the foundation. Wasn't someone from the foundation in touch with him?

He was asked to leave the organization. We've had no contact with him since then.

His hands were very neat, and clean, square-tipped, with clipped nails. He folded a paper clip back and forth between his fingers until it bent.

If he's elsewhere, can he be extradited here if the charges originate here? Sara was ransacking her memory, and as far as she knew, he couldn't be.

You'll have to speak to the police. Or a lawyer.

But isn't it outrageous that he's out there somewhere and might do this again?

Ms. Wheeler, I've explained it to you. We are not the police or a law enforcement organization. We can't charge people.

Gerard said he and the rest of the staff were told not to discuss what had happened.

That was our first impulse, purely to protect the children from exposure and further harm, but we have rethought it.

At every instant she had to be a step ahead of him and here was where she had to swoop in closer and not antagonize him, a man set on wresting as much control of the conversation from her as he could. Gerard also mentioned other men, friends of Mark Templeton's, who came to visit and while here propositioned boys. Someone named Leo Reseltier?

At this, something astonished ran across his forehead and around his mouth, and it was as if he wanted to yank her words out of the air and scrub them from sight.

I said this to Gerard and I'll say it to you. You need to be very careful what you say or intimate about this situation and us. We have evidence of a situation with one man. He was removed. Or asked to leave. As soon as his behaviour came to light, we took immediate action. There is no proof of anything else. Some boys said maybe there were others, but when asked more questions they changed their story. If you start saying anything, anything potentially libellous about us, well, I suggest you be very careful. And think of the children who are in such need. If, for instance, what you say scares away donors, it is the children who will suffer most. And AIDS is making everything worse. More and more children show up on our doorstep every day. Think about that, and how unfortunate it would be for the children if we were not able to continue this work.

Sara thought, You are also in the business of keeping yourselves in business, as all aid organizations are. And you are threatening me. But she didn't say that. There's one man in particular, Raymond Renaud, the Canadian who founded a children's circus in Addis Ababa, did he visit?

The room seemed very bright as she asked this, her mouth chalky. Richard Langley began to flush, colour rising from his jawline up through his cheeks, and she couldn't decide what his pinkness meant: terror, horror, rage, chagrin at the fact that his skin was doing something uncontrollable. Or was he trying to hide something. I believe there was some talk of starting a circus program here and he visited to discuss this proposal. Nothing happened with it. Nothing will happen with it.

Are you aware of the allegations against him?

I've been told.

Gerard said he visited a few times.

As I said, this proposal was discussed and I believe he taught some classes in circus arts, yes. But there will be no more.

For groups of kids or children on their own?

Presumably for groups. That's my understanding. I wasn't here.

Have the children, the boys, been asked if anything, if he did anything?

I have had no word of this.

Can I speak to any of the boys, to Abiye and the other victims?

If they agree to speak to you. And if you do, I hope you will be very clear what you intend. Because they're victims, Ms. Wheeler. Remember that. And you wouldn't want what you're doing to turn into another form of abuse.

He stood, as if dismissing her. But first I'm going to show you what we do here. Because you should also see that for yourself, don't you think?

He led her back through the outer office, under the watchful gazes of Barney Wilcox and Mrs. Fesseha, and, once more, out into the empty yard. Yes, the older children were in their classrooms, Richard Langley said when Sara asked. At noon, they would break for lunch.

Ahead of them, from a round hut, a traditional thatch-roofed tukul set behind the white-walled buildings, beneath the shade of a large tree, issued the babble and shrieks of young children. As they drew close, the hut's open doorway filled with the off-key, high-pitched sound of singing. Worn toys—plastic blocks, part of an alphabet set, a doll, a deflated ball—lay scattered across the ground outside, and when Sara and Richard Langley stepped through the door, the children, perhaps a dozen or so, who had been seated on a rug laid on the hardened earth, clapping their hands, broke and skittered toward them, despite the admonitions of their minders, two women with kerchiefs holding back their hair. A few toddlers tottered about in loose diapers. Little children with runny noses and moist hands clutched Sara's trousers, and even here called out in English, Mother, sister, one birr, two birr. Two girls tried to take her hands. Richard Langley lifted a small boy with a large head into his arms, his blue shirt bunching. He did not strike her as a man who truly liked children, or liked holding them, or liked holding these children, who might or might not be aware of what had happened here. Richard Langley dropped the boy and patted the head of a girl in a dirty white party dress. Only after introducing her to the two women, Meseret and Hawa, did he make introductions to Worku, the boy, and Liya, the girl.

From across the yard came a thrum of music and the faint strains of reedy Bob Dylan: Alazar, running the tape deck off the car battery. He was not in the car but conversing with the watchman in the shade of a patch of metal roofing that formed a raw hut for the watchman, rain or shine. Sara wondered what Alazar and the watchman were discussing, what the watchman had told Alazar about the orphanage. From outside the tukul, she raised a hand and nodded so that Alazar knew she was fine.

Behind the children's buildings lay a semicircle of staff flats. Richard Langley pointed them out, across what passed for a lawn at the end of the rainy season, some hazy tufts of green, bright flowers, geraniums, pushing up from beds at the base of the windows. He said his wife and two boys were back home in Philadelphia.

Sara asked him if each staff member had a separate flat. No, he said, most were shared, but the director had his own. Which was his? He pointed to the second from the end, on the left. Was that where Mark Templeton had lived? No, he said curtly. That one was removed. What about guests, visitors, where did they stay? She was wondering where Raymond Renaud had slept. There was a guest suite, Richard Langley told her, in one of the shared houses.

He gestured toward the children's latrines, took her to the wood-working studio, then to the multipurpose hall, also round and thatched, but plastered and painted pale green and enclosed by a porch, its interior filled with stacks of chairs. He agreed that she could take a few photographs. They moved on to the refectory, where rough wooden benches lined either side of a row of trestle tables covered in plastic cloths. From the kitchen came the clattering of pots. And there was Bethlehem, the cook, stirring a vast vat of pasta while chatting to a tall and astonishingly good-looking blond man who introduced himself as Olaf Olafsson of Sweden. Why did the presence of these white men, and only men, feel odd, and the extreme good looks and blondness of Olaf Olafsson seem somehow tainted? Sara couldn't look at anyone, Bethlehem, Olaf, and not wonder what they knew or had seen or suspect them of some guilt. Through proximity or collusion. She wanted to reach into their heads and pull out exactly what they knew.

In the dormitories, an assortment of thin wool blankets and sheets covered nearly identical rows of wooden bunkbeds devoid of any personal effects. Yet the children must keep at least a few personal things somewhere: in a shared closet, a cupboard drawer. All this being so unlike the dorm room of her youth—in the Ottawa boarding school for wayward girls—the posters on the walls, plush toys hogging the bed covers, toys that she herself had despised, preferring to keep a volume of Anaïs Nin's diaries under her bed.

At last Richard Langley led her toward the building that housed two small classrooms, the junior and the senior, each with a door opening onto a narrow porch. The junior class was in the midst of English recitation, led by a slim white man in pale short shirt sleeves, the bob of dark heads, girls' and boys', turning from within the room to follow Sara and Richard Langley as they passed along the porch. I am very well, the children chorused. There is no problem. I haven't a clue.

When they reached the senior classroom, the teacher, also male but Ethiopian, broke off and stepped toward the door. Some students looked up quizzically at their arrival, some stared with little expression. They didn't wear uniforms, but there was some attempt at uniformity, the girls all in skirts, all the boys and girls in T-shirts, occasionally with jackets or sweaters over them, the girls' hair pulled back in neat braids or corn rows. The children, some of them teenagers, sat on wooden benches, like those in the refectory, at long narrow metal tables that served as their desks. There were some rather battered-looking books on a shelf, a dusty chalkboard with multiplication equations sketched upon it. The boys. How did you identify those who had been violated? Though the ordinariness of these children was different than that of the circus children. These children didn't have families or some did and their families had abandoned them because they couldn't support them. Only a few students spoke among themselves during the pause provided by Richard Langley's low-voiced conversation with the teacher. When the teacher, tapping his metal watch, returned to the front of the classroom, all fell silent.

Minutes later, a tall boy in an old windbreaker worn over a striped shirt and shorts that stopped high above his knees came scuffing across the yard. Yellow flip-flops flapped against the soles of his feet. In the classroom, he'd sat at the end of the middle row, beside the window. At the interruption of their entrance, he'd glanced toward the door, then returned to gazing outside. Now he kept his hands in the pockets of his shorts and his eyes lowered as he approached. When he reached them, he looked up in astonishment or manufactured astonishment. The gaze that he offered Richard Langley was so direct as to seem provocative.

Abiye, Richard Langley said. He held himself stiffly, as if proximity to Abiye's body filled him with fear. This is Sara Wheeler and she wants to talk to you.

He did not say what about. In any case Abiye probably had some idea why he had been singled out to talk.

Sara extended her hand — Hello, Abiye. Some physical gesture seemed wanted, his clasp dry and without weight.

He was surely not eleven or twelve, perhaps thirteen, or even older, nearly as tall as her chin. No facial hair, and she had yet to hear his voice more than the mumble of his reply. A broadening across the shoulders and through the chest, beneath his striped shirt, suggested middle adolescence. There was shame and awkwardness in the air. Sara wanted to do something to set him at ease.

Why don't you two go over to the multipurpose hall, Richard Langley said. It will be quiet there.

What she had expected was that Richard Langley would lead them back toward his office or an office, somewhere he could lurk outside the door or rustle on the edges of her consciousness, and yet here he was suggesting that she take this boy to a place where they would be wholly or largely unmonitored.

Abiye's English is very good, Richard Langley said. He's a very bright boy. Then he flushed, as if he wished he hadn't said this or as if his secret wish was that Abiye vanish.

Abiye began to move off in the direction of the multipurpose hall, his feet in their pale flip-flops scuffing up dust. Red dirt crawled over Sara's black walking boots as she strode after him. He led her up the steps of the round, windowed building, where, a short while before, she had stood with Richard Langley. Instead of continuing through the door, Abiye lowered himself to the cement floor of the porch, at her feet, his back to the wall, legs outstretched, one ankle crossed over the other, his dusty bulbous toes still clutching their flip-flops.

Then his choice made sense: from where he sat, he had a view of most of the yard; he was largely hidden by the low wall enclosing the porch yet could reveal his hiding place by doing no more than moving his legs into the gap where the porch steps led up to the door.

Richard Langley's pale-blue back returned to his office. Alazar and the watchman chatted beside the yellow Lada, the front gate beyond them. Abiye's view was more extensive than Richard Langley's from his office window.

Sara considered bringing out chairs, or a chair, but instead stepped over Abiye's outstretched legs and settled herself beside him, broom tracks visible in the trailings of dust left where wall met floor, aware of Abiye's body, his legs, close but not too close to hers.

Do you often come here by yourself?

He shrugged. Sometime. His voice was a high, light tenor.

Where do you meet the counsellor?

Mrs. Azeze? One time maybe here. Now in the free office. This one that was Gerard office.

Richard Langley was right: his English was good, the English he'd presumably learned from Mark Templeton, the man who had abused him. As soon as Sara took out her tape recorder and set it on the ground, Abiye picked the recorder up and turned it between his fingers, until Sara showed him how to press the buttons to switch it on and off, rewind and fast-forward, and asked him to speak into it.

In English.

Yes. You can hold it if you wish but you don't have to.

Ishee.

An ordinary boy with thick-soled, dusty feet and grey patches of dry skin and the whiter streak of fingernail marks where he had recently scratched his left calf, a scab on his knee, a yeasty musk, a boy desultorily swatting away a fly before it landed on his shin. He did not strike her as obviously docile or easy to take advantage of. Maybe he had once been.

She told him she was a journalist from Canada and she wanted to talk to him about what had happened to him with Mark Templeton, what Mark Templeton had done to him. He nodded, although she felt him vacate part of himself. She wasn't asking him to recount anything he hadn't spoken of before. This was what she did, not cross-examine people but ask questions, often of people in extremity. Sometimes she, too, had to vacate part of herself. Most people, though not all, wanted to tell their stories.

How did it happen? Gerard said you went to Mark Templeton's house. He asked you to his house.

Abiye wandered a fingertip through the trails of dust. Mr. Mark, he teachèd me. He teachèd me many thing. We like him. We play games. He say, we are family. Then he say, Come. You are special boy. He teachèd me English. He say, I look after you. He say, I love you. He touchèd me. I touch. He slep with me like a woman. He pay me two birr each time. He say, It is good.

What kind of games did you play with him?

Tag. Hide-go-seek. He play with all children.

Even after you knew what he wanted, you went to his house.

Abiye nodded.

Abiye, I'm so sorry for the things he did to you.

He nodded again.

How long did this go on?

Two year. I do not tell. Now they teachèd us it is bad thing.

He looked down at his finger and spoke as if he'd been schooled to speak of these matters in this way.

Why did you decide to talk to Gerard?

Gerard askèd me. Abiye's neck, the delicate back of his neck, his ear lobe, rose before her, as he began to pick at the scab on his right knee. He say, I help.

He asked you what?

What I do. He watchèd me come and go to that man house. He say, This is bad thing. We go to doctor and police. Gerard and Sifisse. Abiye offered her a sudden, ravishing smile. Then he yanked the scab free and rubbed at the place where the scab had been.

Who's Sifisse?

He work here. And Gerard. They gone.

Did you know there were other boys?

Something contracted in Abiye's body. In the begin I not know it.

The haze of the sun crept toward the two of them under the overhang of the roof. An ant crawled along the line of dust where floor met wall. Hugging his knees to his chest, Abiye watched the ant. Sara wondered if he felt there was anything to be gained in speaking to her. He had trusted Gerard and Gerard had helped him. He had trusted Mark Templeton also.

Abiye. She waited for the tremour of his attention. I believe all these things you've told me.

He nodded.

After a moment, she asked, Are you angry?

Some time.

How are things now that Mr. Richard is here?

He stared toward the milky horizon. Okay.

She asked him if he'd known his birth family and he said they had left him here when he was very small, during the big famine. They had come down from the north, maybe from Gonder. He did not know how they had made the trip or if they were alive or how to find them.

What will happen to you, and the others, when you are through school, because isn't the Village only a place for children?

In another year, he told her, he would move to a house in town called Transition House where he would learn to fix things, bicycles, maybe televisions, then try to find a job. A chicken whirred and clucked close by, underneath the porch.

She asked him if Mark Templeton had ever had friends or other men visit the orphanage, and when Abiye said yes, she asked if anyone else ever asked him to do the bad things or any other boy that he knew of to do them? He seemed to consider this question before shrugging. Maybe.

Do you have any names?

He shook his head.

Gerard told me about a boy named Tedesse. He said a man approached him.

Mr. Leo. He say he has job for him in Addis Ababa.

Is Tedesse here?

He go.

To Addis?

Abiye nodded.

Do you believe Mr. Leo had a job for him?

He looked at her as if she were a fool. No.

There's a man, Mr. Raymond, who runs a children's circus in —

Oh. Something sprang open in Abiye at the sound of this: joy, excitement travelling out through his legs, his arms. You know it? The circus come. They do it here. The jugglery, the acrobatic. They teach us it.

Abiye, the circus man, Mr. Raymond, did he ever approach any children here, or the children in his circus, did any of them say anything about him doing the bad things Mr. Mark did?

No. One time, Mr. Mark he takèd me and Tedesse and Gerard to see circus in Shashemene.

Gerard came?

Yes. To the big football place, how you say?

A stadium?

That is it. Maybe thousands, so many see it. Lights. Big music. And children, they make all of it.

Do you know if Mr. Mark and Mr. Raymond are friends?

Maybe. Mr. Raymond, he say to me, I make circus here.

He was going to start a circus in the Village?

They teachèd us. The ball toss. The hand walk. I show you.

Abiye scrambled to his feet, lowered his hands to the ground, and tipped himself upside down, flip-flops still attached to his toes, his jacket bunching around his upper arms. Hand over hand, legs in the air, he shuffled over the cement floor.

Abiye, take off your jacket. It looks dangerous, caught around your head like that.

Sara, too, clambered to her feet as Abiye lowered his legs with a thump, stripped his jacket from his arms before upending himself once more, and, legs waggling but perpendicular, made his way along the cement, slap, slap, slap. Out of sight, from around the curve of the porch, came the uneven skitter of his turn, then he reappeared, still up-ended, and made his way back to her. Coming to a standstill, he arched his legs all the way over until his feet met the ground in a backbend, and from there leaped breathlessly upright, then sprang into another, and another backbend. Sara clapped; he was not as agile as the children of Cirkus Mirak but made up for that in strength and the ferocity of his attention and the wildness of his pleasure. And she found pleasure in the presence of his.

Abiye, can I take your photograph?

Someone's feet made a swift passage across the yard. Abiye stopped abruptly as Sara turned, and Olaf Olafsson raised a hand to her.

Abiye said quietly, When Mr. Raymond come, I show him what I do. Or I go to circus in Addis Ababa.

No, Abiye. That's probably not a good plan. Addis is dangerous and a long way off. And, listen, I know Mr. Raymond said he'd come, but I don't think he can come now. He went away. Another man, Tamrat Asfaw, runs the circus.

She'd dealt him a blow. Once more something in his body contracted: a dream that he'd been holding on to snatched away. This was what she'd done for him, ripped away his last, best hope.

Abiye, it's better for you to stay here. Can you do circus here? Make a circus of your own. In the Village. With the other children. There are circuses starting up in other towns too.

Mr. Richard does not like it.

Circus? No, I don't think he does. Can you do it even so? Or do it in secret. Remember the things you saw the children do in the stadium. Practise. Here, in this place. Make up your own acts.

The scraping back of wooden benches sounded through the windows of the classrooms and children's voices rose, along with the clapping of a pair of hands and a man's voice trying to establish order.

Sara pulled her camera out of her bag. Here she was, hypocrite, suggesting Abiye contain another secret. And stay in the place where he'd been violated. Richard Langley might well try to put a stop to any breath of circus. Yet how in her right mind could she counsel Abiye to set off for Addis?

Through the dirt yard, the other children were making their way toward the refectory in weaving lines.

When Abiye asked her if she was coming back, she said, It's not likely. Not soon. I have to go home to Canada. But I will tell Mr. Asfaw about you and the Awassa circus.

The Awassa circus?

Your circus.

She would attempt to tell Tamrat, anyway. She scribbled the Cirkus Mirak phone number on a piece of paper torn from her notebook and handed it to Abiye, knowing how unlikely it was that he would be able to make a phone call, but whatever he chose to do, at least he would have this talisman, and he folded the paper carefully and tucked it in the pocket of his shorts.

You can do this, she said, because, having stolen his story, it seemed the best thing that she had to give him.

Lunch was eaten at one end of the refectory, Sara seated with the two teachers, Richard Langley at her elbow, each of them chewing on the same moist pasta as everybody else. There was something subdued about all the children: she did not know if this was because of what they had been through or was an effect of Richard Langley's new reign of order.

After lunch, he directed her to the free office, as Abiye had called it, which had been Gerard's, although Richard Langley did not mention this provenance and the office had been stripped bare of any personal effects, leaving nothing but two chairs and a desk. He brought two more boys to her: Tesfaye, then Daniel, both younger than Abiye, perhaps ten or eleven or twelve. Sara was aware of their round heads, the delicate shape of their skulls through their cropped hair, as she listened to them, their voices higher, softer, their English more halting than Abiye's. She could have called for Alazar's help. She didn't. The dinners, the special English lessons, the things the man had done to them. What about the circus man? They shook their heads. Tesfaye said, I do the jugglery. And Daniel said, I do backflip. As if these, too, were messages they needed to get out to the world. So there was this trace and legacy of Raymond Renaud. And as yet no confirmation of his participation in any *ring*.

A hoarse-voiced boy named Solomon sat working pleats into his trouser legs, swinging his feet in dirty pink plastic sandals, and muttered, He tell me to say the untrue thing.

Who did?

Gerard did it.

. ·.

The next day, back in Addis Ababa, Sara called the counsellor, Fasika Azeze, who did not seem happy to hear from her but was prepared to talk despite her concern about the possible effects of any public attention on the children.

It is their shame I worry about — Ms. Azeze, at her end of the line, seemed to be thinking out loud. Restitution, it is important, and it is important for them to tell their story when they wish it, but there is the problem of their shame. Yet it is terrible for perpetrators to get away with such crimes, and it is a danger to keep these things hidden.

In person, in her office off the Bole Road, Fasika Azeze was both fierce and polite, a woman of about Sara's age, a scattering of dark freckles across the bridge of her cheeks, her nails painted to a pearly sheen. The room bore a scent of hair oil. She had spent ten years in Italy, working with immigrant women and sexual abuse cases there, she said. Born in Addis. She'd heard about the circus, the allegations, knew only that there would be an investigation. She travelled down to Awassa every other week. I do not think they will tell you all of it. Her voice was reedy but firm. Because they are too damaged. Something in Sara balked at the insistence on their damage.

Because they are confused and frightened, Fasika Azeze went on. They do not know what they should say and they want to say what they think is the right thing to say. I would not nor I cannot tell you exactly what went on in that place, or precisely how many children or for certain how many men. I do not know it yet. Maybe more, but they have all been betrayed.

In the yellow Lada, Sara and Alazar bumped along the maze of dirt and stone-laden streets that led to Yitbarek Abera's house. A dog slunk along beside the car, beneath the overhang of a cinder-block building. A goat stared hypnotically in their direction before bolting out of the way. This time, the flimsy corrugated metal gate was not clamped with a padlock. When Alazar stepped out of the car and knocked upon the metal, the whole expanse shook. He cupped his hand around his mouth and shouted, and a moment later the gate began to judder open, backward upon its shaky hinges, in clanky reverberations, drawn by an as yet invisible person. Alazar drove them through into a small, bare yard in front of a small house. Weedy bamboo pushed up through the corners of the fencing. Behind them, a middle-aged woman in a saffron sweater and flowered housedress fought to close the gate. Three limber boys in the white shirts and dark shorts of school uniforms had slipped out through the open door of the house and stood staring at the car, shifting their balance from foot to foot like delicate storks, until the woman shooed them back inside. Circus children: they looked familiar. The introductions were all in Amharic, Alazar doing his convivial best—Sara caught her own name, and the woman's, Dassala. She is Yitbarek's aunt, Alazar said, as Dassala led them, Sara with her knapsack in one hand and a bag of groceries in the other, through the front door.

The room they entered was disorientingly dark. Then: in the dim, far corner of the room, a boy lying upon a cot turned his head in their direction. The bright flash of his eyes. The other boys, murmuring, moved toward him and cut him off from sight. A television, high on a wooden console in the opposite corner, was flickering greenly at low volume, girls in white shaking their shoulders, folkloric dancing that no one seemed to be watching. Along the near wall, a pair of crutches leaned against a stuffed armchair. There was a second armchair; both had white antimacassars folded over their tops. A cement floor. A curled bedroll tied with a rope was stuffed behind the first chair. At the foot of the cot, a rudimentary wheelchair was parked, the folding kind, with canvas seat and back unfolded, and on the seat lay a square of foam molded in the bumpy shape of egg cartons. David had mentioned using such foam at the worst points of Greta's illness, when she'd been bedridden, to prevent bedsores.

At the end of the cot stood a metal walking frame, and beneath the cot two leg braces were stashed. There were plastic balls—juggling balls?—piled in a plastic bucket. Sara wondered if any of the equipment had been brought back from Montreal by Raymond Renaud in July. Hadn't he mentioned, in his urgency to get to Montreal, his need to pick up some supplies?

The boys were doing something to the boy in the bed, or he was doing something. They were all talking in the insistent monotone beat of spoken Amharic, and Dassala in turn was talking at them. One of the boys, the tallest, pushed the wheelchair close to the side of the bed, and Yitbarek reached for its frame with one hand and pulled himself to sitting, leaning forward and bracing himself with his other arm, while one of the other boys helped or tried to help by giving him a push or support from behind. The mattress beneath Yitbarek was covered by a blue vinyl gym mat like those the circus children used in the rehearsal hall. The boys, and the aunt, gave little yips of encouragement and clapped when Yitbarek sat, braced on both arms, thin legs outstretched. A slight boy: there were socks on his feet but his legs were bare, the muscles obviously atrophied. Paralyzed, at least in the legs: here was evidence that his injury looked as bad as Raymond had feared. And was all this a kind of performance for the benefit of visitors, for her, the presence of strangers heightening his desire to prove he could get up and do as much as possible on his own.

The tall boy, who had performed the chair act in the street show that Sara had seen, stood beside Yitbarek, and although Dassala tried to shoo him away, he waved her off and said in English, I do it. He helped Yitbarek manoeuvre his inert legs over the edge of the bed, first one then the other, feet to the floor, then placed Yitbarek's hands on his shoulders and his own around Yitbarek's waist and lifted him, or helped lift him, into the wheelchair. When Yitbarek's blue sweater rucked above his waist, a stretch of leather brace, clasped around his torso, briefly revealed itself. And any thought that this wasn't how things ought to be done, children caring for a disabled child, had to be chucked away, for here and now this was how things were being done.

Dassala made a universally comprehensible scooting motion in the direction of the three limber-limbed boys. Three nylon knapsacks lay in a tumble on the floor beneath the TV.

Wait, Sara said. Alazar, can you ask their names, and where they live, and if we can talk to them too. And can you ask if any of them lived with Yitbarek at Raymond Renaud's house?

We go to circus, the tallest said. His name was Birook.

Later then. Can we talk to you later?

Yes, we can do it.

Alazar said, Moses — the middle one, who had been one of the unicycling fire jugglers — lived in that house and now lives here. As Moses pointed to the bedroll behind the armchair, then to his chest, and said in English, Me, me, me.

That's his bed, Alazar said.

The third boy, Asefa, one of the acrobats in the street show, having folded the blue vinyl mat into segments, balanced it upright against the wall. On the cot, through the now-exposed sheet, the bumps of more egg crate foam could be seen.

Everything felt chaotic, a jumble of bodies and objects in a space that seemed to shrink around them. Sara tried to hand the plastic bag of Nescafé and long-life milk and cooking oil and biscuits to Dassala, who, still talking to the boys, shook her head and waved her arms as if she could not accept the gift.

Alazar, can you tell her that we brought these things for her. It's a small thing.

What must it be like for Yitbarek to be surrounded by the other boys' bodies, still so limber and racing with fluidity? His face, the beautiful arched brows, the lips, much as when seen in the photographs and on film, caught now out of the corner of Sara's eye, looked watchful, stripped of the animation of previous moments.

Then the other boys, white shirts tucked in, arms thrust through the sleeves of their sweaters, Moses with a nylon gym bag, Birook and Asefa with knapsacks flung over their shoulders, were gone, and the room felt empty without them, and Dassala was holding the plastic bag of groceries and saying, Amesegenallo, and something else.

Alazar said, She wishes to offer us the coffee ceremony. His eyebrows rose in meaningful communication: they'd discussed this in the car, what to do should this occur. It was partly why they'd brought the Nescafé and long-life milk, so it was possible to say no, but we would love a Nescafé, without making their hostess seem inhospitable.

I would actually really love a Nescafé, Sara said to Alazar, who nodded, and spoke to Dassala in Amharic.

There were two doorways that led off the main room, one in the middle of the wall to Sara's left, which was closed off by a length of brocaded fabric slung over a stretch of rope, the other an open doorway through which Dassala in her flowered housedress passed, the room beyond a glimpse of unpainted plank walls, plates on open shelves, a sink, a squat green single-burner kerosene stove set on the floor.

Yitbarek, I'm Sara. She held out her hand to him in his wheelchair and his hand in hers was cold. The air wasn't warm. Yitbarek wore a zip-up cardigan, a blanket thrown over his bare legs, Sara her fleece jacket, only Alazar braving bare arms and a soccer shirt, but perhaps Yitbarek was also cold because he moved less.

How are you, he asked, beating her to it, his voice having the same staccato rhythms as the voices of the other children she'd encountered, each word bearing equal weight.

I'm fine. How are you?

It was an impossible question and impossible not to ask it.

I am well, he said, three even notes, and smiled, and there was curiosity and attentiveness in him if not great force behind the smile.

Once she and Alazar had seated themselves in the armchairs, Yitbarek wheeled himself between them, Dassala calling out something from the kitchen. She says it is okay to move the chairs if we wish it, Alazar said, but there was no need, the two of them like parents on either side of their child. There was room on the upholstered armrest for Sara to lay her tape recorder upon it.

Did you ask if it's okay for me to tape the conversation? Sara said to Alazar, who nodded. She'd told him to explain that she was a journalist visiting from Canada and might be writing about the circus. To tell Yitbarek she'd seen him perform in Copenhagen. To ask his aunt if it was okay to talk to him. To ask Yitbarek if he wanted to talk. It is possible, Alazar said. Yitbarek, she thought, was the one whom Raymond had taught to juggle with fire.

You see me, Yitbarek said in English.

I did, I saw you perform in Denmark. She'd worried that mentioning this, recalling the past to him, might be painful but instead Yitbarek smiled and looked pleased.

Dassala was again saying something in Amharic from the kitchen.

They are in this house one month, Alazar said. Before they were for one month in Mr. Raymond's house. Before that Yitbarek was in the hospital. She has come from their town, which is Dessie, to look after him. Now she works some time as the cook for the circus. His parents, they have a shop, so they cannot come, and it is decided it is best for him to stay here right now. Mr. Raymond found this house and he pays for it, even since he has gone away. He says they are not to worry, he will pay.

Do they know where he's gone or for how long?

And this was so much more the way interviews often went, especially in certain parts of the world, and when translators were involved, not the unusual privacy that she'd shared with Abiye, but something more communal and interrupted. Alazar and Dassala shared another exchange. She does not know, Alazar said. When Alazar spoke in English, Yitbarek watched him intently and sometimes glanced at Sara, while his fingers rubbed back and forth over the blanket or the narrow wooden arms of his wheelchair. He did not say where he is going but it does not seem he will come back soon, Alazar said. He came to say goodbye and to say he is sorry but he must leave and he is crying.

He's crying.

Yes.

Why was he crying? And why did he say he was sorry?

Another exchange, to a chiming of tin against tin in the kitchen, after which Alazar said, He promised to take care of Yitbarek and he is sad to go. It is the turn of Tamrat to look after the circus so he must find another job.

So it really doesn't sound like he's coming back.

It was clear that Yitbarek understood some English, although Sara wasn't sure how much. He seemed to prefer to respond in Amharic, favouring that comfort or fluency.

Can you ask what language he and Mr. Raymond spoke?

Some English, some Amharic, Alazar said.

Dassala reappeared, bearing a small enamel tray on which sat three chipped enamel mugs. At her entrance, Alazar leaped up to pull a small table woven of basketry close to the armchairs. The mug that Dassala handed to Sara was ferociously hot to touch. Yitbarek shook his head at his, the mug with only a tiny amount of milky coffee in it. A moment later, having returned the tray to the kitchen, Dassala positioned herself on the threshold of the room, watching over their conversation. Yitbarek did not seem to be in pain. No, Alazar said, when Sara asked him to ask, he isn't in pain. His neck and arms moved freely, so the injury seemed restricted to his lower body. When he shifted in the chair, a faint scent of urine drifted from him.

How did the accident happen? Yitbarek, can you tell us?

After he and Alazar had conversed, Alazar said, He is at the top of the pyramid and he falls. Maybe his foot caught in the shirt of Moses or on his arm. He is to do a roll to come down but he cannot make his body do the right thing. Then he is on the floor and he cannot move. This is what he remembers.

This was in the rehearsal hall.

Yes.

That's terrible.

Yes, Alazar said, hands clasped between his knees, concern creasing his face.

Now Yitbarek kept a close eye on Sara, and when he spoke again, he pointed to his torso and flexed his arms. Then he is in the hospital, Alazar went on. He has broken a bone in his spine. He can feel some stomach muscles. He can feel a little in his legs, but he cannot move them. He can work his bowel.

At first he must stay very still. Then another doctor comes and tells him he must learn to roll and sit up. He gets a brace. He has strong arms, strong muscles, and they will become stronger. There is a famous Ethiopian, Abebe Bikila, he ran the marathon, and he had the same kind of accident but in a car crash and he became very strong after and an athlete in a wheelchair. The doctor tells him this. So he will become very strong like Abebe Bikila.

Does he see a physiotherapist or anyone who does rehabilitative treatment?

A what?

Okay, who's in charge of his medical care?

A doctor.

She did not think, and Raymond Renaud had intimated in the car that night, that there would be access to specialized care without flying Yitbarek out of the country. And everything, even X-rays, would have to be paid for by someone. Raymond. His family.

Who else looked after him, in the hospital and after?

Mr. Renaud and his aunt.

In the hospital?

Yes. Mr. Raymond came to the hospital to help care for him, to feed him, to wash him, and help turn him. And then his aunt comes, and they move to Mr. Renaud's house. Then Mr. Renaud goes to Australia with the circus, and when he comes back, they move to this house. And Mr. Renaud trains the boys to help his aunt, to roll him and help him sit. Now it is very important for him to sit. And they also do the ball toss and the jugglery. Soon he will begin to stand with the frame and the braces. One day he will do seated jugglery in the circus or he will walk again. Mr. Renaud assures him there will be a place for him in the circus.

Did Mr. Renaud take care of him alone in the hospital? Alone?

Or was there a nurse there with him?

There was another exchange between Yitbarek and Alazar, who in his approaches to Yitbarek seemed gentle and kind. Dassala went on observing them, arms crossed over her bosom, while on the television an Amharic-speaking news anchor warbled.

Sometimes there is a nurse, but Mr. Renaud does these things because there is no one else to do the care, Alazar said.

Couldn't he have hired someone else, a woman, to look after Yitbarek, Sara wondered. Surely he could have found money for a caregiver even if there were other hospital expenses to be paid for. Because the physical intimacy of looking after Yitbarek compromised him — didn't it? He was not the boy's parent. Although the boy had been left in his care. Perhaps he did not trust anyone else to look after Yitbarek. He felt distraught and responsible. He did not want to leave Yitbarek, so vulnerable after his accident, in the hands of a stranger. The intimacy of such care made her uncomfortable. No one would do anything harmful to a boy who had just been paralyzed.

When Sara asked how soon after the accident his aunt had come to stay, Alazar said two weeks. When she asked whether, before the accident, Mr. Raymond had ever washed or bathed Yitbarek or any of the boys, Alazar looked at her strangely, but he spoke to Yitbarek who in turn seemed puzzled or reflected

Alazar's puzzlement back at him as he replied. No, was all Alazar translated.

Sara checked her tape recorder. Before the accident, were you happy in the circus?

Yes, Yitbarek said without waiting for any translation.

Did you feel safe?

He and Alazar discussed this; then, in English, Yitbarek said yes.

Did you feel safe living in Mr. Raymond's house, you and the other boys?

Yes, it is good, Yitbarek said, and Alazar added, They have their own room.

And did you feel safe when you were training? Alazar, can you help me with this—I want to find out if he felt they were properly supervised when doing their circus training, or if they were asked to do unsafe things?

There was some intense discussion about this. Yitbarek, when he spoke, was animated, voluble. He had an expressive face, his hair shorn close to his head, his hands quick in the air, paler palms swivelling, something of his previous quicksilver movements still in him. His aunt interjected something. In Amharic, Sara thanked her for the Nescafé.

Nothing was clear here, nothing felt clear. With Abiye, everything had, in a sense, been easier, despite Gerard's insinuations and rumours and Richard Langley's veiled threats. She'd been seeking confirmation of something already acknowledged, and Abiye had recounted a story he'd told before. She didn't know the extent of abuse at the orphanage, but some boys had clearly been abused. Here, what she encountered were denials and ambiguous intimacy and nothing as yet to corroborate the runaways' allegations. Would Yitbarek protect Raymond, who after all was paying his rent?

He says, Alazar said at last, Mr. Raymond asks them to do things and they want to do them and he believes at all times they can do it. He shows them carefully. He says they can be the best in the world at circus, but they have to work hard. Sometimes even in a big circus an accident happens to a great athlete and such turns of fate must be accepted because it is God's will and overcome.

Do you, does he know some of the circus performers ran away in Australia?

After a moment, Alazar said, He knows it. The boys and Mr. Tamrat tell him. Mr. Tamrat said they ran because they did not wish to be in the circus anymore.

What did the boys say?

They say the others are not happy. They do not like Mr. Raymond. Because he shouts at them.

Why did he shout at them?

Because they're big, and they do not want to do it the way Mr. Raymond wants them to do it.

Do what?

The work.

Did he hurt them?

I do not think so.

Did Mr. Raymond shout at Yitbarek?

He does not. Excuse me — there was a shift in Alazar's tone, a severity that Sara had not experienced from him before. It is enough. He is tired.

Thank you, Yitbarek, Sara said, and it seemed true, there was a loss of focus in him, a wilting, and in her persistence to ask a certain kind of question and pursue a line of thought, she'd been oblivious to it. Of course his strain could be another kind of strain. Yet she would get nowhere without Alazar's assistance.

Can you juggle in your chair? she asked Yitbarek.

Yes, he said quietly, and his head indicated the bucket of balls. Not now. A gust of sadness, rather than anger, swept across him. It was true, he did not seem angry. Then he brightened. Look. And raised himself in his chair from his seat, balancing on the strength of his arms as Alazar explained this was one of the exercises he had to do.

Alazar, can you ask if there's anything they need, any supplies we can bring, medical supplies, anything we can find here in Addis or something I can perhaps get someone to bring back from Canada?

I will ask it.

And is there a toilet?

To stand and walk out of the room felt like the flaunting of a flamboyant gift. The bathroom, off the kitchen, was of a more flimsy construction than the rest of the house, built of scrap wood, slits of light filtering between the boards and underneath them. Outside voices rang from close by. A red plastic bucket filled with water sat beside the toilet, and a row of four buckets in front of the freestanding tub held sheets and possibly cloth diapers, the scent of human waste tamped down by strong wafts of detergent and bleach.

In a hotel in Amman, in the heady wake of their return from Najaf—after the Australian Rafael Nardi's saving of the Iraqi man who'd almost choked to death in front of them, and the carjacking—one of the others, Peter Cross, an American photojournalist, had told Sara how, as a child, he had been sexually attacked by a man known to his parents. The man, who lived in the same building as Peter, had coaxed him into his apartment one day after school, while both his parents were still at work, and tried to molest him, but Peter had fought the man off and escaped into his own apartment and locked the door. The man had called through the locked door and said, If you don't come with me, I'll tell your parents you did and how you touched me and how you liked me touching you, and if you do come with me, I won't say a word.

What did you do? Sara asked. I was so angry I dared him to say something to my mother, and that frightened him. Did you tell her what happened? Yes. And were you believed? Yes. What happened then? She told my father, who beat the man so bad he never went near me again. You were lucky, Sara said. I was, Peter said, but probably others weren't.

In the public change room of the local rink in Ottawa where she'd skated as a teenager, there was a man who bought hot chocolate for boys whose parents left them at the rink on their own, a man whom all the teenagers knew to avoid. A girl she'd known in boarding school had been raped by an uncle in the bathroom of the family home. Another molested by a priest. There were so many different ways for children, and teenagers, to be damaged and abandoned.

The ones who had accused Raymond had not accused him of abusing Yitbarek or not that Sara knew of. As she'd understood it from Sem Le, they'd accused him of abusing them. So many of them, male and female. Possible. Though the story could have altered, been altered. They had altered it. Or they had been misunderstood. They had known or suspected one thing. They'd said another. Or having been misunderstood, they'd agreed to the new version. Turning on Raymond, they'd said what seemed to best serve their case, wanting so intensely to get away from him and from the circus.

She did not see how she could go on in her questioning, not here, not now, without running the risk of hurting Yitbarek further. If nothing had happened, she would be the one forcing him to imagine acts he'd never thought of. She was no police officer or counsellor. Nor was she Gerard Loftus. All she'd gained was more complication and murk, and the ability to hurt someone, her ability to do so lurking in every direction she looked. She was in the presence of some intimacy. She had a day left in her trip. She could try to talk to Yitbarek again. Yet she also wanted to talk to some of the other boys. And girls. Their parents.

What if, walking back out into that room, she were to ask Yitbarek: Did you ever want to run away from the circus? Did you fall on purpose, as a last-ditch means of escape from that man's clutches? Did he touch you like this? Like this?

Always there were the questions you meant to ask and didn't, the questions that came too late, or you were interrupted, the questions that went on yawing inside you.

After peeing, Sara emptied the water from the red plastic bucket into the lidless, rust-stained toilet tank, flushed the toilet, waste water trickling and gurgling away beneath the exterior wall and into the street. She refilled the bucket. The mirror above the sink was backed by a mess of peeling silver, her reflection impenetrable. A car backfiring made her jump. After wiping her wet hands on her jeans, she picked up her bag and returned to the room where Alazar and Yitbarek and Dassala, heads drawn close, spoke quietly to one another.

In the dark of her bedroom in Toronto, Sara was instantly alert at three a.m., which would be eleven in the morning in Addis Ababa. At five, she got up, the heat of the bed still on her, pulled her hair into an elastic, and stepped over her open suitcase. How quiet the room was after Addis, only the low throb of the highway that ran along the lakeshore audible through the closed window at this hour. Without switching on the light, the city night bright enough to see by, she retrieved her notepad from her carry-on bag, altered before leaving Addis to look like a diary, an old trick. And the tapes and rolls of film she'd stuffed into socks and also placed in her carry-on bag, separate from camera and tape recorder, another habit of years past. Just to be safe. And she was back and all was safe, and now she would have to see what happened next. By seven-thirty, wrapped in her blue wool coat, she was stepping out the back door of a streetcar at the corner of King and Spadina, where no children shouted or launched themselves at her and there was no odour of charcoal or diesel fumes, only the rattle of the streetcar clearing the intersection at her back, the zoom of a car trying to overtake it, wind blowing up from the lake, tapes and film and notepad in the bag slung over her shoulder.

At eight, Alan Marker, deputy foreign desk editor, appeared amid the pod of news editors' desks, his wide back shifting within the tight constraints of a mauve shirt, and after Sara approached and asked when Sheila Gottlieb, the foreign desk editor, would be in, Alan said, Sheila's out west this week. Why?

Then can we have a little chat in a meeting room?

Inside the windowless room, Alan took a seat on the far side of the conference table while Sara closed the door behind her. She'd made him curious. She'd spent the whole of the two flights back to Toronto pondering what she was going to do. For some reason she decided to stay on her feet.

I'm just back from Ethiopia and I want to pitch a story to you.

Ethiopia, Sara? I noticed you were away. What the hell were you doing there?

When she said she'd been on vacation, he looked at her askance. When she told him about the orphanage and what had happened there and that as far as she knew the perpetrator had not been apprehended, and the man who'd flushed him out was Canadian, so there was that angle, she had his whole attention. There may be a second suspect, she said.

You went to Ethiopia on holiday and somehow stumbled upon this?

Pretty much. Someone tipped me off. I got introduced to the whistleblower at a party in Addis.

Alan gave a little grunt, as if crediting her with a bullish avidity similar to his own. Blunt yet quick. He'd never reported from overseas but had a good eye, a keenness for what worked on the page. An editor. His coffee mug abandoned in front of him. Sara had worked for him previously, during the years when she'd reported directly to the foreign desk. Sounds like you're getting restless for your days in the field, Alan said. Are you?

Of course he was glad to hear that as far as she knew no one else was on the story. You've got enough we can talk feature-length? We'll discuss details in the story meeting. How soon do you think you can pull something together?

In this way it was decided. Back at her desk, Sara pulled the earphones that she used when transcribing tapes out of a drawer, procrastinated by going upstairs to the world's dreariest cafeteria to fetch an awful coffee, emailed David to say that she was back in town and let's talk soon, and set to work.

How disorienting it was to sit at her newsroom desk and, through her earphones, hear nothing but the insistent inflections of Gerard Loftus, the winnow of wind of that day half a world away and not quite a week ago, the chime of her coffee cup against saucer on the patio of the Addis Ababa Hilton, as she typed out his words, not all but most of them, those that would be of use to her, Gerard so present yet disembodied. A little after nine, she'd spoken to Nuala Johnson, her editor on the national desk, about taking this break from her immigration and multiculturalism work. At ten-thirty, after the story meeting, she returned to her desk and the list of phone calls and emails that she needed to make and to the taped sounds of Gerard's voice. A little before noon, after yanking the earphones from her ears, shrugging her shoulders and shaking out her wrists, she considered the small, nagging voice that said she really ought to get in touch with Juliet Levin. She'd sent Juliet one email from Addis letting her know that Raymond Renaud seemed to have taken off.

You're back, Juliet said at the other end of the phone line. And?

Having called Juliet from her desk, Sara wished she hadn't. To one side, when she checked over her shoulder, Paul Rosenberg had his own headphones on and was clattering away at his keyboard, and on the other side Nellie Wuetherick's chair was empty. No one would be listening to her.

Can I call you back in a minute?

Sure, Juliet said with a note of puzzlement.

At the far end of the meeting room, where she'd conversed with Alan first thing in the morning and gathered with others an hour or so before, Sara perched on one of two faux-leather armchairs and picked up the receiver from the phone on the low table and pressed the button that would give her an open line.

I'm going to be writing something, she told Juliet. Not about the circus. And explained about meeting Gerard and the orphanage and the former director and the boys, that it wasn't clear how many but boys. That Raymond seemed to have left Addis, not just gone on a trip, and Tamrat Asfaw had taken over running the circus, and Yitbarek was indeed paralyzed but making some progress in his recovery and his spirits seemed good. She hadn't been able to substantiate any of the runaways' accusations. Tamrat said Raymond denied them. Tamrat denied them. There had obviously been children in Raymond's home, living there, staying there, and, it seemed, disagreements between him and the teenagers, and who knew if there'd been some laxness in their supervision during training, but none of the children had spoken about inappropriate touch.

Maybe they don't know what it is, Juliet said.

That's possible. Have you heard anything from Raymond? I know it's unlikely but—

No, Juliet said. And I don't expect to ever again.

Or anyone else who has anything to do with the circus?

No. And I'm really not pursuing that project at the moment, I've kind of put the whole thing on a shelf.

To Sara, Juliet seemed oddly incurious. Was her lack of curiosity odd? Don't you want to know what happened?

I don't know if I want to know, Juliet said. And I've kind of been taken up by looking for work.

Mid-morning on Sara's last day in Addis Ababa, she and Alazar had followed the directions given to them by Yitbarek's aunt to the house of Gelila Melesse, the older girl contortionist who'd been one of those who fled the circus in Australia. In this house, too, there was a separate kitchen with a refrigerator in it, and electricity, and a curtain closed off a bedroom. It was a Saturday. Gelila's mother, in skirt and blouse, let them in and insisted on making them Nescafé. Glimpsed through a window, in a tiny stone-walled yard, a younger girl was bashing laundry in a bowl while wet sheets on a line battered themselves around her. There was no sign of a man, a father, no shoes or coat or photograph. On the wall in the small and tidy living room

hung photos of a teenaged boy in a school uniform and one of
a younger Gelila in a gymnast's leotard, another of her in the
sequined pink trousers and top of a circus costume, body curled
in her now familiar upturned spiral. By Addis standards, it was a
middle-class house. Gelila's mother worked in an office, Gelila's
brother, Yordanos, in an electronics shop. Her sister, Hermela,
still in school, brought the Nescafé into the living room.

They had spoken to her one time, Gelila's mother said,
sitting upright in an armchair. Gelila said they had to run away
because they were frightened of the man. She said he'd hurt
them but didn't say how. In Australia, they were living in one
place, but were moving to another, and they were safe and all
together and looked after one another. In school, Gelila had
done gymnastics, but when she saw the circus, it was all she
talked about and all she wanted and circus became her life and
it was all she did apart from school. He took them on trips. He
made them famous here and in other countries. They were in
newspapers and on TV. He told Gelila how talented she was.
He said she had a great gift. She thought Gelila loved it, the
travel, the fame, the circus, and she saw that Gelila was good
at it, and was grateful to the man and the circus for all these
changes in her daughter's life. The opportunities. How he gave
Gelila more opportunities. Gelila liked the fame, yes. Now she
was upset and did not know what to think. Gelila said she was
safe and not to worry, but she did not know if she would see
her daughter again.

They met the girl named Kidsit and her friend Lelise by the
same tree where they were to have met the boys from Yitbarek's
house only Birook and Moses and Asefa had not shown up and

none of the young men lounging near the tree had seen them. When he returned from a brief expedition to Yitbarek's house, Alazar said once more the gate was locked from the outside, and no one answered when he knocked on it. The tree stood in front of a church, and squares of cardboard were strewn around the base of the wall that enclosed the church, the air pungent, young men and other boys wandering about. Kidsit, spirited, twelve-ish, head full of braids, said, The tree is where Alem and Dawit lived when they weren't sleeping at Mr. Raymond's house. They are gone, now, yes. They ran away. They did not like him and they were angry because they wanted to be rich. They thought the circus would make them rich and this made Mr. Raymond angry. No, they did not live at his house all the time, like Moses and Yitbarek and Bereket. Mr. Raymond wanted them to, but they would not because it wasn't free. Free? Too strict, Alazar said that Kidsit said. The shriek of traffic from the street behind them. A babble of voices. He wished them to be all the time in school and doing homework and rehearsing. Sometimes Moses came to join them at the tree, and Kebede, who lived with his mother but his mother took his money and sometimes she beat him. Kebede also ran away. Did you want to run away? Did Mr. Raymond hurt you or make you frightened or touch you in a bad way? It was frustrating, relying on Alazar, who, Sara sensed, had only the roughest idea what she was asking and resisted what he did know. The day before, after their visit to Yitbarek's house, she had tried to explain to him why she was asking these questions, what the sexual abuse of children was. Alazar said, She wants to show us something but only at her house. Overtop of her racing pulse, Sara said, But first can you ask if any of the other boys or young men know a boy named Tedesse who came from the Hope Village orphanage in Awassa or a white man named Mr. Leo Reseltier? It was such a long shot, like tossing a pebble into a swirl of bodies, but she'd had to ask. A young man in dirty, baggy trousers named Mulugeta had come close and said he knew a Mr. Leo. He had been to Mr. Leo's house. In circumstances like this, it was hard to know what to believe, what people would say if they knew you had money and why, in turn, someone like Mulugeta would or should trust her. Oh, how her heart had thundered. Alazar, tell him I'll pay him to take us to Mr. Leo's house when we get back. Internally: Let him be here when we get back.

In a two-room house with magazine photos of blond movie stars glued to the walls and no electricity and no visible parents, Kidsit and Lelise, in their worn T-shirts and sweatpants, had solemnly folded themselves in tandem backward until their hands reached their ankles, lowered their chests to the foam sleeping mat beneath them, and opened their legs in unison above their heads in the splits. Now Tamrat teaches them. At first only the older ones can do this, Alazar told Sara, but now they can do it. And Sara had thought, That's it?

Her night flight to Heathrow left at ten that evening. At four, outside an unassuming gated house not far from the Italian embassy, she and Alazar and Mulugeta had talked to another watchman who said the English man, Leo Reseltier, was gone. He used to work for South Sudan Aid. Sometimes boys stayed at the house. Once the watchman saw a boy climb out a window. The boy looked frightened. The man went back to England. Mulugeta said, I touch him and he pay me five birr.

As Sara had frantically packed her bags in her hotel room, having paid for an extra night so that she could have the room through the evening, the black phone rang, and amid the static of her own adrenaline, Tamrat Asfaw yelled, Leave all the children alone. I try and make circus. It is not helping us what you do.

Had it been luck, or the appalling opposite of luck, or something uncanny that had found her seated, on the London flight, next to a smooth-ish, middle-aged English man who told her he'd taken a trip north to the churches at Lalibela but was planning to retire to Kenya, he liked the climate and the people and he'd decided to do a little good while he was at it and open a home for orphans. Sara hadn't been able to believe her ears. Every word he uttered made her suspicious of his motives. His very ingenuousness could be a front, yet he offered up a business card without hesitation, Rupert Bart of Topsham, Devon, and seemed disinclined to secrecy, and maybe ordinary people did things like this, dumbly altruistic yet not pedophiles. Her suspicion turned them into potential pedophiles. She took his card out of her wallet, laid it on her newsroom desk, and thought, Am I obliged to pass on his name to someone?

The transcribing of her tapes, the emails, the phone calls, the phone interviews. Alan, standing by her desk on Tuesday morning, said, Can you get me something by next Monday? That'll leave three days to edit. Doable? And Sara said, I'll try.

Gerard's voice, Richard Langley's, Fasika Azeze's, not to mention Kidsit's and Mulugeta's and that of the watchman outside the missing Leo Reseltier's house. She left a message with the secretary of Kim Guest, a man and the executive director of the Hope Village Foundation in Mount Laurel, New Jersey, assumed that Richard Langley would have told him about her visit to the Village. She tried Gerard Loftus at the Calgary number he'd given her, his family home she thought he'd said, and a man who might be Gerard's father told her that Gerard was in Vancouver and wasn't expected back until the end of the week.

By phone, Kim Guest confirmed that as soon as he'd been informed of the allegations of misconduct by Mark Templeton, he'd removed Templeton from his position. Yes, Templeton had already fled the Awassa Village. What could he have done to prevent that? No, he didn't know where Templeton was. Yes, the allegations had been passed on to the Ethiopian police. The address and phone number that he had for Mark Templeton were in the United States, but most of Templeton's work experience was overseas. For three years in the early 1990s, he'd directed a project for children in Eldoret, Kenya. Before that, he'd taught at a school in Kandy, Sri Lanka. Before that, he'd directed an orphanage outside of Negombo, also in Sri Lanka. Before that he'd taught in Kerala in southern India.

Her colleague Matt Johansen gave Sara the name of an RCMP contact, a windy talker, who worked in the sex crimes unit and specialized in international pedophile and child smuggling rings, who said yes, it would be extremely hard to track anyone down if they hadn't actually been charged with a crime, and no, there were no formal registries of sex offenders, and no, you couldn't be charged with a crime that had taken place overseas although there was certainly a push to create such registries and to make it possible to be charged for a sex crime that took place in another country. And, yes, the targeting of aid organizations was a growing problem, especially as awareness and oversight increased in the West; some pedophiles had even invented charities to gain access to children, since when it came to small, privately funded organizations that set themselves up in developing countries, it could be hard to monitor precisely what was going on. The man from the Canadian Humanitarian Relief Agency confirmed this. Yes, he was aware of the problem, yes, they were trying to increase monitoring in the NGO sector generally.

Wednesday night, David showed up at Sara's door bearing a bag of groceries and a bottle of wine, saying he'd cook, as he often did. She'd been working from home all day. Three days back and she was already exhausted, as she'd told David by phone. At the sound of his arrival—his ringing of the doorbell, the turning of the key she'd given him in the lock—she surged downstairs, determined not to slather him with her myopic and distracted energy.

Steak, which, when Sara pulled it from the bag, seemed a particularly bloody choice. And a Barolo, nice. David hung his coat on a hook and, in the kitchen, opened cupboards and drawers and pulled out wineglasses and knives and cutting board without asking where anything was. In his way, he was at home in her house, and had stopped making kind jokes about her Goodwill furnishings: the chest of drawers and the sofa that had actually come from a Goodwill, and, apart from her mother's crystal tumblers, her assemblage of mismatched plates and cups in lieu of a set of dishes. Sometimes they went to bed before dinner and sometimes after. The one thing Sara had done, after moving into the house, was buy a new bed. Usually they cooked together, though Sara took her orders from David, since her own approach to meals was decidedly more improvised. Two weeks apart, and in all ways she was ravenous. Touch, the ongoing wonder of it. His skin. The bed of his lips. And they had the whole house to themselves, no whisper of a presence from the basement, since Kumiko was out. No word as yet, David said in response to Sara's question about Greta's latest CT scan. But soon they hoped, and no one had given any sign that there was cause for alarm and no immediate follow-ups had been ordered and if this one was clear they'd go from three-month to six-month monitoring. Greta was back at work part-time, Sara knew, although David had said she still tired easily and had some short-term memory issues. He said she had started to go out by herself. And if this scan was clear, what might this mean for them, as in David and Sara? Across the kitchen table, she tried to read David, what his face and body revealed without words, or revealed without meaning to and here, too, was what she wanted to see obscuring what she ought to be seeing?

Are you allowing yourself to think ahead?

Not really, not yet, David said. After this, after we get these results, if all's well, I think everything will feel different then, given what happened the last time we got to this point. Everything seems to be going well. I can't remember if I felt exactly this way last time.

The last time Greta had reached her third three-month scan, after two all-clears, Sara had asked David an impetuous question. If all went well, could the two of them, she and he, go away together, overnight or for a weekend? It had been close to her miscarriage. She'd felt so many complexities of longing. I'll see if that's possible, David had said, and then came the grim word of the second tumour, which had again changed everything.

On many occasions, they had drifted together toward sleep, dozed entangled, before rousing themselves. They had never accommodated each other's bodies through the hours of a night and woken together in the morning. Yes, they'd spoken of it. Though not recently.

Then there's this. Sara pushed aside her plate, steak aswim in reddish juice, half-eaten, which she noted David noting, distraction circulating through her along with the wine, I have everything that went on at the orphanage. There's the confusion of the boys who recanted and the problem of the man getting away, partly or wholly thanks to Gerard Loftus, but what went on is relatively straightforward. And horrible, and traumatizing, but it's relatively clear what he did. There seems to be this other man, Gerard says he visited the orphanage, and so did Abiye. I don't know if he actually did anything at the orphanage, but he seems to have solicited boys for sex in Addis. I met a boy who attests to that. So I have a lot, really if you want to put it like that, I have plenty. Then there's the circus director. There are the existing allegations. But I couldn't find anything in Addis to substantiate them. The current circus director says he denies them. From what I can gather from the kids I spoke to, the ones making the allegations wanted more money than he paid them, and complained that he was strict. I'm so wary of repeating allegations like these that can be so destructive, that have the power to destroy someone's life.

He visited the orphanage.

Yes, but he was in the process of setting up circus programs in various places, not just there.

You said he knew the orphanage director, the known molester.

According to Gerard Loftus.

And the allegations are in the public record.

Yes, though I don't think they've been reported here.

Well. David took a sip of wine. And, once again, how calm he was. Why can't you say all of what you just said?

Thursday morning: Sara picked up the phone at work and the voice of Gerard Loftus, live, said, Hello, Sara. Gerard, it has to be early where you are. He said, Yes, he'd just got the message she'd called when he arrived back in Calgary the night before, at his parents' house, and he was extremely pleased she was doing this and did she have everything she needed because he would help in any way he could. He made it sound as if they were working on something together. Which was unsettling. And, because the phone number for Mark Templeton that Kim Guest had passed on was disconnected, she had to ask for Gerard's help. Can you think of any friends or colleagues of Templeton's who might have his number?

A little after noon, her RCMP contact, Dan Greco, called and said he'd run some searches with the names of the men she'd mentioned, and a Scotland Yard source had come up with this: a Leo Reseltier, of Maldon, Essex, had returned to the UK about a month previously from Ethiopia and filed a legal application to change his name.

The current director of the school in Kandy, Sri Lanka, where Mark Templeton had taught before coming to Africa, said Templeton had been asked to leave due to management problems, and she knew no other details. Management problems was an ambiguous phrase, Sara thought, which could hide other things.

Toward the end of the next afternoon, a friend of the friend of the friend of Mark Templeton, whose number Gerard had provided, passed on a phone number in Sweetwater, Florida, a town that, Sara discovered when she looked it up online, had once been a retirement community for circus dwarves. The voice of the man who answered the phone sounded more sleepy than wary, a hint of the nasal, but ordinary, even warm. When she asked if he was the Mark Templeton who had worked at an orphanage in Awassa, Ethiopia, he said yes before something seized him and he hung up with a crash. These discoveries leaped in her. She'd found him, he wouldn't speak but she'd located him: an electric shock that nevertheless registered distantly.

That night, listening to phone messages from the kitchen while she poured soup into a saucepan — her friend Soraya Green saying, Where are you, I haven't heard from you in weeks! — Sara cast her mind around the globe trying to land on wherever Raymond Renaud was. If she was going to mention the allegations against him, she wanted to give him the chance to respond. Which meant locating him. The night before, she'd started out of a dream, one whose content seemed blindingly self-evident. He was stepping out of her car, not her actual car but one that nevertheless was hers. When she looked again, he was gone, the world around her dim and enclosed and crepuscular. She went looking for him in a train station, down into the basement of the station, yet there was no sign of him; only his absence registered, like a shape in the place where he ought to be. She had no leads and so little time. Would he have stayed in Africa: it would be easy enough to disappear in Africa, head south or west or north, yet her hunch was he'd gone farther. Why? Somewhere he could get a job with relative ease. Yitbarek had said he'd said he needed to find work. Somewhere he'd been before, had contacts? Sri Lanka, unlikely. Which still left huge swaths of the wide world. Gerard said he had absolutely no idea where Raymond Renaud was and seemed affronted that she'd think he'd know anything. She did not want to scapegoat Raymond.

She pulled a spoon out of the cutlery drawer, and something—a mouse?—skittered in the wall behind the counter. Matt Johansen had told her a story of a man he knew, a teacher accused by a female high school student of sexual abuse. The man denied the accusation and had no prior record of misdemeanour, yet he'd lost his job, and his wife had left him. The girl accusing him was young and seemed vulnerable and why would she lie about so terrible a thing? The man lost access to his own children, Matt said, and was forced to move, and when, later, he won his case in court, the vindication hardly mattered for it was impossible for him to reconstruct his life.

Soup bowl in hand, Sara paced back and forth between kitchen table and stove. She did not want to be shielding herself from the truth, but for the moment something outweighed the reasons for mentioning the allegations against Raymond Renaud. A gnawing discomfort held her back.

Saturday, a week later: through the dark came the tock of a newspaper hitting the wood of the porch. A car engine throbbed its way in slow, accelerated bursts up the street, and half asleep, Sara imagined a dark-skinned man, Tamil, resident of one of the towers on Jameson Avenue down by the lake or, more likely, a house to the east in Scarborough or to the north in Brampton filled with recent arrivals like him, reaching into the back seat of an old sedan for another newspaper from the stacked piles and hurling it houseward through the open car window. Her own words rolled in an elastic band made their way out into the world. She curled in on herself, pushing the pillow under her head, wanting praise or reassurance, which was ridiculous. She was a professional: why this time did she want someone to call her up and tell her she'd done a good job?

The ringing of the telephone roused her. Full daylight, almost eleven, my God. By the time she made it down the hall and into her office, whoever was calling had hung up. And left no message. David? Usually left a message. She was woozy in the way that happens when you are yanked from deepest sleep, the collapsing of two weeks of late nights, writing, editing, the hashing out of the shape of the article's two parts with Alan Marker, and Sheila Gottlieb, back from a conference, and Paula Brown, the features editor. The house was cold, the temperature outside must have dropped overnight. As Sara stumbled down to the first floor, barefoot, having pulled on a sweater and jeans, the phone, phones, both the one in her office upstairs and the portable one on its stand in the front hall, rang again.

Oh you're there, said Gerard Loftus, loud. I was calling back to leave a message. I saw your piece. It takes up a lot of space. That's good. And it's good there are photographs. The photo of Abiye. And most of what you say is good. That you found Templeton and the thing about Reseltier. Amazing. This morning I thought, I'm glad of all the people I could have met, I met you. But I have a few issues. Like what you say about what happened when Templeton left the Village. If you think I should have told the boys to keep on going to his house until someone in New Jersey decided to do something or the police did something, think again. Oh, and it says there's a second part, so is that when you're going to mention Raymond Renaud, because there's nothing here so I'm checking.

How she wished she had never given him her home number. It was only nine in the morning where he was. Determined had been Ed Levoix's word for him, hadn't it? Or adamant. Outrage was not going to be the best response. If he could hear the sleep in her voice, he was not going to acknowledge it. The sun was bright in her eyes through the living-room window. In his eyes, she was nothing but his mouthpiece.

Gerard, Sara said, sinking into the sofa, losing her body heat, aware of the coiled paper out on the cold porch, the headline that she hadn't seen but could guess at, something to do with Abuse and Expats, the photo that she'd taken of Abiye looking angrier than she remembered, glowering in his striped shirt. I appreciate all your help and I understand all you have invested in this story, but it's not up to you what I say. She'd made a few more stabs at finding Raymond Renaud, had even called Sem Le in Sydney, but he knew nothing and so far she'd come up with nothing.

Because if you don't say anything, I'll have to let your editors know.

Let them know what?

We wouldn't want it looking like you're protecting him.

We, Gerard?

Well, I mean you.

Listen—outside, the reddening leaves on the Norway maple trembled like little souls and beneath the floorboards Kumiko sang as she vacuumed—you don't need to threaten me. I've decided to try to find Renaud before repeating the allegations against him. He should have the chance to respond to them.

You need to say there's a ring of them.

And how, she wondered, on her feet with the phone dead in her hand, had she managed to get herself in a position where Gerard Loftus had this kind of menacing power over her?

After the first surges of anger and self-justification, as Sara stepped out of the shower and wrenched a towel from the rack to wrap around her head, another thought came to her, What if Gerard found out that she had driven Raymond Renaud to Montreal? It seemed far-fetched to the point of paranoia to think that he would ever learn of it. She had told no one other than Juliet Levin and David. She had no idea to whom Raymond might have mentioned the trip, or her name. He might have said enough to someone that Gerard, learning of the journey, could figure out the truth. She barely knew Gerard Loftus or who he was or who he knew or what he was capable of. No, she had some sense what he was capable of. She wiped another towel across her face and wrapped it around her body, not frightened but unnerved. And if by some rare chance, Gerard did find out that she had driven Raymond to Montreal, she had no doubt that he would use the knowledge against her to dismantle what semblance of objectivity she had.

She didn't want to hurt the circus. The circus, as far as she could see, meant nothing to Gerard. There was all the joy and hope that seemed to have sprung from it, the good that seemed to have its own life. Surely there was good there. She wanted no hand in destroying it.

Do you have a partner, Gerard? She didn't think he had, perhaps he'd never had anything but fleeting sexual encounters. With men, with women? Why was she wondering about this now: she was trying to parse the source of his insistence. Was he thinking only of the boys, of helping the boys. There was an urge to punish in him. How had he been betrayed? Had he possibly been abused himself, and this was a hidden source of his fire. His father was a minister, she thought he'd said at one point. He was an outsider, with an outsider's needs and grievances.

She had the rest of the weekend to rework her copy. It had been edited, even copy-edited, but she could call Alan or Sheila and say she'd discovered something else. Such things happened all the time. Still wrapped in the towel, Sara dashed upstairs. By car, she could be at the office in less than half an hour. Monday's paper would not go to bed until Sunday night.

Tuesday morning by phone, Juliet said, I thought you should know, their Canadian tour's been cancelled. Remember the circus was supposed to come here in the spring, here and Montreal, and the US? I got a note from their presenter this morning saying they were told the embassy in Nairobi wouldn't issue them visas. The message from Foreign Affairs said they were worried about defections and they didn't necessarily believe the performers were coming here for the reasons stated in their applications. Maybe they read in your piece yesterday about what happened with the performers in Australia and that had something to do with the decision.

Just back from a story meeting, Sara had reached across the expanse of loose pages, faxes, empty packets of dissoluble vitamin C, balled-up tissues, pens, the copies of Saturday's and Monday's papers containing the two parts of her article, to grab the receiver from the ringing phone on her desk. There were reprint requests, Alan had announced at the meeting, from as far away as the UK and Australia, and because this had happened on his watch, he was going to take what credit he could, how pleased, even salaciously pleased he was. On one of the TV monitors overhead, American President Bill Clinton smiled and mouthed a truth or a lie, and the pixellated numbers on the clocks of the world on the far wall switched over from one minute to the next: 11:52 in Beijing became one step closer to midnight.

They don't want defectors, Sara said to Juliet, and swept some of the detritus on her desk into the wastebasket. It has to do with the fact that the performers fled and less to do with why. And it doesn't have to do with him. He wouldn't even be with the circus when it came here.

They've been tainted, Juliet said. By all of this. The whole circus has. It's so sad.

That's not necessarily his fault. You can't hang all that on him, or you can't do it yet.

Whatever, Juliet said. Really, it's your story now, not mine. You've taken it over, and I wish you luck with it.

She sounded cool but not cruel. At least she hadn't used the word *steal*, Sara thought, yet the word hung in the air. If you still want to make a film about the circus, I'm happy to give you access to any of my interviews, help with the research, help in any way I can.

She couldn't believe that she was making this offer: where did the urge come from other than a need to reconfirm Juliet's trust.

As once, long ago, as her trial had approached, then at the trial, she'd lived with the sense that she hadn't been canny enough or given enough forethought to the potential after-effects of some of the anecdotes she'd shared with Juliet during her first weeks in the Esplanade apartment. Nights they'd sat up late in Juliet's bedroom or at the kitchen table, drinking from a bottle of cheap red wine and she'd comforted Juliet in her pining after a student actor and raged about Graham and regaled Juliet with stories from her youth, like the time, during the months she'd spent hitchhiking through Europe two years after high school, when a trucker had fleeced her out of what cash she had as she was making her way south through France so that she'd had to beg a woman in a village pension to give her a free room for the weekend. Or stealing toilet paper from restaurants and sleeping on the beach with a boy at Narbonne Plage. Or about the dwarf trucker who'd ferried her into Spain, along with a girl whom he insisted was his sister, although his hand on the girl's thigh and the way they disappeared together into a tent at night made this unlikely, the girl looking no more than fifteen. How, while they'd slept, she'd eaten food they'd left in the truck cab: baguette, apples, a hunk of salami.

Thanks, Juliet said over the phone. I appreciate the offer, but it's unlikely I'll go back to the film.

Why not?

Because the whole thing's turned so morally icky and that's really not the kind of story I want to tell.

Juliet gone, Sara pulled Monday's paper toward her and opened the front section to World News, her eye roving again to what she'd written.

> Another visitor to the Village was Raymond Renaud, aged 42, the Canadian founder of Cirkus Mirak, a famous, world-travelling troupe of child acrobats

from Addis Ababa. According to Loftus, Renaud had plans to start up a circus program at the orphanage, as he had done in towns such as Jimma and Dire Dawa. Loftus claims Renaud previously met Templeton in Sri Lanka. Renaud himself is currently facing allegations of physical and sexual abuse from nine of his performers. They fled the circus last month in Australia, where they have filed an asylum claim. Renaud has withdrawn from his position with the circus pending an investigation. Circus spokesman, Tamrat Asfaw, says he denies the allegations. Children who remain with the circus in Ethiopia have not substantiated them.

She'd heard nothing from Gerard Loftus since his call on the Saturday morning. There'd been no peep from him when these words had appeared in print the day before. And her words were helping to spread news of the allegations far and wide, and now other journalists would be searching for Raymond too, for him and the other men to whom she'd linked his name, Templeton, Reseltier, journalists potentially more ruthless than she was. She'd emailed Ed Levoix to ask if he knew anyone in Addis who might be in touch with Raymond Renaud, and Ed had responded that other than the circus guy Tamrat and the children he had no idea. She'd sent out queries to schools in south India and Thailand that were hiring or had made recent hires since, that night in the car, Renaud had mentioned travelling to both these places. It was like reaching for a needle in the dark.

David's voice: Sara encountered his jubilation from the instant she picked up the phone; it sprang from the air around him, from his hello, as an email from a school in Kottayam, in Kerala, popped into her inbox. David said, We got the results this morning. All clear. I am breathing a sigh of relief like you cannot believe, I am whooping like a wild dog. I wanted to tell you as soon as I could. I know you've been wondering, and it makes such a difference, all your good care.

Dear Mrs, We are apologetic to be of no service in this matter.

Such good news, Sara said. *Your good care*. I'm so thrilled. For you and for Greta.

I won't be able to see you tomorrow night, David said, his voice tumbling on. Is that okay? I just can't. We may be going out. But next week. I do want to see you. I want you to know that too.

This was the song of his happiness, the swoop of him.

So not tomorrow but what about another night this week? It wasn't even that she wanted to see him exactly, as much as she wanted to know how he'd respond.

Sure, maybe. Let me see.

His wife was in remission. He hadn't been punished, none of them had been, the way she thought David had feared irrationally, with the appearance of the second tumour. She had never wanted to love a man the way her mother loved her father, with such fervid exclusivity, the refusal to be like her mother felt even more strongly after the end of her relationship with Graham, but this also seemed clear: she couldn't or wouldn't love David in an arrangement like this anymore.

I'll call you soon, David said. Did he sense some shift in her? Take good care of yourself.

Take good care. Could he not hear the desolation in her? While over her shoulder, in the dark of her car, Raymond Renaud shifted in his seat and said, My father had to choose between the Désir sisters.

Thursday morning, not long after ten, Monsieur le directeur of La Maison des Enfants de Beau Soleil, an orphanage in Jacmel on the outskirts of Port-au-Prince, having switched, at the sound of Sara's voice, from Creole to more neutral French, said, Monsieur Raymond Renaud, yes, we do have. And the straightforwardness with which this man offered up Raymond's name was stunning.

In French, Sara said, He's new. He hasn't been with you very long.

Yes, Dieufort Alexis said, since September.

Is it possible to speak to him? I'm calling from Canada.

But he's in the classroom. Classes have already commenced for the day.

Is it possible to ask him to come to the phone? It's very important I reach him as soon as possible.

Who I should say is calling?

Please just tell him it's a call from Canada.

Now she sensed the man's caution. Wait, please, he said.

A great fluidity took hold of her. Her free hand waved among the papers on her desk until it located her clip-on microphone, which she attached to the edge of the phone receiver. She pulled a new tape from her top drawer, checked that there were others, in case she needed them, and inserted the tape into her recorder, whose red power light glowed brightly, yes. To one side of her, the wheels of Paul's chair cackled on their piece of hard plastic matting as Paul cleared his throat and said something to someone that sounded like, There's a monster in all of us.

There would be no more privacy than this. No dark car, no hurtling alone together through the night. And if Sara had, instead, simply thanked the director of the House for Children of the Good Sun for that information, hung up, and begun a whirlwind of preparations to take her down to Haiti in order to waylay Raymond Renaud in person? It would have taken days, at least a couple of days, and there was the risk, if Raymond guessed someone had stumbled upon his whereabouts, that he might vanish again. She had a pad of paper and a pen in hand and a back-up pen. By now, presumably, the orphanage director had spoken to Raymond. He could choose not to come to the phone. Who would he imagine was calling him? He was walking toward her, tall, with the supple and muscular gait that she remembered, away from a room full of children along a corridor of painted cinder blocks latticed with petal-shaped holes through which came an uproar of horns and bright fists of light.

A mutter of voices, mesi, mesi, a murmur of footsteps, and then someone lifted the phone and his voice spoke into it, Oui, allo?

In English, Sara said, Raymond, it's Sara Wheeler from Toronto. Do you remember me —

How ridiculous to feel caught out as much as that she was

catching him out. She was doing him a favour, giving him a chance to speak, she had done everything she could to find him. She was cleaving his present from itself and violently realigning it with his past.

Yes, I remember you. She would have been a fool to expect friendliness from him. Thanks again for the lift. How did you get this number?

The lift, she thought, *the lift*? I spoke to a cousin of yours in Montreal. I was looking for your aunt.

My aunt? My aunt's dead.

Yes, I know that now. And that both his parents were also dead.

Which cousin. Oh, forget that, it doesn't matter. What do you want?

Okay then, she thought, I'll return bluntness with bluntness. And said, I want to talk to you about what happened with the circus, about the performers who fled in Australia.

Listen, I am sorry, but that is all over. That was another life. Okay? I understand you want to speak but no. No. This is my place now and these are my people and I have a class of children waiting for me.

Raymond. It was as if he had no idea of the precariousness of his position, at least as seen from where she was. To remind him of the fact that some months ago he had said if there was ever anything he could do for her seemed ludicrous because it was like a promise made before a bomb went off, and trying to retrieve a small thing plaintively across the wreckage of a bombsite. This is your chance—I'm giving you this chance to respond to the allegations. Maybe you want to take this opportunity—

Why? Okay, wait, what kind of call is this. Respond how? Are you saying these things have been reported on? There?

Yes. Yes, here.

You're reporting on them. Your calling me is part of your job.

It's not just a job. Please believe that, but yes.

He didn't swear but from the sucking in of his breath he might as well have done — to him what she was doing registered as betrayal. In his eyes, how could it not? How could she possibly defend herself?

I went looking for you in Addis Ababa.

When was this?

After I heard what happened in Australia, which I read about by chance online, in one of the Australian papers. That some of your performers fled, about the allegations. Three weeks, a little more than three weeks ago. You'd already left Addis.

I don't understand, you happened to be there.

No, I went to Addis. It seemed pointless to say to him, You invited me to Addis.

Why?

I wanted to see the circus.

After you heard about the allegations.

I wanted to see the circus, what Cirkus Mirak was. And speak to you.

What the circus is, because you will know then, it still very much is, despite what happened, despite that some people are trying to destroy it.

So what is your version of what happened?

And you will write all this up in an article for your newspaper, is that it?

With your permission. But you know if I don't, someone else will. I'm taping this, I need you to know that too.

Maybe if I call you back later?

No, Raymond, but if there's somewhere that's quieter—where are you, in the director's office? Do you have your own office?

Her heart beat fast at her own foolishness, because she'd given him an out, an opportunity to slip away. And she was an old hand at this. He could put down the phone, put her on hold, never return. Then again at every instant he had the choice to hang up on her.

A minute, please, he said, and he did put down the phone, and his footsteps tocked across a stretch of floor, and his voice spoke quite conversationally in Creole to someone, a woman who murmured something in reply, and Sara closed her eyes, as if that made it easier to take in everything she could of him, close herself off from the clocks and the bodies surrounding her, Alan Marker in a pink shirt, and then a door closed, and Raymond Renaud's footsteps came close again, and he picked up the phone.

Maybe I should not have taken them overseas. Maybe that was a mistake. They saw what life is like outside Ethiopia and they did not want to go back. For this, can I blame them? Others leave all the time. They started talking to people in the expat communities, Ethiopian expats, or these people spoke to them, when they came to our shows. I know this happened. And people in the communities started feeding them lines, maybe this didn't happen until Australia. Does he do this to you or this? Is he cruel? Does he beat you? They say, You will have to say this, and they ask, Does he touch you? and when they say,

Yes, because when I work with them, yes, I touch their bodies to show them how to do things, the expats say, These are the kinds of things you will have to say if you want to stay. They weren't thinking of me, they were thinking of themselves. I was in the way.

You're saying you think they made the allegations up in order to make an asylum claim.

Exactly.

These are pretty strong accusations — physical and sexual abuse, profound mistreatment. The words were like stones in her mouth.

Well, yes, they needed something strong to make a refugee claim. You would know this. It never occurred to me, never, never, they would do a thing like this. Say these things. It makes me sick. I thought we had a dream, we all shared it, we were all making it together, in a place it had never been done before.

Though it's a children's circus, and the ones who fled are teenagers, aren't they?

They could teach, help, we were building other circuses, you know? Yes, it's hard work, it takes commitment, a desire to think beyond yourself.

So you're saying you did not do what they accused you of.

No. I didn't.

What about Yitbarek —

What about him?

There were children, boys living in your house. And after the accident, from what he said, you were quite intimately involved in his care.

I can't believe you would imply anything about that. I cannot believe it. You went there and —

I'm not implying, I'm simply asking questions. I have to ask. You did not abuse Yitbarek?

No. No, this is sick. He has a terrible injury. I helped care for him. What would you have me do?

And the other boys?

They needed a home. You think they're better off in the street?

Raymond, I have to ask you one more question. There's a man, Mark Templeton, who ran an orphanage outside of Awassa, where I believe you went to set up a circus program, am I right? But you knew him from before, is that right, in Sri Lanka?

The sucking in of his breath, again, but this time a rising volatility, of anger or panic? The shriek of a chair's feet underneath him. You've been digging around. You're not trying to help me, are you? I don't even know what questions you asked Yitbarek. Of all of them.

I'm trying to give you a chance to speak. Do you, did you know this man —

We met, we met as travellers do.

Which is how? What was he doing there, when you met him?

What was he doing — travelling, teaching at a school.

And how did you meet?

In a restaurant, you know, fellow travellers, we noticed each other, we started talking, but that's it.

Where was that?

In Kodikanal, near the beach.

Did you travel together?

Briefly.

How did you re-encounter him in Ethiopia?

He got in touch with me about the circus. Out of the blue. I had no idea he was there. None.

You know what happened at the Hope Village—that he left, why he left?

I heard before I left Addis. You go to Addis to visit the circus and come back with all of this—

Someone told me what happened at the orphanage. I went—

I see exactly what you're trying to do. You think I don't see it, but I do. You who know what this is like. You tell me a story about being wrongly accused. Yes, I remember that. And I think, Okay, I will talk to you. I will trust you. I tell you my story, what has happened to me. And now. You're trying to trap me. I can't believe it.

Raymond, I'm not.

On a turbulent island a long way to the south, he dropped the receiver and was bolting or striding away from the phone, past the woman whose voice had murmured. Or he was standing aghast at a desk, the phone jammed in its receiver, as Sara leaped to her feet, bent forward, Paul Rosenberg glancing at her from his chair. She stopped the tape and pulled her earphones from her ears and stuffed tape recorder and cord and earphones and notepad into her knapsack and shoved her arms into her coat sleeves, the room catching at her throat. The desire to justify her actions was irresolvable. How and why should Raymond care what her motives were? From the middle of the room, Alan, too, had turned in her direction, as if some kind of silent clamour radiated from her, and as soon as he knew what she'd done, Alan would want her to write up her interview as fast as possible. It was a job. And had she not succeeded in doing exactly what she'd hoped to do. She grabbed her bag and took off.

At the multi-limbed intersection where King Street met Queen, Sara climbed out of a cab. Even before she'd stuffed her change into her coat pocket, the cab had vanished. The wind that caught against her face was raw and smelled of murky lake water, the lake just visible beneath churning clouds, beyond the dip of land where ribbons of railroad tracks and the roaring highway lay. It was only a little after eleven in the morning.

Halfway across the footbridge that arced over the highway and led to the lake, she stopped. It would be easy to take the tape of her interview out of her bag and drop it over the metal railing to be crushed by speeding cars below, or walk a little farther and fling it into the grey depths of the water and watch geese swim toward it as wavelets settled over it and it sank. She could pretend she'd never spoken to him. Yet what would be the point of that? She'd found him, which was what she'd wanted. He had denied the allegations. Wasn't this also what she'd hoped for?

What did a true denial sound like? If accused, you were speaking, always, into the wind of the possibility of not being believed, you had to try to convince your listener, and anything might sound defensive or overcompensatory or strident, you battered yourself against the wall of what you had *not* done but others claimed you had, and somehow you had to dissolve this wall or leap over it. She had read somewhere that when a liar retells an account, he or she will often use the same details, offer a version that is too coherent. But the stories of liars who convince themselves they are telling the truth might not be coherent at all.

Back at the intersection of Queen and King, another taxi did a U-turn in front of her, suspension jouncing. A woman with a brace on one leg came out of the Coffee Time and asked, Can you spare a dollar? A small child beneath a small sheet with eyeholes cut in it came toward her, clutching a woman's hand. It was Halloween, or was that tomorrow night?

Whatever she had hoped for in speaking to Raymond — certainty, clarity — she hadn't got it yet. But she would write out his denial. Make his explanations plain. Do this for him. It would not take her long to work up something, drop Sheila Gottlieb or Alan a note saying that she'd have the piece in by the end of the day. It was not her job to say whether she believed him, only to make room for his words.

A cutout of a witch loomed in the window of a bakery as Sara strode north. In giving voice to his denial, she would have to mention where he was, not name the orphanage, but the city, reveal enough of his location that it would no longer be possible for him to hide there. She would out him.

That night, she turned the porch and downstairs lights off, while costumed children roamed the streets begging for candy. Upstairs, in her study, whisky in one hand, Sara pressed play on her tape recorder and Raymond's voice filled the room once more, blunt, shocked, defensive, and her voice as it probed his, persistent and shocking in its own way. It did not take that long to play the tape; they'd talked for close to fifteen minutes, including the gap in the middle when Raymond had walked across the room, spoken to someone, closed a door, returned. From the middle of the room, Sara listened. For moments at a time, she believed him utterly. His version of events made sense. Touch misinterpreted, touch twisted. Their need to tell a story that would succeed as an asylum claim. His defensiveness and anger didn't necessarily spell guilt. That he'd be distraught, and particularly agitated when she began to question him about Mark Templeton, was more than understandable.

Memories of Port-au-Prince at night came back, as she'd glimpsed it from the vantage point of her hotel two years before: the yipping of feral dogs, the report of distant gunfire, orange tufts of firelight from the streets that spread below her, the holler of a speech on a watchman's radio.

The doorbell rang, and rang again, and a third time, though it was late enough that most children had gone home. Raymond's voice rose. I see exactly what you're trying to do. You who know what this is like. His pained calling upon the fellowship of the accused.

On the dark porch, visible through the glass in the front door, were teenagers, a boy with a painted-on black eye, a boy in a hat, a girl wearing a pink Afro, five in total, holding out pillowcases, and when Sara opened the door to them, they seemed almost surprised, raucous and drunk or just intoxicated by feeling invincible and being a bit threatening—as she had once been a teenager like them. One Halloween night, she and three other girls had snuck out of their Ottawa dorm room wrapped in bedsheets to run through the streets, toss eggs at doors and wrap toilet paper around car antennas. Candy-less, she reached for her wallet and gave them what money she had.

Hey, lady. Thanks, lady.

When Sara entered Sheila's windowless office on the news-room's periphery, the next Tuesday morning, Alan Marker was also there, seated in one of the two chairs positioned in front of Sheila's desk. Sheila had called her to come in as soon as she'd arrived at work. Alan heaved himself to his feet and Sheila looked up from her desk, over top of her reading glasses, beneath the sprung coils of her bleached blonde hair. There was something weathered and wild and perspicacious about Sheila, who had seen so much in the field, who either seemed about to leap or caught mid-leap. The sense of scrutiny from the two of them was intense. Nothing suggested this meeting was about more praise, or further reprints. Someone had decided to sue for libel, despite all the care they'd taken in the wording of her copy. Or Gerard. Of course. Gerard Loftus had come up with something.

Have a seat, Sheila said. Ex-smoker, jaw working, she held out a blister pack of gum, to which Sara, seating herself, shook her head while Alan closed the door.

If it's about the piece, Sara said, can we get right to it?

Sheila, who was never much given to pleasantries, asked, Have you had any further contact with Raymond Renaud, the circus director, since you interviewed him?

No.

Alan saw something come in over the wire this morning. AP, from Port-au-Prince. He was found dead in the room where he lived, gunshot wound, apparent suicide. Nothing about the circus, just that he was a Canadian.

Everything in the world contracted to this point.

Still on his feet, Alan said, The orphanage where he was teaching reported him missing.

When did this happen?

It doesn't say.

There was the commotion of Sheila saying, You must not take this on. And from Alan, Are you okay? As Sheila continued, I was going to ask if you would be able to write an obit, we want to run something, but on second thought, maybe Alan can do it, Alan, can you? Or I'll ask Anne and see about someone in Arts. But we'll need access to your files.

Can I go now?

Sheila sounded fierce, not strident. It's a shock. But you must not, must not feel responsible because this person has chosen to do this thing. For his own reasons, whatever they are. Alan, can you pick up the files? You're free to take the rest of the day off.

Sheila, who had reported in her time from the Middle East and Central America and had seen deaths, bodies, body parts, more death, was no sentimentalist. A paper clip shone on the floor beneath her desk. Alan's thick hands squeezed a pen. As Sara, too, had experienced deaths in the fields, near-deaths, body parts, run from bombs and mortar fire, cement dust clinging to her hair. This was different.

Back at her own desk, phone to her ear, she waited for an official at the Canadian embassy in Port-au-Prince to return to the line, her throat a rock, her desperation for more information overwhelming the urge to cry.

After what felt like nearly half an hour on hold, the man gave her a number for a police station where the French of the on-duty officer was extremely hard to understand.

Yes, in his room, a second police officer said at last. It is a very poor neighbourhood where he lived. The shot is in his head. A man in another room found the body. This is how it is written in the police report. There was identification by him, but he left no note. It is very clear from how he is found that he did it.

When, she asked, did the other man find him?

Thursday night.

Do you know or does anyone know when?

When what?

When did he kill himself?

Thursday sometime.

Paul from the desk next to hers materialized behind her shoulder and said, Alan told me what happened. Are you okay?

Her hands were in her lap, her hair not yet dry from her morning shower. Not now. But I'll be okay.

His cousins must know, including the polite young man she'd spoken to in Montreal. Someone would have to make plans for a funeral.

At La Maison des Enfants de Beau Soleil, Monsieur le directeur was not available, so Sara asked the secretary, in French, The man, the instructor, who died, who killed himself, I called and spoke to him by phone the other day, Thursday, do you know, did he go back to class or did he leave right away?

He left.

And did he have a gun all along or had he gone out then to find one, immediately after talking to her. Walked out the gates of the orphanage into a tumult of heat and trucks and people and a surging of wild dogs on a wide road where spools of barbed wire ran along the wall-tops, though all this barely registered given the state he was in. Perhaps in Addis Ababa, he'd first thought of suicide, and thought to outrun it. The children sat in their classroom or wandered away from their desks waiting for him to return, yet he did not. He bought a gun. It could not be so difficult in that place to buy a gun. Or he walked for hours first, through the heat and clamour, before deciding to buy a gun. Her voice in his head, for how, whatever else was churning through him, could he not have given some thought to their conversation and to what she was going to do. Did he eat or drink first? Did he lock the door of his room or leave it unlocked? He was alone in a room. His voice in his head. He was alone in a room with a gun. Did people startle at the sound of the shot, or in a place where gunshots were common, did it pass as the smallest disturbance and hours go by before his discoverer stumbled on him, his body on bed or floor, blood and brains on the sheets and running down the walls, the edges of the bloodstains already drying, the flies the first to find and feast on him.

And the shot to the head: had that been impulse or planned,

it was a thing men did, not heart but head, the choice to knock out consciousness first, the horror of fury and terror and shame colliding, a final detonation of annihilation and self-judgment.

She'd pushed him to that point. Had she pushed him?

The phone sat dumbly on her desk. She did not call David or want to call David and anyway he'd said he would be going to court: dropping his keys and wallet in the tray provided and sliding his briefcase along for the security guard to shove into the mouth of the X-ray machine and picking up his belongings on the far side.

Sara laid her head on her folded arms. She'd spoken to Raymond Renaud and now there was no more of him. Nowhere at all in the world.

Outside the sun shone and, in the parking lot, tucked between the sock factory and the newspaper's production wing, sparrows chirruped on an overhead wire, and a car turned into the lot through the open gate, an old brown Chevy driven by no one she recognized. On the far side of Wellington Street, a crocodile of small children tottered along, linked by a rope with knotted handholds to which they clung, tippy on their feet, led by a jaunty young woman in a pea jacket, who was cajoling them into song, Row, row, row your boat. Another, older woman brought up the rear.

Each loss was particular but pushed up against every other loss.

A car horn howled. To Sara's right, a taxi, green and orange, jerked to a stop, the driver's voice, even within the sealed tomb of his vehicle, audibly yelling at her, and the faces of the children and the women swerved in her direction, as a young woman in a red coat approached along the far sidewalk, leading a black pug on a leash. The trees ahead of her were almost leafless, branches leading to tinier branches, filigreed, dendritic, beautiful in their spindliness. Merrily, merrily, merrily, the children sang. At her back, the taxi lurched into motion. Life is but a dream. That she could have been hit barely registered.

Juliet Levin was the only person she wanted to talk to, although reaching out to Juliet felt risky. Once before, in a moment of crisis, she had turned to Juliet. Or Juliet had been there and held out sympathy. Juliet knew Raymond and knew enough of Sara's past to understand why the possibility that he was not guilty made the horror of what he'd done so much worse. The horror of what she'd done.

Inside a phone booth at the corner of Portland and Wellington, Sara scrambled through her wallet for change. Held a quarter poised, tried to compose herself. And if Juliet wasn't there. She dropped her coin in the slot and was met by the repellent field of a busy signal, Juliet or Max online or talking to someone else.

West and a block north, the wind tunnels of King and Bathurst pulled at her coat and entered the cloth and sucked at her body as she went on leaning toward Juliet Levin. The Friday before, she'd sent Juliet an email saying that she'd found Raymond teaching at an orphanage in Port-au-Prince and spoken to him and her brief interview was in that day's paper. And had heard nothing from her.

On the far side of Stanley Park, by the pedestrian crossing, the yellow rectangular sign above the crosswalk creaking in the wind, Sara pushed through the accordion door of another phone booth and felt its panels push back as the door closed itself behind her.

Juliet's hello sounded artificially bright: maybe this was her looking-for-work voice.

Juliet, Sara said. I've got some news about Raymond Renaud.

I saw your piece, Juliet said. Sorry, sorry, I meant to get in touch. How did he sound to you when you spoke to him? And how did you track him down anyway? In Haiti?

Upset. Distressed. Listen, I found out—

How upset?

I don't know. Julie, I got word at work, he killed himself.

The short, sharp exhalation of Juliet's breath—Oh—oh no—what happened, when? In a small playground, beyond the phone booth, red leaves flattened themselves against a children's slide.

He shot himself in the head. The day I spoke to him. Last Thursday. There was a wire report, giving his name. Maybe I shouldn't have tried so hard to find him. I spoke to him hours before he does this. I feel like I had a hand in his death. I can't help it. Like in a way I killed him.

Yes, Juliet said.

One afternoon, a little more than two weeks after Raymond Renaud's suicide, as Sara returned from the newsroom cafeteria, the blue glint of an airmail envelope in the inbox on her desk caught her eye. The envelope hadn't been there earlier. She picked it up. The American stamp seemed odd because most Americans didn't put letters to Canada in airmail envelopes. There was no return address on front or back, only her name and address written in scrawled block letters, the contents, as she ran the envelope between her fingers, thin but stiff. Seated at her desk, she contemplated waiting to open it. Then, with her index finger, she ripped open the envelope's seal and pulled out a folded sheet of paper, blank on both sides. Unfolded it to find a photograph.

Of a man surrounded by children, a man with the beginnings of an Afro, bearded, in shorts and a striped cotton T-shirt, who knelt, one knee to the ground, arms wide to embrace the darker children around him. Five boys, three girls. He was smiling, as the children were. It took her a long second, mind reconfiguring what she saw, before, through hair and beard, she recognized him. A cinder-block wall filled the background, leaves fronding to one side. The children's clothes had the incongruous theatricality of secondhand, repurposed clothing sent from the north: one girl clad in a puffy blue party dress, a boy in a multicoloured knitted sweater, another in a down vest. The sheen of sweat on the children's upturned faces suggested heat. The turquoise paint on the wall, a quality of light read as tropical. Port-au-Prince, the wall of an orphanage: Sara was guessing, since nothing was written on the photograph or the sheet of paper, and there was nothing else in the envelope. She pried it open to check. Who had sent the photograph? Raymond Renaud and more children: their happiness, his happiness reached out like a hand from a river to pull her under the current again.

The first night had been the worst. In the wake of Juliet's *Yes*, not comfort or sympathy but chasm, she'd kept walking west, west, and farther west rather than south toward the lake and the lake path as she might otherwise have done, since the lake path went right past the parking lot where the Cirque had raised its tent and where she'd met Raymond Renaud in July. West and north. For hours. Then south. Her sense of responsibility, her horror so tiny when set against his. Her grief. She tried to yank him back, to argue with him. Don't do it. Part of the horror was not knowing if he'd killed himself because he was guilty of what he'd been accused of, felt guilty of something, or because he wasn't guilty, the nature of his panic and shame and point of no return unknown. His voice raged at her: You are not trying to help me.

Years back, she'd been walking along a road near dusk outside the Polish town of Tarnow and come upon a Roma encampment. After the first stint in Lebanon and the Middle East, she'd made up her mind to go north, figuring that her ability to speak a bit of Russian and her glancing childhood familiarity with this part of the world might be useful; she had her contacts as a stringer; there was the first anniversary of Chernobyl, the persecution of the Roma, the Pope's trip home to Poland to write about. She'd rented a flat in Warsaw, returned to terrible toilet paper and began living off potatoes.

Outside Tarnow, through the lime-green leaves of late spring, she'd glimpsed battered cars, trailers, and two small dark men walking in the air between two trees. She looked again: two tightrope walkers on a wire. As she watched, silent and entranced, unseen she thought, one man turned a somersault on the wire and fell, oh the jolt of it, no, for he caught the wire in his hands and spun himself around and around the wire until able to pull himself upright. A woman's voice cried out. From another tree, a giant pine, a woman in a red leotard was hanging upside down from a rope as the rope rotated in tiny circles. At the sound of the woman's voice the men turned, and the woman called again, without moving from her upturned pose, and the men lowered themselves from the wire by their hands, jumped to the ground, hurried toward her, then began to twist the rope from which she hung in bigger and bigger spirals, until it became clear the woman's leotard was pinned, its cloth enfolded against the rope: she was stuck and they were endeavouring to free her. One of the men caught sight of Sara. Her gaze must have touched him, for he shouted, as if she'd glimpsed a secret, or her gaze was a violation, or by watching them she had somehow caused his fall and the woman's entrapment, and both men shook their fists and shouted in Romani, and one of the men began to run toward her as she took off.

The house was dark and quiet when she entered. If she had not found him and exposed him. Was it her linking of him to Mark Templeton that had proved his breaking point? Or that her words, her repeating of the allegations, would remain not just in print but online and searchable and inescapable? Or that he could not live with who and what he was? In the kitchen she poured herself a glass of whisky and climbed the stairs, whisky in hand, her body seizing up as she crossed the threshold of the bedroom. And what about Yitbarek—who would pay his rent now?

The next night, David came over. He'd called her at home late in the morning, said he'd seen the obit in the paper and tried her at work. How are you?

I couldn't stand the thought of the newsroom so I've been working from home.

I'll be over as soon as I can this evening. Any estrangement she'd been feeling was immediately overcome by these words.

As soon as Sara opened the door to him, David took her in his arms and there was so much strength and warmth in him, his embrace felt like a home. She leaned into him. In the kitchen, she laid her head against his shoulder as he pressed his hands to her back.

Did you sleep?

Not much.

You must not take this on. It's nothing you did.

It's easy for you to say that.

Did he contract a little at her tone, as if she wasn't going to be as straightforward to console as he'd hoped.

Breaking from him, Sara unhooked the string that held up the window blind and lowered the cloth on the darkness outside and the lights of other people's homes, and said, I keep wondering if others might have died because of things I've written. People have run risks to speak to me, I know that. The ex-general in Islamabad. This Kurdish woman, Khadija Berwani, who wanted to speak out even though her husband had been taken away and was probably being tortured. And even some of the fixers, our translators in Iraq. I've never heard that anyone died but that doesn't mean they haven't. I've spoken to people who were going to die. Not because of anything I did. From their injuries. People living with the threat of death. That's different. Not a suicide. I don't know of another suicide.

David, in shirt sleeves and stockinged feet, said, It's not necessarily because of anything you've done.

He must have seen the day's newspaper out on the porch, Sara realized, and chosen not to bring it in; she hadn't gone out all day, not even to retrieve the paper, had felt no urge to see the obituary that Anne Rauschenberg or someone else had written or be confronted with whatever photograph of Raymond Renaud accompanied it. She wondered how far word of his suicide had spread by now: to Australia, to Addis Ababa, to the circus children.

Okay, but at least admit I was in the vicinity. He did it hours after I spoke to him.

Unshowered, knees pulled to her chest, feet resting on the

vinyl of her kitchen chair, Sara watched David set on the counter a can of gourmet soup that he'd brought, since she'd said soup was all she could think of eating, and pour them each a shot of single malt.

Granted, David said. Have you tried to get in touch with the alleged victims since you heard about his death?

Tomorrow I'll try. I didn't want to be the one to tell them. And I couldn't seem to do much of anything today.

He nodded and his ordinariness, every ordinary gesture, felt so sad. The assumptions of ordinariness. The scent of the whisky, honey and peat, in the glass that David handed her smelled sad and assaultive. If things had gone another way, she might have been mothering their child by now. A toddler, here in this room, right now, across the table in a high chair. This felt unimaginable, and shocking in part because unimaginable, and this made her even sadder, and David in his true desires nearly as unknowable as Raymond Renaud was. A wreckage of sadness.

The table in front of her was a mess of week-old newspapers. Her father often looked at the Canadian papers at the embassy in Moscow: had he by chance read her Ethiopian dispatches? He was used to seeing her name in the paper, even if not reporting from Ethiopia. He might have read them and not have made the connection between the day's obituary, if he'd seen that, and the man she'd written about the week before. She'd had no word from her parents for weeks, for months, and felt too exhausted at the moment to think of phoning them to let them know what had happened. Why let them know? It was an old and ambiguous urge: to seek comfort without any conviction that the longed-for comfort will be found. Maybe she shouldn't feel so fundamentally shaken. And yet: a man's life. Nor had she heard anything further from Juliet Levin.

The Thursday night, two nights after she'd got word of Renaud's suicide, and she'd had to wait until late because of the time difference, Sara placed a call to the office of Sem Le, the Sydney legal agent. She hoped Sem Le and his clients had heard the news by now. It was a week since Raymond Renaud's death; surely they'd have heard somehow.

She had lived through the day as a series of returns: exactly a week ago, I called him; around ten-thirty he hung up; he left the school; at twelve-ten I arrived home; at twelve-forty I started listening to and transcribing our interview; at three-fifty I handed in my copy. Maybe he had shot himself by then, his body lying in that room. Or sometime after that he— She had stashed the cassette tape of her interview in the top drawer of her desk at home. So close at hand. The alarming temptation to listen to it again was cancelled out by her inability to bear the thought of doing so.

G'day, g'day, carolled Sem Le's bright-voiced receptionist. When Sara gave her name, the young woman put the call through immediately.

I've been meaning to ring you, Sem Le said, barrelling forward without pause. You found him. And then he kills himself. How did you manage to find him, by the way?

Luck. Tenacity. I remembered something about his family.

You found them in Haiti?

I spoke to someone in Montreal.

I read your articles. They were reprinted here. I assume you know that. So what happened — did he give any sign he would do this?

No. He was upset. At being found. And at my questions. Linking him to what happened at the orphanage. I don't know what more to say than that.

In Ethiopia, did you find out anything? He visited the orphanage. I presume you visited the circus. Did any of the children you met say anything about what he'd done to them?

No. I wrote what they told me. About your clients being unhappy and wanting more money. That the new circus director discredits the allegations.

Frustration rang from him, and she knew why: dead, Raymond Renaud was of no use, or was nearly useless to him in making an argument that his clients should be granted asylum. He could not argue that Raymond posed a threat if they were returned to Ethiopia. Alive and hidden he'd been not much of a threat but dead he was no threat at all, unless Sem Le could prove that he was part of a larger ring of pedophiles threatening vulnerable young people in Ethiopia, or Sem Le might argue that in speaking out about their abuse, the runaways had made themselves too vulnerable to return. In Sem Le's eyes, she'd had a hand in Renaud's death and in weakening his clients' case, and whether he'd admit to it or not, she presumed that he was furious about it.

Mr. Le, are your clients aware of Renaud's death?

I've told them.

And?

They're shocked. They wanted justice, but they did not want him dead. It is a very unfortunate turn of events.

And they haven't changed their story in any way.

Changed it? They have not. Why would they do that?

Mr. Le, I know I've asked this before, but I would dearly love to speak to one, to any of them. Even briefly.

Why?

To hear their account of what happened to them.

Are you planning to write more about all this?

Maybe. I don't know yet. In part that depends if—

They do not wish to tell their story to the press.

And if I don't write about it? How can I know until I speak to them? If I don't write, can I speak to them?

It was impossible to keep the pleading out of her voice, whisky carrying it forward, out of the dark room and across the world to a Sydney morning where a man whose body she imagined tilted back in his chair seemed intent on rebuffing her.

I do not see how it's in their best interest to speak to you.

The next morning, Friday, Sara tried calling Addis Ababa from work, wanting to hear how people there were taking the news. Elsa Larsen first because she also hoped to ask Elsa for help finding out what would happen to Yitbarek Abera and his aunt now that Raymond Renaud was no longer paying their rent. She couldn't reach Elsa. Elsa might be able to reach phoneless Alazar. In an email, she told Elsa that she'd be happy to pay Alazar for his aid in contacting Yitbarek. Nor could she get through to

Tamrat Asfaw, whom she tried a little hopelessly at the circus number, then by email. She had little hope that Tamrat would want to speak to her. Raymond's colleague, or colleague and friend. Ed Levoix was very cool, all bureaucrat, unwilling to allude in any way to his small but influential part in Renaud's fate by having introduced her to Gerard Loftus. Nor was he going to offer sympathy or acknowledge her feelings of responsibility, presumably because this would mean touching on his own. He said he'd heard the news from the Larsens. Word was going around. Everyone here is just so terribly, terribly saddened by the whole chain of events, and yet, I suppose, there's closure, if the worst sort of closure for some.

He must have known, Sara thought, that in introducing her to Gerard, things would not go well for Raymond. If Gerard was obvious in his desire to bring abuse to light and punish its perpetrators, Ed's intentions remained clouded — Make up your own mind, he'd shouted.

Have you heard from Gerard in the past couple of weeks? Sara asked. Or do you have any idea where he is now? He's apparently left Calgary.

No. No. We're not friends, Gerard and I. I don't want you to get any kind of idea we're in regular touch. Anyway, I've been upcountry and I'm going south in a couple of days.

She had been surprised to hear nothing from Gerard Loftus since Raymond's death, no crowing or gloating call, and so the day before she had called his Calgary number. He isn't here, his father had said. He won't get any message.

Can you tell me where he is? Or when he left?

Not if you're that woman journalist. Better he stay clear of the likes of you.

Has he gone back to Ethiopia, to Africa?

Did you hear what I said? He doesn't need to be messed up in this business.

On the Monday, which marked a week since word of Raymond Renaud's death had come over the wire, Sheila insisted on taking Sara to lunch, waiting until they'd exited the parking lot on foot before asking, How are you doing?

Fine, I'm fine. Actually, she needed two hundred more words to finish up a piece about two Sikh Canadians in Gambia who had set up a racketeering ring to take money from Gambians and stuff them into a shipping container with promises that they would be carried to Canada, only the plan had been intercepted, luckily before the Gambians had been sealed into their metal tomb. She'd been trying to finish the piece all morning; Nuala was waiting for it. Once that was filed, and edited, it would be time to move on to the piece about the Sikh community of Surrey, BC, where one group of worshippers had attacked another group with swords because the former wished to eat on chairs at tables at the gurdwara, and the others on mats on the floor. Sara had been calling around for someone to explain the conflict's religious intricacies to her. There was comfort in work's self-obliterating concentrations.

As they made their way through an alley between warehouses, their voices funnelled upward by the brick walls to either side, Sheila pressed, What about the other one, the former orphanage director, Templeton, any chance of following up on him? Obviously, to Sheila, the time for mourning and sympathetic restraint had passed and she could return to being what she really was: a hound on the crest of a hill, scenting.

I don't think he wants to speak.

Well, he may not want to speak. The question is whether you can get him to speak, the way you did with the first one. Or can you dig up something more about his past behaviour?

The first one, Sara thought, but said, I'm the multiculturalism and immigration reporter, aren't I? Pedophiles aren't my regular beat.

Sheila darted her a quick look. I thought you'd want to follow up. You broke the story.

I'm not sure I want to. Which drew another sharp glance from Sheila.

On the south side of King Street, down a set of stairs, they entered a wine bar and stood waiting for a table, the man behind them bringing a cold wind in with him, the hubbub of voices around them as thick as steak. The closure that Sara wanted was not the closure that Sheila wanted, if Sheila wanted closure at all, not being interested in the dead as much as the living.

Above all, Sara thought at the end of lunch, she needed to find a way to his accusers, to hear from them, for they seemed the best route to further knowledge if not truth. She told Sheila she had to run an errand before returning to work, and it was an errand of a sort as well as an escape from Sheila: ducking into a café on the far side of King Street for an espresso. Everything in her felt on edge. And another espresso would help? Anywhere we can get a good cup of coffee, Raymond Renaud had asked as they'd set out that July night. And she had laughed. And here, and now: the ghost of him.

A hole had opened in her, into which grief poured: work and more knowledge and a dark, syrupy stream of caffeine seemed the best way she could think to fill it.

In the past couple of weeks, she had made a few attempts to contact settlement and Ethiopian cultural organizations in Melbourne and Sydney without making any progress in reaching the runaways. Sem Le seemed a dead end. Maybe someone in a similar organization in Toronto had contacts in Melbourne, or Sydney, knew someone who was in contact with the teenagers.

There was also Rafael Nardi, freelance journalist based in Melbourne, who'd been part of the team Sara had travelled with on her second Iraq trip. He lived in Melbourne but freelanced for the Sydney paper. She'd sent him an email at the beginning of the fall when she'd first heard about the allegations. And not heard back. Which likely meant he was busy and on the road. She took the espresso in the paper cup that the café cashier handed her.

Would Rafael Nardi help? They'd been through a lot together. On the way into Najaf, they'd been stuck at an army roadblock until she, swathed in scarf and long black coat, and Raed, their fixer, had managed to talk their way through it, while Rafael and the American and Norwegian cameramen waited in the van. That night, Rafael had interposed himself between her and the crazed Norwegian who'd insisted on stripping naked to sleep, the four of them in the same hotel room in the previously bombed hotel, squashed like maggots head to toe on the same mattress, the only mattress available to them. The next day, as they were eating a meal in the small restaurant attached to the hotel, Rafael had leaped up and saved an Iraqi man from choking, which was the day before they were held up at gunpoint and almost killed.

Back in the newsroom, the espresso roiling through her, she began to type:

> Rafael, forgive me for getting in touch only when I need something. Do you remember the Ethiopian teenagers, the circus performers I wrote to you about a couple of months ago? They're in Melbourne now. I'm still trying to get hold of them. If you have any time or tips about how to locate them, let me know? I found the man their alleged abuser and after I spoke to him he killed himself, and I'm a bit of a mess about it.

Mark Templeton's phone number in Sweetwater, Florida, was disconnected, Sara discovered when she tried it. She did that much. Others would be on to him, and if someone else dug up something about him, so be it. It was the teenagers who held her attention, out there somewhere.

The photograph of Raymond Renaud lay on her desk. Once more she picked it up. Altered, hopeful, Raymond in his striped T-shirt smiled at her. Just because it had been mailed in America did not rule out its having originated in Haiti. Whoever had sent it could have lucked into someone returning to the United States and asked this person to drop it in the mail, knowing that this way it stood a better chance of reaching its destination dependably and sooner. The postmark from a week ago: in New York. Mailed a week after his death. Did whoever had put the envelope in the mail know that he was dead? Someone wanted her to see him smiling and transformed, wanted her to confront the possibility of his happiness.

Tant a minit, tant a minit, said the same woman who'd answered the first time that Sara had called the Maison des Enfants de Beau Soleil. In French, Sara asked to speak to Monsieur le directeur de l'orphelinat.

And he, Monsieur Dieufort Alexis, guarded and guttural, children's voices audible behind him, a baby wailing somewhere. In English: What is it you want?

Did you by any chance send me a photograph of Raymond Renaud, the man who was teaching for you and—

You say I what?

Someone sent me a photograph of Raymond Renaud, who was teaching for you. I called and spoke to you, then him a few weeks ago. Then he committed suicide. I called you after that to—

I don't know what to say to you. If this is a good thing that has happened, that you have done, or a terrible thing. I cannot know. For the children what happened is a small disaster. The police told me about this, what they say in Australia, and now I must ask the children questions, delicately, you know, but maybe we are and they are saved from a bigger disaster.

But you didn't send me a photograph. Addressed to me at the newspaper where I work. Mailed in the US.

No, I did not send a photograph to you.

Is there anyone who might have done? He's with children, outside, in front of a wall. I thought maybe it was taken at the orphanage.

Maybe it is one Frédeline, she is one of our instructrices, took? But you know, this photograph, it is the least of my worries.

Did you speak to him, that day, after he got off the phone with me? Or do you know anyone who did?

No, no, and maybe, you know, I know even less about what happened than you do.

Do you know people he was friendly with or people he might have confided in?

He was friendly. My first impression was, I liked him. He had good credentials. But he was here only one month. He joined us for dinner. Already he was working with us on a soccer program for orphans and street children. Now—

Did he juggle?

What?

Did you ever see him juggle—jonglait, ou c'est avec les enfants qu'il faisait ça?

Two women were conversing very close to him in French or Creole, closer than the swallowlike swoops of children's voices.

No, no.

Did he say anything to you about the circus?

He said it was time it is run by an Ethiopian. Thank you. There is someone here for me in the office.

She had suggested to David that they meet at a restaurant, as they had done more frequently in the past and hadn't for a while: her house felt overrun with Raymond Renaud's voice and presence and her internal disarray and actual disarray and her failure to do anything to tidy it. There were Polish and Indian restaurants not far off, places where they were unlikely to run into people they knew. Or people they both knew. They tried to avoid running into friends when out together yet had never pretended not to know each other. Why not Indian, David had said, by which he meant the restaurant where he'd once made the wild claim to the men at the next table that the two of them were Russian journalists or Canadian journalists living in Russia who happened to be in Toronto on vacation. I'll meet you there, okay? Even though they were both coming from downtown, their offices not far from each other, it had always been their habit to travel separately, or to arrive separately, David likely by car, in his old green Saab.

Knapsack on her back, Sara stepped through the rubber-lipped back doors of a streetcar and found herself moments later in the Sha-li-mar before David or any other diners. A man in a white jacket popped his head through the swinging door of the brightly lit kitchen and nodded at her. She could have stopped at home first and dropped off her bag. Everything ought to feel ordinary yet didn't. After ordering a Kingfisher beer, she pulled her knapsack onto her lap and the envelope from it and propped the photograph against the small vase in the middle of the table and stared at bearded, Afro-ed Raymond Renaud surrounded by children.

Asked point-blank who had sent the photo, she'd have said Raymond himself. It was possible to imagine him, even in extreme distress, cajoling a friend, an acquaintance, a relative, a blue-helmeted UN peacekeeper like those with whom she'd travelled through Port-au-Prince, or one of the clean-cut evangelical Christian Americans who were all over the place down there, to carry an envelope back to New York and drop it in the mail. As, in a different state of duress, he had convinced her to help him get to Montreal by embarking on a crazy, six-hour night drive. Had he known when he folded the photograph into the envelope and sealed it and wrote her address on the front what he was going to do next, his extremity seeping into the paper through his fingers. If she touched the envelope, she touched this. The letters of her name and address looked to be written at speed, pen lines trailing from letter to letter. She had never seen another sample of his handwriting. When they'd parted in Montreal, she had given him her business card, along with a hundred dollars in bills. Hadn't she? Or had she passed him a business card in the circus tent, when she'd been standing with him and Juliet? She couldn't remember. He'd sent the photograph to her because he wanted her to see something. There was a message here if only she knew how to read it. The new life that one way or another was about to be stripped from him. For her to feel guilty, feel haunted.

David walked past the restaurant window in his wool coat, hand held to his ear. Seated at a table halfway down the restaurant, facing the street, Sara caught sight of him: he was holding a cellphone to his ear and talking into it. She had never seen him with a cellphone; he'd never mentioned owning one. It was new and/or his life was full of secrets. By the time David entered the restaurant, he'd slipped the phone into his pocket. Or she had imagined it. Nothing about him looked different. He was coming toward her, beautiful and familiar, smiling and seemingly unencumbered, but something torqued in her longing for him, a new restlessness asserted itself. There was a deer in her and it was running. She rose to her feet and kissed the bright cold of his lips, touched her fingers to the reddened skin of his neck.

Were you just talking on a cellphone?

He looked surprised. Yes, he said. It's new. Greta wanted me to get one.

He didn't pull the phone out to show Sara but pried himself free of his coat and suit jacket and loosened his tie. A couple of people at the paper had recently got cellphones. That David had one wasn't so extraordinary: he was a lawyer and could certainly afford one. When the waiter appeared, David ordered a beer for himself and began talking about a case at work, something to do with a minute infringement of a patent on floor tiles. It's driving me crazy. You've no idea how many volumes have been written on it. I'm drowning in paperwork. Or the years it's taking to sort this out. It's like the floor-tile version of Jarndyce vs. Jarndyce in *Bleak House*.

Sara handed him the photo across the table. Do you recognize who this is?

She had an advantage. Two photographs of Raymond Renaud had appeared in the newspaper: these were probably the only images of him that David had seen. In the first, which had accompanied her interview, Raymond, clean-shaven, in his baseball cap, had been standing by the road, the circus sign with its painted upside-down figure of the boy atop the wooden pole in the background. In the second photo, which had run with his obituary, Raymond in profile, arms raised, appeared to be giving instructions to a pyramid of backbending circus girls.

David stared at the photograph respectfully.

It arrived for me at work today, Sara said. Sent in an airmail envelope from the US, no return address. And no note, nothing to say who sent it. It's Raymond Renaud, she said, after another moment.

Oh.

I presume it's taken in Port-au-Prince. At the orphanage where he was teaching. I called the orphanage director this afternoon to see if he knew anything about it but he said he didn't. He thought maybe it was taken by a woman who worked there. But he couldn't explain who sent it or why. I've been thinking maybe Renaud sent it, or gave it to someone else to send.

The waiter reappeared with David's beer and only then did they leaf through their menus and fix on some food, the brocaded walls and dimmed lights doing their best to offer an illusion of exotic comfort, the two of them as yet the only diners.

David peered at the photograph again. It's a pretty good disguise.

You see disguise? It was funny: Sara had registered that possibility without really admitting it to herself.

Yes, David said. Why, what do you see?

There are other reasons for people to change their appearance. As a sign of some transformation or new beginning.

Had he grown his hair into an Afro to accentuate his blackness? she wondered. He had chosen to return to the place where his mother's people came from.

When David passed back the photograph, his expression was difficult to read. Even if he sent it. Just say. To make you feel somehow like he's come back from the dead, or more responsible than you already do, don't—don't let yourself get too wrapped up in this. Okay? Get too obsessed. You were doing your job. Whoever sent it is trying to mess with you a little, and you're going to need to let it, let him go.

There was a loose thread in the raffia placemat in front of her. Sara returned the photograph to the cave of its envelope, the photograph of the smiling dead man. How relaxed David's posture was, a faint flush from the cold still visible in his cheeks, and the reddening of his neck, which sometimes happened, he'd told her, in response to the emotional complications of spending time with her. He'd admitted this but not voiced it as something that bothered him.

A pressure was building against her chest, like the weight of a palm. Sara said, There's a piece of all this I haven't told you. Something that makes it all particularly hard. I was once falsely accused of something, something so much smaller than this but. And then she unravelled the story of Colleen Bertucci and the wallet, watching David's face take in her words. As she spoke, the palm on her chest released itself.

You didn't plea? It went to trial? He listened with focused calm: lover and lawyer.

Yes.

How exactly did you get off?

There wasn't enough evidence to convict me.

David nodded. For so long she'd put off telling him this secret because she hadn't wanted to face his inevitable judgment. The risk of his doubt. Anyone to whom she told the story had at least fleetingly to wonder, imagine her as a thief, even if they immediately discarded this thought. Which David did so swiftly that Sara felt no inkling of it, only his belief, and trust.

What was it that Raymond Renaud had said in the car that July night, something about how when people believe a thing to be true it is very hard to convince them it isn't. It is very difficult to prove something in the negative: I did *not* do it. Had he spoken with the vehemence of someone who'd already had an experience of trying to counter another's claim, of not being believed?

Can you understand why it feels wrong to completely let go of the possibility of his innocence? Maybe he isn't guilty of what he's been accused of. Maybe he did something, and they have good reason to be upset with him and lash out. But maybe, by linking him directly to a pedophile, I've helped scapegoat an innocent man. I spent those hours in the car with him. I had no sense of him then as a raging sociopath. Or when I spoke to him. Full of himself, wanting things his way, self-absorbed but not—

It wasn't just her innocence that she wanted David to see or feel but something else that she wasn't sure she could articulate properly. Something about the complicated ways in which innocence could be lost. How, having been accused, you turned a false accusation upon yourself. Maybe you *had*

(290)

done something in order to be accused, even if you couldn't decipher what. The blame wasn't random. There was something about you. The legacy of imagining yourself as others, as your accusers, saw you became internalized. The shame of it. Some countered shame with anger. She had been angry. There was shame in having to defend yourself. And fear. What had happened once could happen again. Mistrust became global. The places you inhabited felt unforgivably tainted, as you grasped at the belief that you could outrun or cover up what had happened.

She had begun to trust again, to trust David, although trust only went so far with him because if she opened herself too much, he'd back off.

Don't go down that path, he said. It's dangerous.

What path, how dangerous?

I don't know any more than what I've read and what you've told me, but from here, he looks guilty. He runs, he goes to ground, changes his appearance, clearly doesn't want to be found — and he denies the allegations only when you press him to.

I didn't press. And I've thought about why he didn't speak before that. Or make a statement. He didn't want more negative attention to the circus. To risk doing more damage to it.

Listen, he goes right back to working with children in another place. When found, he kills himself. I'm not saying he is guilty, Sara, and granted, that kind of allegation is enough to destroy a person's life, and potentially enough to make someone want to kill himself. Yes. But. There are patterns of behaviour. I don't want you to get too knotted up in all this —

Was there something patronizing about David's words? Even dismissive? There was a strange taste in her mouth. Something was missing, some emotional connection, there was something here that David couldn't or wouldn't see. Because it felt too dangerous. Or she couldn't get him to see it. They had never argued. They had shared a beautiful fluency. They had been through so much together. But their mutual habits of self-protection, which had once seemed like a good thing, a way of being that bound them, were for her no longer enough.

I can't do this anymore. She'd had no idea she was going to say this until she did.

Do what?

Do this. Be with you like this.

David looked startled. It isn't possible otherwise, he said. You know that.

In the maelstrom of all that she didn't know, here was some-thing she did. She felt stuck, trapped in a cage. If he wanted her—he wanted her only like this. He would not leave his wife. He had no desire to change things.

Greta knows you still see me, doesn't she?

There are some things—

Do you love me?

Sara, please.

You don't love me or you won't tell me if you do. You must know I love you. Do you know what it's like to love someone who can't or won't love you back?

Both his face and his body contracted, turning inward and away. She'd raised her voice. He would hate that she was making a scene. The door to the kitchen squeaked somewhere beyond her back. Someone had said to her once that all desire begins in the desire to be witnessed. Did it?

David, do you really think we can go on and on like this? Coat pulled on, she tossed a couple of bills onto the table, which David pushed back at her.

Sara. Stop it.

In pain, she spoke the only words she could think to say to him, It's an impossible thing.

She came to a halt by the lake. By then a light, cold rain was falling. She had walked west in the dark to the park gates, the pair of old lamps glowing atop their pedestals, and, once through the gate, followed the path that led alongside the duck pond and traversed the lawns beyond, passed no one, and came out again, crossing first the Queensway, then beneath the expressway, then Lakeshore Boulevard, where the arched entranceway of the old bathing pavilion glowed white on her left and a thin strip of beach waited ahead through a drooping line of leafless willow trees. The water's edge, a line of white froth, curled at her feet. The water smelled fecund and dank. Ducks and geese were small blobs, darker against the tunnel grey of sky and water. Two swans upended themselves and waved about like drowning hands. There was no sign that David had tried to follow her. She did not think he would follow her. To leap from his car and run through the dark across the strip of beach and shout that he loved her, he would leave his wife for her. His mother had left him and part of him would always be leaving, but he would not leave his wife. No, he would speak to the waiter and pay for their food. Once in his car, would he weep? Maybe he would weep and allow himself to feel the loss, some loss of her. Maybe they would speak again, but she'd done something irrevocable and what had been between them was over.

Once, in their very early days, David had driven them west, past her neighbourhoood, to one of the old motels still clinging to the stretch of Lakeshore Boulevard that was becoming a thicket of condominium towers, the wink of their lights visible around the curve of the bay, and in a bleak motel room, lights on, she and David had pulled off their clothes and thrown themselves into sex that had felt combustible and thrilling, their bodies open even if so much else was held back, and at the time that had been enough and now it wasn't. He had not abandoned her or betrayed her exactly. Yet there was failure here. And loss. And grief. And in its wake, the shock of seeing things newly. This openness. And a need to keep moving, to move through something.

When it came to Raymond Renaud, she could not yet see more clearly. Was David right and she wasn't seeing something because she was too busy projecting herself onto Raymond? And therefore excusing him? Was sympathy thinking only the best of someone or imagining everything possible about them? Maybe more clarity would prove elusive, but she did not know that yet.

At the bottom of her street, wet but not soaked through, she passed her old white Toyota, the speckled gleam of it. There was no sign of David's car anywhere ahead of her, amid the row of parked cars. He wasn't on the porch. The house was lightless.

From inside the front door, the red light of her answering machine blinked on its stand at the other end of the hall. Two messages. The first: not David. Sara, it's Rafael, from Melbourne — cheerful and astonishing — they're here, your kids, the younger ones are boarding with a family, the older ones together in one rental unit. They can't work, but they're taking English lessons and spending a lot of time hanging out at a community storefront in Maribyrnong. I've met a woman who's teaching them, and I believe I saw two of the boys out juggling, busking on the river walk, yeah? But when I tried to approach them, they scampered off. I'll keep working on the teacher, her name's Alice, and see what else I can turn up.

The machine beeped, even as Sara was picking up the phone. He hadn't left his number. His business card was somewhere, probably upstairs, or his number scribbled on a scrap of paper. The second message: Sara? Are you there? I guess you're not. The bewilderment in her mother's voice: and the old mystery of her mother's closed-off fear, her mother's stern parents hovering somewhere behind it.

Upstairs, Sara swept her arm across the surface of her desk, searching for Rafael Nardi's card. The little rectangle found in the side drawer, on top of the audiotape of her interview with Raymond Renaud. The phone rang its Australian ring eight times before the line clicked to a machine: Rafael here, I'm not here. Leave a message, will you?

When she pressed the keyboard, the swirls of the screensaver were replaced by black-on-white text and in the top right corner a clock: nine-ish, and so a little after eleven in the morning in Melbourne. What did her mother want? She hadn't said.

Seated, head in her hands, bereft, she waited while the modem sang its dweedling song of connection, then pulled up her email account. Clicked to create a new message, entered Juliet Levin's address, Juliet whom she hadn't heard from since their broken-off conversation about Raymond Renaud's suicide.

> Juliet, I'm sorry the story of the circus didn't turn out as you hoped. I wish it had been otherwise. But if you're not continuing with your film, at least for the moment, can I borrow your tapes. I'll take good care of them, but I'd love to take another look as soon as possible. And could you pass on the email of your assistant Justin? Huge thanks. Sara

She heard nothing from Juliet for days, and began to think she wouldn't hear from her.

Once more Sara sat within the dark walls of an edit suite. And there he was: outside on a white wooden chair, in a pink T-shirt, beardless, cropped hair, a beige stuccoed wall behind him, as Juliet's close but invisible voice called out, Say anything, through a whooshing that must be the wind. Tell me what you had for breakfast.

A cedar branch quivered above Raymond's head. Through the sound like sheets flapping, he said, Oatmeal, coffee, juice.

Another male voice, presumably that of Justin, said, The sound's bad. Juliet's back appeared, huge, in a mauve sweater, jeans, boots, receding as she walked toward Raymond, and leaned over him, her hair falling across his face, her voice audible, through the crackles and pops of his microphone. She unclipped the mike and moved it from his chest to his T-shirt collar, an intimate gesture that looked intimate, the two of them whispering. How's that? Juliet asked. Raymond's hand brushed hers as he responded, Okay. Juliet turned, pink-cheeked, and Raymond began calling out numbers, five, four, three, two, the air still whinnying until Justin's voice broke in, That's not going to work. The tape cut out.

When Raymond reappeared, in the same shirt, same chair, microphone pinned again at his chest, he was seated, as Sara remembered from when Juliet had first shown her the selections from her tapes, in front of the blue wall of his garden, the gaudy orange beak of a bird of paradise flower swaying behind him. And, like that first time, she was struck by his air of hopeful and generous engagement. She'd been thinking a lot about innocence. How it was a state that could only be perceived by someone able to conceive of its opposite. To proclaim your own innocence was to be capable of imagining that you might not be innocent. A true innocent would have no awareness of this. She searched his face and body for signs of strain. Or evasion. Hints that he was dissembling. Projecting a mask. Could staring bring revelation—a glimpse of what lay beyond words? What was felt? She stopped him with the little joystick in her right hand, his mouth half open, eyes narrowed, then set him in motion again. He turned his head full-on to the camera. She felt—Exactly what kind of intimacy had he shared with Juliet?

Can you tell me how you came to Addis Ababa? Juliet called to him.

At the end of the interview the camera was switched off. Then someone turned it back on. Raymond still sat in his chair, miked, but his posture had relaxed, and he settled forward, resting his clasped hands and forearms on his thighs. So when you come back, he was saying, You have to go. There's no one else I can tell this to who will understand how weird it was. I drove up to Lalibela, this was two years ago. Most of the tourists, they fly. It's easier. Driving takes three days. You go by the Chinese highway and then you go into the mountains, and the roads, well, they are a bit wicked. I had the truck. I was giving lifts to people all along the way. Sometimes—he moved, and the mike crackled and Sara lost some of his words—switchbacks. You feel like you are heading for the roof of the world. But the churches. I think it is thirteen in total, all carved, not built but carved out of the rock, okay? You've seen photographs, haven't you? It is so medieval. There are hermits living in holes in the walls of the courtyards, on beds of straw. I love it. I find this tourist shop. Really it's a shack. And I'm looking at these little wooden diptychs and triptychs of religious scenes—crackle—the Larsens—they like that kind of thing. There's a book I notice on a shelf, surrounded by other objects. It has a paper wrapper, and I pick it up because that's odd. To find a book. And then the wrapper, it's a page from a German-to-English language lesson. Someone has taped it over the actual cover. I open the book. Guess what it was?

There was a teasing liveliness in him as he spoke that Sara had never observed before. It was different than what he projected in public, when his manner was more performative, and he seemed to have a need to be in control, and when she had spent time with him, those dark and delirious hours, even when things had relaxed between them, there had inevitably remained in him an undercurrent of turmoil and fear and exhaustion. Was this lightness something that Juliet elicited from him? A sign of intimacy, an aspect of their intimacy?

Unseen Juliet said, How can I possibly guess?

Juliet was frightened of disappointing him and, indeed, a flicker of disappointment crossed his face. His shifting face and body were the screen upon which their entire conversation registered. He said, Astonishing novel. By a writer from Montreal.

Something by Mordecai Richler?

No. Again, the flare of disappointment, matched by new anticipation. Okay. *Beautiful Loser* by Leonard Cohen.

Oh, Juliet said. Right. You mean *Beautiful Losers*.

Raymond twitched toward impatience. Have you read it, do you not know it?

No. Juliet's voice sounded small and humiliated.

Ah, so all this is lost on you. This is like explaining a joke.

Can you tell me, please?

Now he turned performative. Whatever that earlier quality was, it vanished. He hadn't slept with Juliet. It is a very sexually explicit book, it is a bit wild, so you know discovering it there was just so, so, like a little bomb going off. How did it get there? Someone must have left it. What were they thinking?

What did you do?

How do you mean?

Did you buy it, take it?

I don't even know if it was for sale. No, no, I left it, for someone else to discover and have their own shock.

．．

Juliet had left the tapes in a box on Sara's porch. One evening near the end of November, Sara arrived home from work to find the box pushed against the wall beneath her mailbox. There was no delivery slip with it, only her name and address written on the top, and a return address on Havelock Street. If Juliet had delivered the box in person, she had done so at an hour when Sara was unlikely to be home. When Sara lifted the box, which was not heavy, its contents rattled, the giveaway shifting of the plastic cases of videocassettes. Seated on the sofa with the box on her lap, she ripped off the tape that sealed the top and lifted the cardboard flaps to find a row of mini Hi8 tapes, clasped in their hard grey covers like miniature books, tapes that, she realized, she wouldn't be able to watch on her home videocassette player. She would have to find professional equipment on which to do so. Along one side of the box's interior, Juliet had stuffed a regular-sized VHS cassette, and some file folders, which, when opened, revealed the shot lists from her original tapes, time codes, and next to them descriptions of what the tape contained at that instant: 5:11:05: girls getting into pose, photo shoot; 5:12:33: another pyramid, reverse angle, Raymond watching. A separate folder held the shot list of her abandoned film. There was no accompanying note of any sort. Nor had she included Justin's email.

A TV journalist friend, Carol Frank, said, Sure, you can use the equipment here, what do you need, like a couple of hours?

Longer than that. Maybe I'll rent somewhere. There's a lot of footage.

Yours?

No, someone else's.

She was in a room nearly identical to the one in which she and Juliet had sat together at the beginning of the fall, when the days were still long and heat had pressed itself against the walls outside, not in the video post-production facility where Juliet had rented space but in another smaller facility in a smaller warehouse farther west. Her coat hung on a hook on the back of a door and she had arrived in the dark, after work, and would leave, hours later, in the dark, disappearing into the cascade of images in between these times. Leaning back in her chair, Sara stretched out her arms. Was she editing something? Not a film, but editing thought. From the very first jerky shots trained down a hillside toward a wide dirt playing field where men in hats raised a blue canvas scaffold to upright, and one of the men, in a red baseball cap, turned to peer up the hill, she was following Juliet through her trip.

The hungry mouth of the tape player swallowed another small cassette: on the monitor, the interior of the rehearsal hall of painted cinder blocks appeared, and eager children in dirty clothes, who kept looking at the camera, wiggled and hopped in the line they'd been made to form by Gelila Melesse and Kebede Gebremariam and two other older performers. Gelila and Kebede divided the street children into groups, sending boys to one side of the room and girls to the other. Gelila and her partner led the girls in a series of backbends on the blue mats, Gelila shouting to be heard, while beyond the row of cinder-block pillars, Kebede demonstrated how to toss and catch two juggling pins, then three, and the street boys tossed their pins in the air and tried to catch them and sometimes did and at other times pins fell to the floor and rolled or bounced. One boy skittered madly about the room on a unicycle, gleeful arms waving, and two more boys tottered about on stilts. The noise of the room was cacophonous. Raymond was nowhere in sight.

A new shot, still in the rehearsal hall. In a corner of the hall, half-turned from the camera, Raymond wound black electrical cord around one arm, voice raised, directing some of the boys to help him. He wasn't miked. His words weren't clear, only the short bursts of his directions. Something didn't seem to be understood. He appeared to be speaking a mixture of English and Amharic. He set down his looped coils, knelt, pulled out more length of cord. He sounded stern, at instants even sharp with the boys.

He was in the doorway of the hall, in T-shirt and ball cap, gesturing, ordering Kebede and another boy, was it Dawit, to carry some clangy metal poles outside.

Gelila and Kebede stood outdoors against a yellow wall, clad in the T-shirt and tights, T-shirt and trackpants that they had been wearing in the previous sequences. A hard pulse beat at Kebede's chest.

Do you want to stay in the circus? asked Juliet's off-screen voice.

Yes, Gelila said in English with a great, wide smile, her headful of tiny braids quivering. Oh, yes. I wish to stay with circus always.

And Kebede nodded, his gaze veering off and returning.

What will you do when you get too old, if it's a children's circus?

Maybe, Kebede said. We make two circus. One small, one big.

You mean, one circus for children, one for—not children? Have you talked to Raymond about that?

He say we teach, Gelila said. I be secretary to circus.

I teach, Kebede said, nodding vigorously. The faint line of his moustache hovered along his upper lip.

Rewound, in motion again: Do you want to stay in the circus?

Yes, Gelila said. Oh, yes.

In the next shot, Raymond approached across the bumpy ground, pine trees behind him, children leaping around him and hurrying to keep up with him, bodies close to his, girls, was that Kidsit?, and others whom Sara had begun to recognize, Segaye in his floppy running shoes who had delivered her handwritten message to Tamrat. Joy sprang from their feet and swinging arms, an ease with him, and he with them, or something that looked like joy. Behind them, as they approached the door of the rehearsal hall, Kebede and Gelila stood against the wall, Kebede's mouth whispering in Gelila's ear.

Kebede and Dawit dragged rolls of coloured canvas out through the door that Segaye held open while, off to one side, Raymond crouched and listened as Yitbarek and another younger boy chattered to him.

In his nylon tracksuit, Kebede walked through a door in a wall that led into a cramped yard. A reverse-angle shot revealed a small house, mud-walled, at the far end of the yard, with two glassless windows to either side of its open door, through which an older woman stepped, clad in white, sandals on her feet, a white veil over her head, dressed no doubt in her finest, self-consciously opening her arms. Kebede stood stiff within her embrace, her arm around his shoulder. Her speech unfurled in quick Amharic, and when she broke off, an off-camera male voice, Ethiopian, speaking accented English, said, The circus is good because it helps him get a better job and then his mother has a pension.

Outside the community hall once more, Kebede and Gelila and one of the other older girls pulled close to one another in whispered conversation, glimpsed as if at the end of a long corridor, in silhouette, sunlight beyond them, recognizable by the shake of their braids, the line and curves of their changing bodies, by hips and breasts and muscled arms and legs, oblivious, it seemed, to being filmed, and probably Juliet had held the shot because of the beauty of form and light and gesture, the shadow play of it. Until they noticed Juliet, or whoever was filming, and the whispering—again the whispering—broke off.

The ringing of the phone woke Sara, pushed her up through crowds of children, acrobats, streets filled with bodies, and the absent man whom she was searching for, it was the phone, and daylight, brighter than it should have been, a golden brightness, lit the room, the bedside clock turned to face the wall. When had she done that? And what of her alarm? Alan Marker's voice poured out of the answering machine and up the stairs, Sara, are you there? Where are you? Did you hear about the plane hijacking?

She threw on a robe, though he'd hung up before she reached the phone in her study, the shadows of all those bodies clinging to her.

She phoned Alan back, the sky outside so rivetingly blue it was making her blink, and the time: holding the phone to her ear, the bare wood floor shooting cold up through her feet, she woke the computer and checked, closing in on ten. Alan? What plane?

Word came in almost an hour ago, Alan said. Why aren't you at work? Are you sick?

I slept through my alarm. Downstairs, breathless, in the living room, she switched on the television, which sprang to life with a staticky hum, found an on-the-hour newscast, the blue of a TV newsroom, the urgent anchor's voice overridden by Alan's louder voice in her ear. An Ethiopian airliner went down off the Comoros Islands. It looks like the hijackers, three young men, wanted the pilot to fly to Australia. 175 on board. Apparently a few survivors but looks to be the deadliest airline hijacking ever.

Why Australia? Sara sank down on the sofa and muted the television's sound, everything making her feel as if she must still be asleep, yet dry-mouthed and achy, and thus possibly hungover. And dizzy, the world too full of connectivity: her hands, her dreams, her feet, the brush of bodies. As if all young, desperate Ethiopians longed for a new life in Australia.

I don't know why. They wanted political asylum? All I know is the pilot told them there wasn't enough fuel to get there and they insisted so the plane went down and it's a miracle anyone survived.

Behind the coiffed and made-up male news anchor appeared a still photograph of a jetliner, then a map with a red dotted trail that led down the African coast before swooping out into the Indian Ocean.

Alan, do you need me? I'll be in soon.

We're trying to find out who was on board, Canadians, et cetera. You know people in Addis. Can you call them and get back to me?

The longing to contact David was strong and instinctive and no longer possible to fulfill. It was what they'd done for so long, reached out to each other at moments like this: Did you hear, have you heard? A pang. But that time was over.

From the kitchen, wet hair wrapped in a towel, Sara carried a mug of black coffee and a piece of toast clutched between her teeth back to the living room. There were others whom she could call: Matt from work, Soraya, to whom she had confided over the years about David's presence in her life and now his absence although she had never told Soraya his name. On the cable all-news channel, a woman behind a sprawling newsroom desk was saying, The hijackers were little more than teenagers. There was fighting in the cockpit when they noticed the plane hadn't left the coastline of Africa. The pilot turned out over the ocean and headed for the Comoros Islands and managed to bring the plane down in shallow water not far from a tourist beach. We have Amélie Brousson, a French tourist, on the line from Grand Comoros Island. Can you tell us what you saw, Amélie?

A crackly, disembodied voice said, First we thought it was an air show for us. People were playing in the water and windsurfing. Then the crash, it was terrible. People screamed and ran. They took all the boats, motorboats, fishing boats, rowboats, the catamaran, and went to look for survivors.

Had Gelila or Kebede or Senayit or any of the other former circus performers in Melbourne, Australia, heard about this? The coincidence of it. And the hijackers, were they madmen or just desperate, or mad and desperate, intent on transforming the world as they knew it and taking others, innocents, down with them.

On the first three tries, the Larsens' line in Addis Ababa rang busy. On Sara's fourth attempt, Elsa Larsen picked up. It's awful. It's so awful. Mariam Hailemariam, you remember her from that night? We were celebrating her new job. She has two young children. And a husband. She was so eager to be going to Nairobi. Peter worked with her for years. She was going to meet her new Kenyan colleagues. It could have been any of us. We've all been on that flight, the milk run. It hops across the continent. I can't talk long.

Anyone else you knew?

Peter also said maybe someone else, this doctor, Trevor First, he's Canadian, he works for a small NGO in the south. A photographer from here. We don't know for sure who's among the dead.

(307)

The coincidence, the randomness. Two months ago, Mariam Hailemariam, a robust woman in a flowered dress, had stood laughing in the Larsens' living room. She'd stepped onto a plane to go to a meeting and hours later found herself plunging out of the sky.

Elsa, I won't keep you, but can I ask one more thing? About the paralyzed boy —

They've left that house now and moved in with another family. Alazar looked into it. I've got the contact information somewhere. And the circus is planning a benefit.

If I want to get some money to him, wire some money, can you help?

Yes, but not now.

Any word from Gerard, any sign he's come back through Addis?

Nothing. If I hear, I'll let you know. But I need to go, someone else could be trying to get through.

By the time Sara made it in to work, Alan had confirmed that the doctor, Trevor First, had been on the plane and was thought to be among the dead, and Paul turned in his chair as soon as she appeared at the end of their little aisle, and said, The pilot survived two other hijackings, can you believe it? Rumours about the hijackers swirled: they were religious fundamentalists, political extremists, they'd had a bomb on board, they'd escaped from an insane asylum. Whatever humanity they'd once possessed was lost; so many visions of evil adhered to them.

Amid this, there were immigration stories to attend to: that of the young Chinese-Canadian singer recently murdered with a crossbow in Vancouver in retaliation for her lawyer father's tampering, back in Hong Kong, with the immigration applications of several prominent businessmen desperate to get out in the last months before Hong Kong was turned over to the Chinese.

Beneath the cover of the immigration story and the hullabaloo about the hijacking, Sara sent a message to the Yellowknife District Education Authority, grateful for the embracing silence of email. Had a man named Raymond Renaud taught in any school there sometime in the 1980s? She thought he'd said something about this in her car. He had definitely mentioned Yellowknife in the interview that Juliet had done. He'd left Montreal, worked for a few years somewhere on the West Coast, then gone north. At home, she was building a file on him: the transcript of her interview, the photograph, Juliet's transcribed interviews and shot lists, the notes that she was making as she watched Juliet's tapes. Her back ached. She sent a nudge of an email to Rafael Nardi: had he made any progress getting closer to the Ethiopian asylum seekers?

The next morning, an emailed message was waiting for her from Melanie Purchase of the Yellowknife District Education Authority: Raymond Renaud had taught grade seven for a year and a half at Sir Alexander Mackenzie Middle School in Yellowknife in the 1986–87 and 1987–88 school years. A year and a half was odd, and suggested that he'd left in the middle of the year, but the note offered no further explanation. Sara tried calling both the Education Authority and the school. Elsa Larsen's email confirmed both Trevor First and Mariam Hailemariam among the dead. Paul Rosenberg peered around their divider and said, Did you hear a tourist shot some footage of that plane going down?

By the next day the footage was all over the newsroom TV screens: the silver cylinder of an airliner flying low across a line of water, one wing tilling the surface, spewing a wake, as the fuselage tilted and skimmed before erupting in a burst of steam and metal and flame. Blue sky above, the calm and blurry blue of ocean below. Debris bobbed amid the undulations.

Sara placed another call to the principal of Sir Alexander Mackenzie Middle School and this time got put through.

Is there an explanation for his teaching only a year and a half?

Our records show he left at the end of February on medical leave, Carol Lafontaine said. But a complaint was also filed. He drove two boys home from school, which is illegal.

Is there anything else? Were you at the school then?

That was before my time. That's all the information I can give you.

But that's what the record says.

Yes.

Nothing more than that he drove them home.

Yes. He should have known not to do that.

On one occasion?

The complaint originates from one occasion.

Were there any extenuating circumstances? Like it was in a blizzard or extremely cold?

The file doesn't say.

Who lodged the complaint, the parents?

I can't tell you more than what I've told you.

He had driven two boys home from school, at least once,

and someone had filed a complaint. Why? Simply because he'd driven the boys home and broken the rules? Someone hadn't liked that he shrugged his shoulders at authority, wanted to take down his sense of entitlement, or was the visible objection covering up something else that was known or suspected? Inuit boys, Métis boys, white boys? She had to wonder why he had chosen to run this risk: because there were extenuating circumstances, or because he thought the rule arbitrary. Out of kindness? Out of desire? He'd gone north, so far from where he'd come from, where he would have been a different sort of outsider and, with his pale-brown skin and mixed background, perhaps less of an outsider than in other places. He'd left the Yellowknife school ostensibly for medical reasons, and never returned. He'd set off for the far side of the world, Sri Lanka, Thailand, before landing in Ethiopia, where he'd begun to teach again. In her car he'd said, what was it?, it was difficult to prove the negative of something that people believe to be true. Had this happened to him in Yellowknife? Pedophiles could be socially charming. They tended to repeat their behaviour. The images of the exploding plane, the cubicle dividers, the back of Sheila Gottlieb's head, the newsroom clocks, offered no answers to these mysteries.

That night, Sara pushed the one tape that she could watch at home into her videocassette player, not one that Juliet had shot but one that Raymond must have copied for her. *1991*, Juliet had written on a label, *Early Circus*. Sara had watched it before, each time with the thought that something else might make itself visible, if she sat on the floor rather than on the sofa, or stared at the images through the altering lens of this new knowledge: the complaint filed against him for driving two boys home from school in Yellowknife in 1987, a year after she was charged with stealing a wallet in Montreal. She sat on the floor with a glass of whisky beside her.

He was bearded, but his hair was buzzed short, and he looked younger, his youth visible in his lithe slimness. He was juggling on a street, dirt under his feet, a low cement wall behind him. Children in unwashed clothes sat agog on the wall, and Ethiopian men and women formed a loose, inquisitive semicircle in the background. Not juggling balls or pins but green apples: he plucked an apple, took a bite, tossed the apple with a flourish back into the air. He'd said despair had driven him to juggle in the street, and defiance, but there was also a lightness in him and some of the bravura charm that Sara had seen herself in the Highway 401 service centre. So vital. Who was filming him? Someone had shared this experience with him, white, brown, Ethiopian or other, a witness whose presence he had never mentioned.

Raymond lit two metal juggling torches, and at the gusts of flame, adults in the audience shrank back and children clapped their palms across their mouths. He tipped back his head, breathed over the torch held in front of his mouth until flames jutted from it. Then he righted his head, as if the flames were nothing, and beckoned his audience closer, his whole body rippling, alive to the risk of the moment, ferociously alive.

A different shot: children stood in rows, or attempts at rows, on a patch of ground enclosed by rugged shrubs and held water bottles and detergent bottles that looked to be filled with dirt, perhaps to give them weight. In front of the children, Raymond

held two juggling pins, one in each hand, and demonstrated the
motion of tossing the first pin from one hand to the other, the
second pin in reverse. There was sound, but it was impossible
to hear much beyond the chatter of voices. In the back row
stood two tall boys, and one of them was Kebede, a younger,
curly-haired Kebede, and the other was perhaps Dawit. With
severe attention, Kebede watched Raymond and tossed his
plastic bottles from one hand to the other. And so Kebede had
been with the circus from when it began.

The second-last tape brought Juliet and the circus to Shashemene: they'd travelled south to Sodo, and were returning
from the south, packed into three white minivans. At the end
of an afternoon, in a smallish stadium, the sinuous musicians
swayed to one side of the mat-covered playing area, amplifiers
stacked on either side of the stage, and Raymond darted here
and there as the costumed performers, wireless microphones
fixed to the edges of their mouths, spoke and sang and bounded
across the mats in front of wooden stands full of people: black
heads, glimpses of white veils, children.

In the brighter light of morning, on a stadium field now
empty of performing gear, Raymond, Kebede, and a couple of
others gave a juggling lesson to a group of local boys, teenagers,
even a few adult men, using balls and dirt-filled plastic water
bottles. The camera swooped in close to their eager faces, arms,
torsos, before pulling back. Two balls in the air, now three. On
another part of the field, Gelila and Senayit, the singer, worked
with a group of girls, leading them in an arm-swinging, energetic

dance. There were no obvious signs of reluctance and resistance from the older performers.

Out on the field, just the two of them, Gelila and Raymond were engaged in conversation, Raymond's head inclined as if listening, while Gelila, with a toss of her braids and her expressive hands, seemed intent on holding his attention.

In baseball cap and sunglasses, Raymond loomed before the camera, peered into the lens, and said giddily, Soon there'll be circuses everywhere, everyone wants to learn how to do this. Circus has such power. I had no idea it had such power.

At a restaurant table, the brim of his ball cap swivelled to the back of his head, Raymond sat beside Tamrat, and a couple of the musicians, and Justin, Juliet's assistant, beer bottles scattered between them, while at the next table, Gelila, Senayit, Kebede, and a couple of other teenagers swabbed up curry with scraps of injera and murmured among themselves, Kebede in a ball cap like Raymond Renaud's but with brim to the front. Across from the boys, Senayit whispered to Gelila and they both giggled. Tamrat looked less disturbed than when Sara had seen him in life yet watchful, as if he were keeping an eye on Raymond, the animated centre of the group. Raymond glanced at his watch, rose to his feet, and said to the teenagers, It's late. You need to go to bed. Scurrying them off with one hand. Now they breathed reluctance, even resentment as they pushed back their chairs. Raymond left the frame, returned with a fresh bottle of beer, a jut to his hip as he walked, dropped into his chair, loose-limbed, even drunk. A wildness about him. He turned to the camera. It's crazy. This whole thing, it's so crazy. How do we make it work? We have no money. I'm serious. We have no fucking money. How am I to hold it all together? We're running on air.

The last tape — someone walked along the hall outside Sara's suite, it was late, a swish of footsteps. At dusk, from the window of a car, the gate to Raymond Renaud's house drew close, and the watchman, the same cautious man who had been at the gate when she had pulled up with Alazar, swung the gate's metal bars open. There was no sign of the little brown dog in the yard, only three boys and Raymond kicking a soccer ball. Two wooden chairs marked goal posts, and skinny Moses, arms wide over his head, danced between them as beautiful Yitbarek did a jig and waved for the ball, the game breaking apart when the vehicle entered and the boys and Raymond turned to greet it.

Everyone followed the smallest of the boys — Bereket? — as he carried the soccer ball into the house, a jostle of heads and backs making their way down a hall that led into a kitchen.

The kitchen: Bereket tossed the ball onto the floor, and in the dimmer light, a new version of the game started up, the ball kicked beneath the table, boys' arms flailing to a chorus of shouts and huffs, Justin as well as Raymond joining in. It wasn't clear why Juliet was shooting this, the light so dim as to make the tape unusable. Perhaps Juliet didn't know this yet. Or something about the rocky, handheld graininess and spirited bedlam of the swooping, blurry figures appealed to her. On the monitor in the edit suite, everything clamoured to be read as a clue to what was really going on: the eager boys, the photographs of the circus stuck to the fridge, jars lined up at the back of the counter, dirty glasses by the sink, the direction of Raymond's gaze, his gestures.

The boys set the table, Raymond directing them from the stove, beneath an overhead light. Forks and knives, please. The boys themselves now quieted and dutiful. Juliet, who had grown up with a brother and a slew of uncles, likely found nothing unusual about being the only woman in the room. In the frame, she struck a match against the side of a matchbox and leaned toward the centre of the table to light three candles in a soapstone candelabra, as Justin, holding the fridge door open, asked how many bottles of beer he should take out. It seemed the camera had been mounted on a tripod in the corner of the room and left to run.

A new shot: the boys had disappeared from the table, the candles burned to knuckles, the table a glowing disarray of dishes, glasses, bottles, a pot with a wooden spoon sticking from it, and Raymond flattened his hand upon the wooden surface and said, Anyone can learn to juggle. Anyone. I swear it. I'll teach you. Tomorrow.

We're leaving tomorrow, Juliet said, her face flushed.

A boy appeared in the doorway beyond the table, not Yitbarek or Moses, but the one whom Sara thought was called Bereket. In shorts, without a T-shirt, he came forward and climbed without hesitation into Raymond's lap, Raymond helping him settle, hand to the boy's bare waist as the boy wriggled himself into a comfortable position, Raymond's hand smoothing then coming to resting on the boy's bare thigh.

The boy picked up a pen from the table, Juliet's face half-visible, watching him, everyone still happy in the glow of the candlelight, and the boy began to draw on a crumpled piece of paper, his body pressed against Raymond's, Raymond's arm around him, drawing him close, hand still resting on the boy's thigh.

Sara stopped the tape: the boy, in Raymond's embrace, bent over his drawing, Raymond's stilled expression, Justin's arms passing a pile of dirty plates to Juliet. When Sara restarted the tape, Raymond turned to Juliet, and said, Will you turn that damn thing off.

You said there was nothing, nothing that made you uncomfortable.

Nothing at the time.

Sara had written to Juliet as soon as she got home after watching the final tape, could have called her, decided she'd rather talk to her in person, unease walking through her sinews and along her bones. Raymond's face: what had she seen in it? His hand on the boy's bare waist. His leg. His hand left there. He'd pulled the boy close. Asked Juliet almost violently to turn the camera off.

I've watched all the tapes. Can we meet for a drink? she'd asked Juliet in an email, and in less than a day Juliet had written back to say yes.

When Sara swung through the door of the Parkdale bar, Juliet was already seated in one of the wooden booths, tending a glass of white wine, her pink wool coat folded on the bench beside her. She looked older somehow, and chastened. She'd lost a kind of hopefulness. She waved, in her black cardigan, her throat wrapped in a chiffon scarf.

As soon as Sara pulled off her gloves and leaned over to kiss her, Juliet did say, I'm sorry I never phoned you back when you called to tell me about Raymond Renaud's suicide. Her gaze broke away. I was upset.

She didn't say: I didn't mean to imply you're in any way responsible for his suicide even if you feel you are.

When Sara returned from the bar with a half-pint of lager, Juliet began to talk with some intensity about Max's upcoming solo show of photographs. They're beautiful. I didn't understand the project in the beginning. I couldn't see what made them his photographs since he's taking them from web-cams, but the surveillance cameras are recording the images even when no one is looking, and the images vanish unless he sees them and saves them. He blows them up and makes you look at them. They're usually landscapes because that's what he's interested in. There aren't usually people in them or you can't really see the people, so like intersections, streets, the view from an icebreaker in the Arctic Ocean, which is totally haunting. They're impersonal until he makes them personal. Anyway, I'll invite you to the opening and you can see for yourself.

The last tape, Sara said. Thanks by the way for dropping them off at my place. The scene in his kitchen, after dinner, when he's sitting with the boy in his lap, why didn't you mention it to me at any point these last months? When I asked—you said there was nothing that made you uncomfortable.

Nothing at the time.

So what did you feel when you saw him and the boy like that?

At the time I thought—how can I even say this now? It felt familial. And he said something like that, something about how he felt parental, and he was surprised by it. Juliet stared into the bowl of her wineglass.

What happened after he asked you to turn the camera off? He sounds almost angry. You turned it off.

No, Justin turned it off. We all got up. I don't know. Bereket went to bed. The rest of us cleaned the table and washed dishes.

Did he seem agitated or like he wished you hadn't seen that?

I just thought he was tired of being filmed all the time.

Did you not want me talking to Justin about this?

I don't know. Now he's travelling.

Where did the boys sleep?

In their own bedroom. There was one bed they all slept in. It isn't proof of anything.

I agree. It isn't.

I know it doesn't look good. But I didn't want to prejudice you. I didn't want you prejudging him. I wanted you to go and see what you found. I thought if there was anything to find you'd find it. And you did, I guess. And then I didn't want to make that kind of film. You weren't the only one to say I should do it. But I didn't want to tell that kind of story and I really didn't want to tell it about Africa.

That kind of story.

I should have seen something. Something, something was going on in front of me. I should have picked up on it. He shouldn't have been doing that. I don't know how far it went, but even what I saw is wrong and I should have said something.

Of course, Sara thought, Juliet hadn't wanted to show her the tape, given how she was inculpated as witness to whatever it was.

I don't understand why you didn't try to get hold of the teenagers afterward. Even now. You know them a little. Why not ask them—

Because what's the point? Whatever happened, it's in the past. He's dead. I know when you first told me about the circus, you didn't mean it to be like this. At least whatever he was doing, he isn't doing it any longer.

When did you start to doubt me?

What are you talking about?

Was it before the trial or after? Because you did start to doubt me. Lose trust in me. In Montreal. Maybe you didn't want to, but you did.

Colour was rising in Juliet's flustered face. I don't understand what this has to do with the circus. Why bring it up now? Are you talking about what happened at the trial?

She didn't say: You're wrong. I never doubted you.

How was it possible to speak of such a matter without sounding as if she were blaming Juliet or accusing her of something? This was a problem. Naturally Juliet became defensive. Yet something had shifted in Juliet all those years ago and continued to lurk between them, not spoken of, yet subtly distorting and disturbing all this time. Juliet had tried, especially in the weeks and months right after the trial, to cover it up with frantic efforts at friendliness, appeasements of dinner and gifts, until Sara had bolted, first to the McKibbens' house, then overseas.

Once they had both, independently, moved to Toronto, Juliet had kept trying to make amends, or that's what it had felt like.

Had Juliet's doubt begun in the weeks before the trial when they had sat in her bedroom or at the kitchen table, and Juliet had listened to Sara go over and over her version of what had happened at the Y and after, in preparation for speaking on the stand. Juliet had gone to meet Paul Kastner, Sara's lawyer, at his request, to rehearse her own small court appearance. Sara had told him, she may be nervous. This had been her own source of unease: that Juliet was too nervous to make a good witness. Since Sara was banned from setting foot there, her membership revoked, Juliet had visited the women's change room at the downtown Y and made note of its details for her. Juliet had done so much. They had gone together to a Reitman's on Sainte-Catherine and Juliet had helped Sara choose an outfit to wear in the courtroom—demure grey suit and neutral pantyhose—and plain black pumps from Aldo. A costume, nothing like the sweaters and jeans and leggings and secondhand dresses and grimy black boots and ratty old sheepskin coat that Sara ordinarily wore.

Perhaps her own performance on the stand had tipped Juliet into doubt. Something about the way she spoke, what she'd said or hadn't said: she had seemed too sure of herself or not sure enough. The undeniable fact of that hour or so between her leaving the Y and meeting Graham back at the apartment when she'd wandered unaccounted for on Sainte-Catherine, and there had been no ubiquitous store security cameras in those days to monitor her entrances and exits. Graham's refusal to testify. Maybe, to Juliet, Colleen Bertucci's version of events had become the convincing one, or had been convincing enough to upset her belief in Sara. If the wallet had been in Colleen's unlocked locker, yes, Sara had had the opportunity to steal it. The effects of Sara's cross-examination. The difficulty of proving something in the negative. That the police had found no evidence of the stolen goods in her possession might simply mean that she had dumped or fenced them.

All Juliet had to do on the stand was attest to Sara's good character. Juliet had dressed to look sombre yet pretty in an antique black dress and little black cardigan, intent on displaying a hint of the bohemian. In fact, Juliet looked terrified, her hands gripping the sides of the wooden podium. Yes, she said, Sara was a responsible person. She was studious and dependable and always paid her rent on time. It hadn't been a given that the prosecutor would want to cross-examine Juliet, but she had. This made Juliet appear even more terrified. What kind of coat does Sara Wheeler wear, can you describe it? What does Sara Wheeler spend money on? Does she have much money? One last question, Mme Laberge said in her accented English. What colour are Sara Wheeler's eyes? Paul Kastner objected to this, how was it relevant, but the judge in his ravenlike wisdom let the question stand.

Juliet looked then like she was clinging to a raft while lost at sea. This was impossible to forget. How strange, Sara thought from the courtroom bench where she sat beside Paul Kastner, she doesn't know the colour of my eyes. Had she loved Juliet Levin? Not sexually, but in other ways yes, moved by Juliet's kindness and loyalty. Juliet's eyes were brown. But there were those, Graham, for instance, whose eye colour Sara was suddenly less certain of. Friends, intimates. The realization was unnerving. Blue, Juliet said, but her rising voice made her response a question. Then she broke down in tears. I don't know, she said. I really have no idea. Of course it was a small thing, although Juliet's hesitation shook the credibility of all her testimony, as the prosecutor must have hoped for.

It wasn't that moment as much as how Juliet behaved after the trial that had felt so revealing. Her evasiveness and her refusal to acknowledge her evasions. People look through eye colour, not at it, Sara had said, yet Juliet did not want to talk about the trial other than to make effusive apologies for her own part in it and say how glad she was that Sara had gotten off. Her awkwardness made Sara long to put immediate distance between herself and Juliet, get as fast as possible out of the Esplanade apartment.

Doubt: once it enters your mind and body, how difficult it is to get rid of it. If not impossible. In the edit suite, Sara had watched Raymond gather the boy onto his lap and from that moment doubted him.

Maybe I shouldn't have brought up the past, Sara said to Juliet, as, behind the bar, the bartender in his grey wool hat danced along to the music. Maybe that was selfish. It's all so long ago and if you did doubt me, I forgive you.

How strange, she thought, after all these years, that this would prove to be their point of rupture. Juliet looked frozen, as if forced to stare at something she didn't want to see. If that's what you thought, I'm sorry, she said.

It was unlikely, even if they were to run into each other, that they would ever make plans to get together again.

The orphans' Christmas dinner at Soraya Green's was weeks ago, as was the Christmas phone call to her parents, her mother worried about her father and her father consumed by the Russian elections and the state of Boris Yeltsin's heart. One night in January, after an impulsive late-night movie with a couple of others also toiling after hours at work, Sara arrived home to a blinking red light on her answering machine and, when she pressed the play button, out poured Rafael Nardi's voice.

Hello, darling. I tried you at the paper, on the assumption you might be there, but I guess you're out gallivanting. I assume you've heard, but perhaps you haven't, your gang here has had their refugee claim denied. That came down yesterday. It's in the papers here today, not much detail. Insufficient evidence, it seems. Not clear what will happen to them now. I told you, didn't I, about meeting Louise, through Alice, who's been teaching them English. Louise used to be a gymnast, she's a trainer now, and she's got them access to a gymnastics club in Footscray, where they can practise, which I gather is better than wherever they were practising, and it seems they're intent on keeping up their circus skills. They don't have money so she's getting up early to let them in before anyone else is using the place, and letting them stay late, and helping to ferry the younger ones about and generally spending a lot of time with them. Their English is getting better. She says they've begun to talk about what they went through, how domineering he was, how punishing the pace, how they felt trapped, about not being paid. Any minute, I'm sure your machine's going to cut me off.

Anyhow, quickly, they talk about having a hard time, being terrified, and they're desperate to stay, but she also let on, this, obviously, in confidence, that none of them has said anything to her about or alluded in any way to any sort of sexual abuse, which doesn't mean it didn't happen, but I pass this on.

There were no other messages. Sara stood for a long moment, letting Rafael's words settle, wanting to cast them off but feeling them settle. Then she began to hunt for the portable phone, which was not on its stand, not on the little table where the answering machine was, no sign of its small dark carcass in the kitchen when she tugged on the pendant light and glanced about, the pulse of her blood like running footsteps. The phone wasn't in the living room or on her desk upstairs, it was on a shelf behind her desk. Rafael wasn't home, the bastard, the line ringing as Sara stepped onto the landing at the top of the stairs, three doors open around her, the dark like smoke.

Sem Le was in a meeting, said his secretary or receptionist or whatever she was. He was still in a meeting when Sara tried again, an hour or so later, far from sleep, still dressed, at the mess of her desk, the screen an infernal moon, where, four and a half months before, she'd read for the first time about the allegations the teenagers had made against Raymond Rénaud.

And again: I'll keep trying if he's there. Is he there?

He's busy. He's just back from court.

This won't take long, I promise.

It was as if Raymond were in the room, watching her from his white wooden chair, making up his own mind about her. He was draped across the ceiling, across the sky above her head, so that she couldn't look up without seeing him, yet when she put out her hand it went right through him. She couldn't see into him, he who as a child had longed to be seen.

Sem Le said, This has got to be quick. I don't even know why I am talking to you. Are you writing something more about this? I will be making an appeal for them to stay on compassionate grounds, an appeal based on artistic merit. It is a unique case, as it has always been. And they say it is all or none. Either they all stay, or they all go. And there is no question of their exploitation, this man went into an extremely poor country and exploited some extremely vulnerable young people.

What about the specific allegations of sexual abuse?

They were forced to work under extremely dangerous conditions, sometimes to the point of serious injury, were bullied, shouted at, suffered inappropriate touching, and a lot of money was made off them whilst they were never paid a wage.

What about those specific allegations?

The story is more precise now, Ms. Wheeler. It is clearer. We are moving forward with the leave to stay on compassionate grounds.

A story of exploitation isn't a refugee story.

The air kept ringing: she was alone in the dark with this rising thing. They had changed their story or the story had changed, as stories did, because it was necessary to have a credible story, a watertight story that held up to repeated tellings in front of a tribunal or a judge. If something sexually abusive had occurred, perhaps its nature had been murky, or it was something they'd observed, and it would be difficult to prove, and also it wasn't useful in legal terms since he wasn't doing it any longer. Whatever the truth was, there was damage. Someone, somewhere, had been betrayed.

She was cold in a way that no blast from the furnace was going to touch, frost grown like a forest over the windowpane, real cold seeping in around the frame.

At three-fifteen, Rafael Nardi said, You're not sleeping. Here I've just stepped in and am making a cup of tea. That's me slopping milk into it. Have you tried drinking? And it hasn't worked. I take it you hadn't heard.

About their claim being denied. No, but it's not that, it's the other thing, which their legal agent is also no longer willing to talk about. I reported allegations, only allegations of sexual abuse, but the power of an allegation. Raf, what have I done? I feel sick.

This is the one that's gotten under your skin. There's always one, or more than one.

I've tried that line of thought. There must be others, be-trayals, deaths, because of things I've, or you, or any one of us has — think of all those children lying without supplies in the hospital in Najaf, so many of them likely to die, and I felt implicated then, politically, and personally, there are all the things not written about as well as the things that are. But this — can I tell you why this feels so personal?

She was lying on top of the comforter, wrapped in another quilt, shivering as the bedside lamp shared its huddle of light — and he, never a lover, not that kind of spark. Rafael had been married when they'd crossed out of Jordan in that little convoy, although his marriage was disintegrating. Two journos, two photojournos plus one driver-cum-fixer in a white van. She'd seen Rafael unshaven, smelled him unshowered, breathed in the particular odour of fear and adrenaline that was released through his pores as she stared at the black hairs at the back of his neck. Rafael had been sitting in the front seat beside Raed, their driver, when a man stopped them in a Najaf street and pointed his cocked semi-automatic through Raed's open window. The man wore no uniform, maybe he was a former insurgent, and political betrayal was mixed in with his anger at the Americans sticking it to the Iraqis with their embargo and no-fly zones, leaving those like him on the ground to get slaughtered by government soldiers. None of the four of them was American or British, and maybe that enraged him further or it didn't matter, they were outsiders from the so-called West. He shot a bullet through the back windshield, just missed Tobias, the Norwegian, told Raed to get out of the driver's seat, yelled in English that he was going to kill them all. Maybe his desire was simply to blot them out, take the van, their stuff. They offered him money. He took their money. Somehow Rafael and Raed managed to talk him out of killing them.

She told Rafael about seeing the circus in Copenhagen, and her night drive with Raymond Renaud from Toronto to Montreal, and how hearing about the teenagers' allegations had stirred up what had happened to her years before in Montreal and spurred her trip to Addis Ababa. Maybe my own experience made me less objective, but all I've wanted was to leave space for the possibility of a wrongful accusation, in part because such allegations are so damning. I've always been prepared to believe them, and yet now I can't help feeling like I've destroyed or helped destroy someone, and I don't know what to do about it.

It's bound to be complicated.

What is?

Whatever happened.

Yes, yes. So on this tape, he's holding one of the boys on his lap. Maybe he does nothing more than this, but there's desire. And they observe enough of his behaviour to sense it. Have you met them, Raf? Have *you* spoken to them? Do you know if they've said anything about anything like this to, what's her name, Louise?

Not that she's told me. And nothing to me. I did go out the other evening with them and the lovely Louise.

The lovely Louise?

Former gymnast, yoga instructor. I admit at this point to being intrigued—all of this, I remind you, I have undertaken on your behalf. Up before dawn, off to this converted garage in Footscray. And if there are a few perks, well. However, I have not completely trampled on my so-called objectivity. I've seen their billet, these two shoddy rooms they're all squashed into, a kitchen and two mattresses. I can't tell you what you want to know from anything I've heard or seen.

Your marriage?

Long over. And Louise. She's the sort who's able to draw things out of people. She has the knack. I can attest to it. She and some mates have a plan afoot to start a circus school and found some new sort of outreach-oriented circus, so she says, and are on the lookout for a warehouse space, and want this crew involved, I gather that's part of the plan. To work with immigrants and refugees and indigenous communities. They seem very keen on the philosophy that anyone who wants to should be given the chance to try the trapeze, and even those who don't want to should be strenuously encouraged.

As in you, Raf? According to the lovely Louise?

I am currently a target of this democratizing impulse, yes.

Raf, I'm having the wild thought of flying out, not on a trapeze but — and trying to talk to them, to any of them in person. I keep asking myself, What do I owe him now, and what do I owe them? Do you think they would talk to me? Any one of them?

I'll ask Louise. Wild-ish, but can't you write a trip off, and will it help you sleep? Whatever happens. Not just tonight but all the nights ahead. That's my allegiance, sleep, my ship of state. Seems the best way to judge these things.

When the phone rang, it was still dark. Perhaps she'd slept, sleep that grazes the surface of all that churns beneath. And because she was on the verge of travelling, her exhausted fumbling toward waking came with the conviction that it had to be someone calling from far off: Rafael Nardi or her mother or one of the circus performers or Sem Le ready to tell her that the teenagers were altering their story once again. She'd left the phone close at her bedside, just in case. Her desert-dry voice said hello, mind struggling to catch up, and again hello. An ocean of static met her ear, the pause so long that Sara was on the verge of hanging up except that the static itself suggested distance, the familiar sound of someone placing a call in a faraway place and waiting for her voice to reach them.

Did I wake you, Sara? (What time was it anyway? The

glowing hands of the old clock when grasped and turned toward her read nearly six a.m.) I've been trying to reach you —

The voice was instantly recognizable, for all that it failed to identify itself and despite the static and her not having heard from Gerard Loftus since the week before Raymond Renaud's suicide.

When have you been trying to reach me, Gerard? Sliding to her feet, Sara pulled the quilt around her shoulders, as the bed, the floor, and the chest of drawers heaved themselves out of the dark.

Last night and the night before and at work.

I never got a message.

I didn't leave a message and you can't call me back. A motor scooter or car horn beeped behind him above the din of a street and a volley of voices, and the cry of a baby mingled with a clatter of dishes as if he was in some porous place, an interior open to the outside, a house, a fluorescent-lit bar with turquoise walls and clear plastic bags hanging above the counter to ward off flies — somewhere in Africa, or —

Where are you, Gerard?

I can't tell you where I am, but I have some news for you. Mark Templeton is opening another orphanage. In northern Tanzania, in a place called Longido, near Arusha, close to the Kenyan border. He wants to call it Rainbow House. He's building a school —

Wait a sec. How is he managing to do this? How did you find this out?

I can't tell you how I know, but if you look into it, you'll find it's true.

How did he get into Tanzania?

Well, he must have got a visa. There was nothing keeping him in the States. He hasn't been charged with anything there. He's getting money from a church group, and he has friends, people like him, and orphans, everyone's always eager to help orphans.

Have you gone to the police?

The police?

Wherever you are, can't you alert the authorities? Or let the police in Tanzania know? Or the organization that's funding him. There were charges laid against him in Ethiopia.

I thought you could do that. I don't really want to have anything to do with the police because of some stuff that happened to me in Ethiopia.

Are you in Longido?

Sara. I said I can't tell you, but I can tell you it's a very out-of-the way place where he is, and I'm sure he thinks he's safe, and I have worked very, very hard to get this information to you.

You're giving me hearsay, Gerard, rumour. No contacts. Can you spell out the name of the place at least? Or give me the name of the church group?

She dragged the quilt behind her across the floor, out of her bedroom and into the hall, resisting him as something in her had always wanted to resist him, his importunate requests, their moral obligation, his insinuations, the risks of his zealousness to be set against his dedication and utility. His pain. What was he tugging her into, back into, she was heading one way and he was pulling her another, with his ineluctable ability to complicate everything?

You can look into it, Gerard Loftus said. You'll see. I'm trying to help.

During the only trip Sara had taken alone with her father, he had told her a story, which still sometimes returned to her, again as she sat in a jetliner aimed west across the continent, the setting sun tinting the clouds below her window, a bright beam of light radiating from the hard plastic cabinet above her.

They were driving across the province to visit his mother, her grandmother, in St. Mary's, six hours from Ottawa and two hours west of Toronto, not far from the even smaller village where her father had grown up. The visit to her grandmother had been of less interest than the trip itself: the hours in the car alone with her father, seated in the front passenger seat where her mother, off visiting her own family in Nova Scotia, ordinarily sat.

It was early evening. The light was lowering. Her father, shirt sleeves rolled up, sunglasses shielding his eyes, at ease in a way he seldom was, said as they rolled through the cornfields of southwestern Ontario, I'll tell you about a thing that happened to me when I was a boy.

He used to spend long hours with a friend named Sam Atlin. Along with the other boys, they played in the fields and the woods outside of town and came home for dinner and in the summer headed out to play again until dusk.

In a field just beyond the town stood an abandoned house that had suffered a fire, and the fire was bad enough the family who owned the house had moved out, her father said. It had started as a kitchen fire, and most of the damage was on the first floor, and the house was left standing with its smashed and blackened windows, until one day someone came along and boarded the first floor up. Which all the boys knew, because as soon as word got out about the house being boarded up, they went out to inspect it.

One evening, maybe the same day or a few days later, Sam and I were sitting on a fence with the abandoned house in view when I saw a light shining in one of the second-floor windows. The house was a field away, but the light was bright, like a candle flame or a torch. It wasn't dark yet. I guessed someone had broken in, older boys, teenagers, a hobo. This was during the war and there weren't many men around, but there were a few hobos. There were no other signs of anyone, no car or truck pulled up by the house, or a bike.

So I pointed out the light, which to me was obvious, and Sam turned to me and said, What light? I don't see any light.

I showed him the window the light was in. Then the light, whatever it was, winked out, and again Sam said, I don't see any light.

Did you go to the house? Did you find out what it was? she asked her father, sitting with a bag between her legs that her mother, before leaving on her own trip, had packed with various picnicky things, two leather-covered water flasks, a bag of grapes, some muffins, and she'd felt a possessive pride to be sitting in her mother's seat, in charge of the foodstuffs, while her father told his story to her.

Maybe I should have gone out right away, her father said.

I'm pretty sure I didn't. It was about to get dark and Sam wouldn't go with me. I did go the next day with another boy and there were no obvious signs of entry. Maybe someone had let themselves in and when they left nailed up the board they'd taken off? That would be strange, but the boards on all the doors and windows were still in place. Then we ran into Sam and again he said he hadn't seen a light. I didn't know if this was because he was frightened or because he really hadn't seen anything.

It seems like a small thing, right? But from then on a rift began to open between us even though we'd been the best of friends. He insisted he hadn't seen a light. I insisted I had. And we had no way to resolve our difference. I wondered if I'd made it up, but I knew I'd seen something. It was like I carried around a secret that wasn't a secret. And somehow this thing that had happened started to separate me not just from Sam but the other boys. And there didn't seem to be anything I could do about it. And so, when the time came, I decided to go to university far from home and with my Rotary Scholarship went to Mount A in New Brunswick, and there I met your mother.

Sara had not particularly wanted to be reminded of her mother at that moment. She did wonder, then and later, what her father wanted her to take from this story. He might have told it as a ghost story but hadn't. Nor had he told it as a story you would tell a child; in part it had felt like he was talking to himself. He had wanted to point out how small differences can become irreparable. That some mysteries will remain mysteries. Perhaps talking about one thing was a way of gesturing toward something else that could not otherwise be spoken of. He'd said he was *pretty sure* he hadn't visited the house that first night. Sara had never asked him what he'd meant by any of it. She could still ask him. It was a story that helped explain how he'd come to be who he was and leave the small place that he'd called home.

One other thing stood out about that trip. Her father had decided not to drive back the way they'd come but to take a northern and more scenic route home. They had stopped for a night at a guest house in Bancroft, and the next morning the car wouldn't start. The woman who ran the guest house offered to take Sara for the day while her father stayed in town to get the car fixed. And so she had gone off with the woman and her husband to a nearby lake where the woman's family had a cottage, and for a day she was gathered into someone else's family as if she were someone else's child. The woman was someone who projected the sense of loving children without anxiety, although she didn't have any of her own or didn't yet have any. She was full of brio and warmth and had an irrepressible laugh, and for a day Sara had run about in the glow of this woman's attention, which was so unlike her mother's distracted love, the sense of being surplus in her parents' lives. When they'd left Bancroft the next morning, she'd climbed into the car beside her father, sun-sated and gluttonous with longing, after hugging the woman and her husband one last time goodbye. Four months later, they'd headed back overseas to her father's next posting in Berlin. She never saw the woman again.

Dusk was falling in Melbourne, the sky a smudgy square of aqua, a plane groaning above the patio where Sara sat with Rafael Nardi, outside the room that he called the lounge. My parents are coming back to Canada, she said. My mother called a few days ago. Moving back to Ottawa. I'm still a bit in shock. I keep wondering if something's wrong, though she didn't say anything was.

When was the last time you saw them, Rafael asked, his shadow falling across Sara's feet, her arms, her shadow climbing the wooden slats that fenced them in, the building's small parking lot beyond, lorikeets chirruping in the branches of a eucalyptus tree. Her second day in Melbourne: it did no good to think about what time it was anywhere else.

Ah, years? Let me count, they were back on a visit, oh, four years ago?

In any event, they're alive.

Yours?

Aren't.

So you're suggesting I still have a chance to sort some things out.

Rafael tapped at a crumpled box of Iranian cigarettes, tilting the box in Sara's direction. She shook her head. She'd smoked one with Rafael for old times' sake but one, raw and bitter, was enough, the burn in her throat eased by the can of beer that was perhaps a mistake since it was making her sleepier.

Rafael lit another cigarette, exhaling smoke to his left in a little cloud. He said he loved the taste of Iranian cigarettes, got people to bring him boxes whenever he could, an attraction that was either fetish or nostalgia. Indonesian kreteks were easier to get, but he could only take so much of the clove thing. He'd smoked 57s and Bahmans in the Intercontinental in Amman before they'd set off for Iraq and again on their return, though not while they were in Iraq. He said he had no contact whatsoever with his ex-wife.

And wasn't setting off in the wake of war and insurgency into southern Iraq, as they had done, or northern Iraq, as she'd done with three other female journalists a year before their trip to the south, a greater madness than crossing the globe in the hope of a conversation with those you weren't sure were going to speak to you, which was surely no madder than balancing on the shoulders of two bodies balanced on three bodies balanced upon four bodies before leaping into the air in a somersaulting dive.

The day before, Rafael had met Sara at Tullamarine Airport, shorter and stockier than she remembered, without the beard he'd had in Iraq, partly a stranger yet they'd hugged like the old friends they also were. From the airport, he'd driven them straight to the beach, her exhaustion catching on the domes of the palm trees and in the corona of the sun, for it was summer in Melbourne, and after coffee at a beachside café they'd walked into the salty, delirious water of the bay and Rafael had said, I'm still so very angry, I go out, I'm off to East Timor again next week, I see things, I come back and I'm still angry, that people here haven't seen the things I've seen makes me angry, and I box but I stay angry, and Sara had said, I'm not here because I'm angry, all I want is to hear what they're willing to say and bear witness to it somehow.

They may not tell you the truth.

They may not be able to tell me the truth, whatever it is. I do know that.

A wave had burst and sloshed about their thighs.

Back at Rafael's apartment, she'd slept for hours and hours, waking sometime late in the evening only to fall asleep again on the futon on the floor of his spare room, a greater exhaustion gripping her, and came to consciousness in the afternoon to the sound of Rafael hammering away at a keyboard on the far side of the wall, his collection of weight-lifting equipment, barbells and dumbbells, scattered around her.

She'd roused herself, made them each a cup of tea in Rafael's small kitchen, showered, read the newspaper that Rafael offered her, made more tea, and cooked herself some scrambled eggs. Rafael, still at his computer table in the lounge, insisted he wasn't hungry.

I lost a man in the midst of all this, Sara called to him from the kitchen, scooping the eggs onto a piece of toast, and there was freedom and necessity in being able to summon up David this way. Not exactly because of this, though somehow it got entangled.

Had it been going on a while?

A while. She leaned in the doorway between the two rooms as Rafael looked up from his work. Since shortly after our trip to Najaf. But it had to end.

So then I'm sorry and not sorry.

An hour or so after that, the doorbell had rung, and Rafael opened the door of the flat to a petite, coffee-skinned, dark-haired young woman. Imagined Louise vanished in a puff of dust. An effervescence, a darting busyness to her like a hummingbird, arms bare in a sleeveless shirt. She said she was off to pick up the younger ones from their billets in her ute. If you drop by around half-nine or ten? We should be through or nearly through. You can meet everybody then.

Sara stepped forward to join them in the doorway, and Rafael made the introductions. Louise, Sara. Sara, Louise. The clasp of Louise's warm, small hand. Her quick, inquisitive gaze. She said thanks, but she wouldn't step in. Rafael touched Louise's arm as he closed the door.

She dropped by to check me out, Sara said as Rafael pulled a bag of pistachios and another of rice crackers from a cupboard and a slab of cheese and two cans of beer from the fridge and, tucking everything under his arms except for one can of beer, which he handed to Sara, opened the sliding door that led outside. Raf, let me carry something else—

Yeah, she probably sort of was.

From her seat on the patio, Sara drew a pistachio from the bowl of accumulating shells, cracked it with her teeth, and pried free the green fruit. I have a confession to make—

A confession, Sara?

Three nights ago, no wait, whatever it was, two nights before I left, I got a phone call in the middle of the night. I thought it was going to be you, but it was this man, this strange man, one of my contacts in Ethiopia, the whistleblower from the orphanage. With some new news.

Which she told Rafael.

What did you do?

I made one phone call. Is that reprehensible?

To?

A police contact, RCMP, someone I've spoken to about international pedophile rings, and I sent an email to the foreign desk editor at the paper, outlining what I knew and saying I was going to be out of town and out of reach for a week. And that's all I did.

You didn't tell them where you were going?

No.

You won't check email?

Not today, anyway. She'd written Sheila, copied Alan, passed on Gerard's name and the Calgary number, the number of the police contact, and all the information Gerard had passed on to her about Mark Templeton and the new orphanage in Tanzania, presumed Sheila, or Alan, would do something with what she'd handed to them, she'd given them enough information to do something. In addition to which she had a hunch that Gerard Loftus would not let the matter rest until he knew for certain that word was out or Mark Templeton's plans were thwarted.

Carry-on bag packed, she'd sent off the email in the hour before the taxi arrived to take her to the airport for a Thursday evening flight to Los Angeles. Also, an email to Nuala on the national desk, saying she'd been unexpectedly called out of town.

You could have told me, Rafael said, stubbing out his cigarette. Let me break the story.

I couldn't leave and do nothing. You wouldn't have either. I'm telling you now.

Will he tell anyone else?

I don't know. I can't speak to what he'll do. He's a bit of a wild card. You can follow up or move on it tomorrow. If you want. But I needed to see this thing through, I don't know, unimpeded.

In an hour or so we should head out.

Louise did say one of them would speak to me?

What she said was she'd talked to them about it. No one's making any promises.

Did she tell them I was a journalist?

I said you were a friend, journalist, you'd seen the circus, written about it, spoken to him. She knows pretty much what happened. I said you'd come all this way because you wanted to hear their side of the story.

The privilege of being able to do what she had done felt acute, charging a flight that she couldn't really afford to a credit card, knowing that whatever else happened, she'd be able to work up a travel piece to pay for it. The ease with which she'd travelled to LA, then on to Sydney, then the connecting flight to Melbourne, despite the journey's length. Stepping through immigration control with a passport easy to travel on, in this case visa-less. No one had asked if she had a police record and in the eyes of the law, hers had been eradicated. How radically different her experience was from that of the asylum seekers, stuck in their legal limbo. Or even that of the hijackers, their names released the day before, whose violent attempt to get to Australia had taken 125 others down with them even if 50 had survived.

Shall we go out for dinner? Rafael was asking. Where are you on food, or are you too discombobulated to know?

Let me take you out for dinner.

How about Ethiopian over in Footscray?

Ethiopian, really?

There's a few along near where we'll be. I took Louise and some of the gang to one the other week. They're cheap.

If you want. Whatever you want. Only I'd love another quick shower first, if that's not too decadent.

Yeah, yeah, go ahead.

In the shower, Sara shook shampoo into her palm from a small, yellow-tinted bottle that, to judge by its label, Rafael had snatched from a hotel in Dubai, worked the liquid into her hair under a stream of hot water, and thought about forgiveness. What was it, a word that spread in many directions. You extended it to others if you felt they'd done something wrong, and wanted others to ask you for it if they'd done something wrong or you felt they'd done something wrong. Or you asked others for it if you'd done something wrong, or felt you'd done something wrong. And you attempted to extend it to yourself.

There was no way back to before, before you or anyone had done whatever it was. The teenagers were in their own particular limbo, legally neither one thing or another, in so many ways neither one thing or another. They couldn't go back to before whatever had happened between them and Raymond Renaud, that harm or their awareness of possible harm. Any more than he, or she, or anyone, could go back to the state of being un-accused. Something had happened. They had all been changed by it. By him. He'd pushed her back into her own past. And what was there to hope for now: the possibility of being released from the hold of the past, however outwardly large or small its traumas. To be able to re-enter the past without being returned to the you, and only the you, who'd been damaged in the past. To be able to look back and move forward.

In a wrinkled skirt and linen shirt and sandals, Sara stepped from the spare room into the hall to find Rafael exiting the bathroom in a patterned shirt that looked to have been ironed, an aura of aftershave about him. The risks of unintended harm lay everywhere. And hope. Oh, life, what was there but the risk of it.

Outside, climbing in on the left side of his little hatchback, she waited for Rafael to enter the driver's side on the right, a row of palm trees parading along the wide, nearly suburban road, the grass losing its emerald hue as the light retreated, the rumble of trams, as they were called here, borne from farther off. And there was the moon—Raf, the moon!—rising not in the south but the north, waxing not from the left but from the right, so many things here an inversion of the known.

At the bottom of her leather knapsack, in its little grey plastic case, was a tape, the last tape that Juliet had shot of Raymond with the boys over dinner in his kitchen. The boy in his arms, on his lap. In the bar that night, Juliet had insisted that she didn't want the tapes back. You keep them. Or don't. Do whatever you want with them. Destroy them, I don't care. The plastic case pressed against Sara's foot. Somewhere on that tape he was forever and forever embracing the boy. An offering, depending on what they said. Maybe it could be used to bolster their cause. Or not. Depending on what they said. Whichever way things went, it would be an ambiguous offering.

From the freeway, the towers of the central city jutted up like scabbards across the river, a bridge bearing them up and over the water, the anticipatory sky ahead of them pinking, the teenagers so close. The night before Sara had left home, she'd received an email from Soraya Green, saying, If you're open to it, there's someone, a man, a photojournalist who recently moved here from Chile, who I'd like to introduce you to.

She hadn't responded yet but the invitation rode with her, along with the words that she would write back: I'm open to it.

Don't look at the moon through glass, Rafael said. That's what my grandmother used to say, but how the hell are you supposed to avoid looking at the moon through glass? And never leave a hat on the bed.

I'm always looking at the moon through glass.

Well then we're screwed, you and me both. He rolled down the driver's side window and the wind bashed in and the moon swung in the air beyond his shoulder.

On an extending street of two-storey Victorian buildings, painted lighter, brighter colours than those at home, some with ornate cornices, some with no more than plain rectangular signs for low-rent businesses, a discount furniture shop, a pawnbroker, legal services, Rafael pulled up just past a row of little triangular flags, yellow, red, green, the Ethiopian colours, strung across the top of the Little Lalibela restaurant, its frontage shining amid a motley row of blinking, illuminated signs. With a squeak of the emergency brake, he rooted the car in place.

Or we can do Chinese, he said. In front of them, on a vertical sign, yellow pictograms fell down a red backdrop. I confess, there's nothing terribly fancy in these parts.

Whatever you want, Raf. I'm not very hungry, but I'd love some coffee. Can we get a good cup of coffee around here?

They entered a dim room filled with small tables and metal-framed chairs that might have belonged in an office, the air tinged with frankincense. A couple of Ethiopian men sat at a table over bottles of beer. To the woman who came to take their order, Rafael introduced himself as the man who'd been in the week before with a young woman and the Ethiopian teenagers.

Oh, yes, said the woman, folding her arms with lively authority, Yes, yes, yes, I remember it. The big table, the circus.

The circus, Sara thought.

Rafael introduced her as his friend from Canada. Sara's been to Ethiopia and she's seen the circus. Now, this may be utterly unorthodox, but you think we can have the coffee, the Ethiopian coffee, yeah, at the same time as our food?

Really? You have? Okay, for no one else will I do it but for you.

You'll see me here every week, every night then. Well, nearly every night. You saw them perform, didn't you? Rafael went on. Somewhere here, at some kind of community event?

At the Timkat celebration, the woman said. And by the grace of God I hope they stay.

Minutes later, she wafted a small clay pot of incense beneath their noses, and set a bowl of popcorn on the table, and a small charcoal brazier over which she heated green beans in a flat little pan. Somehow she made space on the table for the wide tin plate of injera and meat that Rafael had ordered, and the coffee, drunk in three rounds out of small handle-less clay cups. For the first time, Sara began to feel the dead man truly settle. Raymond Renaud was loosening his hold with the approach of the living.

Rafael said, Louise says the youngest two, Alem and Tewodros, have discovered skateboarding. She brought them a skateboard she found at an opportunity shop and now it's all they want to do. So maybe they'll work it into their show. You have to understand about Louise. She's become an advocate, and she's looking for help, and like I said, she's got this plan for a circus school with some mates, and for going out into communities with the whole social circus thing, and working with this gang is part of it. Did I give a toss about circuses before this? The answer is no. Am I a convert to the idea of circuses as a transnational and transcultural means of communication and circus arts as a way, ah, of working through trauma? Possibly. Is it obvious that I'm a little in love with the lovely Louise?

Yes, Sara said. And good luck with that.

I may need it.

Raf, you're a catch. Get yourself on a trapeze and you'll be fine.

In the dark, partway along another wide tract of street, beside a Catholic services centre, Rafael pulled into a parking space in front of a small brick warehouse with a garage door covering its front like a wide, closed mouth, and wedged his car between what was presumably Louise's aging utility vehicle and an older sedan. The metal panels of the garage door were painted brown. On the wall to one side, above an ordinary door, a floodlit yet unassuming sign read *Footscray Gymnastics Club*. Once Rafael switched the engine off, music lifted toward them through the garage door, the jangle of guitar, plucked bass, the reedy swoop of saxophone, a line of melody that burst along then cut out.

Am I mad, Raf?

No madder than the rest of us.

Sara checked the interior of her bag: her audio recorder, the little Hi8 tape that had been Juliet's, her notepad, her camera, a pen. Maybe none of these would be needed. And maybe nothing would be learned tonight, it would take time, she had a bit of time, and whatever they offered would have to be enough. And they would all find their way onward.

She and Rafael made their way to the door, where after tugging on the locked handle, Rafael gave the metal surface a couple of sharp raps.

An Ethiopian boy, in T-shirt and sweatpants, opened it, bashful, a wrangle of limbs. He ducked his head of longish, curly hair and mumbled something, and Rafael leaned close, canting toward the boy before turning. Alem, Sara. Sara, Alem. Gaze still lowered, Alem held out his hand, and Sara shook it, aware of the energy of bodies and voices and movement behind him, the air thick with the smells of sweat and chalk.

An archipelago of running shoes and sandals and flip-flops extended in front of them, and as the musicians started up again and a reverberation of amplified sound hit them, Sara slipped her heels free of her sandals, and Rafael tugged off his running shoes, reduced to greying socks. Beside the shoes: two skateboards. To her left, behind two small amps, were three young men: saxophonist, guitarist, and bass player. The saxophone and bass players she recognized from the show in Copenhagen, and from Juliet's tapes. They stopped at the end of their riff, leaving an amplified buzz in their wake, as if they'd just taken in the arrival of strangers. She lifted a hand in greeting and they nodded. The guitar player, not familiar, was also Ethiopian. He's from here, Rafael said. And there was Senayit, the singer, Gelila's friend, in sweatpants and T-shirt, a red kerchief over her hair, sitting on a bench against the far, mirrored wall, chugging from a plastic water bottle.

Alem, who had picked up a set of white juggling balls from the floor, was speaking into the ear of a girl around his age, also in trackpants and T-shirt like Senayit and the boys. Beside them, an older teenaged boy in a fedora kept his own juggling balls in motion, until, with a shout from the girl, Alem began to circle his four balls, and from behind the taller, fedora-wearing boy, the girl grabbed one of his white balls as it rose upward and passed it to Alem, then caught one of Alem's and passed it to the older boy, who was a moustache-less Kebede. They were real, and they were here. And they were aware of being watched. How could they not be? What was she to them? Their desires being so different from hers.

A sea of blue mats spread behind the jugglers, beneath the caged lamps that hung in a row from the high ceiling. In the middle of the long and narrow room, a body flew in a somersaulting dive over the head and outstretched hands of another: two more Ethiopian teenagers worked with two non-Ethiopian young men. And these were Tewodros and Dawit, Rafael said. And the girl juggler was Nazanette. The whoop of voices. Louise called and waved from the far end of the room, where a figure, in tights, Gelila—it had to be Gelila—balanced upside down on one hand atop a tower of bricks. Louise was spotting her. As they approached along the mats, Gelila began to reverse herself, lowered her legs slowly to the ground without losing her balance or disturbing the bricks, more extraordinary than ever in her extreme flexibility and fluid calm. Upright, she shook herself out, hair still in its tumbling little braids, though she looked leaner, having lost an adolescent plushness that she'd had when Juliet had filmed her. She wiped her chalked hands over her black tights. Even on tape, she'd had such self-composure, which her actual presence made more ripply and intense.

Without hurrying, Gelila stopped to pick up a square of towel bunched on the bench and patted her face with it, lifted a water bottle, and drank in short bursts as she and Louise drew close. The others, Sara thought, must also be aware of what her visit was about, even if they went on doing what they were doing. When she glanced over her shoulder, Kebede stood with his arms at his sides. The jugglers had stopped.

Louise said with a grin to Rafael, voice raised in the din, Don't hug me, I'm all sweaty, but it sounded like a dare, and Rafael hugged her anyway, then said to Gelila, Can you teach me to do that thing you were doing? Which made Gelila smile.

Gelila, Louise said, this is Rafael's friend, Sara. You've met Rafael.

Gelila's handshake was hot from her exertions, palm sticky with chalk, a drop of sweat visible at her throat, breath beating beneath her white T-shirt.

I saw you perform in Copenhagen, Sara said.

Oh. Yes. Pleasure lit Gelila's face; then she extinguished it.

I'm amazed by what you do. Even if you tried to teach me, I don't think I could do it.

Gelila nodded.

I came here, did Louise say, because I want to talk to you about the circus and what happened to you and how you came to be here. Not necessarily now. It can be now or whenever's a good time.

Yes. I know it. Gelila's speech was direct and firm. Louise tell me. She tell us what you do, what you want. We think about it, we talk about it. We all talk about it. We decide together. And this is it.

She drew herself upright, vibrating with conviction and hope. We do not wish to speak about these things to you. We wish to begin again.

From: Ed Levoix <elevoix@rcross.net>
Subject: Re: circuses
Date: March 19, 1997 2:00:18 PM EST
To: Sara Wheeler <wheelrs@globe.com>

Sara,
I'm not sure where you are but hope this reaches you. I was in Nairobi
reading newspapers at the embassy a couple of weeks back and saw
the brief piece on Mark Templeton. But it was not by you. Anyway
there was a lot of relief here, as you can imagine, plus amazement at
his capture, and that after he managed to slip across the Tanzanian
border into Kenya — someone must have tipped him off — he'd
get on a plane in Nairobi that stopped over in Addis. I suppose he
thought they didn't know or they'd never take him off the plane.
Anyway, when they did, it was all over the English-language paper
here, and I gather he'll be staying in jail in Addis until he goes to trial.
But this is not why I am writing. Last week I was on my way back
from the south and saw something I think will interest you. I was
preparing to overnight in Awassa and pulled into town at the end of
the day and saw a crowd at the roadside and stopped to see what
the commotion was. Tumblers, jugglers, children, a circus act, plus
acting and singing, and the leader of all this was, as maybe you've

guessed, Abiye Alemu. Apparently he led a little insurrection, some months back, walked out of the orphanage taking a lot of the other children with him, and they've set themselves up in a house in town. I have no idea how they are managing to support themselves, but they have a local woman looking after them. I didn't know who he was until I spoke to him after the show, which is rudimentary but performed with huge amounts of verve. I told him I would put him in touch with the man who's now running the circus here in Addis, and see if we might be able to help with some funding. He's interested in putting together an AIDS awareness show. Also, there's a British actor I've met here who wants to get involved. Abiye hadn't heard the news about Mark Templeton until I told him. Please don't think me an opportunist for offering to help after some previous comments made regarding the future of circuses in this country. Things have changed, and I believe what is going on now is different than what was going on previously. And Abiye is a remarkable young man, so self-directed, so full of energy and talent. He has great plans for his circus, and if you come back this way you really must go down and see it. He performs, by the way, an amazing fire-breathing act.

Regards,
Ed

Hello

Thanks a lot for you to contact me our Circus is alive
if some body likes to know about us any body welcome
You must know it, we are here

Heartfelt thanks to those who read early drafts of the manuscript, including Michael Helm, Terry Jordan, Kathryn Kuitenbrouwer, Michael Redhill, and Shyam Selvadurai.

Thanks to the following funding agencies for their generous support: the Canada Council for the Arts, the Ontario Arts Council, and the Toronto Arts Council. Thanks also to the Writer-in-Residence programs of the University of Alberta, the University of Guelph, McMaster University, and the University of New Brunswick.

Thanks to all who shared their stories and helped in my research, including Stephen Anderson, Sophia Bush Anderson, Dan Brodsky, Jennifer Bush, Robert Everett-Green, Marina Jiminez, Clare Pain, Robert Rotenberg, Richard Scrimger, Kathleen Smith, Cheryl Sourkes, and Shelley Tepperman.

Particular thanks to Nigel Hunt for generously sharing the written files for his documentary *The Unexpected Circus*. I'm also indebted to a series of articles in *The Guardian* by Audrey Gillan. Also *There Is No Me Without You* by Melissa Fay Greene and *Youth Gangs and Street Children: Culture, Nurture and Masculinity in Ethiopia* by Paula Heinonen, and *Identifying Child Molesters* and *The Socially Skilled Child Molester* by Carla van Dam.

The epigraphs are from Robert Browning's *The Pied Piper of Hamelin* (London, UK: Frederick Warne and Co., 1888) at http://www. indiana.edu/~librcsd/etext/piper, and from Ryszard Kapuscinski's *The Emperor* (English translation copyright © 1983 by Ryszard Kapuscinski, New York: A Helen and Kurt Wolff Book / Harcourt Brace Jovanovich).

Thanks to agent Samantha Haywood for her belief in this project and for taking me on at a crucial moment, and to Bethany Gibson for being the ideal reader and everything I could possibly hope for in an editor. Thanks to everyone at Goose Lane. And to Mike Hoolboom, for listening so closely to all these words and for shining a light that saw me through the final stages of this project.

All individuals and most organizations described in this novel are fictional, including the circuses. Yet there is an actual and vibrant Ethiopian circus movement, part of the larger social circus movement in which circus skills are a means of educating and reaching out to at-risk populations in various parts of the world. For more information on the contemporary Circus Ethiopia, please go to www.circusethiopia.org.